"Som... suspense writing in years"
—Bari Wood, co-author of *Twins*

The erupting nightmare of murder after murder cannot stop him. The crazed townspeople cannot stop him. Miles has returned for a reason.

Now he holds the photograph. He and Alison, hand in hand. As they must have been seen by all, their spirits flowing toward each other, more one than two drops of blood in one bloodstream. This is not what he expected. It is what must be.

And now he knows what has drawn him into the horror which surrounds him—horror at the hands both of the living and the dead!

"A snapping story of the occult, suspenseful to the last" —*New Haven Register*

"Compulsive reading. It has marvelous atmosphere, suspense, and a truly grand Guignol ending." —Dorothy Eden

Books by Peter Straub

If You Could See Me Now
Julia
Marriages

Published by POCKET BOOKS

PETER STRAUB

IF YOU COULD SEE ME NOW

PUBLISHED BY POCKET BOOKS NEW YORK

'There's a long statement in the papers, sir, about a murder . . .
But someone is always being murdered, and I didn't read it.'

David Copperfield

You can walk away from anything but a strong smell: it haunts
you, calls you back.

Book of the Cranberry Islands,
RICHARD GROSSINGER

July 21, 1955

"Winter has already started," said Alison.

"Huh?"

"Winter started a month ago."

"I don't get you."

"What day is it?"

"The twenty-first of July. Thursday."

"God, look at those stars," she said. "I'd like to take a big step off the planet and just go sailing through them." He and Alison, cousins from opposite ends of the continent, lay side by side on their grandmother's lawn in that part of rural Wisconsin nearest the Mississippi River, and looked up past the dark massive heads of the walnut trees to the sky. Oral Roberts' country voice came drifting to them from the porch of their grandmother's house. "My spirit is passing into you," Oral Roberts was shouting, and Alison's mother, Loretta Greening, softly laughed. The boy turned his head sideways on the coarse, springy grass and looked at his cousin's profile. It was fox-sharp, ardent, and if will could lift her off the earth she would already be sailing away from him. He caught her smell of cold, bracing water. "God," she repeated, "I'd just buzz around up there, wouldn't I? I feel that way sometimes when I listen to Gerry Mulligan. Do you know about him?"

He did not.

"Boy, you should really live in California. In San Francisco. Not just because we could see each other more, but Florida is so damn far away from everything. Gerry Mulligan would just slay you. He's really cool. Progressive jazz."

"I do wish we lived near you. That would be neat."

"I hate all my relatives except for you and my

3

father." She turned her head toward his face and gave him a smile of brilliant, heart-stopping whiteness. "And I suppose I see him even less than I see you."

"Lucky me."

"You could look at it that way." She turned away from him again. They could hear their mothers' voices mingling with the noise from the radio. Their grandmother, Jessie, the shrewd center of the family, was doing something in the kitchen, and from time to time through the crossweave of the sisters' conversation on the porch slid her softer voice. She had been closeted all day with cousin Duane (pronounced *Dew*-ane), who was about to be married. Their grandmother opposed the marriage, the children knew, for reasons tenuous but forceful.

"You got into trouble again last year," Alison said.

He grunted assent, embarrassed, not wanting to talk about it. She was not supposed to know about the side of him that got into trouble. Last time it had very nearly been serious, and the entire messy context of the trouble raged in his dreams several nights a week.

"You get into a lot of trouble, don't you?"

"I guess so."

"I get into a little trouble, too. Not like you, but enough to make them notice me. I had to change schools. How many times have you changed schools?"

"Four times. But the second time was—the second time was just because one of the teachers hated me."

"I had an affair with my art teacher."

He looked at her sharply, but could not tell if she were lying. He thought that she probably was not.

"Is that why they made you leave?"

"No. They kicked me out because they caught me smoking."

Now he knew that it was true—lies were never as anticlimactic as that. He felt intensely jealous and intensely interested. Both of these feelings were mixed with a large measure of admiration. At fourteen, a year older than he, Alison was part of the passionate adult world of affairs and cigarettes and cocktails. She had previously revealed to him her enthusiasm for martinis "with a twist," whatever a twist was.

"Old Duane would like to have an affair with you," he said.

She snickered. "Well, I'm afraid old Duane doesn't have much of a chance." Then, rushing at him with all of her unexpected, ardent force, she rolled rapidly over onto her side and faced him. "Do you know what he did yesterday? He asked me if I wanted to go out for a ride in his pickup, this was while you and your mother were visiting Auntie Rinn, and I said sure, why not, and he took me for a drive and he put his hand on my knee as soon as we left the driveway. He only took it off when we passed the church." She laughed again, as if this last detail were the conclusive proof of Duane's unsuitability as a lover.

"You let him?"

"His hand was *sweating,*" Alison said through her laughter—indeed said it so loudly that the boy wondered if Duane could hear it—"and it felt like he was rubbing tractor grease or something all over my knee. I said, 'I bet you don't have much luck with girls, do you, Duane?' and he pulled over and made me get out."

"Are there any boys you like up here?" He wanted her to give a flat negative, and her reply at first made him flush with satisfaction.

"Here? Are you kidding? First of all, I don't like the boys very much, they're so inexperienced, and I don't like the aroma of the barnyard that surrounds most farmboys. But I think Polar Bears Hovre is sort of goodlooking."

Polar Bears, so called because of the whiteness of his hair, was the son of the Arden Township policeman, and he was a tall, rather chunky boy of nearly Duane's age who had several times driven over to the Updahl farm to ogle Alison. He was a famous tearaway, though as far as the boy knew, he had not yet been made to leave any schools.

"He thinks you're goodlooking too, but I suppose even a lout like Polar Bears would notice that."

"Well, you know that I only love you." But she said it so lightly that the phrase seemed smooth with overuse.

"I'll accept that," he said, thinking it sounded sophisticated—the kind of thing her art teacher might say.

Duane had begun to shout in the kitchen, but they, like their mothers on the porch, ignored it.

"Why did you say that about winter? That winter was starting?"

She touched his nose with a finger, and the gesture made his face blaze. "Because on this day last month we had the longest day of the year. Summer's lease is fading, dear one. Do you like Auntie Rinn? I think there's something spooky about her. She's really off the wall."

"Yeah," he said vehemently. "She's eerie. She said something to me about you. When Mom was out looking at her herbs."

Alison seemed to stiffen, as if she knew that the old woman's comment would not have been complimentary. "What did she say about me? She listens to my mother too much."

"It was . . . she said I should watch out for you. She said you were my snare. She said you'd be my snare even if we weren't cousins, even if we didn't know each other, but since we are cousins, that it was much more dangerous. I didn't want to tell you."

"Snare," Alison said. "Well, maybe I am your snare. It sounds like a nice thing to be."

"Nice for me, you mean."

She smiled, not agreeing or disagreeing, and rolled back to look again at the shining starry sky. When she spoke, she said, "I'm bored. Let's do something to celebrate the beginning of winter."

"There's nothing to do."

"Polar Bears could think of something," she said

sweetly. "I know. Let's go swimming. Let's go up to the quarry. I'd like to go swimming. Hey? Let's do it."

It seemed like a dubious proposition to him. "They won't let us do it."

"You wait and see. I'll show you how we swim in California."

He wondered aloud how they would travel the eight miles to the quarry. It was in the hills just outside Arden.

"Wait and see." She jumped up from the grass and began to march toward the farmhouse. Oral Roberts had ceased faith healing for another week, and now the sounds of a dance band mingled with the voices of their mothers. He ran to catch up with her and followed her through the screen door of the porch.

Loretta Greening, a softer, taller version of Alison, was sitting on the porch sofa with his mother. The two women looked very much alike. His mother was smiling; Alison's wore her perpetual look of nervous excitement mixed with discontent. After a moment the boy noticed Duane seated on a wicker chair at the far end of the porch. Slapping a fist noiselessly against his thigh, he appeared to be considerably more discontented than Mrs. Greening. He was staring at Alison as though he hated her, but she blithely ignored him.

"Give me the keys to the car," Alison said. "We want to go for a drive."

Mrs. Greening shrugged to her sister.

"Oh, no," said the boy's mother. "Alison is too young to drive, isn't she?"

"It's for practice," Alison said. "Just on the back roads. I have to practice or I'll never pass the test."

Duane was still staring at her.

"I have this theory," Mrs. Greening said to the boy's mother. "You always let them do what they want to do."

"Because I'll learn from my mistakes."

"Well, don't you think—" his mother began.

"Here," said Mrs. Greening and tossed her the keys. "For God's sake watch out for that old fool Hovre.

He'd rather give you a ticket than chew that disgusting tobacco."

"Oh, we're not going anywhere near Arden," Alison said.

Duane had put his hands on the arms of his chair. The boy realized with sickening certainty that Duane was going to invite himself along, and he feared that his mother would insist on their allowing him to drive the Greening Pontiac.

But Alison acted too quickly for either Duane or his mother to speak. "Okay, thanks," she said and wheeled back through the door of the porch. By the time the boy could react, she was already sliding into the car.

"We pulled that one off all right, didn't we?" she said minutes later, as they were swinging out of the valley road onto the state highway to Arden. He was looking out the back window, where he thought he had seen the lights of Duane's pickup truck. But it could have been any truck from one of the farms in the valley.

He was about to agree with her when she spoke again, strangely counterpointing his thoughts. It was a common experience between them, this access to each other's thoughts and fantasies, and the boy thought that it was what Auntie Rinn had noticed.

"Old Duane was just about to invite himself along, wasn't he? I wouldn't mind him if he wasn't so *path-et-ic*. He sort of can't do anything right. Did you see that house he was building for his girlfriend?" She began to giggle. The house had become a subterranean family joke, unmentionable before Duane's parents.

"I just heard about it," he said. "It sure sounds funny. He didn't want me to see it. Duane and I don't really get along. We had a big fight last year."

"And you didn't even sneak out there just to take a peek? Jesus H. Christ, it's amazing. It's . . ." she broke down into giggles, unable to characterize the house any better. "And," she said gasping, "you're not supposed to mention it to Duane, you can't make just the

teeniest tiniest little comment . . ." She was laughing
uncontrollably.

Because the car was weaving in and out of its lane,
he said, "How did you learn to drive? My parents
won't even let me touch the car."

"Oh, from these greasers I sometimes hang around
with."

He merely grunted, having no idea what greasers
were, and thinking that they sounded even worse than
the art teacher.

"Do you know what we should do?" Alison said.
"We should make a pact. A really serious pact. A
vow. To make sure that whatever happens, you know,
no matter who we marry, since we can't really marry
each other, that we stay in touch—no, stay together."
She looked at him oddly for a moment, and then
swung the car to the side of the road. "Let's make a
vow. This is important. If we don't, we can't be sure."

He looked at her dumbly, amazed by this sudden
emotion. "You mean, promise to see one another when
we're married?"

"Married, not married, if we're living in Paris or
Africa—anything. Let's say—let's say we'll meet here
on some date. On this date in ten years. No, that's not
far away enough. In twenty years. I'll be thirty-four and
you'll be thirty-three. That's lots younger than our
mothers. July twenty-first, um, 1975. If there's still a
world in 1975. Promise. Make me a vow." She was
looking at him with such intensity that he did not
even attempt to turn the absurd promise into a joke.

"I vow."

"And I vow. At the farm, twenty years from now.
And if you forget, I'll come after you. If you forget,
God help you."

"Okay."

"Now we have to kiss."

His body seemed to become lighter in weight. Alison's face seemed larger than its true size, more chal-
lenging and mask-like. Behind the mask her eyes shone
at him. With difficulty, he made his body move on

the carseat. He bent toward her. His heart began to gong. When her suddenly enormous face drew near his, their lips brushed. His first sensation was of the unexpected cushiony softness of Alison's lips, then this was supplanted by an awareness of her breathing warmth. Alison pressed her mouth harder against his, and he felt her hands at the back of his head. Her tongue darted through his lips.

"This is what Auntie Rinn is afraid of," she whispered, her mouth publishing warmth over his. She kissed him again, and he became a pinpoint of sensation.

"You sort of make me feel like a boy," she said. "I like it."

When she withdrew, she glanced down at his lap. He looked dazedly into her face. He would have given her anything, he would have died for her on the spot.

"Did you ever go swimming at night?" she asked.

He shook his head.

"We'll have so much fun," she said, and started the car again. With a flourish, she pulled out into the road.

He turned his head to look again out of the rear window, and saw the high headlights of another vehicle swing out thirty yards behind them. "I think Duane is following us."

She hastily looked into the rearview mirror. "I don't see him."

He looked back. The headlights had disappeared. "But he was there before."

"He wouldn't dare. Don't worry about old Du-ane. Imagine having a name like that anyhow."

As he laughed, relieved, he was stopped short by an appalling realization. "We didn't bring our suits! We'll have to go back."

Alison glanced at him oddly. "Don't you wear underwear?"

Again, relief made him laugh.

When they reached the rutted dirt road leading up the hill to the quarry, the boy quickly checked for the following headlights, but saw nothing except the lights of a farmhouse far down the road. Alison flicked on the radio, and "Yakety Yak" blared out at them. She sang the words as they sped up the hill. *"Don't talk back."*

A thick screen of bushes separated the irregular steps to the quarry from the grassy, rock-strewn flat space where she stopped the car. "Oh, this is going to be good," she said; on an afterthought, she snapped the radio back on. "—and for Johnny and Jeep and all the A.H.S. gang at Reuter's Drive In, Les Brown and His Band of Renown playing 'Lover Come Back To me,' " came the announcer's low oily voice. "And for Reba and LaVonne in the Arden Epworth League. Les Brown and 'Lover Come Back To Me.' "

From the flat space where workmen's sheds had once stood, a beaten trail of dust and grass led through an opening in the screen of bushes to the rocky steps down to the lip of the quarry. When he had followed Alison down the steps, they stood on the slablike platform, two feet above the black water. As with all quarries, it was said that this one was bottomless, and the boy could believe that—the black skin of water seemed inviolate. If you broke through it, you would never cease to fall, you would go down forever.

No such reflections troubled Alison. She was already out of her blouse and shoes, and was now removing her skirt. He realized that he was staring at her body, and that she knew he was staring, but did not mind.

"Get out of those clothes," she said. "You're awfully slow, cousin. If you don't hurry up I'll have to help you."

He quickly pulled his shirt over his head. In bra and pants Alison stood and watched him. Shoes, socks, and then his trousers. The night air drifted coolly down onto his shoulders and chest. She was looking at him with approval, grinning.

"Do you want to do what we do in California?"

"Uh, sure."

"So let's skinny-dip."

"What's skinny-dip?" Though he thought he knew.

"Watch me." Smiling, she pushed her pants down over her hips and stepped out of them. Then she reached up and unhooked her bra. The car radio sent them Ray Anthony playing a languid torchy song. "You too," she said, smiling. "You won't believe how good it feels."

A sound from above them, from near the rocks, made him jump. "Was that someone coughing?"

"Do birds cough? Come on."

"Yeah." He removed his underpants, and when he looked up at her, she was just diving into the water. Her body gleamed whitely beneath the dark surface of the water, gliding for a long time out toward the center of the quarry. Then her head broke the water and she flipped back her hair, a movement full of competent womanly life.

He had to be near her. He went to the lip of rock and made a flat dive into the water: the shock of the cold seemed to flash through his nervous system and burn his skin, but the simple womanly efficiency of her gesture had been a greater shock. More than her talk of greasers and art teachers, it made her a foreign creature.

By the time he got to the surface, his body had adjusted to the temperature of the water. Alison was already knifing away from him, moving smoothly through the water. He realized with chagrin that she was a better swimmer than he, who was proud of his swimming. And she was a stronger swimmer too, for when he set out after her, she effortlessly increased the pulse of her strokes and widened the distance between them. At the far end of the quarry she flipped under the water in a racing turn and came up gracefully and powerfully, her shoulders and arms gleaming in the darkness. The rest of her body gleamed too, mysterious and warped by the water. He began to tread water, waiting for her.

Then he heard, muffled by the drifting snatches of dance music from the car, another sound from above them, and he looked up sharply. Something white ran flitting behind the sparsest of the bushes. For a moment he thought it was a white shirt, and then it stopped and was too motionless for it to have moved at all—moonlight on a rock. From the other side of the quarry's top, up above and behind him, came a short calling whistling sound. He looked up over his shoulder but saw nothing.

Alison was now near him, making her beautiful strong strokes which barely disturbed the surface of the water. She bent at the waist, her bottom flashed for a moment, and she was gone. He felt her hands braceleting his calves and he managed to hold his breath before he went under.

In dark water, Alison was clasping him now at the waist, grinning. He touched her cold smooth hands. Then, bravely, dared to touch her spreading hair and round skull. She gripped his middle more firmly and, using her shoulder muscles, levered him down and slid her body along his until her arms were clasping his chest. Her mouth nipped at his neck. Their legs lay parallel, twin forks, touching. Trouble started in his mind.

When what she had caused to come to life brushed her stomach, she released him and went smoothly up to the surface. Holding the final seconds of his air, he saw her body dangling headlessly down, an unbelievable bounty of almost mystical perfection. Her small breasts bobbed in the water, her legs bent to a heartbreaking curve of calf. Her hands and feet were white stars, flashing. The trouble spread thickly through his mind, canceling all else. He glided up beside her, bruising all that foreign heartland and wilderness of skin.

For a second he was unable to see, and Alison's arm clamped about his neck: when his eyes cleared, he was looking into a sleek wet fall of hair. Her hard cheekbones pressed his jaw. Using all his strength, he broke the hold of her arms and turned her into him. His head went under water, forced to the hollow of her neck, and he heard her yell of laughter. His legs kicked around hers. They were back under, thrashing, and the trouble in his mind forced them to roll deeper into the cold water. His ears boomed as she struck them.

Booming was everywhere. The water blanketed him, her slippery perfection fought him. They reached the surface again and gulped air a second before the water exploded with trouble. Her laughter ceased and she gripped his head, crushing his ears forward painfully and then there seemed to be more than two of them, fighting the trouble, fighting the water and fighting for air and fighting *for* trouble. The water boomed and whenever all their bodies, their one body, broke the surface, geysers of spray were booming too.

To Get to Arden

One

No story exists without its past, and the past of a story is what enables us to understand it (perhaps that I believe this is the reason I teach novels and not poems, where the internal history may be only a half dozen slewfoot lines), but because—precisely because—I am so aware of the past pressing in on my story, I wish to allow it to leak in when it must, and not butter it over the beginning. I know, and here speaks the lecturer in literature, the sort-of professor of contemporary fiction, that each story, however freighted with history, is a speaking present unit, a speaking knot, a gem. We may appreciate a diamond more if we know its history of association with bloody feuds and failed dynastic marriages, but we do not understand it better. The same point could be made of love, or of lovers—the history of indifferent wives' or loafing husbands, even the paraphernalia of personality, is strewn about there on the floor, waiting to be put on with their clothing. So I begin this story, so far along in this maladroit paragraph, with myself driving my car, a decade-old Volkswagen, from New York to Wisconsin in the last breathless weeks of June. I was in that limbo between youth and middle age when change is most necessary, when new possibilities must replace the old dying visions, and I had been divorced a year. Divorced

spiritually, not legally: because my wife had died six
months after she had left me, I would never need the
formal decree. (Impossible to conceal the bitterness,
even after Joan's death.)

I had been driving for a day and a half, going as
fast as my Volkswagen and the highway patrol would
permit, and I had spent the intervening night in an
Ohio motel of shabby aspect—a motel so characterless
that I forgot its name and the town on the heel of
which it squatted the moment I rejoined the freeway.
Having had a particularly disturbing nightmare, I was
gasping for freedom, for new air. Every cell and nerve
of my body was choked with malignancy, the residue
of gasoline fumes and repressed outrage; I needed
dull green peace, fresh days in which to finish (actually, to write most of) the dissertation which would
enable me to keep my job.

For as I have said, I am not a professor: not even,
to be truthful, a "sort-of" professor. I am an instructor. An instructor of the last gasp.

Automobiles, especially my own, make me irritable
and prone to accidents of temperament. Each man sits
alone in his six-foot metal coffin, and traffic jams are
like noisy graveyards. (I may be mechanically incompetent, but I can reduce death to a metaphor—the
day after dreaming of it!) I am likely to "see" things,
whereas normally all my hallucinations enter through
another organ—I mean my nose. (Some people see
things, I smell 'em.) In Massachusetts once, during a
time when I was teaching *Tom Jones,* I was driving
late at night on a country road well out of Boston.
The familiar roadsign picked out by my headlights
indicated a sharp curve. Entering it, I saw the road
begin to ascend steeply, and pushed the accelerator
down hard to the floor. I like to go up hills as fast
as possible. When I had swung fully into the curve
and had begun to ascend—little Schnauzer engine bark-
ing furiously—I heard a terrific clatter from the brow
of the hill. A second later, my blood thinned: just beginning to careen down the hill was a stagecoach, ob-

viously out of control. I could see the four horses racing in the straps, the carriage lamps flickering, the driver hauling uselessly on his reins. His face was taut with panic. The high wooden box of the coach jounced down at me, veering crazily across the road. It seemed like my last moment on earth. I fumbled in fear at the controls of my car, not knowing whether to change gears, shut off the engine, or risk my luck on speeding past the plunging carriage. At the last moment my mind began to work and I turned sharply to the right. The coach sped past me, missing the car by four or five inches. I could smell the sweat of the horses and hear the creaking of leather.

When I had calmed down, I continued up the hill. It must have been a fraternity or club prank, I thought, college madmen from Harvard or B.U. But after I had gone on no more than a quarter mile, I realized that it was very late for that sort of prank—past three in the morning—and that you don't race stagecoaches downhill. They crash. And I could not be sure that I had seen it at all. So I turned around and went back. I followed the road five miles the way I had come— long enough to catch up, more than enough to find the wreck. The road was empty. I went home and forgot about it. A year later, idly listening in my bath to a phone-in program about the supernatural, I heard a woman say that while she had been driving on a country road well out of Boston, she had turned up a hill late at night and seen a careering stagecoach racing toward her. My asthmatic heart nearly folded in half with shock. Driving, I still remember this. When the other world comes up and slaps me in the face, it will happen when I am in a car.

Teagarden's the name, pomposity's the game.

I was sweating and in bad temper. I was perhaps thirty miles from Arden, and my engine was rattling, and on the back seat noisily shook a carton of books and papers. I had to do that book or the Advancement and Promotions Committee—seven well-padded scholars on Long Island—would fire me. I was hoping that my cousin Duane, who lives in the newer farm-house on what used to be my grandparents' farm, would have got my telegram and had the older wooden house cleaned up for my arrival. Duane being himself, this seemed unlikely. When I reached a town I knew called Plainview, I stopped at a lunchroom for chili, though I was not hungry. Eating is affirmation, greed is life, food is antidote. When Joan died, I stood up beside the refrigerator and gobbled an entire Sarah Lee creamcake.

Plainview is where my family always stopped for lunch when we drove to the farm, and I had to make a longish detour to get there. In those days, it was a hamlet of one street lined with feed stores, a five and ten, a hotel, a Rexall pharmacy, a tavern, our diner. Now I saw that the town had grown, and the second feed store had been replaced by the Roxy cinema, which itself had bankrupted so that the marquee read C ARLTO HESTO IN   HUR. Good work, Carlto! The diner was externally unchanged, but when I stepped inside I saw that the churchy wooden booths along the wall had yielded to new banquettes padded with that plastic luncheonette leather which is forever gummy. I sat at the far end of the counter. The waitress idled over, leaned on the counter staring at me and missed a few beats with her gum while I gave my order. I could smell baby oil and tooth decay, mostly the latter.

Though she smelled of nothing of the kind. As I've said, I have olfactory hallucinations. I smell people even when I'm talking to them on the telephone. In a German novel I once read about this phenomenon, and there it seemed almost charming, pleasant, a sort of gift. But it is not charming or pleasant, it is dis-quieting and unsettling. Most of the odors I catch hook the nerves.

She wandered away, scribbling on a pad, and re-joined a group of men attending to a radio at the other end of the counter. The men were huddled together, ignoring their plates of hash and steaming cups of coffee. I could see it was a matter of serious local interest, both by the men's attitudes—anger in those hunched shoulders, anger and bafflement—and by the broken phrases which came to me from the radio. "No progress in the shocking . . . discovery of the twelve . . . a bare eight hours since . . ." Some of the men glanced sullenly at me, as if I hadn't the right to hear even so much.

When the waitress brought my bowl of chili I asked, "What the devil's going on?"

One of the men, a skinny clerk in rimless glasses and a shiny double-breasted suit, clapped his hat on his elongated pink head and left the diner, slamming the screen door.

The waitress blankly watched him go and then looked down at her stained blue uniform. When she brought her gaze up to my face I saw that she was older than the high-school girl I had taken her for; her sprayed white bubble of hair and bright lipstick rode uneasily on her aging face. "You're not from around here," she said.

"That's right," I said. "What happened?"

"Where're you from?"

"New York," I said. "Why does it matter?"

"It matters, friend," came a male voice from down the counter, and I swiveled to look at a burly young moonface with thinning blond hair and a high corrugated forehead. The others grouped behind him, pretending not to hear, but I could see their bicep muscles tensing in their short-sleeve shirts. My friend with the football forehead leaned forward on his stool, palms on knees so that his forearms bulged.

I deliberately took a spoonful of chili. It was warm and bland. Greed is life. "Okay," I said, "it matters. I'm from New York. If you don't want to tell me what's happening you don't have to. I can hear it on the radio for myself."

"Now apologize to Grace-Ellen."

I was dumbfounded. "For what?"

"For swearing."

I looked at the waitress. She was leaning against the wall behind the counter. I thought she was trying to look offended.

"If I swore at you, I apologize," I said.

The men sat staring at me. I could feel violence thickening about them, not sure which way to flow or whether to flow at all.

"Get the shit out of here, wiseass," the young man said. "Wait. Frank, get the number of bigshot's car." He held up a massive palm in my direction while a small man in suspenders, a natural flunky, jumped up from his stool and ran out and stood in front of my car. Through the window I saw him pull a piece of paper from his shirt pocket and write on it.

My friend lowered his meaty palm. "I'm taking that number to the police," he said. "Now are you gonna sit and bullshit me some more or are you gonna leave?"

I stood up. There were three of them, not counting no 'count Frank. Sweat glissed coldly down my sides. In Manhattan such an exchange might last fifteen minutes with all parties knowing that they will do nothing more violent at the end than walk away. But the muscular balding blond young man had no trace of New York relish in insult and feigned toughness, and I risked only one further remark.

"I only asked a question." I hated him, his distrust of strangers and his manner of the village bully. I knew I would hate myself for fleeing.

He looked at me with flat eyes.

I walked slowly past him. All of the men were looking at me now with expressionless faces. One of them edged a contemptuous half inch out of my way so that I could open the door.

"He's got to pay for that chili," said Grace-Ellen, coming to life.

"Shut the fuck up," said her defender. "We don't need his goddam money."

I hesitated for a second, wondering whether I dared to drop a dollar on the floor. "Whatever it was," I said, "I hope it happens again. You deserve it." Then

I wheeled through the door and flipped the little pinwheel catch on its outside and sprinted toward the
Volkswagen. Grace-Ellen's voice was screaming *don't
bust that door* when I got the car started and drove off.

Five miles out of Plainview, my mind was a stew
of fantasies. I imagined retorts witty and threatening,
attacks sudden and brutal. I saw a hundred things I
might have done, from reasonable discussion to mash-
ing my bowl of chili into Wrinklehead's face. Eventually, I was trembling so severely that I had to stop
the car and get out. I needed release. I slammed the
door so hard that the whole car vibrated; then I raced
to the back and kicked one of the rear tires until my
foot ached. For a while I hammered on the beetle's
engine cover, pounding with my fists, seeing Wrinklehead's face in my mind. When I was exhausted I half-
fell into the dust and grass at the side of the road.
Hot sun scored my face. My hands throbbed, and I
noticed finally that I had torn a triangular flap of skin
from my left hand. The palm was filling with blood.
I clumsily wound my handkerchief around it. When
I held the handkerchief tightly, the wound throbbed
more but hurt less, both satisfactory sensations. A
memory hit me and came pulsing out with my slow
blood.

This was a memory of marital disharmony. A memory of disorder. Most of my marriage was disordered,
in fact, the blame for which was neither Joan's nor
mine but lay in the mis-mating of two wildly diver-
gent temperaments. It was tomaytos–tomahtos, eether–
eyether in every possible sphere. My favorite movies
had people shooting guns, hers had people speaking
French; I liked to read and listen to records in the
evening, she liked parties where she could pick fights
with stuffy gents in white shirts and striped ties; I
was monogamous by nature, she polyandrous. She was
one of those people for whom sexual faithfulness is
simply not possible, for whom it would be something
like death of imagination. Seven months before Joan
died, she had gone through, to my knowledge, five

lovers during our marriage, each of them wounding
to me: the last of these was one (let's call him)
Dribble. She was swimming with him, drunk, when
she drowned. On the occasion I remembered, we had
gone for dinner at Dribble's house. Amidst the usual
posters of the time (Che's iconic face, War Is Unhealthy for Children and Other Living Things) and
the paperbacks by Edgar Rice Burroughs and Carlos
Castaneda, we ate chili and drank Almaden Mountain
Red. Only during the musical part of the evening, while
Joan and Dribble were dancing to a Stones record, did
I realize that they had become lovers. Once home I
became a Mars of the coffee table and the dining room
curtains—I had thought we were in a good patch, I
felt betrayed. I accused. She denied hotly and then
hotly refused to deny. I slapped her. Oh, these errors
of an optimistic heart. She gasped, then called me a
"pig." She said that I had never loved her, that I had
stopped loving anything but Alison Greening. It was all
that could be said, it was a deliberate foray onto my
sacred territory. She stormed off to Dribble, I drove
to the all-night university library and played clown to
students in the corridors. My six years' marriage was
over.

It was the memory of that last messy scene that
assaulted me while I sat in the dust beside my car. I
almost smiled. It may have been from shame—it makes
me blaze with shame, that I struck her—and it may
have been in response to an odd and powerful sensation
which visited me then. This sensation was, centrally,
of freedom: of having a purer vision of myself settling
down upon me, of being cast out forever from my old
life. It felt like cold air, like blue cold water.

The connection between these two scenes, as you will
have noticed, is anger—as it was anger, I only now
observe, which rebounded back on me to grant the
sensation of a central freedom. Anger is an emotion
not typical of me. Generally, I mess through life, seeing
everybody's point of view. But the month to come,

certainly the strangest of my life, brought as much anger as it did fear. In my normal life, back on Long Island, I was shy and something of a clown, a clown from shyness. Since my adolescence, there seem to have been secrets of competence and knowingness from which I was locked away. Innocently, I had always imagined that anger created its own moral authority.

I rose from the dust and got back into the car, breathing hard. Blood had seeped through to the outer layers of the handkerchief, and I was vaguely aware of blood on my shoes, which I scuffed against the backs of my trouser legs. An echo of a dream caught in my mind, dislocating and severe. This I shook off by attempting to start the car. My assault on the engine must have offended the touchy little motor, because it sputtered and tut-tutted a long time and then eventually flooded. I sat, still breathing noisily, for a while and then tried it again: it chuffed, and went back to work.

When I had gone about half of the distance to Arden I turned on the radio and twisted the knob until I found the Arden station. Then I discovered what the peculiar scene in the diner had been all about. My up-to-date reporter, Michael Moose (so it sounded), was coming to me with the news and all the news on the hour and the half-hour with a full five minutes of local roundup and world events. In his deep hollow announcer's voice, he said, "Police report no progress yet toward discovery of the perpetrator of the most shocking crime in Arden's history, the sex-murder of Gwen Olson. The discovery of the body of the twelve-year-old sixth-grader was made early this morning by fishermen crossing a deserted area of waste ground near the Blundell River. Chief Hovre reports that he and his team will be working on this case full time until it is solved. A bare eight hours since . . ." I turned it off.

Though any urban American gets this story with most of his breakfasts, it was not callousness that made me switch off the radio, but the flicker of a penetrating

certainty—the certainty that I would be seeing Alison
Greening again, that she would honor a pact we had
made twenty years before. My cousin, Alison Greening—I had not seen her since that night, when the
consequence of a nude swim had been our total separa-
tion.

I cannot explain this sudden half-conviction that
Alison would keep her vow, but I believe it had its
birth in that earlier flood of wonderful high feeling,
that grip of freedom as I bled into my handkerchief.
When I knew and loved her, she embodied freedom
to me, freedom and strength of will—she obeyed only
her own rules. Anyhow, I savored this sensation for
a moment, my hand still on the knob of the radio, and
then I packed it away in my mind, thinking that what
would happen, would. I knew that the keeping of my
half of our vow was an equal part of my return to
Arden.

Eventually the four-lane highway ascended a hill I
knew, and then, going sharply down, traversed a high
metal bridge which was the first true landmark. Going
down the hill, my father would say, "We'll fly over it
this time," and pull back on the wheel while accelerat-
ing. I would scream with expectation, and even as we
raced past the bolts and girders of the bridge it was
as though we had for a moment taken flight. From here
I could have jogged to the farmhouse, bad heart, thick
waistline, suitcases and cartons and all, and I glanced
at the long flat cornfields on both sides with spirits
momentarily high.

But between the bridge and my grandmother's farmhouse were many more landmarks—I knew the roads,
the few buildings, even the trees by rote from my childhood, when they had been all washed in the glow of
being on vacation—all of them important, but at least
three of them vital. At the first crossroads past the
bridge I left the highway, which continued, going over
another, low metal bridge, on to Arden, and joined
the narrower road into the valley. At the very edge

of the entrance to the valley, when one first becomes
aware of the wooded hills sloping up from the far side
of the fields, was the yet narrower and rougher road
to Auntie Rinn's house. I wondered what had happened
to that sturdy little wooden structure now that the
old woman was surely dead. Of course children have
no proper idea of the ages of adults, forty to a ten-
year-old is only a blink away from seventy, but Auntie
Rinn, my grandmother's sister, had always been old
to me—she was not one of the fat vital shouting farm
women conspicuous at church picnics in the valley,
but of the other common physical type, drawn and
thin, almost stringy from youth on. In old age, these
women seem weightless, transparencies held together
by wrinkles, though many of them work small farms
with only the most necessary assistance. But Rinn's
day had long passed, I was sure: my grandmother had
died six years before, aged seventy-nine, and Rinn had
been older than her sister.

Rinn had owned a considerable reputation for ec-
centricity in the valley, and visiting her always partook
a bit of the adventurous—even now, knowing that the
old wraith's home was probably inhabited by a redfaced
young farmer who would prove to be my cousin at
several removes, even now the little road up the hill to
her house looked eerie, winding up past the fields to
the trees. Her house had been so thickly surrounded
by trees that little sunlight had ever fought through to
her windows.

I think Rinn's oddness had been rooted in her spin-
sterhood, always something of an anomaly in farm
country where fertility is a sign of grace. Where my
grandmother had married a neighboring young farmer,
Einar Updahl, and prospered, Rinn had been tenuously
engaged to a young Norwegian she never met. The
match was arranged by aunts and uncles in Norway.
It is the only sort of engagement I can imagine Rinn
accepting—to a man thousands of miles away, a man
in no danger of impinging upon her life. The story, as
I remember it, was that the young man ceased to threat-

en Rinn's independence at the very time he drew nearest to it: he died on board the boat bringing him to America. Everyone in the family, save Rinn, thought this was a tragedy. She'd had a house built for her by her brother-in-law, my grandfather, and she insisted on moving into it. Years later, when my mother was a child, my grandmother had visited Rinn and come upon her talking volubly in the kitchen. *Are you talking to yourself now,* asked my grandmother. *Of course not,* said Rinn. *I'm talking to my young man.* I never saw any sign that she was on excessively familiar terms with the departed, but she did look as though she were capable of tricks not available to most of us. I knew two versions of the story of Rinn and the heifer: in the first, Rinn was walking past a neighbor's farm when she looked at his livestock, wheeled around and marched up the track to his house. She took him down to the road and pointed to a heifer in the pen and said that animal will die tomorrow, and it did. This is the predictive version. In the causal version, the neighboring farmer had offended Rinn somehow, and she took him into the road and said, that heifer will die tomorrow unless you stop—what? Crossing my land? Diverting my water? Whatever it was, the farmer laughed at her, and the heifer died. The causal version was certainly mine. As a child I was scared to death of her—I had half-suspected that one glance of those washed-out Norwegian blue eyes could turn me into a toad if it was a toad she thought I deserved to be.

She must be imagined as a small hunched thin old woman, her abundant white hair loosely bound by a scarf, wearing nondescript farm dresses—working dresses, often covered by various amazing coats, for she had kept poultry in an immense barnlike structure just down the hill from her house, and she sold eggs to the Co-op. Her land never was much good for farming, being too hilly and forested. If her young man had come, he would have had a hard time of it, and maybe when she talked to him she told him that he was better off wherever he was than trying to plant corn or alfalfa on a heavily wooded hillside.

To me she had chiefly spoken of Alison, whom she had not liked. (But few adults had liked Alison.)

Six minutes from the narrow road to Rinn's old house, set off the main valley road on a little dog-leg behind the valley's only store, was the second of my landmarks. I spun the VW into the dirt parking area before Andy's and walked around in back to have another look at it. As comic and sad as ever, but with all of the windows broken now and its original slight listing become a decided sprawl of the whole structure, it sat in a wilderness of ropy weeds and high grass at the edge of a vacant field. I see now that these first two landmarks have both to do with marriages frustrated, with lives bent and altered by sexual disappointment. And both of them are touched with strangeness, with a definitive peculiarity. I was sure that in the past fifteen years, Duane's monstrous little house had acquired among the valley children a reputation for being haunted.

This was the house that Duane built—my father's apposite joke—the house he had singlehandedly built for his first love, a Polish girl from Arden detested by my grandmother. In those days, the Norwegian farmers and the Polish townsmen mingled very little. "Duane's Dream House," my parents had said, though only to one another: his parents pretended that nothing was wrong with the house, and any jocularity about the subject met with insulted incomprehension. Duane had worked to plans in his head, and they had evidently been stunted there, for the house he had lovingly built for his fiancée was about the size of a small granary—or, say, a big dollhouse, a dollhouse you could stand up in if you were under five foot seven. It had two stories, four equal tiny rooms, as if he had forgotten that people had to cook and eat and shit, and all of this weird construction now leaned decidedly to the right, as if the boards were stretching—I suppose it was about as substantial as a house of straw.

As was his engagement. The Polish girl had fulfilled my grandmother's worst expectations of those whose parents did not work with their hands, and had run off one winter day with a mechanic at an Arden garage—"another shiftless Pole without the brains God gave him," my grandmother said to my mother. "When Einar was trading horses—Miles, your grandfather was a great horsetrader here in the valley, and there never was a lazy or a stupid man yet who could see what a horse was made of—when he was going off for a few days with a string, he always used to say that the only thing an Arden Pole knew about a horse was he was supposed to look at its teeth. *And* that he didn't know which end to find them at. *And* that if he found them he didn't know what he was supposed to see. That girl of Duane's was just like the rest of them, running off into damnation because a boy had a fancy car."

She had not even seen the house he had just finished building for her. As the story gradually came to me, Duane had wanted the girl's first sight of her house to be as he was carrying her into it after the ceremony. Had she come out with her mechanic one night for a look and run off on the spot? Duane had gone into Arden to see her, the week before Christmas in 1955, and her parents had been weepy and hostile. It was a long time before he learned from them that she had never come home the night before—they blamed him, a Lutheran and a Norskie and a farmer, for the loss of their daughter. He ran up to her room and found everything gone: all her clothes, everything she had cared for. From there he raced down to the five and dime where she clerked and heard that she had told the supervisor that she wasn't going to come in any more. And from the store he went to the filling station to meet the boy whose existence had never exactly been confirmed. He too had disappeared: "Run off last night in that new Stude," the owner said. "Musta been with your girl, I spoze."

Like a character in a parody of a Gothic novel, he had never spoken of the girl again, nor had he ever visited this terrible little house. It was never mentioned before him: he was pretending that his engagement had never happened. Four years later he met another girl, the daughter of a farmer in the next valley. He married her and had a child, but that too turned out badly for him.

The absurd frame structure was leaning as though a giant had brushed against it, in a hurry to get somewhere else; even the window frames had become trapezoidal. I walked across the dust and into the thick high weeds and grass. Burrs and bits of fluff adhered to my trousers. I looked in through the two windows facing the rear of Andy's store and the valley road. The room was, to be straightforward, a mess, a mess of desolation. The floorboards had warped and rotted so that weeds thrust up at various places into the room, and bird and animal droppings littered the floor—it looked like a filthy vacant coffin. One corner held a tangle of blankets from which radiated a semi-circle of dead cigarette butts. On the walls I could distinguish the scrawls left by felt-tip pens. My spirits began to dwindle as I looked in at my cousin's folly, and I turned away, snaring my left foot in a thick fist of weeds. It was as though that malignant dwarf of a house had snatched at me, and I kicked out with all my force. A thorn stabbed my ankle as decisively as a wasp. Swearing, suddenly cold, I walked away from Duane's little house and went through the dust around to the front of Andy's.

This, the third of my landmarks, was much more comfortable, much more touched with the grace of normality. My family had always made a ritual stop at Andy's before continuing on to the farm, and there we invariably loaded up with bottles of Dr. Pepper for me and a case of beer for my father and Uncle Gilbert, Duane's father. Andy's was what people used to mean when they said general store, a place where you could buy almost anything, workshirts and trousers, caps, ax handles and heads, meal, clocks, soap, boots, candy, blankets, magazines, toys, suitcases, drills and punches, dogfood, paper, hoes and rakes, chicken feed, gasoline cans, silage formula, flashlights, bread . . . all of this ranked and packed and piled into a long white wooden building raised up on thick stilts of brick. Before it, three white gaspumps faced the road. I reached the steps and went up through the screen door to the dark cool interior.

It smelled as it always had, a wonderful composite odor of various newnesses. When the screen door banged behind me Andy's wife (I could not remember her name) looked up at me from where she was sitting behind the counter, reading a newspaper. She frowned, glanced back at her paper, and when I began to thread my way through the aisles of things, turned her head and muttered something toward the rear of the store. She was a small darkhaired aggressive-looking woman, and her appearance had become dryer and tougher with age. As she glanced suspiciously back, I remembered that we had never been friendly, and that I had given her reason for her dislike of me. Yet I did not think that she recognized me: I have changed greatly in appearance since my early youth. The chemistry of the moment was wrong, I knew this; my earlier elation had ebbed away, leaving me flat and depressed, and I should have left the store at that moment.

"Anything I can do for you, Mister?" she asked, in her voice the valley's lilt. For the first time it sounded unfriendly and alien to me.

"Andy in?" I asked, coming closer to the counter through the massed smells of newness.

She wordlessly left her chair and disappeared into the cavernous rear of the store. A door closed, then opened again.

In a moment I saw Andy walking toward me. He had grown fatter and balder, and his pudgy face seemed sexually indeterminate and permanently worried. When he reached the counter he stopped and leaned against it, creasing his belly. "What can I do you for?" he said, the jokiness of the phrase out of key with his rubbery defeated face and his air of country suspicion.

I saw that gray had eaten nearly all of the brown in his fringe of hair. "You're not one of the drummers. Reps, they call themselves now."

"I wanted to come in and say hello," I said. "I used to come in here with my parents. I'm Eve Updahl's boy," using the shorthand that would identify me in the valley.

He looked at me hard for a moment, then nodded and said, "Miles. You'd be Miles, then. Come back for a visit or just a look-see?" Andy, like his wife, would remember my little errors of judgment of twenty years before.

"Mostly to work," I said. "I thought the farm would be a peaceful place to work." An explanation when I had planned to give none—he was making me defensive.

"Don't think I recall what kind of work you wound up doing."

"I'm a college teacher," I said, and the demon of irritation made me take pleasure in his flicker of surprise. "English."

"Well, you were always supposed to be brainy," he said. "Our girl takes shorthand and typing over to the business college in Winona. She's getting on real good up there. Don't suppose you teach around here anywhere?"

I told him the name of my university.

"That's back East?"

"It's on Long Island."

"Eve always said she was afraid you'd wind up back East. So what's this work you got to do?"

"I have to write a book—that is, I'm writing a book. On D. H. Lawrence."

"Uh huh. What's that when it's at home?"

I said, "He wrote *Lady Chatterley's Lover*."

Andy swung his eyes up to mine with a surprisingly roguish gesture which was somehow girlish at the same time. He looked as though he were about to lick his lips. "I guess it's true what they say about those colleges out East, huh?" But the remark was not the invitation to masculine revelation that it could have been: there was a sly malice in it.

"It's only one of a lot of books he wrote," I said.

Again I got the wink of roguishness. "I guess one Book's good enough for me." He turned to the side, and I saw his wife lurking in the back of the shop, staring at me. "It's Miles, Eve's boy," he said. "Coulda fooled me. Says he's here writing a dirty book."

She came forward, glowering. "We heard you and your wife got divorced. Duane said."

"We were separated," I said a bit harshly. "Now she's dead."

Surprise showed in both their faces for a second.

"Guess we didn't hear that," said Andy's wife. "Was there something you wanted?"

"Maybe I'll pick up a case of beer for Duane. What kind does he drink?"

"If it's beer he'll drink it," said Andy. "Blatz, Schlitz or Old Milwaukee? I guess we got some Bud around here too."

"Any one," I said, and Andy lumbered away to the back room where he kept his stacked cases of beer.

His wife and I looked uncomfortably at one another. She broke the contact first, darting her eyes away toward the floor and then out to where my car was parked. "You been staying out of trouble?"

"Of course. Yes."

"But you're writing filth, he says."

"He didn't understand. I came here to write my dissertation."

She bristled. "And you think Andy's too dumb to understand you. You were always too good for us up here, weren't you? You were too good for ordinary folk—too good to follow the law too."

"Wait, hold on," I said. "Jesus, that was a long time ago."

"And so good you don't think about taking the Lord's name in vain. You haven't changed, Miles. Does Duane know you're coming?"

"Well sure," I said. "Don't be so bitchy. Look, I'm sorry. I've been driving two days and I've had a couple of funny experiences." I saw her glance at my hand-kerchief-wrapped left hand. "All I want here is peace and quiet."

"You always made trouble," she said. "You and your cousin Alison were just alike that way. I'm glad neither of you was raised in the valley. Your grandparents were our people, Miles, and we all took to your father like he was one of us, but now I think maybe we got enough trouble without having you here too."

"Good lord," I said. "What happened to your hospitality?"

She glared at me. "You wore out your welcome here the first time you stole from us. I'll tell Andy to take your beer down to your motor. You can leave the money on the counter."

Portion of Statement by Margaret Kastad:
July 16

I knew he was Miles Teagarden when he first set foot in our store even though Andy says he didn't know until he said he was Eve's boy. He had that same look he always had, like some bad secret was on his mind. I used to feel so sorry for Eve, she was straight as a die all her life, and I guess you don't know what will happen to your children if you bring them up in funny places. But Eve never was to blame for that boy Miles. Now we know all about him, I'm glad Eve passed away before she could see just how bad he turned out. On that first day I just turned him out of the store. I said Miles, you ain't fooling none of us here. We know you. Now you just get on out of our store. Andy'll take that beer of yours down to your motor. I could tell he was in a fight or some-thing—he looked weak or scared, the way they do, and his hand was still bleeding. I told him, and I'd tell him the same again. He never was

*any good, was he, for all those brains they said
he had? He was just funny—just funny. If he was
a dog or a horse you'd have penned him up or just
shot him. Right off. Him and that sneaky look and
that handkerchief around his hand.*

I silently watched Andy load the beer into the back
seat of the Volkswagen, shoving in the case beside
the paper boxes full of notes and books. "Hurt your
wing, huh?" he said. "Wife says you paid up there.
Well, give my regards to Duane, and I hope your mitt
gets better." He backed away from the car, wiping his
hands on his trousers as if he'd dirtied them, and I
wordlessly got in behind the wheel. "Bye now," he
said, and I looked at him and then took off out of the
dusty little lot. In the rearview mirror I saw him shrug-
ging. When the curve in the road by the red sandstone
cliff took him out of sight I snapped the radio on,
hoping for music, but Michael Moose was droning on
again about Gwen Olson's death and I impatiently
turned it off.

When I had got as far down the valley as the shell
of the school where my grandmother had taught all
eight grades I pulled over and tried to relax. There is a
special feeling in the mind that represents the creation
of alpha waves, and I deliberately sought that mild
state. This time I failed, and I merely sat in the car,
staring alternately at the road, the long green field of
corn to my right, and the shell of the schoolhouse.
I began to hear the buzz of a motorcycle, and soon I
saw it flying down the road toward me, growing in size
from the dimensions of a horsefly to the point where I
could see the black-jacketed, helmeted rider and the
blond passenger behind him, her hair whipping out in
the wake and her thick thighs gripping him. At the
curve by the sandstone cliff the sound altered, and then
it died away altogether.

Why should your old sins be permanently pinned to
your jacket? For all to read aloud? It was stupidly
unfair. I would do my shopping in Arden, despite the

inconvenience of making a ten-mile drive whenever I wanted anything. The making of this decision helped to dispel my temper and after a minute or two of further brooding I began to feel as though I might be producing an at least feeble tranquility.

Where, you might ask, was the clown, the reluctant wag I have proclaimed myself to be? My own abrasiveness surprised me. A woman like Andy's wife would think the word "bitch" scandalous applied to any sphere but the canine. It was an emotional morning. My former thefts! Yet I supposed that it was too much to expect anyone to have forgotten them.

A hundred yards past the deserted school was the church: Gethsemane Lutheran church is a red brick building with quite a sturdy, pompous, peaceful air to it, probably conferred by the Palladian columns at the top of the stairs. For the sake of my grandmother, who was already very weak, Joan and I had been married in this church. (My mother's idea.)

After the church the land seems to open up, and the corn takes over. I passed the Sunderson farmhouse —two pickup trucks parked on the high sloping lawn, a rooster strutting in the red dust of the driveway— and saw a burly man in overalls and a cap just coming out of the house. He stared at me and then decided to wave, but I had not generated sufficient alpha waves to return his greeting.

Half a mile past the Sunderson farm I could see my grandmother's old house and the Updahl land. The row of walnut trees at the edge of the lawn had put on weight, and now they looked like a row of heavy old farmers standing in the sun. I drove by the front of the property and swung into the driveway, passing the trees and feeling the car jounce on the ruts. I expected to feel some strong upwelling of feeling, looking at the long white house again, but my emotions seemed flat and dull. It was just a two-story house with a screen porch, an ordinary farmhouse. Yet when I got out of the car I smelled all the old odors of the farm, a rich compound of cows and horses and fertilizer and milk and sunshine. This pervades everything: when people from the farm had visited my family in Fort Lauderdale, it hung on their clothes and hands and shoes. Smelling all this again made me momentarily feel thirteen years old, and I lifted my head, straightening out the kinks in my neck and back, and saw a heavy form moving down the screen porch. By his shovel-handed, lumbering walk I knew it was Duane, who had been sitting invisible in the corner of the porch just as he had been on that terrible night twenty years before. When Duane came out of the porch into the sun I tried to smile at him. What the first sight of my cousin had brought back to me was how much hostility there had always been between us, how little we had liked one another. It would be different now, I hoped.

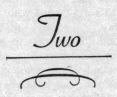

Two

"Have a case of beer, Duane," I said, mistakenly trying for a bluff friendliness.

He appeared to be confused—really, confusion was stamped all over his big plain face—but his mechanism was set for holding out his hand and saying hello, and that was what he did. His hand was huge, a true farmer's hand, and so rough it felt made of a substance less vulnerable than skin. Duane was a short barrel-like man, but his extremities might have come from someone a foot taller. As we clasped hands and he blinked at me, half smiling, trying to figure out what I meant about the beer, I noticed that he had obviously come in from a morning's work: he wore heavy stained denim coveralls and workboots crusted with mud and excrement. He radiated all of the usual farm odors, compounded with sweat and underlain by his true odor, his inner smell, which is of gunpowder.

Finally he released my hand. "Did you have a good drive?"

"Sure," I said. "This country isn't as big as we think it is. People zip back and forth on it all the time." The persistence of habit: although he was nearly a decade older, I had always taken this tone with Duane.

"I'm glad you had a good drive. You sure surprised me when you said you wanted to come out here again."

"You thought I was lost among the fleshpots of the East."

He distrusted the word "fleshpots," being not quite sure what it meant. That was twice I had taken him off balance. "I was just kind of surprised," he said. "Say, Miles, I was sorry about your wife. Maybe you wanted to get away?"

"That's it," I said. "I did want to get away. Did you take time off from your work to greet me?"

"Well, I didn't want you to come in and find nobody to home. The kid's gone out somewhere, and you know kids, you can't count on them for anything. So I thought I'd wait around after lunch and say hi. Make you feel welcome. And I thought I might listen to the radio in the porch there, see if anything new happened on that terrible business. My kid knew that Olson girl."

"Will you help me get these bags and things inside?" I said.

"Huh? Oh, sure," and he reached in, bending over the seat, and lifted out two heavy boxes of books and notes. Upright again, he asked, "Is that beer in there for me?"

"I hope it's your brand."

"It's wet, ain't it?" He grinned. "I'll put it in the tank when we got you squared away." Before we went toward the porch, Duane twisted his head and looked at me with a surprisingly embarrassed expression on his face. "Say, Miles, maybe I shouldn't have said that about your wife. Because I only met her that once."

"It's all right."

"No. I should never open my mouth about anyone else's woman troubles."

He was referring, I knew, to his own history of marital disaster and to something else as well. Duane was suspicious of women—he was one of those men, sexually normal in every other respect, who are at ease only in male company. I think that he had a radical dislike of women. For him they primarily had been sources of pain, with the exception of his mother and grand-

mother (about his daughter I could not then speak).
After his first disappointment, he had married a girl
from one of the farms in French Valley, and this girl
had died giving birth to their child. He'd had one numb-
ing humiliation at the hands of a girl (the humiliation
not salved by his grandmother's evident satisfaction
in it) followed by four years of being between women,
his romantic life joked about in Arden bars, then eleven
months of marriage and the rest of his life without
adult feminine companionship. I suspected that his suspicion of women contained a fair portion of hate. For
Duane they had approached and then abruptly with-
drawn, still holding whatever mysterious sexual secret
they possessed. In the old days, when the Polish girl
had been giving him trouble, I had often sensed that
his attitude toward Alison Greening was edged with
something darker than mere desire. I think he hated
her, hated her for evoking desire in him and for finding
his desire laughable, a thing of no consequence or
value. Alison *had* found him absurd.

Of course Duane was physically vigorous, and his
celibacy must at times have been a torment: yet I
suspected him of being the kind of man who is shocked
and upset by his own fantasies, and is comfortable
with women only when they are safely married to his
acquaintances. He had submerged his sexuality in work
for so long that he expected other men to do the same,
habit had become transformed into principle, and he
had his success to justify him. Duane had purchased
two hundred neighboring acres, and was now at the
limit of what a man could farm by himself if he worked
ten hours a day; as if to demonstrate the physical law
that actions have equal reactions, sexual starvation had
fattened his bank account.

The immediate evidence of his prosperity struck me
when we carried the boxes and suitcases into my grandmother's old house. "My God, Duane," I said, "you
bought new furniture for the place!" Instead of my
grandmother's spare old wooden furniture, her threadbare old sofa, the room held what I suppose could be

called nineteen-fifties lounge furniture: heavy patterned chairs and matching couch, a blond coffee table, starkly functional table lamps instead of kerosene lamps, even framed reproductions of mediocre paintings. In the setting of the old house, the nondescript new furniture had a tactless chic. The effect of all this on the austere farmhouse living room was to make it resemble a freeway motel bedroom. But there was another resemblance I did not immediately identify.

"I suppose you think it's funny to get new stuff for an empty house, don't you?" he asked me. "The thing is, I get people stopping up here more often than you'd think. In April, George and Ethel were here, and in May Nella from St. Paul, and—" He went on to enumerate a lengthy list of cousins and their children who had stayed in the house for a week or more at a time. "Sometimes this place is like a regular hotel. I guess all these city folks want to show their kids what a farm looks like."

While he talked I noticed that the old photographs of the grandchildren still hung on the walls, as they always had. I knew them all: I identified a picture of myself at nine, my hair in a cowlick like a ruff, and one of Duane at fifteen, scowling suspiciously at the camera as if it were about to tell him something he wouldn't like. Below this was a photograph of Alison which I sensed glowing at me but lacked the courage to look at directly. The sight of that beautiful wild face would have knocked the wind out of me. And then I noticed that the house was immaculately clean.

"Anyhow," Duane was saying, "up over to Arden, a warehouse full of office furniture had a clearance sale just when I got my rebate. So I thought I'd do the old place up since all the furniture was going pretty cheap. Took the truck down and just humped all this stuff back with me."

This was the resemblance I had been unable to name: the room looked like an office in a down-at-heels concern.

"I like the modern way it looks," said Duane, perhaps a shade defensively. "And it cost less than a second-hand disc." He glanced at me, then added, "Everybody seems to like it."

"It's great," I said, "I like it too," distracted by the throbbing and glowing of Alison's photograph on the wall. I knew this photograph well. It had been taken in Los Angeles near the end of her childhood, before the Greenings were divorced and Alison and her mother moved to San Francisco. It showed only her face. Even when she was a child, Alison's face was beautiful and complicated, magic, and her father's photograph showed it all, the beauty and the magical complications. She looked as though she knew and embraced everything. The thought of that overwhelming expression on her childhood face made my stomach tingle, and to avoid looking at the photograph I said, "I wish you had picked up a desk while you were at it. I need a desk to work at."

"That's no problem," said Duane. "I got an old panel door and a couple of sawbucks we could lay it across."

"Well," I said, and turned toward him. "You're a good host, Duane. The place looks clean, too."

"Mrs. Sunderson down the road, you remember her? Tuta Sunderson? Her husband died a couple of years back, and she lives up there now with her boy Red and his wife. Red farms pretty near as good as Jerome did. Anyhow, I talked to Tuta and she said she'd come over here every day to cook your breakfast and dinner and clean for you. She was in here yesterday." He paused, having something further to say. "Said it would be five dollars a week and you'd have to buy your own groceries. She can't drive since she had her cataract operation. That okay?"

I said it was fine with me. "Actually, let's make it seven dollars," I said. "Otherwise I'd feel like I was stealing from her."

"Whatever you say. She said five, though, and you probably remember her. Let's get that beer into the tank." He clapped his hands together.

The two of us went back outside into the hot sun and the farm smells. Duane's gunpowder odor was stronger in the open air, and to escape it I reached into the car first and pulled out the case of beer. He trudged beside me up the long path past the baking metal of the pole barn, the granary, and well past that, his white clap-boarded house, to the tank beside the cattle barn.

"You said in your letter you were working on a book."

"My dissertation."

"What's that on?"

"An English writer."

"Did he write a lot?"

"A lot," I said, and laughed. "A hell of a lot."

Duane laughed too. "How'd you pick that?"

"It's a long story," I said. "I expect to be pretty busy, but is there still anyone around here that I used to know?"

He considered that as we passed the brown scar where the summerhouse used to be. "Didn't you know Polar Bears Hovre? He's the Police Chief over to Arden now."

I almost dropped the case of beer. "Polar Bears? That wildman?" When I was ten and he seventeen, Polar Bears and I had spitballed the congregation from the choir loft at Gethsemane church.

"He settled down some," Duane said. "He does a good job."

"I ought to call him up. We used to have fun together. Even though he always liked Alison a little too much for my taste."

Duane gave me a peculiar, startled look, and contented himself with saying, "Well, he keeps pretty busy now."

I remembered another figure from my past—really, the sweetest and most intelligent of all the Arden boys I had met years ago. "What about Paul Kant? Is he still around? I suppose he went off to a university somewhere and never came back."

"No, you can see Paul. He works in Arden. He

works in that Zumgo department store they got over there. Or so I hear."

"I don't believe it. He works in a department store? Is he manager or something?"

"Just works there, I guess. He never did much." Duane looked at me again, a little shyly this time, and said, "He's a little funny. Or so they say."

"Funny?" I was incredulous.

"Well, you know how some people talk. Nobody would mind if you called him up, I guess."

"Yes, I do know how they talk," I said, remembering Andy's wife. "They've said enough about me. Some of them are still saying it." Now we were at the tank, and I leaned over the mossy rim and began putting the bottles down into the green water.

Portion of Statement by Duane Updahl:

July 16

Sure, I'll tell you whatever you want to know about Miles. I could tell you lots about that guy. He never fit in up here, you know, when he was nothing but a shrimpy kid, and I could tell right off that he wasn't going to fit in any better this time. He looked weird, I guess you could term it. He talked like he had a crab hanging on his asshole, city fashion. Like he was making jokes at me. When he said he wanted to see Chief Hovre you coulda knocked me down with a feather. (Laughs.) I guess he got his wish, didn't he? We were carrying beer to put down into my little tank I got there beside my barn, you know, and he said that about Polar Bears, I mean Galen, and then he said he wanted to see Kant (laughs), and I said, sure, you go ahead, you know (laughs), and then he said something, I don't know, about people talking about him. Then he damn near popped those beer bottles slamming them against the bot-

*tom of the tank. But when he really acted strange
was when my daughter came in.*

The cap on one of the last beer bottles caught my
handkerchief when I was pulling my hand out of the
tank, and the wet cloth separated from my hand and
sank down on top of the bottles. Chilly water tingled
and ached in the exposed wound, and I gasped. Blood
began to come twisting out like smoke or a flag—I
thought of sharks.

"You meet up with something that didn't like you?"
Duane had insinuated himself beside me and was staring heavily down at my hand bleeding into his tank.

"It's a little difficult to explain." I snatched my paw
out of the cold water and leaned over the tank and
pressed my palm against its far edge, where moss grew
nearly an inch thick. The throbbing and stinging immediately lessened, inhibited by application of magic
substance. If I could have stayed there all day, pressing
my hand against that cool slimy moss, my hand would
have healed, millions of new cells would have formed
every second.

"You dizzy?" Duane asked.

I was looking out across the road to his fields. Alfalfa
and tall corn grew in alternate bands on either side of
the creek and the line of willows and cottonwoods; a
round shoulder of hillside further up was perfectly bisected by the two crops. It was for silage—Duane had
years before given up everything but beef cattle. Up
from the bifurcated hillside grew the woods climbing
to the top of the valley. They seemed impossibly perfect, like a forest by Rousseau. I wanted to take a
handful of moss and go up there to camp, forgetting
all about teaching and my book and New York.

"You dizzy?"

Blood was oozing down through the thick moss into
the water. I was still looking at the edge of the field,
where the rise of trees began. I thought that I had
seen a slim figure duck momentarily out of the trees,
glance toward us and then slip back into cover like a

fox. It might have been a boy. By the time I was fully aware of it, it had vanished.

"You okay?" Duane sounded a little impatient.

"Sure, I'm fine. Do you get many kids wandering around up in those woods?"

"They're pretty thick. Nobody goes in them much. Why?"

"Oh, nothing. Nothing, really."

"We still got a few animals up there too. But they're no good for hunting. Unless you got a rifle can shoot around trees."

"Andy's probably got a few of those." I lifted my hand from the moss. It immediately began to sting and pulse. Due to removal of magic substance.

Portion of Statement by Duane Updahl:

July 16

He was planning something all along, something that had control of him, you could say. You should . . have seen him grab onto the tank with that cut mitt of his. I should have known there'd be trouble up in those woods, just by the way he was staring at 'em and asking funny questions.

Magic substances are those with a sacred, soothing and healing content. When Duane said, "Let's go up to the house and I'll bandage that mitt of yours," I surprised him by ripping out a handful of the thick moss, exposing a gray, rusting section of the tank, and by gripping the green slippery stuff in my wounded hand. I squeezed it tightly, and the stinging pain lessened a bit.

"Used to be an old Indian woman around here who'd do that for you," Duane said, looking at the pulpy mess in my hand. "Make medicine out of herbs and like that. Like Rinn did, too. But what you got there is liable to get pretty dirty. We'll wash her out before we put on the gauze. How'd you get a thing like that, anyhow?"

"Oh, it was just a stupid fit of temper."

The moss had become dark with blood, an uncomfortably soggy thing to hold, and I dropped the messy handful onto the grass and turned to walk up the drive to Duane's house. A dog lying panting by the granary looked attentively at the bloody pad.

"You get into a fight?"

"Not really. I just had a little accident."

"Remember that time you totaled that car just outside Arden?"

"I don't think I could forget it," I said. "I just about bought it."

"Wasn't that after that time out at the—"

"It was, yes," I broke in, not wanting him to utter the word "quarry."

"That was a hell of a time," he said. "I was in my truck going down the road right after you, but when you turned right on 93, I went the other way toward Liberty. I just drove around. After about an hour—"

"Okay, that's enough."

"Well, you know, I was going to—"

"That's enough. It's all in the past." I wanted to shut him up and was desperately sorry we had ever got on this topic. Several steps behind me, the dog began growling and whining. Duane bent down and picked up a stone and threw it at the animal; I kept walking straight ahead. I was holding my hand out from my side, letting my blood drip steadily down my fingers, and I imagined that skulking creeping black-and-white beast crawling toward me. The stone connected; the dog yelped, and I could hear it pelting off to a safe distance. I looked around and saw a trail of bright drops on the grass.

"You gonna call Auntie Rinn today?" Duane had reached the cement steps to his house, and was standing down there, his head tilted up at me. "I told her you were coming, Miles, and I guess she understood. I think she wants to see you."

"Rinn?" I asked, incredulous. "Is she still alive? I was just thinking that she must have died years ago."

He smiled—the infuriating disbelief of an insider. "Dead? That old bird? Nothing can kill her."

He came up the stairs and I followed him into his house. The door opened onto a hallway off the kitchen, which was much as it had been when Uncle Gilbert had been alive: patterned linoleum on the floor, a long Formica-topped dining table, the same porcelain stove. But the walls looked yellowish, and the entire room had an air of dirt and neglect only partially explained by the greasy handprints on the refrigerator and the stack of dishes by the sink. There was dust even on the mirror. It looked like the sort of room where an army of ants and mice are poised behind the walls, waiting for the lights to go off.

He saw me gazing around. "The damn kid's supposed to keep the kitchen clean, but she's about as responsible as a . . ." He shrugged. "A cowflop."

"Imagine what your mother would say if she could see it."

"Oh, I'm used to it this way," he said, blinking. "Besides, it don't do to hold to the past like that."

I thought he was wrong. I have always held to the past, I thought that it could, would, should be repeated indefinitely, that it was the breathing life in the heart of the present. But I couldn't speak of this to Duane. I said, "Tell me about Auntie Rinn. Were you hinting that she's deaf?" I went to the sink and held my dripping hand over it.

"Hang on while I get the gauze and tape," he said, and lumbered away toward the bathroom. When he returned he took my hand and held it under a stream of cold water from the tap. "You couldn't say she was deaf. You couldn't say she was blind. The way I make it out, she sees what she wants to see and hears what she wants to hear. But don't mess around with her. If she wants to hear it, she'll hear. She's sharp. She knows everything that's going on."

"Can she get around?"

"She doesn't leave her place much. Neighbors buy her groceries, the little she needs, but she still has her egg business. And she rents out her little field to Oscar Johnstad. I reckon she gets by. But now she's in her eighties, we don't even see her at church."

Surprisingly, Duane was a good nurse. As he talked, he quickly dried my hand with a dishtowel, pressed a big pad of absorbent cotton onto the wound and wrapped a broad strip of tape around the base of my hand, winding it around both sides of my thumb. "Now," he said when he was finishing. "We're gonna make you look like a farmer."

Farms are notorious for accidents: slings, bandages and amputated limbs are commonplaces in rural communities, as are suicides, mental instability and sullen temperaments. In the latter particulars, but not the former, they resemble academic communities. Both are usually thought of as havens of serenity. I entertained myself with these reflections while Duane made his final pass with the roll of tape, tore it with his blunt fingers, and anchored the loose end firmly at the base of my hand. I looked like a farmer: a good omen for the completion of my dreadful work.

Oh, for it was dreadful, an insult to spirit. As the fingers of my left hand began to tingle, suggesting the possibility that Duane might have wound the tape over-tightly, I realized how much I disliked writing academic criticism. I decided that once I had finished my book and had made my job secure, I'd never write another word of it.

"Anyhow," Duane said, "you could call her up or just go over."

I would. I thought I would drive over to her farm in the next day or two, after I had settled in at the old farmhouse. Auntie Rinn, I thought, was inhabited by spirit, she *was* spirit in one of its forms, like the girl whose photograph could make my tongue a stone. I heard the door open and close behind me.

"Alison," Duane said matter-of-factly but with an undertone of anger. "Cousin Miles has been wondering where you were."

I turned around, aware that I did not look normal.

Gazing sardonically, even contemptuously at me, though with a trace of interest—the contempt seemed defensive and automatic—was a rather thickset, thoroughly Nordic blond girl of seventeen or eighteen. His daughter. Of course. "Big deal," she said. She was the girl I had seen that morning, clinging to the rider of the motorcycle. "He looks sick. You threaten him or something?"

I shook my head, still trembling but beginning to recover. It had been stupid of me not to remember her name. Heavy-breasted in her T shirt, large in hip and thigh, she was still an attractive girl, and I was aware of what an odd figure I appeared to her.

Duane looked over at me, then looked again, observing that I was shaken. "This is my girl Alison, Miles. You wanta sit down?"

"No," I said. "I'm fine, thanks."

"Where were you?" asked Duane.

"Why is it your business?" said this stocky warrior with lank blond hair. "I went out."

"Alone?"

"Well, if it's any of your business, I was with Zack." Again, that flat glass-breaking glare. "We passed *him* on the road. He'd probably tell you anyhow, so I might as well."

"I didn't hear the bike."

"Jesus," she groaned, her face an ugly mask of disdain. "Okay. He stopped down by the other house so you wouldn't hear. I walked up the road. You satisfied? Okay?"

Her face twitched, and I saw that what I had taken for disdain was only embarrassment. It was that torturing embarrassment of the teens, and aggression was her weapon against it.

"I don't like you seeing him."

"Suppose you try and stop me." She strode past the two of us into another part of the house. A television set went on a moment later; then she called from another room, "You ought to be out working anyhow."

"She's right," Duane said. "What do you want to do? You look a little funny."

"I just felt a little faint. What's wrong with Zack? Your daughter—" I was not yet ready to call that surly warrior Alison; she seemed, in my imagination, to be stalking and slashing through a forest, lopping trees off at their knees. "She seems to know her own mind."

"Yeah." He managed to smile. "That's one thing she really does know. She's a good girl though. As good as you can expect anything built female to be, anyhow."

"Sure," I agreed, though the qualification made me uneasy. "What's wrong with Zack?"

"He's no good. He's a weirdo. Listen, Alison's right, I ought to be out doing some work, but we still should set up your desk. Or I could just tell you where everything is and you could set it up yourself. It's no work."

Over the noise of the television set, Duane told me where to find the door and the trestles in his basement and then said, "Make yourself at home," and went outside. I watched him through the side windows of the kitchen as he lumbered toward the pole barn and emerged from it atop a giant tractor. He looked comfortable and at ease, as some men look natural on a horse. Somewhere he had acquired a peaked cap which I could see when the tractor had taken him behind the tall rows of corn up in the far field.

The sound of the television drew me into the unexpected room where Alison Updahl had gone. When I was a child this room had been cramped, linoleum-tiled like the kitchen, and occupied chiefly by a sprung davenport and an inefficient television. Duane had evidently rebuilt it; his skills had grown since the days of the Dream House. Now it was three times its former size, thickly and luxuriously carpeted, and furnished in a manner which suggested a great deal of expense. My cousin's daughter, sprawled on a brown couch and watching a color television, looked, in her T shirt and jeans and bare feet, like a teenager in an affluent suburb of Chicago or Detroit. She did not look up when I entered. She was rigid with self-consciousness.

I said, "What a nice-looking room. I haven't seen it before."

"It stinks." She was still looking at the television, where Fred Astaire was sitting in a racing car. After a second I saw that the car was up on blocks in a closed garage.

"Maybe it just smells new," I said, and earned a glance. But no more than that. She snorted through her nose and returned to the movie.

"What's the film?"

Not bothering to look up again, she said, *"On The Beach.* It's great." She waved off a fly which had settled on her leg. "Suppose you let me try and watch it?"

"Whatever you say." I went to a big comfortable chair at the side of the room and sat. I watched her for a minute or so without either of us speaking. She began to jerk her foot up and down rhythmically, then to toy with her face. After a while she spoke.

"It's about the end of the world. I think that's a pretty neat idea. Zack said I should watch it. He saw it before. Do you live in New York?"

"On Long Island."

"That's New York. I'd like to go there. That's where everything is."

"Oh?"

"You should know. Zack says everything is going to end pretty soon, maybe with people throwing bombs, maybe with earthquakes, it doesn't matter what, and that everybody thinks it'll happen in New York first. But it won't. It'll happen here first. There'll be bodies all over the Midwest, Zack says."

I said that it sounded like Zack was looking forward to it.

She sat up straight, like a wrestler on the mat, and took her attention off the screen for a moment. Her eyes were very pale. "Do you know what they found at the Arden dump a couple of years ago? Just when

I was starting high school? Two heads in paper bags. Women's heads. They never found out who they were. Zack says it was a sign."

"A sign of what?"

"That it's beginning. Pretty soon there won't be any schools, any government, any armies. There won't be any of that shit. There'll just be killing. For a long time. Like with Hitler."

I saw that she wished to shock. "I think I can see why your father doesn't like Zack."

She glared at me and returned her gaze sullenly to the screen.

I said, "You must have known that girl who was killed."

She blinked. "Sure I knew her. That was terrible."

"I suppose she helps prove your theories."

"Don't be creepy." Another pale-eyed, sullen stare from the little warrior.

"I like your name." In truth, and despite her foul manners, I was beginning to like her. Lacking her confidence, she had none of her namesake's awesome charm, but she had her energy.

"Ugh."

"Were you named after anybody?"

"Look, I don't know and I don't care, okay?"

Our conversation seemed to be concluded. With an air which suggested that she would stay in that position for life, Alison had returned to the television set. Gregory Peck and Ava Gardner were strolling across a field arm in arm, looking as if they too thought the end of the world was a neat idea. She spoke again before I could rise and leave the room.

"You're not married, are you?"

"No."

"Didn't you get married? Didn't you used to be married?"

I reminded her that she had been at my wedding.

Now she was staring at me again, ignoring Gregory

Peck's twitching jaw and Ava Gardner's trembling breast. "You got divorced? Why?"

"My wife died."

"Holy cow, she died? Were you upset? Was it suicide?"

"She died by accident," I said. "Yes, I was upset, but not for the reasons you're imagining. We hadn't lived together for some time. I was upset that another human being, one to whom I had been close, had died senselessly."

She was reacting to me strongly, in an almost sexual way—I could almost see her temperature rising and I thought I could smell blood. "Did you leave her or did she leave you?" She had curled one leg beneath herself and straightened her back on the couch so that she was sitting up and staring at me with those flat sea-water eyes. I was better than the movie.

"I'm not sure that's important. I'm not sure it's any of your business either."

"She left you." Accent on both pronouns.

"Maybe we left each other."

"Did you think she got what she deserved?"

"Of course not," I said.

"My father would. He'd think that." I saw the point of these odd questions finally, and felt an unexpected twinge of pity for her. She had lived all her life within her father's suspicion of womankind. "So would Zack."

"Well, people can surprise you sometimes."

"Hah," she grunted. It was a proper rejection of my cliché; then she twisted herself back around, almost flouncing on the couch, to watch the movie again. Now my audience was truly over, and this complicated little warrior queen was bidding me leave.

"You needn't bother to show me the way out," I said, and left the room. On the other side of the kitchen, in the little vestibule before the door, was the entrance to the basement. I opened this second door and fumbled for the light. When I found the switch and flicked it up, the bulb illuminated only the wooden staircase and a pool of packed earth at its foot. I began carefully to descend.

It still bothers me that I did not go to Duane to discuss his daughter's loony theories. But I have heard proposals more bizarre from my students—many of them my female students. And as I navigated Duane's basement, stooping over, hands extended, going to what I hoped was the west wall, I considered that he had surely heard it all by now, his daughter's ventriloquial act: he had said this Zack was a weirdo, and I was inclined to agree. We had presumably judged on the same evidence. And their family problems were secondary to me, or tertiary, or quaternary, if I counted Alison Greening, my work and my well-being as my interlocking priorities. *Mea culpa.* Also, I would not have given Alison Updahl more problems than daughterhood had.

The pad of my bandage bumped a clean flat surface and sent it rocking. With my right hand I reached to steady it, and grasped by accident a smooth long wooden handle. It too was swinging. The object, I realized after a moment's further groping, was an ax. I saw that I could have jostled it off its peg and severed my foot. I swore aloud, and felt gently around for more axes in the air. My hand brushed another long depending handle, then another, and after it a fourth. By this time my eyes had begun to adjust to the cellar's darkness, and I could discern the four shadowy handles hanging down in a row from one of the ceiling supports; rakes and garden hoes hung beside them. I worked my way around them, threading through bags of cement and Qwik-Ferm. I stepped over a stack of equipment catalogs. Beyond them a row of things like skinny dwarf mummies leaned against the wall. After a second I knew they were rifles and shotguns in soft cases. Shell boxes were stacked up at one end of the row. Like most farmers, Duane did not find it necessary to put his guns on display. Then I saw what I was looking for. Leaning against the wall, just as Duane had described it, was an old white paneled door, a perfect flat surface for a desk. It had odd doorknobs, but they could easily be taken off. Perhaps Duane would want them—as I got closer to the door, I saw that the knobs were glass, thousand-sided. Beside the door were stacked two trestles, Duane's sawbucks, like insects in the act of copulation. And beside these was a case of empty Coke bottles, the old eight-ounce variety. The top had been ripped off to expose the open, sucking mouths of the bottles.

I thought of calling for Alison Updahl's help, but decided not to. It had been a morning of mistakes, and I did not wish to commit another and upset the delicate peace between us. So I took the trestles up first and put them on the grass outside Duane's back door, and then went back down for what would be my desktop.

The long heavy wooden rectangle was far more awkward to handle, but I managed to get it up the stairs without knocking down a shotgun or dislodging an ax or shattering the old cello-hipped Coke bottles. After I had muscled it up the steep wooden steps, I was sorry I had not called for Alison's help, for my chest leapt and pounded as though a trout were dying in it. My torn hand ached. I slid the door across the linoleum, crumpling several small hooked rugs, and then banged the screen door open with my elbow and wrestled the door outside and down the concrete steps. I was sweating and breathing hard. Mopping my forehead with my sleeve, I propped the door against the trestles and looked at it in dismay. Spider webs, dust and insects made scurrying lacy patterns over the white paint.

The solution, a garden hose, lay at my feet. I twisted the knob set into the base of the house and played the hose over the door until all the filth had been sluiced away. I was tempted to run it over myself. My hands were black and my shirt was ruined, and sweat poured out of my scalp. But I merely held my hands one after the other in the jet of cold water, wetting the bandage as little as possible. Application of magical substance.

Cold water!

I dropped the still-spurting hose and went across Duane's patchy lawn in the direction of the barn. When I looked to the right I could see my cousin's head and upper body grinding along atop the invisible tractor, as if he were floated by a perverse, bumpy wind. I went over the gravel and dust of the drive. The dog began to curse me with big windy arrogant curses. I reached the tank and plunged my good hand into the greenish water and closed it over a beer bottle to which clung my bloody handkerchief. This I threw into the weeds. I extracted the dripping bottle. I had just twisted off the cap and begun to pour into me the tingling liquid when I saw the blond-fringed face of the Tin Woodsman staring at me from the kitchen window. She winked. Suddenly we were grinning at each other, and I felt the snarl of emotion which the day had caused in me begin to loosen. It was as though I had found an ally. Really, it could not have been easy for a high-spirited girl to have my cousin Duane for a father.

Three

After I had stripped it of the knobs and set it up in the empty upstairs bedroom of my grandmother's house, the desk looked sturdy and serviceable, a present-day echo of all the desks I have known and used. The room itself, small, white and pine-floored, was a perfect place for literary work, since the bare walls offered vistas for contemplation and the single window which faced the barn and the path to Duane's house, opportunity for distraction. Soon I had all my paraphernalia arranged on the desk—typewriter, paper, notes, the beginning of my draft and my outline. Typex, pens, pencils. paperclips. The novels I placed in several neat piles beside the chair. For a moment I felt that spirit lay in labor. in hard work, the more recondite and irrelevant the better. My dogged dissertation would be my linkage with Alison Greening; my work would summon her.

But that day I did no work. I sat at my desk and looked out of the window, watching my cousin's daughter cross and recross the grass and the path as she went to the equipment shed or down to the barn, glancing curiously at my window, and then watching Duane ride up from the road on his giant tractor. He put it in the pole barn and then lumbered back across to his house, scratching himself on the bottom. I felt—I suppose I felt—lonely and elated, primed for an event and still flat and hollow at the same time, as though I were not what I was pretending to be, but were merely an actor waiting for the role to begin. It is a feeling I often have.

I sat there watching the sky darken over the barn as the path lost its definition and the tops of Duane's house and the barn first stood out with greater clarity against a background of darkening blue and then were absorbed into the sky, as if bites were taken out of them. Lights appeared in Duane's house in series, each window lighting up as though it were timed to go on a moment after its neighbor. I thought Alison might appear on the path, her T shirt shining in moonlight as she sulkily walked toward me, the lank ends of her hair swinging in rhythm with her heavy thighs. After a time I fell asleep. I could have been out no more than an hour, but when I opened my eyes only one light was on in Duane's house and the territory between our two dwellings seemed as dark and pathless as a jungle. Hungry, I groped my way downstairs and into the kitchen. The house was clammy and musty, and everything was cold to my touch. When I opened the refrigerator I found that either Duane or Mrs. Sunderson had stocked it with enough food for that night and the following morning—butter, bread, eggs, potatoes, two lamb chops, cheese. I fried the chops and wolfed them down with slices of bread and butter. A meal without wine is not a meal for a grown man. I gnawed at the block of cheddar for dessert. Then I dumped the dishes in the sink for the cleaning woman and went burping back upstairs to the bedroom. When I looked in at my workroom I saw a single light still on in Duane's house, but at its far end. Alison's bedroom, presumably. As I stood looking at it I heard the buzz of a motorcycle going up the road. It increased in volume until it came about level with my position and then it abruptly shut off. My desk looked malevolent, like the fat black center of a spider web.

My bedroom, of course, had been my grandmother's. Yet I see that it is not of course, for she had moved to the chillier, smaller bedroom upstairs only after the death of my grandfather; for this reason it had a newer bed, and for that reason I chose it. It was as far as you could get from the old bedroom and still be in the house—on the opposite side and up the narrow stairs. My grandfather had died when I was a small child, so all my memories of my grandmother are of her as a widow, a wrinkled old woman who climbed the narrow stairs to go to bed. As some old women do, she swung in size between extremes of heaviness and thinness, alternating every three or four years, and finally settled on being thin, and died like that. Given that the narrow little room had this history, it is unsurprising that I had a dream about my grandmother; but I found the emotional violence of the dream shocking.

I was in the sitting room, which was furnished not with Duane's office contraptions but in the old way. My grandmother was seated on her wooden-backed sofa, nervously looking at her hands.—Why did you have to come back?

—What?

—You're a fool.

—I don't understand.

—Haven't enough people died already?

Then she abruptly stood up and walked out of the room onto the porch, where she sat in the rusty old swing.—Miles, you're an innocent. She raised her fists to me and her face contorted in a way I had never seen.—Fool, fool, fool! Fool innocent!

I sat beside her. She began to beat me around my head and shoulders, and I bent my neck to receive her blows. I wished for death.

She said—You put it in motion and it will destroy you.

All the life went out of me, and the setting receded

until I was suspended in a blue fluid, far away. The distance was important. I was in a far blue drifting place, still weeping. Then I understood that it was death. Distant conversation, distant laughter filtered to me, as though through walls. When I became aware of other bodies floating as mine was, hundreds of them, thousands of bodies spinning as if from trees in that blue horror, I heard the sound of loud handclaps. Three of them. Three widely spaced loud claps, unutterably cynical. That was the sound of death, and it held no dignity. It was the end of a poor performance.

Sweating, I rolled over on the bed, gasping. The dream seemed to have lasted for hours—I seemed to have been caught in it from the first moments of sleep. I lay panting under the great weight of guilt and panic. I was held responsible for many deaths; I had caused these deaths, and everybody knew.

Only gradually, as I saw light begin to crawl through the window, did rationality appear. I had never killed anyone. My grandmother was dead; I was in the valley to get work done. *Easy,* I said out loud. Only a dream. I tried to produce alpha waves, and began to breathe deeply and evenly. It took a long time for the enormous sense of guilt to dissipate.

I have always been a person with an enormous excess of guilt. My true vocation is that of guilt expert.

For three-fourths of an hour I tried to fall asleep again, but my system would not permit it, my nerves felt as though doused in caffeine, and I got out of bed just past five. Through the bedroom window I could see dawn slowly beginning. Dew lay silvery over the old huge black iron pig trough in the field near the house where my grandfather had kept hogs. The field was now used for grazing a horse and a neighbor's cows. Beside humped cows, the tall chestnut mare was still asleep, standing with its long neck drooping down. Further up began a sandstone hill, pocked with shallow caves and overgrown with small trees and intensely curling vines and weeds. It looked much as it had during my childhood. A very light gray fog, more like a stationary mist than fog, hung in the lowest parts of the field. As I stood by the window, absorbing peace from that long green landscape edged with fog, two things happened which made me momentarily and at first without realizing it hold my breath. I had let my eye travel up across the road and the fields—the colors of Duane's corn were beautifully muted by the gray light, and the woods seemed blacker than in the sunlight. Light fog like smoke came curling out of the mass of trees. Then I unmistakably saw a figure emerge, embraced by the fog, and hover for a moment at the boundary between wood and field. I remembered my mother telling me of seeing a wolf come from those woods forty years before—of seeing a wolf pause perhaps at that exact spot and stand tense with hunger, leveling its muzzle at the house and barn. It was, I was almost certain, the same person I had seen the previous afternoon. Like the wolf, it too stood and paused and looked toward the house. My heart froze. I thought: a hunter. No. Not a hunter. I didn't know why not, but not. In the same second I heard the bee-noise of a motorcycle.

I glanced at the empty road and then back up to the tree line. The figure had disappeared. After a moment, the motorcycle entered my frame of vision.

She was hanging on behind him, wearing a blanket-like poncho against the morning chill. He wore uniform black, jacket to boots. He cut the engine just after they passed out of my sight, and I wrestled myself into my bathrobe and hurried down the narrow stairs. I quietly stepped onto the screen porch. They were not kissing or embracing, as I had expected, but were merely standing in the road, looking in different directions. She put her hand on his shoulder; I could see his skinny intense enthusiast's face, a wild face. He had long up-swept old-fashioned rock 'n' roll hair, raven black. When she removed her hand, he nodded curtly. The gesture seemed to express both dependence and leadership. She brushed his face with her fingers and began to walk up the road. Like me, he watched her go, walking along with her stiff Tin Woodsman's walk, and then he jumped back on his bike, gunned it, wheeled around in a flashy Evel Knievel circle and roared away.

I stepped back inside and realized that the inside of the house was as cold and moist as the porch. On my chilled feet I went into the kitchen and put a kettle of water on the stove. In a cupboard I found a jar of instant coffee. Then I stepped back outside onto the damp boards of the porch. The sun was just beginning to appear, huge and violently red. After a minute or two Alison reappeared, coming quietly around the side of her house, taking long slow strides. She crossed the back of her house until she reached the last window, where the light still burned. When she stood before it she levered the window up until she stood on tiptoe and then she hoisted herself into the bedroom.

After two cups of the bitter coffee, gulped while standing in bathrobe and bare feet on the cold kitchen floor; after two eggs fried in butter and a slice of toast, eaten at the old round wooden table with the sun beginning to dispel the traces of fog; after appreciation of the way cooking had warmed the kitchen; after adding more greasy dishes to those in the sink; after undressing in the bathroom and with distaste scrutinizing my expanding belly; after similar scrutiny of my face; after showering in the tub; after shaving; after pulling clean clothes out of my suitcase and dressing in a plaid shirt, jeans and boots; after all this I still could not begin to work. I sat at my desk and examined the points of my pencils, unable to rid my mind of that awful dream. Although the day was rapidly warming, my little room and the entire house seemed pervaded with cold breath, a chill spirit I associated with the effect of the nightmare.

I went downstairs and took the photograph of Alison off its hook in the living room. Back upstairs I placed it on the back of the desk, tilting it against the wall. Then I remembered that there was another

photograph which had hung downstairs—indeed there
had been many others, and Duane had presumably
packed most of them away with the furniture after our
grandmother's death. But only one of all those photographs of various grandchildren and nephews and children of nephews concerned me. This was a photograph
of Alison and myself, taken by Duane's father in 1955,
at the beginning of the summer. We were standing before a walnut tree, holding hands, looking into the in-
comprehensible future. Just thinking of the picture now
made me shiver.

I looked at my watch. It was still only six-thirty.
I realized that it would be impossible to get any work
done in my mood and at such an hour. At any rate, I
was unused to doing any sort of writing before lunch.
I felt restless, and had to get out of my workroom
where the typewriter, the pencils, the desk itself re-
buked me.

Downstairs, I perched on Duane's uncomfortable
sofa while I sipped a second cup of coffee. I thought
about D. H. Lawrence. I thought about Alison Updahl's
nighttime excursion. I rather approved of that, though
I thought her company could have been better chosen.
At least the daughter would be more experienced than
her father; there would be no Dream Houses for her.
Then D. H. Lawrence began to rant at me again. I had
written much of the middle portion of the book, but
I had saved the beginning and ending for last—the
ending was fully outlined, but I still had no idea of how
to begin. I needed a first sentence, preferably one with
several scholarly clauses. From which forty introductory
pages could eloquently, commandingly flow.

I went into the kitchen, once again cold and damp.
I lowered my cup into the sink with the other dishes.
Then I walked around the table and took the telephone
book from its shelf beneath the old wall phone. It
was a thin volume, about the size of a first collection
of poems, and on the cover was a pastoral photograph
of two small boys fishing from a pier. The boys were
surrounded by blue cold-looking river water nicked

by a million ripples. Though barefoot, the boys on the pier wore sweaters. Across the river massed a thick unbroken line of trees—like an eyebrow across a thug's face. When I had looked at it for longer than a second, the photograph seemed less pastoral than ominous. It was menacing. My own feet had been bare on cold boards; I too had been suspended above indifferent blue water. In the photograph the sun was dying. I folded the cover back and flipped to the page I wanted and dialed the number.

While the phone trilled at the other end I gazed dumbly through the window facing the lawn and the road, and through the trunks of the walnut trees saw Duane already mounted on his tractor, plying majestically across the field near where the trees began. He reached one end of his course and made the heavy tractor twirl around as easily as a bicycle. On the third ring the receiver was lifted. She did not say hello, and after a moment I spoke myself.

"Rinn? Is that you, Auntie Rinn?"

"Of course."

"This is Miles, Auntie Rinn. Miles Teagarden."

"I know who it is, Miles. Remember to speak loudly. I never use this terrible invention."

"Duane said he told you I was coming."

"What?"

"Duane said—Auntie Rinn, could I come up to see you this morning? I can't work, and I couldn't sleep."

"No," she said, as if she already knew.

"May I come? Is it too early for a visit?"

"You know farm people, Miles. Even the oldsters get up and doing early in the day."

I put on a jacket and walked across the dew-sodden lawn to the Volkswagen. Condensation streamed off the windshield. As I swung into the road where I had seen the Tin Woodsman make her curious and emotionless departure from the boy who could only be Zack, I heard my grandmother's voice, speaking quite clearly some words she had uttered in my dream. *Why did you have to come back?* It was as though she were seated beside me. I could even smell her familiar odor of woodsmoke. I pulled off to the side of the road and wiped my face with my hands. I wouldn't have known how to answer her.

The trees which began toward the end of the rutted road to Rinn's house, just where the valley begins to climb up into the hills, had grown taller and thicker. The pale early sunlight came slanting down, spangling the corrugated trunks and the spongy, overgrown earth. A little further along the narrow road, some of the rags of light struck the side of Rinn's chicken coop, the top of which was fully illuminated by sunlight. It was a big barnlike structure, long and high as a two-story house, painted red; little comic-strip windows like missing pieces of a jigsaw puzzle arbitrarily dotted the side facing me. Further up the rise stood her house, which had once been of white boards but now badly needed paint. The three-room structure looked as though a cobweb had settled over it. The trees had marched right into her tiny area of lawn, and big thick branches wove together over her roof. As I got out of the car, Rinn appeared on her little porch; a moment later she opened the screen door and came outside. She was wearing an ancient blue print dress, calf-high rubber boots and an old khaki army jacket with what seemed to be hundreds of pockets.

"Welcome, Miles," she said, with that Norwegian lilt in her voice. Her face was more wrinkled than ever, but it was luminous. One of her eyes was covered with a film like milk. "Well. You haven't been here since you were a boy, and now you're a man. A nice tall man. You look like a Norwegian."

"I should," I said, "with you in my family." I bent to kiss her, but she held out her hand, and I took it. She wore knitted fingerless gloves, and her hand felt like loose bones wrapped in cloth. "You look wonderful," I said.

"Oh, goodness. I have coffee on the stove, if you're a coffee drinker."

Inside her tiny, overheated kitchen she thrust sticks of wood down into the heart of her stove until the iron pot bubbled. Coffee came out in a thin black stream. "You're not always up so early," she said. "Are you troubled?"

"I don't really know. I'm having trouble getting started on my work."

"It isn't your work though, is it, Miles?"

"I don't know."

"Men should be workers. My young man was a worker." Her good eye, almost as pale as Alison's and a thousand times more informed, examined me over her cup. "Duane is a good worker."

"What do you know about his daughter?" I was interested in her opinion.

"She was misnamed. Duane should have named her Jessie, after my sister. That would have been right, to name her after his mother. The girl needs to be guided. She's high strung." Rinn peeled a cloth off a plate loaded with round flat discs of a breadlike substance I knew well. "But she is much nicer than she wants you to think."

"You mean you still make lefsa?" I said, laughing, delighted. It was one of the great treats of the valley.

"Lefsa and sonnbockles. Of course I make them. I can still use a rolling pin. I make them whenever I can see well enough."

I spread thick butter on a piece and rolled it up into a long cigar shape. It was still like eating bread prepared by angels.

"Are you going to be alone this summer?"

"I'm alone now."

"It's better to be alone. Better for you." She meant me specifically, not mankind in general.

"Well, I haven't had much luck in my relationships."

"*Luck*," she snorted, and hunched further over the table. "Miles, do not court misery."

"Misery?" I was genuinely startled. "It's not that bad."

"Miles, there is great trouble here now. In the valley.

You have heard the news. Do not associate yourself with it. You must be alone and apart, doing your work. You are an outsider, Miles, a natural outsider, and people will resent your being near. People know about you. You have been touched with trouble in the past, and you must avoid it now. Jessie is afraid that you will be touched by it."

"Huh?" It was with talk like this that she had terrified the wits out of me when I was a child.

"You are innocent," she said—the same words my grandmother had used, in my dream. "But you know what I am talking about."

"Don't worry. No matter how provocative they get, little girls don't tempt me. But I don't get what you mean by innocent."

"I mean that you expect too much," she said. "I think I am confusing you. Do you wish more to eat or do you care to help me gather my eggs?"

I remembered her comments about work, and stood. I followed her outside and through the trees down the slope to the henhouse. "Go in quietly," she said. "These birds can be excited easily, and they might suffocate each other in panic."

Very gently, she opened the door of the tall red structure. A terrible stench came to me first, like ashes and dung and blood, and then my eyes adjusted to the dark and I saw hens sitting on their nests, in tiers and rows like books on a bookshelf. The scene was a parody of my Long Island lecture halls. We stepped inside. A few birds squawked. I was standing in a mess of dirt, sawdust, feathers, a pervasive white substance and eggshells. The smell hung acrid and powerful in the air.

"Watch how I do," Rinn said. "I can't see in this light, but I know where they all are." She approached the nearest nest and inserted her hand between the bird and the straw without at all stirring the hen. It blinked, and continued to stare wildly out from either side of its head. Her hand reappeared with two eggs, and a second later, with another. A few feathers were glued to them with a gray-white fluid. "You start at that end, Miles," she said, pointing. "There's a basket on the floor."

She covered her half before I had coaxed a dozen eggs out of half as many unhappy hens. Duane's thick bandage made for clumsy work. Then I went up a ladder where the air was even denser and stole more eggs from increasingly agitated birds; one of the last ones pecked me in the hand while I held her three warm products. It was like being stabbed with a spoon.

Finally we were done, and stood outside in the rapidly warming air beneath the looming trees. I inhaled several deep, cleansing breaths. At my side, Rinn said, "Thank you for helping me. You might make a worker some day, Miles."

I looked down at the thin hunched figure in the outlandish clothes. "Did you mean to tell me that you talk to my grandmother? To Jessie?"

She smiled, making her face look Chinese. "I meant that she talks to me. Isn't that what I said?" But before I could respond, she said, "She is watching you, Miles. Jessie always loved you. She wants to protect you."

"I guess I'm flattered. Maybe—" I was going to say, maybe that's why I dreamed about her, but I was hesitant to describe that dream to Rinn. She would have made too much of it.

"Yes?" The old woman was looking alerted to a current inaudible to me. "Yes? Did you say more? Often I don't hear properly."

"Why did you think I would get involved with Alison Updahl? That was a little far-fetched even for me, don't you think?"

Her face shut like a clamp, losing all its luminosity. "I meant Alison Greening. Your cousin, Miles. Your cousin Alison."

"But—" I was going to say *But I love her,* but shock choked off the startled admission.

"Excuse me. I can no longer hear." She began to move away from me, and then stopped to look back. I thought the milky eye was turned toward me. She appeared to be angry and impatient, but inside all those wrinkles she may just have been tired. "You are always welcome here, Miles." Then she carried her basket and mine back up to the little house darkened by trees. I was already past the church on the way home when I remembered that I had intended to buy a dozen eggs from her.

I parked the car in the gritty driveway and went along the porch and through the front room to the narrow staircase. The house still felt damp and cold, though the temperature was now in the upper seventies. Upstairs I sat at my desk and tried to think. D. H. Lawrence seemed even more foreign than he had the previous day. Auntie Rinn's final words about my cousin both thrilled and upset me. To hear another person allude to Alison Greening was like hearing someone else recount your dreams as his own. I riffled the pages of *The White Peacock,* far too nervous to write. Mention of her name had set me on edge. I had used her name as a weapon against Duane, and Rinn had used the same trick on me.

From downstairs I heard a sudden noise: a door slamming, a book dropped? It was followed by a noise of shod feet hushing across the floor. Alison Updahl, I was sure, come around to flirt while expounding her boyfriend's crazy philosophy. I agreed with Rinn, Alison was a far more agreeable person than she wished anyone to know, but at that moment I could not bear to think of anyone casually usurping my territory.

I thrust my chair away from the desk and went thundering down the narrow steps. I burst into the living room. No one was there. Then I heard a rattling noise from the kitchen, and imagined her nosily exploring the cupboards. "Come on, get out of there," I called. "You tell me when you want to come over, and maybe I'll invite you. I'm trying to get some work done."

The clattering ceased. "Get out of that kitchen right now," I ordered, striding across the room toward the door.

A large pale flustered-looking woman appeared before me, wiping her hands on a towel. The gesture made her large loose upper arms wobble. Horror showed on her face, and in her eyes, magnified behind thick glasses.

"Oh my God," I blurted. "Who are you?"

Her mouth worked.

"Oh my God. I'm sorry. I thought you were someone else."

"I'm—"

"I'm sorry, I'm sorry. Please sit down."

"I'm Mrs. Sunderson. I thought it would be all right. I came in to do work, the door was open . . . You're —you're Eve's boy?" She backed away from me, and almost fell as she stepped backwards over the step down into the kitchen.

"Won't you please sit down? I'm honestly sorry, I didn't mean to—" She was still retreating from me, holding the dishtowel like a shield. Her eyes goggled, the effect made even worse by her glasses.

"You want cleaning? You want me to clean? Duane said last week I should come today. I didn't know if I should, what with, I mean since we, since this terrible . . . but Red said I should, take my mind off, he said."

"Yes, yes. I do want you to come. Please forgive me. I thought it was someone else. Please sit for a moment."

She sat heavily in one of the chairs at the table. Her face was going red in blotches.

"You're very welcome here," I weakly said. "I trust you understand what I want you to do?"

· She nodded, her eyes oily and glazed behind the big lenses.

"I want you to come early enough to make breakfast for me, wash all the dishes, and keep the house
clean. At one I'll want lunch. Is that what you agreed
to do? Also, please don't bother about the room I'm
working in. I want that room undisturbed."

"The room . . . ?"

"Up there." I pointed. "I'll be up and working most
mornings when you arrive, so just call me when you
have breakfast ready. Have you ever done any work
like this before?"

Resentment showed in the puffy face for a moment.
"I kept house for my husband and son for forty years."

"Of course. I should have thought. I'm sorry."

"Duane explained about the car? That I can't drive?
You will have to do the shopping."

"Yes, okay. I'll go out this afternoon. I want to see
Arden again, anyhow."

She continued to stare dumbly at me. I realized that
I was treating her like a servant, but could not stop.
Embarrassment and a fictitious dignity made me stiff.
If she had been the Woodsman, I could have apol-
ogized.

"I said five dollars a week?"

"Don't be silly. You deserve seven. I might as well
give you the first week's wages in advance." I counted
seven dollar bills out onto the table before her. She
stared resentfully at the little pile of bills.

"I said five."

"Call the extra two dollars hardship allowance. Now
you don't have to worry about making breakfast this
morning since I got up early and made my own, but
I'd like lunch somewhere around one. After washing
the lunch dishes, you'll be free to leave, if the downstairs rooms look clean enough to you. All right? I
really am sorry about that shouting. It was a case
of mistaken identity."

"Uh," she said. "I said five."

"I don't want to exploit you, Mrs. Sunderson. For
the sake of my conscience, please take the extra two."

"A picture is missing. From the front parlor."

"I took it upstairs. Well, if you will get on with your work, I'll get on with mine."

Portion of Statement by Tuta Sunderson:

July 18

People who act like that aren't right in the head. He was like a crazy man, and then he tried to buy me back with an extra two dollars. Well, we don't work that way up here, do we? Red said I shouldn't go back to that crazy man, but I went right on going back, and that was how I learned so much about his ways.

I wish Jerome was alive yet so he could give him what-for. Jerome wouldn't have stood for that man's way of talking nor his ways of being neither.

Just ask yourself this—who was he expecting, anyhow? And who came?

I sat dumbly at my desk, unable to summon even a single coherent thought about D. H. Lawrence. I realized that I had never liked more than two of his novels. If I actually published a book about Lawrence, I was chained to talking about him for the rest of my life. In any case, I could not work while imagining that guilt-inducing woman shifting herself about through Duane's furniture. I bent my head and rested it on the desk for a moment. I felt Alison's photograph shedding light on the top of my head. My hands had begun to tremble, and a vein in my neck pulsed wildly. I bathed in that melting, embracing warmth. Application of you know what. When I got up and went back downstairs, I found that my knees were shaking.

Tuta Sunderson peeked at me from the corners of her eyes where she knelt before a pail of water as I went wordlessly by. Understandably, she looked as though she expected me to aim a kick at her backside. "Oh, a letter came for you," she uttered. "I forgot to tell you before." She gestured weakly toward a glass-fronted chest and I snatched up the envelope as I went out.

My name was written in a flowing hand on the creamy outside of the envelope. After I got into the baking interior of the VW I ripped open the letter. I pulled out a sheet of stationery. I turned it over. Confused, I turned it over again. It was blank. I groaned. When I grabbed the envelope up from the ffoor of the car I saw that it bore no return address, and had been posted the night before in Arden.

I shot backwards out of the driveway, not really caring if another vehicle were coming. At the sound of my tires squealing, Duane far off in the field turned his head. I sped away as if from a murder, the blank page and envelope lying on the seat beside me. The car's engine began to sputter, lights flashed as if the hand of Spirit had momentarily thrust in and touched them; by instinct I looked up across the fields to the woods. No one stood there. No figure not a hunter but a wolf. If it was a trick, a worthless joke, who? An old enemy in Arden? I wasn't sure I still had any; but I hadn't expected Andy's wife still to carry hostility toward me like a raised knife. If a sign, of what? Of some future message? I grabbed the envelope again and held it clamped to the wheel with both hands. "Damn," I muttered, and dropped it back on the other seat as I floored the accelerator.

It was from this moment that all began to go wrong, askew. My mistake with Tuta Sunderson, the maddening letter—perhaps I would have acted more rationally if the threatening scene in the Plainview diner had never occurred. Yet I think I knew what I was going to do in Arden long before it was a conscious thought. My old response to stress. And I thought I might know the handwriting on that envelope.

Speeding, I recklessly zoomed up the twisting hilly road to Arden. I nearly forced a tractor off the road. Bunny

Is Good Bread; Surge Milking Machines; This Is Holsum Country; Nutrea Feeds; Highway 93; DeKalb Corn (orange words on green wings); Broiler Days: the billboards and roadsigns flashed by. At the crest of the long hill where the road opens into a view like that in Italian paintings, endless green and varied distance dotted with white buildings and thick random groups of trees, a tall sign with a painted thermometer and pointer announced that the goal of the Arden Community Chest was $4,500. I switched on the radio and heard the hollow, spurious voice of Michael Moose. ". . . report no progress in the shocking—" I turned the dial and let loud rock music assail me because I hated it.

An area of frame Andy Hardy houses, the R-D-N Motel, and I was going down Main Street, past the high school, where Arden lay at the bottom of the last hill. Pigeons were circling over the brick fortress of the courthouse and town hall, and in the odd quiet of the moment I could hear their wings beating after I had swung into a parking space before the Coast To Coast Store and shut off the motor. Wingbeats filled and agitated the air like drumming; when I got out of the car I saw that the birds had wheeled away from the courthouse-town hall and bannered out over Main Street. Apart from an old man sitting on the steps to Freebo's Bar, they were the only visible living things. A tin sign clacked and banged somewhere behind me. It was as though some evil visitation had drawn everyone in Arden inside behind locked doors.

I went into the store and picked up enough groceries for a week; the two women in the aisle looked at me oddly, and would not meet my eye. The atmosphere in the grocery seemed almost ostentatiously hostile, almost theatrical—those women glanced at me, then quickly lowered their eyes, then pierced me with covert glances from the sides of their eyes. *Who are you and what are you doing here?* It was as though they had spoken. I counted my money down onto the counter and went hurriedly back outside and locked the grocery bags in the VW. I had to get a bottle of whisky.

Down the street, just passing the corner of the Annex Hotel and the Angler's Bar, walking toward me with his hunched bustling walk, accompanied by his sour-looking wife, was Pastor Bertilsson. He was my least favorite clergyman. He had not yet seen me. I looked around in panic. Across the street was a two-story building labeled Zumgo, a name I recalled having heard before. It was where Duane had said Paul Kant was working. I turned my back on the Bertilssons and hurried across the street.

Unlike the Plainview diner, Zumgo's had resisted any efforts to bring it up to date, and my first response was to relish the old-fashioned fittings of the store—change was sent, enclosed in metal cylinders, racketing down on wires from an office suspended below the ceiling, the counters were wooden, the floors of boards worn smooth and sent rippling by time. A moment afterwards I noticed the threadbare, depressed look of the place: most of the tables were only scantily covered by goods, and the salesladies—even now staring at me with displeasure—were aged shabby horrors with rouge enameling their cheeks. A few overweight women desultorily picked at underwear strewn across a table. I could not imagine Paul Kant at work in such a place.

The woman I approached seemed to share my attitude. She drew her lips back over false teeth and smiled. "Paul? You a friend of Paul's?"

"I just said, where is he working? I want to see him."

"Well, he isn't working. Are you a friend of his?"

"You mean he doesn't work here?"

"When he's in he does, I guess. He's home sick. Least that's what he told Miss Nord. Said he couldn't come in today. Looks funny, I think. You a friend of his?"

"Yes. I used to be, at least."

For some reason, this caused her canine, hungry interest in me to become merriment. She gave me a glimpse of her plastic-coated gums and called to another woman behind the counter. "He's a friend of Paul's.

Says he doesn't know where he is." The other woman
joined her laughter. "A friend of Paul's?"

"Christ," I muttered, turning away. I went back
to ask, "Do you know if he will be in tomorrow?" and
got only malicious staring eyes for my answer. I noticed
that two or three of the customers were staring at me.
Auntie Rinn's advice came back to me. Certainly some
of the women seemed to resent the presence of a
stranger.

Baffled, still angry, I paced around the store until
even the first old woman had ceased to giggle and
gossip about me with her partner. I had a purpose I
did not then wish to admit to myself. I examined un-
speakable clothing; I regarded sad toys and dusty
envelopes and yards of material best suited to the backs
of horses. The old response to stress became conscious:
I took a five-dollar bill and folded it into my palm.

I was helpless before my own advice to *get out*.

On the second floor I spun a rack of paperback
books. One of the jackets and titles snagged my attention. My Ph.D. supervisor, a famous scholar, had
written it. It was Maccabee's most popular book, *The
Enchanted Dream*. Actually a mechanical treatise on
nineteenth-century poets, it had been tricked out with
a jazzy cover showing a long-haired young man apparently inhaling an illegal substance while a slightly
less beautiful nude maiden coiled lambent legs and
tendrils of hair about him. Unable to control the impulse which was my purpose—I hadn't thought of
such amazing luck—I took the book off the rack and
slid it into my jacket pocket. It had been Maccabee
who had suggested I write on Lawrence. Then I turned
cautiously around (when it was too late for caution)
and saw that no one had witnessed my theft. My chest
thumped with relief; the book hung unobtrusively in
my pocket. I twitched the pocket flap up over the top
of the book. When I passed the cash register I dropped
the bill on the counter and continued out onto the
street.

And nearly into the arms of Bertilsson. That hyp-

ocritical pink moonface and wet smile were directed,
I swear, toward the pocket with Maccabee's book before Bertilsson decided he wished to favor my face with
them. Balder and fatter, he was even more repulsive
than I remembered him. His wife, several inches taller
than he, stood stock-still beside him, her posture suggesting that I might be expected at any moment to
commit an act of disgusting perversity.

As I suppose I had, in her eyes. When Joan and
I were married, Bertilsson had taken pains to in-
corporate into his homiletic address some allusions to
my past misdeeds; later, on a drunken night during
our honeymoon, I wrote him an abusive letter and
posted it on the spot. I think I said that he did not
deserve to wear his collar.

Perhaps the recollection of that statement was what
put the malicious icy chips in his eyes, far behind the
sanctimony, when he greeted me. "Young Miles. What
have we here? Young Miles."

"We heard you were back," said his wife.

"I'll expect you at tomorrow's services."

"That's interesting. Well, I must—"

"I was grieved to hear of your divorce. Most of my
marriages are of the enduring kind. But then few of
the couples it is my privilege to unite are as sophisticated as you and your—Judy, was it? Few of them
write notes of thanks as distinctive as yours."

"Her name was Joan. We never did get divorced in
the sense you mean. She was killed."

His wife swallowed, but Bertilsson, for all his oili-
ness, was no coward. He continued to look straight at
me, the malice behind the sanctimony undimmed. "I
am sorry. Truly sorry for you, Miles. Perhaps it's a
blessing that your grandmother did not live to see how
you . . ." He shrugged.

"How I what?"

"Seem to have a tragic propensity for being nearby
when young women are lost to life."

"I wasn't even in town when that Olson girl was

killed," I said. "And Joan was anything but nearby when she died."

I might as well have been speaking to a bronze Buddha. He smiled. "I see I must apologize. I did not intend my remark in that way. No, not in the least. But in fact, since you bring up the matter, Mrs. Bertilsson and I are in Arden on a related mission, a mission of mercy I think I may describe it, of the Lord's mercy, related to an event of which you seem to be in ignorance."

He had long ago begun to speak in the cadences of his tedious sermons, but usually it was possible to figure out what he was talking about. "Look. I'm sorry, but I have to get going."

"We were just with the parents." He was still smiling, but now the smile expressed great sad meretricious gravity.

My God, how could he think that I had not heard of that?

"Oh, yes."

"So you do know about it? You have heard?"

"I don't know what I've heard. I'll be going now."

For the first time, his wife spoke. "You'd be wise to keep going until you get back where you came from, Miles. We don't think much of you around here. You left too many bad memories." Her husband kept that grave, falsely humble smile on his face.

"So write me another blank letter," I said, and left them. I recrossed the street and stepped over the nodding drunk into Freebo's Bar. After a few drinks consumed while listening to a half-audible Michael Moose compete with the mumbled conversation of men who conspicuously avoided catching my eye, I had a few more drinks and attracted a little attention by dismembering Maccabee's book on the bar, at first ripping out one page at a time and then seizing handfuls of paper and tearing them out. When the barman came up to object I told him, "I wrote this book and I just decided it's terrible." I shredded the cover so that he could not read Maccabee's name. "Can't a man even tear up his own book in this bar?"

"Maybe you'd better go, Mr. Teagarden," the bartender said. "You can come back tomorrow." I hadn't realized that he knew my name.

"Can tear up my own book if I want to, can't I?"

"Look, Mr. Teagarden," he said. "Another girl was murdered last night. Her name was Jenny Strand. We all knew that girl. We're all a little upset around here."

It happened like this:

A girl of thirteen, Jenny Strand, had been to the Arden cinema with four of her friends to see a Woody Allen movie, Love and Death. *Her parents had forbidden her to see it: they did not want their daughter to receive her sex education from Hollywood, and the title made them uneasy. She was an only daughter among three boys, and while her father thought the boys could pick things up for themselves, he wanted Jenny to be taught in some way that would preserve her innocence. He thought his wife should be responsible: she was waiting for Pastor Bertilsson to suggest something.*

Because of the death of Gwen Olson, they had been unusually protective when Jenny said that she wanted to see a friend, Jo Slavitt, after dinner. —Be back by ten, her father said. —Sure, she agreed. The picture would be over an hour before that. Their objections were silly, and she had no intention of being restricted by anyone's silliness.

It did not bother her that she and Gwen Olson had looked enough alike to be taken, in a larger town— one where everyone's family was not known—for sisters. Jenny had never been able to see the resemblance, though several teachers had mentioned it. She was not flattered. Gwen Olson had been a year younger, a farm girl, in another set. A tramp had killed her—everybody said that. You still saw tramps, bums, gypsies, whatever they were, hanging around town a day or two and then going wherever they went. Gwen Olson had been dumb enough to go wandering alone by the river at night, out of the sight of the town.

She met Jo at her house and they walked five blocks in sunshine to the theater. The other girls were waiting. The five of them sat in the last row, ritually eating candy. —*My parents think this is a dirty movie,* she whispered to Jo Slavitt. Jo put her hand to her mouth, pretending to be shocked. In fact they all thought the movie was boring.

When it was over, they stood on the sidewalk, empty of comment. As always, there was nowhere to go. They began to drift up Main Street toward the river.

—*I get scared just thinking about Gwen,* said Marilyn Hicks, a girl with thin fair hair and braces on her teeth.

—*So don't think about her,* snapped Jenny. It was a typical Marilyn Hicks comment.

—*What do you think happened to her?*

—*You know what happened to her,* said Jenny, who was less innocent than her parents supposed.

—*It could have been anyone,* said another girl in a shuddery voice.

—*Like Billy Hummel and his friends over there?* said Jenny, ridiculing the other girl. She was looking across the street, where some of the older boys from A.H.S., football players, were wasting time hanging around the telephone company building. It was getting darker, and she could see the white flock of the letters on their team jackets reflected in the big phone company window. In ten minutes the boys would be sick of watching themselves in the window and would drift off down the street.

—*My dad says the police better watch someone real close.*

—*I know who he means,* said Jo. They all knew whom Marilyn's father meant.

—*I'm hungry again. Let's go to the drive-in.*

They began to trudge up the road. The boys took no notice of them.

—*The food at the drive-in is junk,* said Jenny. They put garbage in it.

—*Sourpuss. Look at ole sourpuss.*

—*And that movie was dumb.*

—*Sourpuss. Just because Billy Hummel didn't look at you.*

—Well, at least I don't think he murdered anyone.

Suddenly she had had enough of them. They were standing in a circle around her, waiting for her to move, their shoulders slumping, their faces empty. Billy Hummel and the other boys in team jackets were walking the other way, back into town. She was tired and disappointed—with the boys, with the movie, with her friends. For a moment she wished passionately that she were grown up. —I'm fed up with the drive-in, she said, I'm going home. I'm supposed to be home in half an hour anyway. —Awcomeonnn, moaned Marilyn. The whine in her voice was enough to make Jenny turn decisively away from them and begin to walk quickly down the street.

Because she could feel them staring at her she turned into the first side-street. Let them gawk at an empty street, she thought, let them my goodness! one another.

She walked straight down the middle of the unlighted street. Windows shone in the houses on either side. Someone was waiting up ahead, just a shape on the grassy sidewalk, a man washing his car or getting cool evening air. Or a woman getting away from the kids.

At that moment she nearly saved her life, because she realized that she was hungry after all, and almost turned around to go back to her friends. But that was not possible. So she put her head down and walked up to the next corner, vaguely planning a route that would take most of the half hour she had of freedom. When she went past the shape on the sidewalk, she half-noticed that it was not a man but a fat bush.

The next street was shabbier, with two vacant lots between the mean houses like vast blots of darkness. Trees towered and loomed overhead, black and without definition. She heard slow steps behind her. But this was Arden and she did not begin to be fearful until something hard and blunt touched her back. She jumped and whirled around and when she saw the face looking at her she knew that the worst moments of her life were beginning.

Four

At that moment I would have been skeptical about the odds on my returning to take up the bartender's invitation for Sunday, but twenty-six hours later I was in Freebo's, not this time at the bar but in a booth and not alone but in company.

I realized that I was drunk only when I found that I was pounding the VW along in second gear; chanting to myself, I messily, grindingly slotted the shift up a gear, ending the howl of anguish from the engine, and zoomed home, no doubt weaving through lanes as rakishly as Alison Greening had done on one night years before—the night I had first felt her mouth issuing warmth over mine, and felt all my senses rubbed by her various odors of perfume, soap, powder, contraband cigarettes and fresh water. About the time I reached the red thermometer in the Italian vista I recognized that the Strand girl's death had been the reason for the hostile stares I'd received from the Arden townspeople. After I spun into the driveway I left the car slewed at a telltale angle before the garage and lurched out, half-sprawling over the front fender. The maddening envelope and blank sheet of paper, along with several torn balled-up pages of Maccabee's book, bunched in my pocket. I heard footsteps inside the house, a door closing. I went unsteadily across the lawn to the door of the screen porch and entered. It seemed I could feel the chill of the boards even through my shoes. The cold house seemed full of noises. Tuta Sunderson appeared to be in two or three rooms at once. "Come on out," I said. "I won't hurt you."

Silence.

"It's okay," I said. "You can even go home, Mrs. Sunderson." I looked around, called her name in the direction of the old downstairs bedroom. Duane's furniture was immaculately cleaned and dusted, but no one else was in the room. I shrugged and went into the bathroom.

When I emerged, the noises in the old house had magically ceased. I heard only the singing of the plumbing in the walls. She had nervously decamped; I swore to myself, wondering what I would have to do to get her back.

Then I heard a cough unmistakably originating from my workroom. That I had yet to complete a sentence in that room made her offense against its privacy triply serious. I gave myself a shove toward the stairs.

But when I burst into the cold little room I stopped short. Through the window I could see the stout form of Tuta Sunderson huff-puffing down the road, her handbag bobbing on its strap; and seated in the desk chair, absolutely at ease, was Alison Updahl.

"What—" I began. "I don't like—"

"I think you scared her off. She was already pretty upset. but you finished her off. But don't worry, she'll come back."

Portion of Statement by Tuta Sunderson:

July 18

When I saw him get out of that car, I knew he was drunk, just pig drunk, and when he started that yelling I thought I'd better skedaddle. Now we know he was just back from that time he argued with the pastor on the street, down in Arden. I

*think the pastor was right in everything he said,
next day, and he could have said it even stronger.
Red was home from the police station by then—
all shook by what he'd seen, of course—and he
said, Ma, don't you go back to that crazy man, I've
got a few ideas of my own about him, but I said
his five dollars is as good as anyone else's, isn't it?
I put that other two dollars under a lamp. Oh, I
was going to come back, you can bet on that, he
didn't scare me any. I wanted to keep my eye on
him.*

We stayed there silently for a moment—oddly, she
made me feel as though I was intruding on her. I could
see her assessing my condition. To forestall any comment, I said, "I don't like people in this room. It has
to be kept private, mine. Other people louse up the
atmosphere."

"She *said* she wasn't supposed to come in here.
That's why I did. It was the only quiet place to wait
for you." She stretched out her blue-jeaned legs. "I
didn't take anything."

"It's a question of vibrations." At least I did not say
"vibes." Alcohol cheapens the vocabulary.

"I don't feel any vibrations. What do you do in
here, anyhow?"

"I'm writing a book."

"On what?"

"It doesn't matter. I'm stuck anyhow."

"A book about other books, I bet. Why don't you
write a book about something real? Why don't you
write a book about something fantastic and important
that other people can't even see? About what's really
going down?"

"Did you want to see me about anything in particular?"

"Zack wants to meet you."

"Swell."

"I told him about you and he was really interested.

I said you were different. He wants to know about
your ideas. Zack cares a lot about ideas."

"I'm not going anywhere today."

"Not today. Tomorrow around noon. In Arden.
Do you know Freebo's bar?"

"I suppose I could find it on a bright day. Did you
hear about another of your pals getting killed?"

"It's on all the news. Don't you pay attention to
the news?" She blinked, and I saw the fright beneath
her pretended indifference.

"Didn't you know her?"

"Sure I did. In Arden you know everybody. Red
Sunderson found her body. That's why old Tuta was
so touchy this morning. He saw her in a field off Highway 93."

"Jesus." I remembered how I had treated her, and
then I could feel my face begin to burn.

So the next day I found myself entering the scene of
my second disgrace in the company of Alison Updahl.
Underage though she was, she sailed through the door
as if, given any resistance, she'd knock it down with
an ax. By now I of course knew to what extent this
was purely a performance, and I admired its perfection.
She had more in common with her namesake than I
had thought. The bar was nearly empty. Two old men
in coveralls sat before nearly full glasses of pale beer
at the bar and a man in a black jacket sat at the last
booth. The same fleshy grayhaired bartender who had
been there yesterday leaned against the wall beside
the cash register, surrounded by the flashing sparkling
lights and perpetual waterfalls of beer advertisements.
His eyes glided over Alison, but he looked at me and
nodded.

I followed her to the booth, watching Zack as we
went. His eyes flicked back and forth between us and
his mouth was a taut line. He appeared to be charged
with enthusiasm. He also looked very young. I recognized the type from my youth in Florida—the misfits
who had gathered around gas stations, paying great

attention to their hair, cherishing their own failure even
then. Dangerous kids, at times. I didn't know the type
was still in style.

"This is him," said my cousin's daughter, meaning
me.

"Freebo," Zack said, and nodded to the bartender.

As I sat in the booth facing him I saw that he was
older than I had at first taken him for; he was not a
teenager but in his twenties, with those wrinkles embedded in his forehead and at the corners of his eyes.
He still had that look of displaced, unlocated enthusiasm It gave a sly cast to his whole character. He
made me very uneasy.

"The usual. Mr. Teagarden?" asked the bartender,
now standing at the side of the booth. Presumably he
knew what Zack wanted. He avoided looking at Alison.

"Just a beer," I said.

"He didn't look at me again," said the Woodsman
after the bartender had turned away. "That really slays
me. He's afraid of Zack. Otherwise he'd throw me out
on my butt."

I wanted to say: don't try so hard.

Zack giggled in the best James Dean fashion.

The bartender came back with three beers. Alison's
and mine were in glasses, Zack's in a tall silver mug.

"Freebo's thinking of selling this place," the boy
said, grinning at me. "You ought to think about buy-
ing it. You could snap it up. Be a good business."

I remembered this too: the ridiculous testing. He
smelled of carbon paper. Carbon paper and machine
oil. "For someone else. I'm about as businesslike as
a kangaroo."

The Woodsman grinned: I was proving whatever it
was she'd said about me.

"Far out. Listen. I think we could talk."

"Why?"

"Because we're unusual. Don't you think unusual
people have something in common? Don't you think
they share things?"

"Like Jane Austen and Bob Dylan? Come off it.

How do you get your seventeen-year-old girlfriend served in here?"

"Because of who I am." He grinned, as though that were both Jane Austen and Bob Dylan. "Freebo and I are friends. He knows what's in his interest." I was getting a full dose of his sly enthusiasm. "But almost everybody knows what's in his interest. The Big One. Right? It's in our interest to talk, to be seen together, to explore our ideas, right? I know some things about you, Miles. People still talk about you up here. I was knocked out when she said you were back, man. Tell me something. Do people keep laying their trips on you?"

"I don't know what that means. Unless it's what you're doing now."

"*Hoo,*" Zack uttered softly. "You're cozy, man. Make 'em work, huh? I can see that, I can dig it. Make 'em work, yeah. You're deep. You're really deep. I got a lot of questions for you, man. What's your favorite book of the Bible?"

"The Bible?" I said, laughing, spurting beer. "That was unexpected. I don't know. Job? Isaiah?"

"No. I mean, yeah, I can dig it, but that isn't it. Revelations is it. Do you see? That's where it's all laid out."

"Where what is all laid out?"

"The plan." He showed me a big scarred palm, lines of grease permanently printed in it, as though the plan were visible there. "That's where it all is. The riders on the horses—the rider with the bow, and the rider with the sword, and the rider with the scales, and the pale rider. And the stars fell and the sky disappeared, and it all came down. Horses with lions' heads and snakes' tails."

I glanced at Alison. She was listening as if to a nursery story—she had heard it a hundred times before. I could have groaned; I thought she deserved so much better.

"That's where it says that corpses will lie in the streets, fires, earthquakes, war in heaven. War on earth too, you see? All those great beasts in Revelations, remember? The beast 666, that was Aleister Crowley, you know, Ron Hubbard is probably another one, and then all those angels who harvest the earth. Until there's blood for sixteen thousand furlongs. What do you think of Hitler?"

"You tell me."

"Well, Hitler had the wrong thing going, you see, he had all this heavy German stuff around him, all that shit about the Jews and the master race—well, there is a master race, but it's nothing crude like being a whole nation. But he was one of the beasts of Revelations, right? Think about it. Hitler knew that he was sent to prepare us, he was like John the Baptist, see, and he gave us certain keys to understanding, just like Crowley did. I think you understand all this, Miles. There's like a brotherhood of those who catch on to all this. Hitler was a screw-up, right, but he had insight. He knew that everything has to go smash before it can get better, there has to be total chaos before there can be total freedom, there has to be murder before there can be true life. He knew the reality of blood. Passion has to go beyond the personal—right? See, to free matter, to set matter free, we have to get beyond the mechanical to, uh, myth maybe, ritual, blood ritual, to the physical mind."

"The physical mind," I said. "Like the dark seat of passion and the column of blood." I quoted these catchphrases despairingly. The end of Zack's tirade had depressingly reminded me of ideas in Lawrence's writing.

"Wow," said Alison. "Oh, wow." I had impressed her. This time I nearly did groan.

"I knew it, man," continued Zack. He was just gleaming at me. "We gotta have more talks. We could talk for centuries. I can't believe that you're a teacher, man."

"I can't believe it either."

This sent him into such happiness that he slapped Alison on the knee. "I knew it. You know, people used to say all this stuff about you, I didn't know if I could really believe it all, about the stuff you used to do—I got another question. You have nightmares, don't you?"

I thought of being suspended in that blue drifting horror. "I do."

"I knew it. You know about nightmares? They show you the revelations? Nightmares cut through the shit to show you what's really going on."

"They show you what's really going on in the nightmares," I said. I didn't want him to analyze my dream-states. I had ordered another two beers while he ranted, and now I asked Freebo for a double Jack Daniels to soothe my nerves. Zack was looking as though oil had come pouring out of his scalp, as though he expected to be either stroked or kicked. His face was wild and skinny, framed by thick sideburns and that complicated ruff of hair. When the whisky came I drank half of it in one gulp and waited for the effect.

Zack went on. Didn't I think the situation had to be loosened up? Didn't I think violence was mystic action? Was selfhood? Didn't I think the Midwest was where reality was thinnest, waiting for truth to erupt? Didn't two killings prove that? Couldn't they *make* reality happen?

Eventually I began to laugh. "Something about this reminds me of Alison's father's Dream House," I said.

"My father's house?"

"His Dream House. The place behind Andy's."

"That place? Is that *his?*"

"He built it. You must have known that."

She was gaping at me. Zack was looking irritated at this interruption in his sermon. "He never said anything about it. Why did he build a place like that?"

"It's an old story," I said, already sorry that I had mentioned the place. "I thought it would have a reputation for being haunted."

"No, nobody thinks it's haunted," she said, still looking at me with determined curiosity. "Lots of us kids go there. Nobody bothers you there."

I remembered the mess of blankets and cigarette butts on the ruined floor.

Zack said, "Listen, I've got plans—"

"What was it *for?* Why did he build it?"

"I don't know."

"Why did you call it his dream house?"

"It's nothing. Forget about it." I could see her begin to look impatiently around the bar, as if to find someone who would tell her all about it.

"You've got to know about my plans—"

"Well, I'll find out from someone else."

"I've been doing some things—"

"Just forget about it," I said. "Forget I ever mentioned it. I'm going home now. I have an idea."

The bartender was beside us again. "This is an important guy, you know," he said, putting his hand on my shoulder. "He wrote a book. He's some kind of artist."

"Also," I said, "I think I'm going to give you some novels. You'll like them. They're right up your street."

"I considered we might see you in church today." Duane was still wearing his suit, the old double-breasted pin-stripe he had been wearing to church for ten years or more. But the new informality had touched him too: beneath the jacket he wore a tieless open-collared shirt, blue with patterns of lighter blue. Alison must have given it to him. "Do you want some of this? It's Tuta's day off over at your place, isn't it?" He lifted one big hand toward the mess that Alison had left bubbling on the stove—it looked like pork and beans, with too much tomato sauce. Like the general disorder of the kitchen, this too would have riled his mother, who had always prepared gigantic lunches of roasted meat and potatoes boiled so long they crumbled like chalk. When I shook my head no, he said, "You should go to church, Miles. No matter what you believe in, going could help you out in the community."

"Duane, it would be the most blatant hypocrisy," I said. "Does your daughter usually go?"

"Sometimes. Not always. I reckon she has little enough time to herself, taking care of me and doing for me the way she does around here, so I don't grudge her some extra sleep on Sunday. Or a couple of hours with a girlfriend."

"Like now?"

"Like now. Or so she says. If you can ever trust a female. Why?"

"I was just wondering."

"Well, she has to get along to see her friends sometimes. Whoever the hell they are. Anyhow, Miles, this is one day you should have gone."

Then I heard the emphasis I should have heard the first time. And wasn't it unusual that Duane was still wearing his suit an hour after the service? And that he was sitting in his kitchen instead of doing an hour or so of work before lunch?

"I'll bite. Why today, especially?"

"What do you think of Pastor Bertilsson?"

"I'll spare you. Why?"

Duane was crossing and uncrossing his legs, looking very uncomfortable. On his feet were heavy black brogues, immaculately polished. "You never exactly liked him, did you? I know. He maybe did go a little out of line when you and Joan got married. I don't think he was right to bring up all that old stuff, even though he did it for your own good. When I got married, he didn't talk about any of my old mistakes."

I hoped that his daughter would forget all about my reference to the Dream House—it had been a serious betrayal. While I was trying to think how I could tell him that I had let his secret slip out to his daughter without actually telling her anything about it, Duane got over his own nervousness and finally got to the point.

"Anyhow, like I was saying, he said a few words about you today. In his sermon."

"About *me?*" I yelped. My guilt disappeared like flash powder.

"Wait, Miles, he didn't actually name you. But we

all knew who he was talking about. After all, you made yourself known around here, years ago. So I guess most everybody knew who he was talking about."

"You mean I'm actually having sermons preached about me? I guess I really am a success."

"Well, it would have been better if you'd been there. See, in a community this size—well, a small community like this sort of draws together if any trouble happens. What happened to those two girls was a terrible thing, Miles. I think a man that can do something like that ought to be slaughtered like a pig. The thing is, we know none of us could have done it. Maybe some over in Arden, but none of us here." He shifted in his chair. "While I'm talking on this I ought to say something else. Look. It might be better if you didn't go around trying to see Paul Kant. That's all I want to say about that."

"What are you saying, Duane?"

"Just what I said. Paul might have been okay when he was a kid, but even then you didn't know him all that well. You were only here in the summers."

"To hell with that," I said. "Suppose you tell me what was the point of this sermon of Bertilsson's."

"Well, I guess he was just saying how some people—"

"Meaning me."

"—some people put themselves outside normal standards. He said that's dangerous, when everybody's got to pull together, times of trouble, like now."

"He's guiltier of that than I am. Now I wish you'd tell me what crime Paul Kant is supposed to have committed."

To my surprise, Duane flushed. He turned his eyes toward the pot bubbling on the stove. "Well, it's not a crime, exactly, not that you could say a crime, exactly. He's just not like the rest of us."

"He puts himself outside normal standards. Good. That makes two of us. I'll make a point of seeing him."

We stared at one another for a moment or two, Duane fidgeting, looking out of his depth. He appeared to be afflicted with moral uncertainty. In a dubious cause he had acted dubiously. He obviously wished that he had never brought up the questions of Bertilsson and Paul Kant. I remembered the idea I'd had in Freebo's Bar—an idea brought up by my tactless mention of the Dream House. "Shall we change the subject?"

"Hell, yes." Duane looked relieved. "Do you feel like having one of those beers?"

"Not now. Duane, what did you do with the rest of the stuff from Gramma's house? The old pictures, and all the furniture?"

"Well, let me think. I put the furniture down in the root cellar. It didn't seem right to sell it or throw it away. Some of that stuff might be valuable someday, too. Most of those old pictures I took down I put in a trunk in the old bedroom." That was the bedroom on the ground floor, where my grandparents had slept during my grandfather's life.

"All right, Duane," I said. "Don't be surprised by anything you hear."

Portion of Statement by Duane Updahl:

July 17

So that was what he said just before the really strange business began. Don't be surprised, something like that. Don't be surprised by anything. Then he went off toward the old house like a rocket was in his pants. He was all sort of excited —he was drunk some too, Sunday morning or no Sunday morning. I could smell the booze on his breath. Later I found out from my kid that he'd been over to Freebo's, down on Main. You know? He was just sittin' there with Zack, suckin' up drinks like it was Saturday night. Kind of funny, considering what he tried to do to Zack later. Maybe he was sort of trying him out, you know? Testing him? That's what I think, anyhow. I

*think maybe he was keeping his mind on Paul
Kant too, to see if he could use him like he tried
to use Zack. What a choice, huh? But I don't
know. I don't understand that whole Paul Kant
business. I guess none of us will ever know what
happened there.*

I found the trunk immediately. In fact, I had known
where it was the moment Duane had said that it was
in the old bedroom; it was an ancient Norwegian sea
chest, not truly a trunk, a small brass-bound wooden
case brought to America by Einar Updahl's father. It
had carried everything he owned in a space just about
large enough to hold four electric typewriters. It was
a beautiful old thing—the wood was handcarved,
filigreed with scrolls and leaves.

But the beautiful old thing was also padlocked, and
I was too impatient to go back and ask Duane where
he'd misplaced the key. I slammed out of the house
onto the porch and went down its length to the far
door. In surprising heat, I tugged open the old sliding
doors of the garage and went inside. It smelled like a
grave. Damp earth smells, a general odor of mold and
beetles. Old tools hung on the walls, just as I had
remembered. Rusted saws from the log-clearing days,
three ten-gallon gas cans, hatchets and hammers, all
on nails driven into the walls. I took a crowbar off its
nail and went back into the house.

The lip of the crowbar fit neatly into the gap between
the lid and the body of the chest; I pressed hard on
the bar, and felt wood yielding. The second time I
pressed on the bar I heard a splintering sound; I put
all my weight on the bar, and the wood above the
lock popped away from the lid. I fell to my knees, the
wound on my palm throbbing where I had unknow-
ingly, unfeelingly been gripping it against the crowbar.
With my right hand I banged open the lid of the chest.
The inside was a disorder of framed and unframed
photographs. After a second of pawing through them
ineffectually and seeing several versions of Duane's

square face and my vanished cowlick and many pictures of orthodontia at work on the toothy Updahl smile, I impatiently turned the entire chest over and sent the sheets and frames across the hooked bedroom rug.

It stared up at me from four feet away, self-isolated from the other photographs; someone had removed it from its frame, and it was curling slightly at either end. But there it was, and there we were, seen by Uncle Gilbert as we must have been seen by all, our spirits flowing toward each other, more one than two drops of blood in one bloodstream, no longer children but trapped in the beautiful amber chrysalis of the teens, our hands clasped and our faces smiling out in the summer of 1955.

If I had not already been kneeling, it would have brought me to my knees—the force of that face next to mine squeezed all the breath from me. It was like being punched in the stomach with the handle of a rake. For if we were both beautiful, stuck there in ignorance and love in June of 1955, she was incomparably more so. She burned my intelligent young thief's face right off the paper, she canceled me, she was on another plane altogether, where spirit is incandescent in flesh, she was at the height of being, body and soul together. This live trumpet-blast of spirit this illumination, put me altogether in shadow. I seemed almost to be levitating, carried by the currents of magic and complication of spirit in that face which was her face. Levitating on my knees, my knees already rubbed sore by the hooked rug!

That face which was her face. By telepathy, we had been in communication all our lives—all my life I had been in touch with her.

Then I knew that all my life since our last meeting had been the project of finding her again. Her mother had retreated in shock back to San Francisco; after I had stolen a car and wrecked it in a spectacular crash not forty feet from the spot where the painted thermometer overlooked an Italian distance, my parents had clapped me in a prison-like boarding school in Miami. She was in another state; she was in another condition. We were apart but (I knew) not finally apart.

After an incalculable number of minutes I rolled over onto my back. Moisture dripped into the hair at my temples. The back of my head was embedded in crushed photographs and long splinters of Norwegian wood. I knew I *would* see her, that she would return. That was why I was there, in my grandmother's house—the book had been an evasion. Wood dug into the back of my head. I had never intended to finish the dissertation. Spirit would not permit it. From now until she came, I would prepare for her coming. Even the blank letter was part of the preparation, part of the necessary trial of spirit.

I was in the final stages of the transformation (I thought) which had begun when I had torn open my hand on the VW's engine cover and felt the freedom which was her freedom invading and sluicing through me. Reality was not a single thing, it broke through the apparently real like a fist. It was this knowledge which had always trembled in her face. Reality is merely an arrangement of molecules held together by tension, a veneer. In her face was there not the face she'd had at six? Also the face of herself at fifty? As I lay sprawled on the hooked rug in a confusion of paper and splintered wood, the white ceiling above me seemed to dissolve into white sky. I thought fleetingly of Zack, and smiled. Harmless. Harmless clueless nut. When I lost normal consciousness, I dreamed not of being suspended adrift in a far blue horror, but of Alison swimming toward me.

This image rang through my suspended mind. Everything was a part of this surge of feeling, my ripped hand, the unimportant discomfort in my neck, even Zack's prattle about reality being thinnest in the Midwest, even my theft and destruction of Maccabee's terrible book. The proof would occur on the twenty-first of July. There were no impossibilities. I slept. (I passed out.)

And woke full of purpose. When I had said to Duane, don't be surprised by anything you hear, I'd had a plan which I now saw to be absolutely necessary. I had to begin the preparations. I had to be ready for the day. I had about three weeks. It was more than enough time.

I began by tearing a photograph out of the nearest frame that looked the right size and sliding the picture of Alison and myself inside it. Idly, I tore the other photograph in half, and doubled the pieces and tore it again. Dropping the torn bits of glossy paper and letting them flutter to the littered floor, I took the photograph into the living room and hung it where the first photograph of Alison had been.

Then I looked around at the room. Most of it was going to have to go. I was going to make an Alison-environment: I was going to recreate, as nearly as possible and with a few added embellishments, the room of twenty years before. Duane's office furniture could go down into the root cellar where my grandmother's old furniture now sat. I wasn't sure that I could singlehandedly manage some of the heavier pieces down the rough steps of the root cellar, but there was no other choice It was what I was going to do.

The doors to the root cellar were set into the ground at a slightly elevated angle just at the end of the porch. You swung them up and let them drop open to the sides—it was the most oldfashioned and rural of arrangements. and I suspected that Duane's dark cellar, though modernized by the introduction of a staircase leading down from the body of the house, was originally of similar construction. With some effort I pulled one of the doors up and open, nearly straining my back; time had cemented the two doors together.

The earthen stairs looked treacherous, half-crumbled away and very steep. Some of the damage was old, but Duane had shredded some of the steps when he had taken the old furniture down. I put one foot on the first of the stairs and tested my weight. The earth was reassuringly resilient and firm. After trying a few more steps I became careless and put my foot down without looking, and the earth gave way beneath it, sending me sliding three or four feet down across a terrace of crumbling dirt. When I was steady again I put my feet solidly on a thick step and braced my shoulder under the other door and pushed with my body and legs. The door strained and flew open on complaining hinges. Now light entered nearly the whole of the root cellar. That wonderful old furniture lay in heaps and piles like stew bones. Like the garage, the cellar smelled like a grave. I began to pull my grandmother's furniture out of the dark hole of the root cellar and up into the sunlight.

I worked at this task of reclamation until my shoulders and legs ached and my clothes were covered with dirt. There was more furniture in the cellar than I had thought, all of it essential. I needed every footstool and end table, every lamp and bookcase. Too exhausted to continue, I went inside and made sandwiches from Saturday's groceries. When I had pushed down the food, I went back out with a pail of soapy warm water and washed off what was on the lawn; that completed, I went back down the crumbled steps and began to wrestle out more things. I could remember where every stick of it had been placed, I could see the room as it had been twenty years before and would be again. She had touched every bit of this furniture.

By the time the light had begun to fail, I had it all out on the lawn and washed. The fabrics were worn, but the wood was clean and shining. Even on the lawn beside the white house in the fading light, it all looked magically appropriate—that is to say no more than that it had the rightness of all things made and used with care. That beautiful worn old stuff could make you weep. The past was enshrined in it. Just sitting out there on the lawn in the dusk, it evoked the entire history of my family in America. Like them, it was solid, it was right.

Unlike Duane's office furniture, which merely looked naked and stunned and stupid when dragged outside. There was less of it than there had seemed. It had a negative relation to spirit.

I made the mistake of taking the lighter pieces, the dreadful pictures and lamps and chairs, down into the root cellar first. Under one of the lamps I found two neatly folded dollar bills. Under different circumstances, I might have admired the gesture, but it was proof of how badly I had acted. I finished with the light things in a disproportionately bad temper. That left me with the job of handling the heavy couches and the two heavier chairs when I was almost too tired to move them further, and in the dark. I had only the light from the porch and pale early moonlight, and the battered earthen steps, in many places now worn to a continuous pitted incline, were visible only at their top. The first chair went down easily; I carried it in my trembling arms and felt my way slowly along the ruined steps. But when I tried it with the second chair, I lost my footing on an incline of dirt and fell all the way to the bottom.

To complete that Buster Keatonish stunt I should have landed on the dirt floor seated comfortably in the embrace of the chair; but I landed sprawled half-over, half-under it, with pain radiating out from all of my left leg ankle to thigh. It did not feel broken, but one of the chair's legs was, dangling from ripped fabric like a dead tooth. Cursing, I ripped it off and threw it into a corner. I disposed of the chair in much the same way.

After that, I had no patience with the couches. I was not going to baby them down the slope. I shoved the first up to the lip of the cellar, nudged it over until it was set, and let go of the arm. It crashed down to the bottom. I grunted with satisfaction and was turning to the second when I became aware of a flash-light bobbing toward me.

"Goddam you, Miles," Duane said. The flashlight was held on my face. In a moment he had moved into the area of light from the porch.

"You don't need a flashlight to see it's me."

"No, even on a dark night I'd know it was you." He flicked off the flashlight and stepped closer to me. His face was savage. "Goddam you. I wish you'd never come back here. What the hell were you thinking of anyhow? You fucking bastard."

"Look," I said, "I know it looks funny, but—" I realized that as far as anger was concerned I was an amateur. Duane's face seemed to be inflating.

"Is that what you think? You think it *looks* funny? Now *you* look. If you had to go and talk about that goddam house, why did you have to talk about it with my daughter?"

I was too stunned to reply.

He glared at me for another long moment, and then whirled to the side and banged his hand against one of the porch supports.

That was when I should have started to worry—when I was given special dispensation.

"Don't you have an answer? You shit, Miles. Everybody's forgotten about that house by now. Alison was never going to find out. In a little while, the goddam thing was going to fall over anyhow. She'd never know. Then you come along and tell her it was my 'dream house,' huh? Then she can get one of the drunken bums in Arden to tell her all about it, can't she? I suppose you wanted to get her to laugh at me, just the way you and your cousin used to do."

"It was a mistake, Duane. I'm sorry. I thought she knew already."

"Bullshit, Miles, bull *shit*. My dream house, isn't that what you called it? You wanted to make her laugh at me. You wanted to humiliate me. I should pound you into the ground."

"Maybe you should," I said. "But if you're not going to, then listen to me. It was an accident. I thought it was something everybody knew."

"Yeah, that makes me feel real good. I should break you up."

"If you want a fight, give it a try. But I'm apologizing to you."

"You can't apologize for that, Miles. I want you to stay away from my daughter, hear that? Stay away from her, Miles."

He might not ever have noticed the furniture around us if he hadn't thumped his hand into the couch. Pure furious astonishment replaced the rage in his face.

"Now what the hell are you doing?" he screamed.

"I'm putting back the old furniture," I said, my heart sinking and the foolishness of my entire project momentarily clear. "When I go you can change it all back again. I have to do it, Duane."

"You're putting back—nothing's good enough for you, is it, Miles? You have to spoil everything you touch. You know, I think you're crazy, Miles. And I'm not the only one around here who thinks so. I think you're dangerous. You oughta be locked up. Pastor Bertilsson was right about you." He flicked the flashlight on again and shone it into my eyes. "We're quits, Miles. I'm not gonna throw you off the place, I'm not gonna pound the crap out of you, but I'm sure as hell gonna keep my eye on you. You can't get away with squat from now on without my knowing it."

The light came off my face and played on the few items of furniture still dotted around the lawn. "Goddam you, you're out of your skull. Somebody ought to put you away." For a moment I thought that he probably was right. He turned away without bothering to look at me. After he had stomped five or six feet away, I got the flashlight treatment again, but this time he was unable to hold it steadily on my face. "And remember, Miles," he called. "You stay away from my kid. Just keep off of her."

It was too much like Auntie Rinn.

I wrestled the other couch over to the abyss and savagely pushed it down. It crashed satisfactorily into the one already at the bottom. I thought I heard wood breaking. I kicked the doors over and shut. It took me another half hour to get the old furniture inside the old house. I just let it sit where I dropped it. Then I opened a bottle and took it upstairs.

Five

All my life I have been engaged in Sisyphean and hopeless tasks, and given the ache and flutter in my muscles, it may not be odd that I dreamed of pushing my grandmother uphill in a wheelchair through an obscure territory. We were surrounded by brilliant light. My grandmother was surprisingly heavy. I felt great dread. The smell of woodsmoke burned my nostrils. I had committed a murder, a robbery, something, and forces were closing in. They were vague as yet, but they knew about me and they would find me.

—Talk to Rinn, my grandmother said.

She repeated—Talk to Rinn.

And again—Talk to Rinn.

I ceased pushing the wheelchair. My muscles could no longer bear the strain; we seemed to have been going uphill for hours. I placed my hand on her head and bent over. Gramma, I said—I'm tired. I need help. I'm afraid. The woodsmoke smell swarmed up, occupying the spaces within my skull.

When she turned her face to me it was black and rotten.

I heard three bare, cynical handclaps.

My screams woke me up—think of that, a man alone in a white bedroom, screaming on his bed! A man alone, pursued only by himself. My body seemed heavy and incapable of motion. My mouth burned and my head felt stuffed with oily rags. Result of abuse of magic substance. I gently swung my legs out of bed and sat up, bowing my back and holding my forehead in my palms. I touched the place where my hairline used to be, now smooth and oily skin instead of soft hair. My foot encountered the upright bottle. I risked a glance. It was more than half empty. Evidence of mortality lay all about me. I stood on long sensationless legs. Except for the boots, I still wore Sunday's clothes, now smudged and crusted with dirt from the root cellar. I could taste my screams.

The stairs were navigable as long as I planted my hands on the close walls.

The furniture at first startled me. It was the wrong furniture in the wrong places. Then I remembered the scene of the previous night. Duane and the flashlight stitching into my face. That too seemed to have the quality of drunkenness. Effects can leak backward and forward in time, staining otherwise innocent events. I sat heavily on the old couch. I feared that I could fall straight through it into another dimension. On Sunday I had told myself that I knew the precise, proper location of all my grandmother's things. Now I saw that was an illusion. I would have to experiment until the room clicked shut like a tumbler in a lock, itself again at last.

The bathroom. Hot water. Drinking water. I pushed off the couch and avoided the haphazard furniture and came into the kitchen.

Alison Updahl was leaning against the counter, chewing something. She wore a T shirt (yellow) and jeans (brown). Her feet were bare, and I could feel the chill of the floor as if it were penetrating my own feet.

"I'm sorry," I said, "but it's too early for company."

She finally finished chewing, and swallowed. "I have to see you," she said. Her eyes were large.

I turned away, aware of the presence of a complication I was in no condition to handle. On the table was an untouchable plate of congealed scrambled eggs and shriveled bacon.

"Mrs. Sunderson made that for you, I guess. She took one look in the other room and said she would clean in there after you decided how you wanted the furniture. And she said you busted that old sea chest. She said that was a valuable antique. Her family has one like it and a man from Minneapolis said it was worth two hundred dollars."

"Please, Alison." I ventured another look at her. Beneath the tight yellow shirt her large breasts hung heavily, comfortably. They looked like Claes Oldenburg torpedoes. Her feet, surprisingly, were small, white, slightly puffy, beautiful. "I'm too wrecked to go public."

"I came for two reasons. The first is, I know I did a stupid thing by talking to Daddy about that house. He really blew up. Zack warned me, but I went right ahead and asked him anyhow. That was stupid, all right. What's the matter with you, anyhow? Are you hung over? And why are you putting all that old furniture and stuff back upstairs?" She was speaking very quickly.

"I'm working on a project."

That stumped her. I sat down at the table and shoved the cold food away before I could smell it.

"You don't have to worry about Daddy. He's real mad, but he doesn't know I'm here. He's out in the new fields. That's way down the road. He doesn't know about lots of things I do."

I finally saw that she was being very chatty—too chatty.

The telephone began to shrill. "Shit," I said, and weakly stood. When I plucked the earpiece off the box, I waited for the caller to say something. Silence. "Who is it?" I got no response. "Hello, hello." I heard a noise like wings, like the whuffle of a fan, like beating air. The room was cold. I slammed the earpiece down on the metal hook.

"They didn't say anything? That's weird. Zack says

that telephones can lock you into these waves of energy from outer space, and he said that if everybody took their phones off the hook at exactly the same second all over the world you could get pure outer space energy coming in waves through the receiver. Another idea he had was that if everybody in the world called the same number at exactly the same split second, there'd be some kind of energy explosion. He says that electronics and things like telephones are all making us ready for the apocalypse and the revelations." There was a doll-like brightness in all of this.

"I need a glass of water," I said. "And a bath. That's a hint." I went to the sink and stood beside her while I watched cool water rush into a glass. I drank it in two or three large inhalations, feeling the water seem to sparkle along veins throughout my chest. A second glass failed to reproduce these sensations.

"Did you ever get any of those calls in the middle of the night?"

"No. I wouldn't answer it if I did."

"I'm surprised. It looks like a whole lot of people around here don't like you very much. They talk about you. Didn't something bad happen to you once a long time ago? Something did, didn't it—something all the old people know about?"

"I don't know what you're talking about. My life has been limitless bliss from infancy. Now I'm going to take a bath."

"Daddy knows about it, doesn't he? I heard him say something well he didn't really *say* anything, he was talking about it without saying it straight out, on the telephone a couple nights ago. I think he was talking to Zack's father."

"It's hard to think of Zack having parents," I said. "He's more the head-of-Zeus type. Now scram. Please."

She wasn't going to budge. The water had awakened a sharp floating pain high behind my forehead. I could sense the tension in her, stronger now than my hangover. Alison crossed her arms over her stomach, consciously squeezing her breasts together. I caught her blood smell. "I said I had two reasons. I want you to make love to me."

"Jesus," I said.

"He won't be back for at least two hours. It doesn't take very long anyhow," she added, giving me more insight than I wished to have into Zack's sexual life.

"What would good old Zack think about it?"

"It's his idea. He said it was so I could learn discipline."

"Alison," I said, "I'm going into the bathroom now. We can talk about this later."

"We could both fit into the bathtub."

Her voice was light, her face miserable. I was terribly conscious of her thighs in the tight brown jeans, of the large soft breasts, the plump pretty feet on the cold floor. If Zack had been there, I would have shot him.

Mildly, I said, "I don't think Zack is very fair to you." She abruptly turned and wheeled out, slamming the door.

After my bath I remembered what my conversation with Duane on Sunday had resolved me to do, and I went immediately to the telephone book jacketed with the two small boys suspended over cold water. Paul Kant lived on Madison Street in Arden, but when he picked up the telephone his voice was so faraway and small that he might have been in Tibet.

"Paul, this is Miles Teagarden. I've been around for a week or so, and I tried to see you a few days ago."

"The women told me," he said. "I heard you were in town."

"Well, I heard *you* were in town," I said. "I thought you would have been off long ago."

"Things didn't happen that way, Miles."

"Do you ever see Polar Bears any more?"

He gave an odd, bitter laugh. "As little as possible. Look, Miles, it might be better . . . it might be better if you didn't try to see me. It's for your own good. Miles. Mine too, probably."

"What the hell? Are you in trouble?"

"I don't know how to answer that." His voice was strained and very small.

"Do you need help? I can't figure out what's going on, Paul."

"That's two of us. Don't make things worse, Miles. I'm saying that for your own good."

"Christ I don't understand what all the mystery is about Didn't we used to be friends?" Even through the telephone I could detect an emotion I had begun to recognize as fear. I said, "If you need any help, Paul, I'll try to help All you have to do is ask. You should have been out of that burg years ago. It's not the right place for you. Paul. I'll be coming into Arden later today Could I drop in to see you at the store?"

"I'm not working at Zumgo's any more."

"That's good." I don't know why, but I thought of the Woodsman.

"I was fired." His voice was flat and hopeless.

"Then we're both out of a job. And I'd think it's an honor to be fired from a mausoleum like Zumgo's. I'm not going to force myself on you, Paul, I've gotten involved in something that will probably take up nearly all of my time but I think I should see you. We were friends way back then."

"I can't stop you from doing what you're determined to do." he said "But if you're going to come, it'd be better to come at night."

"Why do you—"

I heard a click a second of the silence Zack had told my cousin's daughter was laden with waves of energy from outer space, and then the noncommittal buzz of the dial tone.

While I was pushing the old wooden furniture around, trying to reconstruct the sitting room as it had been twenty years before, I heard from the second of my two old Arden friends. I set down the chair I had been moving across the room and answered the telephone.

A man asked, "Is this Miles Teagarden?"

"That's me."

"One moment, please."

In a few seconds another telephone lifted. "Hello, Miles. This is Chief Hovre."

"Polar Bears!"

He laughed. "Not many folks remember that any more. Mostly people call me Galen." I had never heard his real name before. I preferred Polar Bears.

"Doesn't anyone dare call you Polar Bears any more?"

"Oh, your cousin Du-ane might. I hear that you've been making a few waves around here since you came in."

"Nothing serious."

"No, nothing at all serious. Freebo says if you went in every day he wouldn't have to be thinking of selling his bar. Are you workin' on another book now, Miles?"

So Freebo had passed on my impromptu story about Maccabee's book. "That's right," I said. "I came up here for the peace and quiet."

"And walked smack into all our troubles. Miles, I was wondering if I could arrange to see you sometime soon."

"How soon?"

"Like today?"

"What's it about?"

"Just for a friendly talk, you could say. Were you going to make it in here today?"

I had the disturbing feeling that he had telepathically overheard my conversation with Paul Kant. "I thought you'd be pretty busy these days, Polar Bears."

"Always time to spare for an old buddy, Miles. How about it? Could you drop in for a talk sometime this afternoon? We're still around the back of the court-house."

"I guess I can make it."

"Looking forward to it, Miles."

"But I wonder what would happen if I said I couldn't."

"Why do you think something would happen, Miles?"

But *why?* It sounded almost as though Polar Bears (Galen, if I must) had been monitoring my movements since I had come to the valley. Had one of Paul's enemies seen me pocket Maccabee's fraudulent book? If so, they would surely have stopped me before I left the store.

Still thinking of this, a little upset by the seriousness of Polar Bears' tone, I went upstairs and into the work room and sat before the panel desk. It all felt unbelievably remote, as though another man had removed those diamond-faceted doorknobs and set the flat door upon the trestles. My pitiful notes, my pitiful drafts. I flipped open a folder and read a sentence. "Recurrent in Lawrence's work is a moment of sexual choice which is the choosing of death (or of half-life) over fully engaged, personalizing life." Had I actually written this sentence? Uttered stuff like this before students? I bent down and scraped a random lot of books off the floor. I tied them into a bundle with twine and went out of the house and up the path.

"I'll never read these," Alison Updahl told me. "You don't have to give me anything."

"I know. You don't have to give me anything either." She looked at me unhappily. "But at least this was my own idea."

"Would you mind—would you mind if I gave them to Zack? He's the big intellectual, not me."

"Do anything you want with them," I said. "You're just saving me the trouble of throwing them away." I started to turn away.

"Miles," she said.

"It's not that I wasn't tempted," I said. "I find you extremely tempting. But I'm too old for you, and I'm still your father's guest. And I do think that you ought to get away from Zack. He's screwy. He'll never do anything but injure you."

She said, "You don't understand." She looked terribly unhappy, standing just outside the door on the concrete steps and holding the little heap of books.

"No, I guess I don't," I said.

"There isn't anyone else like him around here. Just like there isn't anyone like you around here either."

I wiped my hand over my face. I was sweating like a band drummer on a hot night. "I won't be here long, Alison. Don't make me into something I'm not."

"Miles," she said, and stopped, embarrassed. Her habit of assertion saw her through. "Is something wrong?"

"It's too complicated to explain." She did not reply, and when I looked into her blunt face I saw the expression of another person whose problems were too complex to be fit easily into verbal patterns. I wanted to take her hand, and nearly did. But I could not lay claim to the spurious authority of age which that would imply.

"Ah . . ." she said as I turned to go again.

"Yes?"

"It was partly my own idea. But you probably won't believe me."

"Alison, be careful," I said, meaning it as much as I have ever meant anything in my life.

I went back to the old house through the sunlight. My hangover had receded to a not unpleasant sensation of light emptiness. By the time I reached the VW parked before the frame garage I realized that the sun was warming my face and shoulders. Twenty yards to my right, the mare grazed in the torn uprooted field, pretending for the sake of a full belly that it was a cow like its neighbors. The walnut trees ahead of me were thick and burly, emblems of long health. I wished the same for Alison Updahl and myself. I could feel her back there on the concrete porch, watching me go. I wished that I could do something, something strong and direct, to help her. A hawk swung far above the hills across the valley. Down the drive and across the road stood the birdhouse mailbox on its metal stalk.

Tuta S. had probably left before the arrival of the mail-man in his dusty Ford.

At the box I pulled out a thick pad of folders and envelopes. One after the other I sailed into the ditch letters addressed to Occupant. The last of the letters came in the same envelope as the one addressed to me, and it was written over in the same flowing handwriting. For a moment I thought I read my name on it. Like the previous letter, it had been posted in Arden.

When I finally saw what the envelope said I glanced across the cornfields to the beginning of the woods. No figure stood there gazing with waiting aloof Olympian calm. My hands were trembling. I looked again at the envelope—I was not mistaken. It was addressed to Alison Greening. Care of (my name), RFD 2, Norway Valley, Arden. The sun seemed to penetrate behind my pupils and give me a searing touch. Clumsily, still trembling, I inserted a finger beneath the flap and tore it open. I knew what I would find. The single sheet unfolded itself in my hands. Of course. It was blank. Neither a heart pierced by an arrow nor a black spot nor anything but creamy paper.

Down the road, her handbag pumping at her side, Tuta Sunderson toiled toward me. I waited, gasping with emotion, as long as I could and then ran toward her.

"Something come for you?"

"No, yes," I said. "I don't know. Mrs. Sunderson, you can't clean the living room yet. I'm not through in there. You might as well go home. I have to go some-where." Remembering the phone call of the morning, I added, "If the phone rings, don't answer it." I pelted up the road toward my car.

Smashing the gears, making the VW howl in torment, I shot across the lawn, twisting the wheel at the last moment to avoid the walnut trees. I came rocketing out onto the valley road in the direction of Highway 93. Fat Tuta Sunderson still stood where I had left her; mouth open, she dully watched me zoom past.

But this was not how I wanted to meet Polar Bears,

I could not be dragged manacled before him by a slack-faced Arden constable, and I slowed to forty descending the hill past the R-D-N motel. By the time I reached the flat near the high school, I was proceeding at an almost-legal thirty. People were visible on the sidewalks, a cat cleaned itself on a windowsill, other cars trolled before mine: Arden did not have the deserted, eerie look it had had on my earlier visit, but was a normal small town in a normal condition of sleepy bustle. I pulled into an empty spot before Zumgo's and stopped as gently as a dove. I felt like a man poised on an eggshell. The folded envelope distended my pocket. I knew only one sure way to conquer that awful weightless expectant eggshell feeling. Hearing no wingbeats but the sound of voices, I crossed the pavement to enter Zumgo's.

Happily, the store had a good crowd of women shoppers. Mostly overweight, dressed in obscene halters and skirts excessively short, they would be the audience for my autotherapy. From them rose a mass smell of compost and barren backyards, of dime taps of Leinenkugel beer and soggy pretzels. I began to drift, in an attitude of abstracted busy specific search, through the aisles and around the tables. The women, including the harridan of my previous visit, scarcely noticed me. I was some husband on some errand. I thought and felt myself into this role.

I am no kleptomaniac. I have a letter from an analyst setting that down in black and white, pica type. I took a ten-dollar bill from my wallet and folded it between the second and third fingers of my right hand.

Now it is time for two comments. The first is obvious. I thought that I knew the handwriting on that envelope. I thought that Alison Greening had sent it to me. This was crazy. But it was no crazier than that she would return on the twenty-first of July to keep her vow. Perhaps she was signaling to me, telling me to hold out until that day. The second comment has to do with stealing. I do not think of myself as a thief—except perhaps at a gritty subconscious level that pumps guilt up into my dreams. I hate stealing. Except for Maccabee's book, I had not stolen anything for at least fifteen years. Thinking of the thefts of my boyhood, I once asked an analyst if he thought I was a kleptomaniac. He said, of course not. Put it in writing, I said. He told me it was my fifty minutes and typed it out on a piece of notepaper. Yet at moments of great unease, I know that I can put my mind right—if at all, if at cost of a wider displacement—by only one means. It is like eating—like stuffing food down your throat long after your hunger has died.

So what I intended doing was a repetition of my mime of thievery: I was going to surreptitiously pocket goods and then drop the ten dollars at the cash register on the way out. Temptation struck first in household novelties, where I saw a corkscrew on a table. Next to it lay a rank of clasp knives. I hovered over the table, ignoring a dozen opportunities for palming the corkscrew and one of the knives. The whole business suddenly seemed labored and stupid.

Revulsion for the charade made me turn away. I was too old for these tricks, I could not allow myself to be so foolishly self-indulgent. But still I suffered. I went upstairs where the books were kept.

Slowly I revolved the rack: you will not steal again, I said to myself, you will not even pretend to steal. Romantic novels with jacket pictures of girls running from castles predominated. I could see no more copies of *The Enchanted Dream*. Finding even one had been fantastic luck. With feigned idleness I scanned the spines side-view. Still nothing.

And then I saw a natural second choice. There, crammed in one of the bottom divisions, was a novel written by Lamont Withers, who had been the gabbiest, most annoying member of my Joyce seminar at Columbia and now taught at Bennington—*A Vision of Fish*, an experimental novel disguised by its jacket drawing of two embracing androgynes as a romance. I extracted the book and examined the back of the cover. "A sensi-

tive tour de force . . . *Cleveland Plain Dealer*. Stunning,
witty advance . . . *Library Journal*. Withers is the coming man . . . *Saturday Review*." My facial muscles con-
tracted; it was even worse than Maccabee. Temptation
reared up, and I nearly tucked the book between arm
and elbow. But I would not give in to this gluttony; I
could not be ruled by the responses of twenty years
past. I gripped the book in my hand. I went down the
stairs. At the cash register, an orderly man, I paid for
the book and accepted my change.

Breathing hard, flushed of face, at peace, I sat in my
car. Not stealing was so much a better feeling than
stealing, or mime-stealing. Not stealing, as I had in
fact known for years, was the only way to shop. I
felt like an alcoholic who has just turned down a drink.
It was still too early to see Polar Bears, so I touched
the folded letter in my pocket and decided to go—
where else?—to Freebo's, to celebrate. In the midst of
death and breakdown, a successful mission.

As I walked across the street, a sharp atom neatly
bisected my back between the shoulder blades. I heard a
stone clatter on the surface of the road. Stupidly, I
watched it roll and come to rest before I looked at the
sidewalk. People were there, still simulating that sleepy
smalltown bustle, walking from Zumgo's to the Coast
To Coast Store, looking in the bread-filled windows of
Myer's bakery. They seemed to be avoiding looking at
me, avoiding even looking in my direction. A second
later I saw the men who had probably thrown the
stone. Five or six burly middle-aged men, two or three
in dungarees and the others in shabby business suits,
stood in front of the Angler's Bar. These men were
watching me, a general smile flickering between them.
I could not stare them down—it was like the Plainview
diner. I recognized none of them. When I turned away,
a second stone flew past my head. Another struck my
right leg.

Friends of Duane's, I thought, and then realized I
was wrong. If they were merely that, they would be

laughing. This business-like silence was more ominous than stone-throwing. I looked over my shoulder: they still stood, bunched together and hands in pockets, before the dark bar window. They were watching me. I fled into Freebo's.

"Who are those men?" I asked him. He came hurriedly down the bar, wiping his hands on a rag.

"You look a little shook up, Mr. Teagarden," he said.

"Tell me who those men are. I want their names."

I saw the drinkers at the bar, two thin old men, pick up their glasses and move quietly off.

"What men, Mr. Teagarden?"

"The ones across the street, standing in front of a bar."

"You mean the Angler's. Gee, I don't see anybody there, Mr. Teagarden, I'm sorry."

I went up to the long narrow window overlooking the street and stood beside him. The men had vanished. A woman with her hair in curlers pushed a baby carriage in the direction of the bakery.

"They were just there," I insisted. "Five, maybe six, a couple of farmers and a few others. They threw rocks at me."

"I dunno, Mr. Teagarden, it could have been some kind of accident."

I glared at him.

"Let me get you a drink on the house," he said. He turned away and put a shot glass beneath one of the upended bottles. "There. Put that inside you." Meekly, I drank it in one gulp. "You see, we're still all upset around here, Mr. Teagarden. It was probably because they didn't know who you were."

"It was probably because they did know who I am," I said. "Friendly town, isn't it? Don't answer, just get me another drink. I have to see Polar Bears, Galen I mean, in a little while but I'm going to stay in here until everybody goes home."

He blinked. "Whatever you say."

I drank six whiskies, taking my time over them.

Several hours passed. Then I had a cup of coffee, and after that another drink. The other men in the bar regarded me surreptitiously, shifting their eyes toward the mirror when I raised my glass or leaned on the bar. After an unendurable time of this, I took Withers' book out of my jacket pocket and began to read it on the bar. I switched from whisky to beer and remembered that I'd had nothing to eat.

"Do you have sandwiches in here?"

"I'll get one for you, Mr. Teagarden. And another cup of coffee?"

"And a cup of coffee *and* another beer."

Withers' book was unreadable. It was unbearably trivial. I began to tear out pages. If you find a pattern, you should stick to it. Now the other men in the bar no longer bothered to conceal their stares. I recognized in myself the buzzing frontal lobes of intoxication. "Do you have a wastebasket, Freebo?" I asked.

He held up a green plastic bucket. "Is that another one you wrote?"

"No, I never wrote anything worth publishing," I said. I pitched the ripped pages into the green bucket. The men were staring at me as they would at a circus ape.

"You're shook up, Mr. Teagarden," Freebo said. "See, it won't help any. You've had a few too many, Mr. Teagarden, and you're kinda upset. I think you ought to go out in the fresh air for a little bit. You're all paid up in here, see, and I can't serve you any more. You oughta go home and have a rest." He was walking me toward the front of the bar, talking in a low, calming voice.

"I want to buy a record player," I said. "Can I do that now or is it too late?"

"I think the stores just closed, Mr. Teagarden."

"I'll do it tomorrow. Now I have to see Polar Bears Galen Hovre."

"That's a good idea." The door closed behind me. I was standing alone on a deserted Main Street; the sky and the light were darkening, though it would not be dusk for at least two hours. I realized that I had spent most of the day in the bar. Signs on the bakery and department store doors read CLOSED. I glanced at the Angler's Bar, which seemed from the outside to be as empty as Freebo's. A single car went past in the direction of the courthouse. Once again, I could hear the beating of pigeons' wings, circling way up above.

At that moment the town seemed haunted. The Midwest is the place for ghosts, I realized, the truest place for them; they could throng up these wide empty Main Streets and populate the fields. I could almost feel them around me.

With these thoughts in my mind, I started when I heard footsteps behind me. I looked over my shoulder and saw only an empty street lined with cars like the deserted hulls of insects. When I turned my neck, I again heard the footsteps, a crowd of them. I began to walk quickly, and heard them follow. The street lay wide and deserted before me, lined with empty cars and blank deserted shops. I heard the electric buzz of a neon sign in the window of a kitchen supplier's. Reality's veneer seemed on the verge of dissolution, even the pavement and the brick storefronts were stretched taut over a drumming void. I began to run, and heard them running behind me. I turned my head again, and was almost relieved to see a crowd of thick-waisted men making down the street toward me.

The courthouse was four blocks away, in a straight line up Main Street, but I didn't have a chance of getting there before they caught me. In the brief glimpse I had, some of them seemed to be carrying sticks. I pumped around the next corner and doubled back into an alley. When I reached the rear of Freebo's I hunched down beside a group of large silver garbage cans; I did not have time to reach the end of the alley. The group of men had clearly divided; two of them appeared at the alley's entrance and began to half-trot toward me. I crouched as low as I could get behind the big silver cans. Their footsteps approached, and I heard them breathing hard. They were even less accustomed to running than I was.

One of them distinctly exclaimed, "Shit."

I waited until I heard them returning; they passed my hole, and then clattered toward the alley's entrance. When I peeked out, I saw them turning right to follow the rest of the group. My back to the buildings, legs ready to spring, I edged down the alley's length. I looked cautiously out at Madison Street. Two blocks down, they were rocking an old car parked before a peeling, shabby house. One of them swung at the car with a long stick, ax handle or baseball bat. Glass popped and exploded.

I couldn't make sense of it. Were they just rowdy drunks looking for the nearest target? Hoping that the noise they were making while destroying the car would keep them from hearing me, I ran across Madison Street into the alley on the other side. Shouts and yells told me that they had seen me. I nearly fell down in terror. I pelted through the alley and came out on Monroe Street, turned right with the thick boiling noise gathering behind me, and wheeled around the corner back onto Main. At the last possible second, I yanked at the door-handle of a car and rolled inside. Then I scrambled over the seat and lay, heart pounding, in the well before the back seat. A candy wrapper fluttered before my nose; dust seemed to pour dryly up from the floor, acrid and foul. I closed my nostrils with my fingers, and after a time the impulse to sneeze left me. I could hear them coming quickly up the street, banging with fists or clubs on cars in frustration.

The edge of a greasy shirt passed the window I could see. A hand pressed against it, flattened and white like a dead starfish. Then I saw only darkening sky. I thought: what if I die here? If my machinery fails and dumps my corpse into this odorous car? Who would find me? It was an image of utter hopelessness. After a while I was strong enough to sneak a look over the top of the seat. They were not far down the block, evidently confounded by my disappearance. There were only four of them, fewer than I had thought; they did not look like the men who had stoned me. They were younger. They ran ahead a few steps. Then they began to walk up Main, looking from side to side, rapping their bats on the sidewalk. They were the only people on the street. When a car passed, they bent to examine the driver's face. I waited until they had gone several blocks past the courthouse and then I crawled over the seat and came crouching out onto the sidewalk.

The four men were across the street now, far up ahead, nearly to the bridge over the Blundell River. The courthouse lay about halfway between us. I began to walk toward it. The men had reached the bridge, and I saw them leaning on it, talking, lighting cigarettes. Bent over, moving as quickly as possible without running, I gained another fifty feet. Then one of the men threw down his cigarette and pointed at me.

I lifted my elbows and knees and discovered for the first time in my life what running was. It is rhythm, all rhythm, long easy beats made by coordinating every muscle. They were confused that I ran toward them, but when I reached the courthouse and turned easily on one leg and pounded, stepping high, to the back, they flew shouting after me. I fisted my hands and made arcs in the air with them, my chest bowed out and my legs sailing across the asphalt parking lot. I reached the police cars just as they came into the lot. I heard them slow down, scuffling, calling out to me.

The words were inaudible. A roaring sound kicked to life in the corner of the parking lot, and I saw a black-jacketed man tear off on a motorcycle. It looked as though it could have been Zack; I wasn't sure. The sudden noise made my followers panic. By the time I reached the yellow door with thick glass inset above the word POLICE, they had scattered. My throat felt like burning paper.

The uniformed man rolling a sheet of paper into a typewriter turned his chubby face toward me. I closed

the door and leaned back against it, breathing hard.
Still holding the paper in his hands, he half-rose, and
I saw the stumpy pistol strapped to his hip. "My name
is Teagarden," I said, "and I have an appointment with
the Chief."

"Oh yeah," he said, and lowered the paper with
deliberate slowness on top of the typewriter. My chest
was heaving.

"I just won a race. Try not to shoot."

"Just hold it right there." He came around to the
front of the desk, not taking his eyes from me nor removing his hand from within panic distance of the
revolver. His left hand found the telephone; when he
had the receiver to his ear, he glanced at the row of
buttons at the base of the phone and punched one and
then dialed a single number. "Teagarden's here." He
set the phone down.

"You can go right in. He's been waiting for you.
Take that door right there, and then it's the door
marked Chief."

I nodded, and moved toward the door "right there."
Polar Bears' office was at the end of the hall; it was
about ten by twelve, mostly filled with green filing
cabinets and a worn old desk. Most of the rest of it
was filled by Polar Bears.

"Sit down, for God's sake, Miles," he said, waving
at the chair before his desk. "You look like you had
a hard old day." Looking at him, I could see the difference in our ages more clearly than I ever had before—he had been nearly Duane's age, though his
cheerful rowdiness had made him younger in my eyes.
In this solidly massive man with a serious square face
I could see few traces of the boy who had spitballed
Bertilsson's sheep. Even the reason for his name had
vanished: his furry cap of astonishingly white hair had
darkened and receded to a brownish dusting from his
ears to his rubbery-looking scalp.

"You look like you've had a hard old life, but it's
nice to see you again," I said.

"Yeah, we had some good times together, didn't we? Some real good times."

"I had an especially good time on the way over here. A gang of your citizens chased me with baseball bats. I barely made it."

He tilted his head back and pushed his lips out. "Would that be the reason you're sort of late for our reunion?"

"Our reunion is the reason I'm here at all, and not broken up in the alley behind Freebo's. They only stopped chasing me because I made it into your parking lot."

"You were at Freebo's. I'd say you spent quite a time in there."

"Does that mean you don't believe me?"

"Some of the bucks around town are getting all riled. I can believe you, Miles. I don't suppose you saw these boys close enough to identify them."

"I was trying hard not to get that close."

"Simmer down, Miles. They're not going to get you. You're going to be safe in here, having a little talk. Just simmer down. Those boys will leave you alone."

"Some others of your local boys threw rocks at me this noon when my back was turned."

"Is that so? You get hurt any?"

"It's so and no, I didn't. Do you want me to forget about that too? Just because they didn't dent my skull?"

"I don't want you to go getting yourself worked up over a bunch of hotheads. I'd say that some of the good people decided that you'd be better off leaving town."

"Why?"

"Because they don't know you, Miles. It's simple as that. You're the only man in about a century and a half had a sermon preached about him. You weren't thinking of being run off, were you?"

"No. I have to stay here. I'm involved in something."

"Um hum. Real good. Any idea how long that might take you?"

"Until the twenty-first. After that I don't know."

"Well, that's not far away. I want to ask you to consider staying up there at Duane's until we get some things straightened out around here. Is that all right?"

"What the hell is this all about, Polar Bears? Don't leave town until the police give me permission?"

"I wouldn't put it like that. I'm asking you for a favor."

"Am I being questioned?"

"Hell no, Miles. We're having a talk. I want your help on something."

I leaned back in the stiff chair. I couldn't feel the alcohol any more. Galen Hovre was regarding me with a half-smile which held little warmth. My senses were confirming a theory of mine, that when a man's nature changes his essential smell changes with it. Polar Bears once had carried a dense, pleasant odor of closely packed earth, strongest when he was racing a jalopy at seventy down the curves of Highway 93 or stuffing a mailbox with rocks; now, like Duane, he smelled of gunpowder.

"Can I count on your help?"

I looked at this large square-faced man who had been my friend, and didn't trust a thing he said. "Sure."

"You've heard about these girls who were killed. Gwen Olson and Jenny Strand. Your neighbor Red Sunderson found that Strand girl, and she wasn't a pretty sight. My deputy, Dave Lokken out there, lost his cookies when he saw her."

"He's still upset," I said.

"Any normal man would be," Hovre said amiably. "Truth is, we're all upset around here. This crazy son of a bitch is still walking around. He could be anybody, and that's the one that gets them by the nuts, Miles. We pretty well know everybody, and folks don't know what to think."

"Don't you have any ideas about who it might be?"

"Oh, we're sort of keeping an eye on someone, but

even he's not very likely, according to the way I see it. Now I'd like to keep this local. I've been Chief here for four years, and I want to get re-elected so I can keep my family in hamburgers. Now you're new around here. You might see things we don't notice. You had a good education, you're observant. I wonder if you've seen or heard anything that might help me out?"

"Wait a second," I said. "Do those people who chased me think I did those things? Those killings?"

"You'd have to ask them."

"Christ," I said. "I've scarcely even thought about them. I've been busy with my own problems. I didn't come here for this."

"Seems to me it might help you out too if you could think of anything."

"I shouldn't need that. I shouldn't have to help myself that way."

"Seems to me should doesn't have much to do with it."

He had a point. "Okay, I can see that. I don't think I've noticed anything. Just a lot of people acting queer, afraid. Some of them hostile. I met one strange kid, but . . ." The "but" was that I did not want to say anything that would bring suspicion on Zack or Alison. Zack was just a nutty theorist. Polar Bears lifted his eyebrows in a gesture of uninvolved patient anticipation. "But he was just a kid. I don't even want to name him. I don't know what I could say that would help."

"Not yet, maybe. But you might remember something. Just keep it in mind, will you, old buddy?"

I nodded.

"Yeah. We could have this all on a plate by the twenty-first, so don't do any unnecessary worrying. Now I got a few other little points to bring up with you." He put on a pair of thick black glasses, making himself look like a scholarly bald bull of melancholy temperament, and took a sheet of paper off a messy pile. "I guess you got into a little trouble over in Plainview a while ago. I got a report on it just yesterday. A fellow named Frank Drum took the number of your car."

"Jesus," I said, thinking of the slinking little clerk who had been dispatched out of the diner.

"This was after an incident in Grace's Restaurant over there. Do you remember it?"

"Of course I remember. They were like your gang of happy hooligans who tried to beat in my head with bats."

"Who chased you." He looked sharply up from the paper.

"It's the same thing. What happened was ridiculous. I saw these guys listening to a radio and they looked like some trouble had happened and I asked what it was. They didn't like my face. They didn't like my coming from New York. So they threw me out after they took my license number. That was all. It was around one of the day somebody found the first girl."

"Just for the record, do you know where you spent the previous night?"

"Somewhere. In a motel somewhere. I don't know."

"You don't have a receipt or a check stub?"

"It was in a crummy little dive off the freeway. I paid with cash. What the hell do you want to know for?"

"I don't want to know. There's a cop named Larabee over there who wanted me to ask, that's all."

"Well, tell Larabee to shove it up his ass. I was in a crummy motel in Ohio."

"Just fine, Miles, that's fine. Real good. No need to get lathered up all over again. How did you hurt that hand of yours?"

I looked in surprise down at my bandaged hand. The tape was filthy and beginning to unravel. Loose wispy trails of dirty gauze leaked from beneath the tape. I had nearly forgotten about Duane's bandage. "I had an accident with my car. On my car. I cut myself."

"Dave Lokken can fix you up with a new bandage

before you leave. He's real proud of his first aid skills. When did that accident happen?"

"That same day. After I left the diner."

"According to another fellow in that restaurant, a fellow named Al Service—he's the official weedcutter in that part of the county—you made a funny remark before you left. According to Service, you said you hoped another girl would be killed."

"I didn't mean that. I was angry. I didn't even know anyone had been killed then. I just said something like, 'Whatever it was, you deserve to have it happen again.' Then I ran like hell."

He took off the glasses. He rested one jowl in his meaty hand. "I guess that makes sense, Miles. They got you riled. It happens to everybody. Why, you even got old Margaret Kastad worked up, I hear."

"Old who?"

"Andy's wife. She gave me a call after you left the store. Said you were writing pornography and I should run you off."

"I won't waste time talking about that," I said. "She holds a few ancient mistakes against me. I'm a different person now."

"All of us are, I guess. Guess it doesn't mean we can't help each other out. You could do something for me right now, and write out what happened in that restaurant and date it and sign it so's I can have a copy sent to Larabee. It's for your own good." He fished around on his desk and pushed a sheet of paper and a pen across the surface. "Just in general terms, Miles. It doesn't have to be long."

"If I have to." I took the paper and wrote down what had happened. I returned the paper to him.

"You'll give me a call whenever you remember or notice anything?"

I put my hand in my pocket and felt folded paper. "Wait. Just wait a second. Here's something you can help me with. Who do you think sent this to me? There was a blank sheet of paper inside it." I took out the envelope and smoothed it on his desk. My hands were shaking. "It's the second one. The first was addressed to me."

The glasses went back on, and he bent over the desk to take the envelope. When he saw the name, he glanced up at me. It was the first genuine response I'd had from him. "You got another one of these?"

"Addressed to me. With a blank sheet of paper in it."

"Would you let me keep this?"

"No. I want it. What you can do is tell me who sent it." I had the sense of taking a great risk, of making a huge error. It was strong enough to weaken my knees.

"I hate to say this, but it looks like your writing, Miles."

"What?"

He held up my statement alongside the envelope and then turned them so I could see them together. There was a certain superficial similarity. "It's not my writing, Polar Bears."

"Not many people around here remember this particular name any more."

"All it takes is one," I said. "Just give me the envelope back."

"Whatever you say. Only experts can really tell about these handwriting things anyhow. Dave!" He was bellowing at the door. "Get in here with your first aid kit! Pronto!"

"I heard you callin' him Polar Bears. Not many does that any more."

Lokken and I were walking down Main Street in the late humid darkness. The few streetlights had come on; I could again hear the buzz of neon signs. Lights burned in the windows of the Angler's, spilling a rectangle of yellow onto the sidewalk. My hand was encased in gleaming white.

"We're old friends."

"You'd have to be. That name Polar Bears just drives

him up the wall. Where's your car at, anyhow? I think you'd be safe now."

"I'm not taking the chance. He said for you to walk me to my car, and that's what I want you to do."

"Shit, there's nothing to be ascairt of. There ain't nobody out."

"That's what I thought last time. If you don't call him Polar Bears, what do you call him?"

"Me?" Lokken guffawed. "I call him Sir."

"What does Larabee call him?"

"Who?"

"Larabee. The chief over in Plainview."

"Excuse me, but you musta lost some of your marbles, Mr. Teagarden. There ain't nobody named Larabee over there in Plainview and even if there was he wouldn't be chief because Plainview ain't even *got* a Chief of Police. They got a sheriff named Larson, and he's my second cousin. Chief Hovre calls in there once or twice a week. It's his jurisdiction, like all these little towns roundabout, Centerville, Liberty, Blundell. He's chief of it all. Where's your car at, now?"

I was standing motionless in the middle of the wide dark street, looking at the VW and trying to assimilate what Lokken had said. The condition of my car made it difficult.

Lokken said, "My God, that's not yours, is it?"

I nodded, my throat too dry to form words.

The windows were smashed, the top and hood bent and battered. One of the headlights protruded like an eyeball on a thin stalk. I ran to look at the front tires, and then went around in back. They were untouched, but the rear window had been smashed in.

"That's property damage. You want to come back and tell the Chief about it? You should fill out a report. I gotta make a report too."

"No. You tell Hovre about it. This time he'll believe me." I could feel anger building up in me again, and I gripped Lokken's arm and squeezed it hard, making him yelp. "Tell him I said I wanted Larabee to handle it."

"But I just told you my second cousin—"

I was already in the car, torturing the ignition.

The dangling headlight clattered onto the street before I had gone a block, and as I gunned the car up the first of the hills, just past the high school, I heard a hubcap roll off into the weeds beside the road. Through the starred windshield, I could see only a quarter of the road, and even that was fogged and blurred by the condition of the glass. My single headlight veered between illuminating the yellow line and the weeds, and my emotional condition swung wildly about a giant sense of betrayal. Larabee, was it? Was it Larabee who wanted to know how I'd cut my hand? Was it Larabee who wanted to get re-elected?

I suspected that it was Larabee who would not push very hard to find the men who had tried to attack me, and who had wrecked my car in their frustration.

Fighting the shuddering car around a tight, ascending curve, I realized that the radio was playing: I had accidentally brushed the button some miles back, and now it was unreeling yards of drivel. ". . . and for Kathy and Jo and Brownie, from the Hardy Boys, I guess you girls know what that means, a good old good one, 'Good Vibrations.'" Teenage voices began to squeal. I slammed into a lower gear, trying to watch the turning of the road through the web of the windshield as the announcer inserted a voice-over. "The Hardy Boys, far out." Headlights raced toward me, then slipped past, flaring like the car's horn.

The next car flipped its lights up and down twice, and I realized that my single headlight was on bright; I hit the dimming button with my foot.

"Too much, really too much. Those were the good old days talkin' at ya. Now for Frank from Sally, a real tender one, I guess she loves you, Frank, so give her a call, huh? Something from Johnny Mathis."

On the rises I could see nothing but black empty air beyond the roadbed; I kept the accelerator to the floor, releasing it only when I had to change gears or when the bolts in the car's body began to shimmy. I flew past the Community Chest thermometer, seeing it only for a second in the headlight. All the beautiful green distance was one-dimensional dark.

"Hey, Frank, you better watch that little fox, she's gonna get you, baby. She's just stone in love with you, so be cool. Little change of pace now—for the junior gym class and Miss Tite, a blast of soulful Tina Turner, from Rosie B—'River Deep, Mountain High.'"

My tires complained as I suddenly braked, seeing a high wooded wall of stone before me instead of the black road; I cramped the wheel, and the back end fished out and then righted itself in that way which suggests that an automobile is constructed of a substance far more elastic than metal. The oil light flashed and went dead again. Still going dangerously fast, my mind filled with nothing but the mechanics of driving, I came over the last hill and began the straight slope down to the highway in a deep well of unheard music.

Without bothering to brake I spun out onto the deserted highway. The music pulsed in my ears like blood. Over the low white bridge, past where Red Sunderson must have found the second girl's body; then a sharp left onto the valley road. I was breathing as hard as if I'd been running.

"Whoo-ee! Tell that to anyone, but don't tell it to your gym teacher! All the weirdos are out tonight, kiddies, so lock your doors. Here's something for all the lost ones, I kid you not, that's what the card says, for all the lost ones, from A and Z. Van Morrison and 'Listen to the Lion.'"

At last I became conscious of the radio's noise. I slowed, passing the narrow drive to Rinn's house. Dark mounted high on either side—I seemed to be entering a tunnel of darkness. From A and Z? Alison and Zack? "Listen to the Lion"—that was the name of the song. An untrained high baritone glided through words I could not distinguish. The song seemed to have no particular melody. I switched the radio off. I wanted only to be home. The VW sped past the shell of the old school, and a few moments later, the high pompous façade of the church. I heard the motor grinding arhythmically, and pushed the button to bring the headlight back up to bright.

Before the Sunderson farm the road makes a tight bend around a red outcropping of sandstone, and I leaned forward over the wheel, putting all my attention onto the two square inches of clear glass. The beam of yellow light flew over the corn. Then I saw something that made me slew the car over to the side of the road and brake. I hurriedly got out and stood on the ridge beside the seat so that I could look over the top of the car to the end of the fields.

It had not been a mistake: the slight figure was there again, between the field and the black rise of the wood.

I heard a screen door bang shut behind me and looked up over my shoulder, startled. Lights in the Sunderson home showed a tall husky man in outline on the high sloping lawn. I looked back across the fields, and it was still there. The choice was simple because it was not a choice at all.

I jumped down onto the road and ran around the front of the car.

"Hey!" a man shouted.

In the next second I was over the ditch and already running down the side of the cornfield, going toward the woods. Whoever was up there was watching me, I thought, letting me approach.

"Stop! Miles! Wait up!"

I ignored him. The woods were a quarter of a mile away. I could almost hear music. The voice behind me ceased to shout. As I ran toward it, the figure went backward into the woods and disappeared.

"I see you!" the man shouted.

I didn't bother to turn around: the vanishing of the figure into the woods made me run even harder, even more clumsily, forgetting the technique I had learned in the police parking lot. The ground was hard and dry, covered with a light stubble, and I pounded along, keeping in view the place where the figure had last been. Beside me, the corn was higher than my head, a solid dark mass beyond the first rows.

The boundary of the first row of fields, from the highway to the farm just beyond Duane's, is formed by a small creek, and it was this that gave me my first difficulty. The plowed and farmed land ended about eight feet on either side of the creek; when I reached the end of the corn planting, I looked to my left and saw an area of beaten-down tall grass and flattened weeds where apparently Duane customarily drove the tractor through to the upper fields. When I ran there and began to approach the creek, I saw that the ground had been churned by the tractor so that the whole area was a muddy swamp. There the creek was four or five feet wider than anywhere else, spilling out into the depression the tractor had made. I walked back along the bank; birds and frogs announced themselves, joining the cricket noises that had surrounded me since I had left the road. My boots were encased in soft mud.

I pushed tall fibrous weeds apart with my arms and saw a narrowing of the creek. Two hairy grassy bulges of earth made an interrupted bridge over the water; the bulges, about a yard and a half apart, were supported by the root systems of two of the cottonwood trees which grew all along the creek's length. I circled one of the trees and edged out on the root-hump and jumped across, banging my forehead and nose into the trunk of the tree on the opposite side. Crows took off in noisy alarm. Still clutching the tree with both arms, I looked back over the cornfield and saw the VW parked on the valley road before the Sunderson house up on its hill. Light came beaming out from both house and car—I had forgotten to turn off the engine. Worse, I had left the key in the ignition. Mrs. Sunderson and Red were standing at one of the windows, cupping their hands to their eyes and staring out.

I jumped down from the humped tangle of roots and, after struggling through another area of thick weeds, began to jog up through the next field. I could see the place where I thought the figure had slipped into the woods, and pushed myself up over a rise where alfalfa gave way to corn again. In a few minutes I was at the beginning of the trees.

They seemed sparser, less a thick homogeneous mass than they had appeared from the road. Moonlight made it possible for me to see where I was going once I had begun to run through the widely spaced trees. My feet encountered the edges of large rocks and the yielding softness of mould and beds of pine needles. As I ran deeper into the trees the impression of sparseness quickly diminished: the ghostly pines and birches slipped behind me, and I was moving between oaks and elms, veterans with rivered barks which blocked out nearly all the light. I came to a jog and then stopped, hearing an excited rustle of movement off to my left.

I turned my head in time to see a deer bounding for cover, lifting its haunches like a woman leaving a diving board.

Alison. I plunged blindly off to the right, hindered by my heavy boots. She had appeared to me, she had signaled. Somewhere, she was waiting for me. Somewhere deep in the darkness.

A long time later and after I entered a circle of trees, I admitted that I was lost. Not finally lost, because the slope of the forest's floor told me which way the fields and the road were, but lost enough not to know if I had been circling. More disturbingly, after I had fallen and rolled against a lichen-covered boulder, I had become unsure of lateral direction. The woods were too dark for me to see farmhouse lights in the distance—in fact, distance did not seem to exist at all, except as an infinity of big close dark trees. I had edged my way into one clearing, perhaps half a mile back; but it may have been *up*, not *back*, and was at least some distance up, for I had come down the slope before going right again. All in all I thought I had been looking for nearly an hour, and the trees about me seemed familiar, as if I had been at this same spot before. It was only the little clearing, blackened at its center with the cold ashes of a fire, which proved I had gone anywhere at all, and not turned and turned in the same place before the same trees until I was lost and dizzy.

Because, really, it did look familiar—the giant bulge of a trunk before me had been before me earlier, I had looked up at an identical thick curve of branch, I had knelt on an identical shattered log. I shouted my cousin's name.

At that moment I had an essentially *literary* experience, brewed up out of Jack London and Hawthorne and Cooper and Disney cartoons and Shakespeare and the brothers Grimm, of panic which quickly passed into fear. The panic was at being lost, but the fear which rushed in after it was simply of the woods themselves, of giant alien nature. I mean that the trees seemed inhabited by threatening life. Malevolence surrounded me. Not just nature's famous Darwinian indifference, but active actual hostility. It was the most primitive apprehension of evil I had ever known. I was a fragile human life on the verge of being crushed by immense forces, by forces of huge and impersonal evil. Alison was a part of this; she had drawn me in. I knew that if I did not move, I would be snatched by awful twigged hands, I would be shredded against stones and branches, my mouth and eyes filled with moss. I would die as the two girls had died. Lichen would pack my mouth. How foolish we had been to assume that mere human beings had killed the girls!

From this frozen encounter with spirit it was terror that finally released me, and I ran blindly, plungingly, in any direction I could find—in far greater fear than I had run from the hooligans in Arden. Low branches caught my stomach and brought me crashing down, rocks skittered under my slippery feet, twigs clutched at my trousers. Low leaves rustled at my eyes. I was just running, glad for running, and my heart whooped and my lungs caught at breath.

I fell many times. The last time, I peered up through creepers and nettles and saw that the malevolence had gone; the god had departed; human light was darting into the vegetation, the light which represents our conquering of unreason, and I brought my body complaining up into a squatting position to see from where the light was coming. I could feel Alison's letter in my pocket. My personality began to reassemble. Artificial light is a poem to reasonableness, the lightbulb casts out demons, it speaks in rhymed couplets, and my body began to shake with relief, as if I had stumbled into the formal gardens of Versailles.

Even my normal cast of mind returned to me, and I regretted my momentary betrayal of belief. It was betrayal of Alison and betrayal of spirit. I had been spooked, and spooked by literature at that.

As this specific Teagardenish guilt whispered through me, I finally saw where I was and knew the house from which light fell. Yet my body still trembled with relief when I made it stand and walk through the domesticated oaks.

She appeared on the porch. The sleeves of a man's tweed jacket hung below the tips of her fingers. She was still wearing the high rubber boots. "Who is that out there? Miles? Is that you?"

"Well, yes," I said. "I got lost."

"Are you alone?"

"You're always asking me that."

"But I heard two of you."

I just stared at her.

"Come on in, Miles, and I'll pour you some coffee."

When I came up on the porch she scrutinized me with her good eye. "Why, Miles, you're in a terrible condition! You're all over dirt. And you've torn your clothes." She looked down. "And you'll have to take off those boots before you can come into my kitchen."

Gently I removed the mud-laden boots. I was aware of numerous small aches and sores on my face and hands, and I had somewhere banged my leg in the same place I had when I had accompanied the chair down the stairs of the root cellar.

"Why, you're limping, Miles! What were you doing out there at night?"

I lowered myself into a chair and she placed a cup before me. "Auntie Rinn, are you sure you heard someone else in the woods? Someone besides me?"

"It was probably one of the chickens. They do get out and make an awful ruckus." She was sitting poised on a chair across the old wooden table from me, her long white hair falling to the shoulders of the gray tweed jacket. Steam from the cups rose wispily between us. "Let me take care of your face."

"Please don't bother," I said, but she had already bounced up and was at the sink, dampening a cloth. Then she took a covered pot from a shelf and returned. The cloth was cool and soothing against my cheek-bones.

"I don't like saying this to you, Miles, but I think you should leave the valley. You were troubled when you first came here, and you are more troubled now. If you will insist on staying, I want you to leave Jessie's house and come to stay here."

"I can't."

She dipped her fingers in the pot and dabbed a thick green mixture on my cuts. It made my entire face throb. A woodsy fragrance snagged in my nostrils. "This is just an herbal mixture for your cuts, Miles. What were you doing out there?"

"Looking for someone."

"Looking for something in the woods at night?"

"Ah, yes, someone broke most of the glass on my car and I thought I saw them running up this way."

"Why were you trembling?"

"I'm not used to running." Her fingers were still rubbing the green mixture into my face.

"I can protect you, Miles."

"I don't need protection."

"Then why were you so frightened?"

"It was just the woods. The darkness."

"Sometimes it is right to fear the dark." She looked at me fiercely. "But it is never right to lie to me, Miles. You were not looking for a vandal. Were you?"

I was conscious of the trees bending over the house, of the darkness outside her circle of light.

She said, "You must pack your things and leave. Come here or go back to New York. Go to your father in Florida."

"I can't." That thick smell hung over my face.

"You will be destroyed. You must at least come here to stay with me."

"Auntie Rinn," I said. My entire body had begun to shake again. "Some people think I have been killing those girls—that was the reason they attacked my car. What could you do against them?"

"They will never come here. They will never come up my path." I remembered how she had terrified me when I was a child, with that look on her face, sentences like that in her mouth. "They are only town people. They have nothing to do with the valley."

The little kitchen seemed intolerably hot, and I saw that the woodstove was burning, alive like a fireplace with snapping flames.

I said, "I want to tell you the truth. I felt something monstrous out there. Something purely hostile, and that's why I was frightened. I guess it was evil I felt. But it all came out of books. Some toughs chased me through Arden, and then Polar Bears shook me up, as he would say. I know the literature about all this. I know all about Puritans in the wilderness, and it caught up with me. I've been repressed and I'm not myself."

"What are you waiting for, Miles?" she asked, and I knew that I could prevaricate no longer.

"I'm waiting for Alison," I said. "Alison Greening. I thought it was her I saw from the road, and I ran up into the woods to find her. I've seen her three times."

"Miles—" she began, her face wild and angry.

"I'm not working on my dissertation any more, I

don't care about that, I've been feeling more and more that all of that is death to the spirit, and I've been getting signs that Alison will come soon."

"Miles—"

"Here's one of them," I said and took the crumpled envelope out of my pocket. "Hovre thinks I sent it to myself, but she sent it, didn't she? That's why the writing is like mine."

She was going to speak again, and I held up my hand. "You see, you never liked her, nobody ever liked her, but we were always alike. We were almost the same person. I've never loved any other woman."

"She was your snare. She was a trap waiting for you to enter it."

"Then she still is, but I don't believe it."

"Miles—"

"Auntie Rinn, in 1955 we made a vow that we would meet here in the valley, and we set a date. It's in only a few weeks from now. She is going to come, and I am going to meet her."

"Miles," she said, "your cousin is dead. She died twenty years ago, and you killed her."

"I don't believe that," I said.

I Light Out for the Territories

Six

"Miles," she said, "your cousin died in 1955 while the two of you were swimming in the old Pohlson quarry. She was drowned."

"No. She drowned," I said. "Active verb. I didn't kill her. I couldn't have killed her. She meant more to me than my own life. I would rather have died myself. It was the end of my life anyhow."

"You may have killed her by accident—you may not have known what you were doing. I am only an old farm woman, but I know you. I love you. You have always been troubled. Your cousin was also a troubled person, but her troubles were not innocent, as yours were. She chose the rocky path, she desired confusion and evil, and you never committed that sin."

"I don't know what you're talking about. She was, I don't know, more complicated than I was, but that was part of her beauty. For me, anyhow. No one else understood her. And I did not kill her, accidentally or any other way."

"Only you two were there."

"That's not certain."

"Did you see anyone else that night?"

"I don't know. I might have. I thought I did, several times. I got knocked out in the water."

"By Alison's struggles. She nearly took you with her."

145

"I wish she had. I haven't had a life since."

"Not a whole life. Not a satisfied life. Because of her."

"Stop it," I shouted. The heat of the kitchen was building up around me, seeming to increase with every word. The stuff on my face was beginning to burn. My shout had frightened her; she seemed paler and smaller, inside all those wrinkles and the man's baggy jacket. She slowly sipped at her coffee, and I felt a great sad inevitable remorse. "I'm sorry. I'm sorry I shouted. If you love me it must be the way you'd love some wounded bird. I'm in a terrible state, Auntie Rinn."

"I know," she said calmly. "That's why I have to protect you. That's why you have to leave the valley. It's too late now for anything else."

"Because Alison is coming back, you mean. Because she is."

"If she is, then there is nothing to do. It is too late for anything. She has hooks in you too deep for me to remove them."

"Thank God for that. She means freedom to me. She means life."

"No. She means death. She means what you felt out there tonight."

"That was nerves."

"That was *Alison.* She wants to claim you."

"She claimed me years ago."

"Miles, you are submitting to forces you don't understand. I don't understand them either, but I respect them. And I fear them. Have you thought about what happens after she returns?"

"What happens doesn't matter. She will be in this world again. She knows I didn't kill her."

"Perhaps that doesn't matter. Or perhaps it matters less than you think it does. Tell me about that night, Miles."

I let my head drop forward, so that my chin nearly touched my chest. "What good would that do?"

"Then I will tell you. This is what Arden people

remember about you, Miles. They remember that you were suspected of murder. You already had a bad reputation—you were known as a thief, a disturbed, disordered boy with no control over his feelings. Your cousin was—I don't know what the word is. A sexual tease. She was corrupt. She shocked the valley people. She was calculating and she had power—I recognized when she was only a child that she was a destructive person. She hated life. She hated everything but herself."

"Never," I said.

"And the two of you went to the quarry to swim, no doubt after Alison had deceived your mothers. She was ensnaring you even more deeply. Miles, there can exist between two people a kind of deep connection, a kind of voice between them, a calling, and if the dominant person is corrupted, the connection is unhealthy and corrupt."

"Skip the rigamarole," I said. "Get on with what you want to say." I wanted to leave her overheated kitchen; I wanted to immure myself in the old Updahl farmhouse.

"I will." Her face was hard as winter. "Someone driving past on the Arden road heard screams coming from the quarry and called the police. When old Walter Hovre got there he found you unconscious on the rock ledge. Your face was bleeding. Alison was dead. He could just see her body, caught on a rock projection down in the water. Both of you were naked. She had been . . . she had been abused." Her complexion began to redden. "The inference was there to be made. It was obvious."

"What do you think happened?"

"I think she seduced you and died accidentally. That she died by your hand, but that it was not murder." Now her blushing was pronounced: it was a ghastly effect, as if she had rubbed rouge into her cheeks. "I have never known physical love, Miles, but I imagine that it is a turbulent business." She raised her chin and looked straight at me. "That is what everybody thought.

You were not to be charged—in fact, many women in Arden thought that your cousin had gotten just what she deserved. The coroner, who was Walter Hovre in those days, said that it was accidental death. He was a kindly man, and he'd had his troubles with his own son. He did not want to ruin your life. It helped that you were an Updahl. People hereabouts have always looked up to your family."

"Just tell me this," I said. "When everybody was silently condemning me while hypocritically setting me free, didn't anyone wonder who had made that phone call?"

"The man didn't give his name. He said he was frightened."

"Do you really think screams from the quarry can be heard on the road?"

"Evidently they can. And in these times, Miles, people remember your old story."

"Goddam it," I said. "Don't you think I know that? Even Duane's daughter has begun to hear rumors about it. Her crazy boyfriend, too. But I'm bound by my past. That's the reason I'm here. I'm innocent of the other thing. My innocence is bound to come out."

"I hope with all my heart that it does," she said. I could hear the wind rattling the branches and leaves outside, and I felt like a character from another century—a character from a fairy tale, hiding in a gingerbread house. "But that is not enough to save you now."

"I know what my salvation is."

"Salvation is work."

"That's a good Norwegian theory."

"Well, work, then. Write! Help in the fields!"

I smiled at the thought of Duane and myself mowing hay side by side. "I thought you were advising me to leave the state. Actually Polar Bears won't let me leave. And I wouldn't, anyhow."

She looked at me with what I recognized as despair. I said, "I won't let go of the past. You don't understand, Auntie Rinn." At the end of this sentence, I shocked myself by yawning.

"Poor tired boy."

"I am tired," I admitted.

"Sleep here tonight, Miles. I'll pray for you."

"No," I said automatically, "no thanks," and then thought of the long walk back to the car. By now the batteries had probably run down, and I would have to walk all the way back to the farmhouse.

"You can leave as early as you like. You won't bother a dried up old thing like me."

"Maybe for a couple of hours," I said, and yawned again. This time I managed to get my hand to my mouth at least half-way through the spasm. "You're far too good to me."

I watched her bustle into the next room; in a moment she returned with an armful of sheets and the fluffy bundle of a homemade quilt. "Come on, youngster," she ordered, and I followed her into the parlor.

Together we put the sheets on the low narrow seat of her couch. The parlor was only marginally cooler than the kitchen, but I helped her smooth the quilt over the top sheet. "I'd say, you take the bed, Miles, but no man has ever slept in my bed, and it's too late to change my habits now. But I hope you won't think I'm inhospitable."

"Not inhospitable," I said. "Just pig-headed."

"I wasn't fooling about praying. Did you say you've seen her?"

"Three times. I'm sure I did. She's going to come back, Auntie Rinn."

"I'll tell you one thing certain. I'll never live to see it."

"Why?"

"Because she won't let me."

For a solitary old woman close to ninety, Rinn was an expert in the last word. She turned away from me, switched off the lights in the kitchen, and closed the door to her bedroom after her. I could hear fabrics rustling as she undressed. The immaculate tiny parlor seemed full of the smell of woodsmoke, but it must have come from the ancient stove in the kitchen. Rinn began to mumble to herself.

I slipped off my jeans and shirt, sat down to remove my socks, still hearing her dry old voice rhythmically ticking away like a machine about to die, and stretched out between the papery sheets. My hands found one nubbly patch after another, and I realized that they had been mended many times. Within seconds, to the accompaniment of the dry music of her voice, I passed into the first unbroken and peaceful sleep I'd had since leaving New York.

Several hours later, I woke to two separate noises. One was what seemed an incredible rushing clatter of leaves above me, as though the woods had crawled up to the house and begun to attack it. The second was even more unsettling. It was Rinn's voice, and at first I thought her praying had become a marathon event. After I caught its slow, insistent pulse I recognized that she was saying something in her sleep. A single word, repeated. The whooping clatter of the trees above the house drowned out the word, and I lay in the dark with my eyes open, listening. The smell of woodsmoke hung unmoving in the air. When I heard what Rinn was saying, I folded the sheet back and groped for my socks. She was pronouncing, over and over again in her sleep, my grandmother's name. *"Jessie. Jessie."*

That was too much for me. I could not bear to hear, mixed up with the windy racket of the woods, the evidence of how greatly I had disturbed the one person in the valley who wanted to help me. Hurriedly I put on my clothes and went into the kitchen. The undersides of leaves, veined and white, pressed against the back window like hands. Indeed, like the pulpy hand of one of my would-be assailants in Arden. I turned on a small lamp. Rinn's voice went dryly on, scraping out its invocation to her sister. The fire in the woodstove had died to a red glowing shadowy empire of tall ashes. I splashed water on my face and felt the crust of Rinn's herbal mixture. It would not wash off: my fingers simply bumped over it, as over the patches on the sheets. I inserted a fingernail beneath the edge of one of the crusty spots, and peeled it off like a leech. A thin brown scale fell into the sink. I peeled off the rest of the dabs of the mixture until they covered the bottom of the sink. A man's shaving mirror hung on a nail by the door, and I bent my knees to look into it. My heavy bland face looked back at me, pink in splashes on forehead and cheek, but otherwise unmarked.

Inside a rolltop desk crammed with the records of her egg business I found the stub of a pencil and paper and wrote: *Someday you'll see I'm right. I'll be back soon to buy some eggs. Thanks for everything. Love, Miles.*

I went out into the full rustling night. My mud-laden boots felt the knotted roots of trees thrusting up through the earth. I passed the high cartoon-windowed building, full of sleeping hens. Soon after that, I was out from under the dense ceiling of branches, and the narrow road unrolled before me, through tall fields lighter than the indigo sky. When it traversed the creek I once again heard frogs announcing their territory. I walked quickly, resisting the impulse to glance over my shoulder. If I felt that someone or something was watching me, it was only the single bright star in the sky, Venus, sending me light already thousands of years old.

Only when the breeze had dissipated it over the long fields of corn and alfalfa did I notice that the odor of woodsmoke had stayed with me until I had gone halfway to the road, and left Rinn's land.

Venus, light my way with light long dead.

Grandmother, Rinn, bless me both.

Alison, see me and come into my sight.

But what came into my sight as I trudged down the valley road was only the Volkswagen, looking like its own corpse, like something seen in a pile of rusting hulls from a train window. It was a misshapen form in the dim starlight, as pathetic and sinister as Duane's Dream House, and as I walked toward it I saw the shattered rear window and the scooping dents on the engine cover and hood. Eventually it hit me that the lights were out; the battery had died.

I groaned, and opened the door and collapsed onto the seat. I passed my hands over the pink new patches of skin on my face, which were beginning to tingle. "Damn," I said, thinking of the difficulty of getting a tow truck to come the ten miles from Arden. In frustration, I lightly struck my hand against the horn mechanism. Then I saw that the key was gone from the ignition.

"What's that for?" asked a man approaching me from the high slope of the Sunderson drive. As he crossed the road I saw that he had a thick hard belly and a flat face with no cheer in it. He had a pudgy blob for a nose, signaling his family connection to Tuta Sunderson. Like the hair of most men called "Red," his was a dusty tobaccoish orange. He came across the road and laid an enormous hand on top of the open door. "Why do you wanta go honkin' that horn for?"

"Out of joy. From sheer blinding happiness. My battery's dead, so the car won't move, and the damned key's gone, probably lying somewhere in that ditch. And you might have noticed that a few gentlemen in Arden decided to work over the car this evening. So that's why I was honking the horn." I glared up into his doughy face and thought I saw a glint of amusement.

"Didn't you hear my callin' you before? When you jumped out of this-here jalopy and tore on up toward the woods?"

"Sure," I said. "I didn't have time to waste."

"Well, I been waitin' on the porch to see you come back. I sacked out up there a little bit—didn't think you'd be so long. But just in case, I took your keys out of your jalopy. And I turned off your lights to save your battery."

"Thanks. I mean it. But please give me the keys. Then we can both get to bed."

"Wait up. What were you doin' up there anyhow? Or were you just runnin' away from me? You were sure goin' like a jackrabbit. What are you tryin' to get away with, Miles?"

"Well, Red, I can't really say. I don't think I'm trying to get away with anything."

"Uh huh." The amusement became more acid. "According to my ma, you been doin' some pretty peculiar things up to Updahl's. Says that little girl of Duane's been hangin' around more than she should. Specially considering the problem we got here lately. You kinda got a *thing* about hurting girls, don't you, Miles?"

"No. I never did, either. Quit wasting my time and give me my keys."

"What's so good you got up in those woods?"

"Okay, Red," I answered. "I'll tell you the truth. I was visiting Rinn. You can ask her yourself. That's where I was."

"I guess you and that old witch got somethin' going."

"You can guess all you want. Just let me go home."

"This ain't your home, Miles. But I guess you can go back to Duane's. Here's your keys for this piece of shit you're driving." He held them out by extending one big blunt finger protruded through the keyring so that ring and keys looked dwarfed, like toys. It was a gesture obscurely obscene.

Portion of Statement by Leroy
("Red") Sunderson:

July 16

It was just eatin' at me that Ma had to be working in the same house as that Miles Teagarden—I'll tell you, if I'd been in Duane's shoes, I wouldn't of let my daughter hang around a man with a

*reputation like that. And some say he learned,
good. I'd have run him off first thing, with a load
of birdshot. So I thought, let's see what we got
here, and started comin' down the drive to talk to
him as soon as I saw his car begin to slow down
outside below our house. Well Miles he jumps out
of his car and looks away like he was seein' things,
and he just begins to run like crazy. When I yelled
he just kept on running.*

*Now there's two ways of looking at that. Either
he was in one hell of a hurry to get at something in
these woods, or he was runnin' away from me. I
say both. I'll tell you, he was scared as hell of me
when he came back. And that means he sure as
hell was plannin' out what was gonna happen up
in those woods—see?*

*I just said to myself, Red, you wait on him.
He'll be back. I went down and switched off the
lights in that beat up junker of his. Then I waited
for him. Ma and me both looked out for him for a
little, and then she went up to bed, and I laid out
on the porch. I had his keys, so I knew he wasn't
going anywhere without me.*

*Well, a long time later, he comes back. Steppin'
light. Loose as a goose. Walkin' like a city nigger.
When I got up close to him he was workin' away
at his car, swearin' and bangin' on the horn. Then
I saw his face. He looked all burned or something—he had big red spots all over. The way
Oscar Johnstad did when he got alcohol poison-
ing a few years back. Maybe somebody coulda
been scratching on him.*

*I said, well Miles, what the hell you been up
to?*

I been makin' myself happy, he says.

I says, up in the woods?

*Yeah, he says, I go up there to make myself
happy. I been seein' Rinn.*

How do we know what those two was up to?

*Funny things go on with these old Norwegians
in the valleys around here—I'm a Norwegian myself, and I won't say a word against 'em, but some
of those old people get up to crazy things. And
that Rinn was crazy as a coot all her life. Sure
she was. She was just about the only friend Miles
had around here. You remember about old Ole,
down at the Four Forks? Well, he was related to
half the people in this valley, me included, and
when he started going crazy he tied that half-wit
daughter of his to a beam up in his attic and he
started usin' his other daughter as his wife. On
Sundays he stood there at the back of the church
lookin' like an angry chunk of God that happened
to land near Arden. That was twenty-thirty years
ago, but funny things still go on. I never did trust
Rinn. She could put the spooks in you. Some folks
say Oscar Johnstad started drinking heavy because
she put the evil eye on a heifer of his and he was
afraid he was next.*

*The other thing you got think about is Paul
Kant. Pretty soon after this, no more than a
couple of days, is when he saw Paul. And then he
tried to kill himself, didn't he?*

*I think he wanted to get out of it, fast—maybe
Rinn told him to do it, crazy as she was. Maybe
little Paul did too. Well, if he didn't he sure was
sorry later. I mean, whatever Paul Kant did to
make himself happy, he didn't go up into the valley
woods at night to do it.*

*I feel all involved in this, you know. I found
that poor Strand girl and talked to you fellows a
couple of hours that day. I almost puked too, when
I saw her—I knew nothing normal had been at
that girl. She was damn near ripped in two. Well,
you were there. You saw it.*

*So after we finally found out about the next one
I got a call from one of the boys who drinks down
at the Angler's, about that car idea, and I said,*

sure go ahead, I'll give you all the help you want.
You set it up, and I'll help over at this end.

By the time I got the car into the driveway, my face
had begun to burn and itch; my eyes watered, and I
left the car just past the walnut trees and walked
diagonally across the lawn, pressing the palm of my
unbandaged hand to my face. It felt as cool and healing as water. My face was blazing. The night air too
seemed oven-like and composed of a million sharp
needling points. I was moving slowly, so that the
rush of hot gelatinous air would not scrape at my face.

As I approached the house, all the lights came on
at once.

It looked like a pleasure boat on dark water, but it
made me feel cold. I lowered my hand from my face
and went slowly toward the screen door. The mare in
the field to my left began to whinny and rear.

I half-expected a jolt from the metal doorknob. I
almost wished that I were back on that bed of mold,
beneath those giant dark trees.

I crossed the porch, hearing no noise from the interior of the house. Through the mesh of the screen,
I looked sideways to see the mare's body plunging up
and down, scattering the dumbfounded cows. Then I
swung open the door to the sitting room and looked
in—empty. Empty and cold. The old furniture lay
randomly about, suggesting an as yet unlocated perfect
order. All the lights, controlled by a single switch beside the doorframe, were burning. I touched the switch,
aware that the mare had ceased her whinnying. The
lights went off, then on, apparently working normally.

In the kitchen the overhead bulb in its shade illuminated the evidence of Tuta Sunderson's work: the
plate of cold food had been removed from the table,
the dishes washed and put away. When I touched the
light switch, it too worked in the usual fashion.

The only explanation was that the wiring had gone
massively wrong. At the moment that this possibility
came to me I became aware that something—some-

thing important—was out of place in the living room. And that my face was still reacting painfully to contact with air. I returned to the kitchen and turned on the taps over the sink and splashed water over my forehead and cheeks. The feverish sandpapered feeling began to lessen. The only soap within reach was dishwashing liquid, and I squeezed a green handful into my right palm and brought it to my face. It felt like balm. The stinging disappeared. Delicately I rinsed away the soap: my skin felt tight, stretched like canvas over a frame.

This transformation, temporary as it was, apparently also made me more acute, for when I was in the living room again, I saw what had caused my earlier sense of dislocation. The picture of Alison and myself, the crucial picture, no longer hung on the nail over the doorway to the stairs. Someone had removed it. I looked around at the walls. Nothing else had been changed. It was an unthinkable violation, a rape of my private space. I rushed into the old bedroom.

Tuta S. had evidently been at work. The mess I had left on the floor had been bundled back into the broken sea chest and the splinters of wood from the chest's lid were laid out beside it like gigantic toothpicks. I knelt to open the chest and threw up the lid to see Duane's unhappy mulish countenance scowling at me. I lowered the lid gently. Pandora's box.

Unless it had been stolen, there was only one place where the photograph could be, and it was there I found it—in fact, even while I was ascending the narrow staircase I knew where I would find it. Propped between wall and desk, beside the earlier photograph of Alison.

And I knew—if the unknowable can be at all said to be known—who had put it there.

Following what seemed to be a general rule about nights spent in the old Updahl farmhouse, my sleep was interrupted by a succession of disturbing dreams, but all I could remember of them when I awoke—too late, I noted, to witness the parting of the lovers on the road and Alison's athletic, comic entrance through her window—was that they had made me start into wakefulness several times during the night. If you cannot remember them, nightmares lose all of their power. I was as hungry as I could remember ever being, another sign of renewed health.

I was as certain as if she'd left a note that Alison Greening had moved that photograph, and the information that she had influenced another hand to do it for her did not alter my conviction.

"You don't mind my moving that picture, do you?" said Mrs. Sunderson when I came down for breakfast. "I thought since you had that other one up there, you might want them both. I didn't mess with anything in that writing room of yours, I just put the picture on your desk."

Startled, I looked at her. She was working her fat arms over a frying pan. Grease spat, flames jumped. Her face was set in an expression of sullen obduracy.

"Why did you do it?"

"Because of the other one. Like I said." She was lying. She had been Alison's agent; it was also clear that she had disliked having the photograph within her view.

"What did you think of my cousin? Do you remember her?"

"Not to speak of." She went firmly back to the eggs.

"You don't want to talk about her."

"No. What's past is past."

"In one sense," I said, and laughed. "Only in one sense, my dear Mrs. Sunderson."

The "my dear" made her look toward me with magnified goggling eyes. More brooding, puzzled silence over the sizzling eggs on the gas burner.

"Why did you tear up that picture of Duane's girl? I saw it when I straightened up your mess in the front bedroom."

"I don't know what you're talking about," I said.

"Oh I do remember. I didn't really know what it was. It was a random gesture. A reflex."

"So some would say," she pronounced as she brought me the eggs. "Maybe some would say the same about that car of yours."

I could still taste those eggs two hours later when I stood on the asphalt of the Arden filling station beside a squat young man with *Hank* blazoned over his heart and listened to him groan about the condition of the VW.

"This is some mess," he said. "I sure hope you got insurance. First off, we ain't even got a man these days who can beat out those dents for you. And all these is foreign parts. This glass here, and that headlight and missing hubcap. They might be a long time in coming. It's gonna cost plenty."

"You don't have to get them from Germany," I pointed out. "There must be a VW agency around here somewhere."

"Maybe," the boy reluctantly agreed. "I heard about one somewheres, but I can't remember where it is right now. And we're all backed up on work. We're doubling up."

I looked around at the deserted gas station.

"You can't see it all," Hank said defensively.

"I can't see any of it." I was thinking that it must have been at this station that the Polish lover of Duane's fiancée had worked. "Maybe this will help you squeeze it into your schedule." I took a ten dollar bill from my pocket and folded it into his hand.

"You live here, Mister?"

"What do you think?" He just coolly regarded me. "I'm a visitor. I had an accident. Look. Forget about the dents, they're not too important, just get the glass and headlights repaired. And take a look at the engine to see if it needs any work. It's been acting up."

"Okay. I need a name for the slip."

"Greening," I said. "Miles Greening."

"That Jewish?"

The boy reluctantly parted with one of the garage's loaners, a 1957 Nash that steered like a lumber wagon; further into Arden, I took the precaution of parking it in a sidestreet in an area where the houses appeared to be at least moderately prosperous.

An hour and a half later, I was listening to Paul Kant say to me, "You put yourself and me in trouble just by coming here, Miles. I tried to warn you. You really should have listened. I appreciate your friendliness, but there are only two people that the good folks around here think could have done these crimes, and here we are together. Cozy. If you're not scared, you should be. Because I'm terrified. If anything else happens, anything else to a child I mean, I think I'm a dead man. They took baseball bats to my car last night, just to let me know they're watching."

"Mine too," I said. "And I saw them working on yours, but I didn't know whose it was."

"So here we are, waiting for the other shoe to drop. Why don't you just get out while you have the chance?"

"I can't, for several reasons. One of them is that Polar Bears asked me to stay put until everything is over."

"Because of the Alison Greening business?"

I nodded.

He let out an enormous, scooping sigh, too large for his small body. "Of course. Of course. I didn't even have to ask. I wish my sins were as far in the past as yours." I looked up, puzzled, and saw him trying to light a cigarette with a trembling hand. "Hasn't anybody warned you about being associated with me, Miles? I'm quite a notorious character."

"Hence the ritual."

"It's been a long time since anyone in Arden used a word like hence, but yes, hence the ritual."

I had come to Paul's by way of Main Street, where I first stopped in at a shop to buy a portable record player. The clerk looked at the name on my check and disappeared with it into an office at the rear of the shop. I was aware of my presence causing a little flurry of attention among the other customers—they were pretending not to look at me, but they moved with that exaggerated carelessness of people trying to catch every nuance. After a while the clerk returned with a nervous man in a brown suit and a rayon tie. He informed me that he could not accept my check.

"Why not?"

"Ah, well, Mr. Teagarden, this check is drawn on a New York bank."

"Obviously," I said. "They use money in New York too."

"But we only accept local checks."

"How about credit cards? You don't refuse credit cards, do you?"

"Ah, no, not usually," he said.

I yanked a lengthy strip of cards from my wallet. "Which one do you want? Mastercharge? American Express? Diners' Club? Mobil? Sears? Come on, you make the choice. Firestone?"

"Mr. Teagarden, this isn't necessary. In this case—"

"In this case, what? These things are as good as money, aren't they? Here's another one. BankAmericard. Take your pick."

The other customers by now had dropped the pretense of not listening, and a few were threatening to come forward to take a closer look. He decided to accept Mastercharge, which I could have predicted, and I waited while he took one of the portable stereos from stock and went through the usual business with the card. He was sweating by the time he had finished.

I spent some time looking through the record racks at Zumgo's and the Coast To Coast Store, but could not find what I needed for the Alison-environment. At a little stationery shop a block from Freebo's I found a few of the books I remembered Alison had liked: *She, The White Guard,* Kerouac, St. Exupéry. These I purchased with cash, having conquered for good that other childish business.

I cut through sidestreets to get back to the Nash,

locked my purchases inside it, and then went back to Freebo's.

"Can I make a phone call?" I asked him. He looked relieved, and pointed to a pay phone in the rear corner. I knew by his demeanor what his next words would be before he spoke them.

"Mr. Teagarden, you been a good customer here since you came in town, but some people came to see me late last night, and I wonder if . . ."

"If I might lay off? Take my business elsewhere?" He was too embarrassed to nod.

"What did they say they'd do? Break your windows? Burn your place down?"

"No, nothing like that, Mr. Teagarden."

"But you'd be happier if I quit coming in."

"Maybe just for a week, just for a couple of days. It's nothing personal, Mr. Teagarden. But, well, some of 'em decided—well, it might be better to wait it out for a while."

"I don't want to make trouble for you," I said.

He turned away, unable to face me any further. "The phone's in the corner."

I looked up Paul Kant's number. His whispery voice greeted me hesitantly. "Stop hiding," I said. "This is Miles. I'm in Arden, and I'm coming over to talk about what's happening to us."

"Don't," he pleaded.

"You don't have to protect me. I just wanted to prepare you. If you want people to draw conclusions from the sight of me banging on your front door, then let me bang away. But I want to find out what's going on."

"You'll come even if I say not to."

"That's right."

"In that case, don't park near my house. And don't come to the front door. Pull into the alley between Commercial Street and Madison, and then walk up through the alley so you can come around to the back. I'll let you in the back door."

And now, in a dark shabby living room, he was

telling me that he was a notorious character. He looked
the way you'd expect one of Freud's case studies to
look—frightened, his body a little shrunken and bent,
his face prematurely aged. His white shirt had been
worn too many days; his face was small and monkey-
like. When we had been boys, Paul Kant had radiated
intelligence and confidence, and I thought that he was
the person my age in Arden whom I most respected.
On summers when Alison was not at the farm, I had
divided my time between raising hell with Polar Bears
and talking with Paul. He had been a great reader. His
mother was an invalid, and Paul had the grown-up,
responsible, rather bookish demeanor of children who
must care for their parents. Or parent, in his case—his
father was dead. Another of my assumptions had been
that Paul would get a good scholarship and shake the
traces of Arden from him forever. But here he was,
trapped in a shabby musty house and a body that
looked ten years older than it was. If he radiated anything, it was bitterness and a fearful incompetence.

"Take a look out the window," he said. "Try to do
it without being seen."

"You're being watched?"

"Just look." He stubbed out his cigarette and immediately lit another.

I peeked around the edge of a curtain.

Halfway down the block a big man who looked like
he could have been one of the party which had shied
stones at me was sitting on the fender of a red pickup,
directing his eyes at Paul's house.

"Is he there all the time?"

"It's not always him. They do it in shifts. There are
five, maybe six of them."

"Do you know their names?"

"Of course I know their names. I live here."

"Can't you do anything about it?"

"What do you suggest? Telephoning our benevolent
Chief? They're his friends. They know him better than
I do."

"What do they do when you go out?"

"I don't go out very often." His face worked, and ironic lines tugged deeply into his skin. "I suppose they follow me. They don't care if I see them. They want me to see them."

"Did you report that they wrecked your car?"

"Why should I? Hovre knows all about it."

"Well, *why*, for Christ's sake?" I burst out. "Why all this fire in your direction?" He shrugged, and smiled nervously.

But of course I thought I knew. It was what had occurred to me when Duane had first suggested that Paul Kant was better left alone: a man with Duane's history of sexual suppression would be quick to react to any hint of sexual abnormality. And a town like Arden would maintain a strict nineteenth-century point of view about inversion.

"Let's just say I'm a little different, Miles."

"Christ," I blustered, "nobody's different any more. If you're saying that you're gay, it's only in a backwater like Arden that you'd have problems because of it. You shouldn't allow yourself to be terrorized. You should have been out of here years ago."

I think for the first time I understood what a wan smile was. "I'm not a very brave man, Miles," he said. "I could never live anywhere but Arden. I had to drop out of life to take care of my mother, and after she died she left me this house." It smelled of dust and decay and damp—Paul had no smell at all. He was like something not there, or there in only one dimension. He said, "I've never really been . . . what you're implying. I thought I was, I guess, and I guess other people thought I was. But the opportunities here are rather limited." Again I got that pale, self-mocking half-smile that was only a lifting of the edges of the mouth. He was like something in a cage.

"So you just sat here and put up with Zumgo's and what your neighbors whispered about you?"

"You're not me, Miles. You don't understand."

I looked around at the dim room filled with old lady's furniture. Lumpy uncomfortable chairs with antimacassars. Cheap china figurines: shepherdesses and dogs, Mr. Pickwick and Mrs. Gamp. But there weren't any books.

"No," I said.

"You don't even really want me to confide in you, do you? We haven't seen each other since we grew up." He stubbed out the cigarette and scratched his fingers in his tight black curly hair.

"Not unless you're guilty," I said, beginning to be affected by the air of despairing hopelessness which surrounded him.

I suppose the sound he uttered was a laugh.

"What are you going to do? Just wait until they break in and do whatever it is they have in mind?"

"What I'm going to do is wait it out," he said. "It's what I'm best at, after all. When they finally catch whoever it is, maybe I'll get my job back. What are you going to do?"

"I don't know," I admitted. "I thought we might be able to help each other. If I were you I'd scram out of the back door in the middle of the night and go to Chicago or someplace until it's all over."

"My car won't move. And even if it did, I'd be picked up in a day or two." He sent me that ghastly smile again. "You know, Miles, I almost envy that man. The killer. I'm almost jealous of him. Because he wasn't too afraid to do what he had to do. Of course he is a beast, a fiend I suppose, but he just went ahead and did what he had to do. Didn't he?" The small monkey's face was pointing at me, still wearing that dead smile. Mixed in with the smells of dust and old lady's possessions was the odor of long-dead flowers.

"Like Hitler. You sound like you should talk to Zack."

His expression altered. "You know him?"

"I've met him."

"I'd keep away from him."

"What for?"

"He can hurt you. He could hurt you, Miles."

"He's my biggest fan," I said. "He wants to be just like me."

Paul shrugged; the topic no longer interested him.

I said, "I think I'm wasting my time."

"Of course you are."

"If you ever need help, Paul, you can come out to the Updahl farm. I'll do whatever I can."

"Neither one of us can help the other." He looked at me blankly, wishing I would leave. After a moment he spoke again. "Miles, how old was your cousin when she died?"

"Fourteen."

"Poor Miles."

"Poor Miles, bullshit," I said, and left him sitting there with the cigarette smoke curling around him.

Outside the warm air smelled unbelievably fresh, and I recognized that my chest was tight, clamped by an emotion too complex to identify. I inhaled deeply, going down Paul's wooden steps to his tiny yard. It seemed to me that I could almost hear the paint peeling off that hopeless house. I looked both ways, knowing that if anyone spotted me I was in trouble, and saw something I hadn't noticed when I had come in. In a corner of the yard beside Paul's low fence was a doghouse, empty and as in need of paint as the house. A chain staked to the front of the doghouse trailed off into the weeds and bushes beside the fence. The chain seemed taut. The hairs on the back of my neck rose, and I was aware of the texture of the shirt next to my skin. I did not want to look, but I had to. I took two steps across the dying lawn. It was lying in the weeds with the chain around what was left of its neck. Maggots swarmed over it like a dirty blanket.

The tightness in my chest increased by a factor of ten, and I got out fast. The dreadful thing stayed in my vision even when my back was turned to it. I went through the gate and began to walk quickly down the alley. It had been a wasted gesture, the visit. I wanted only to get away.

When I was no more than thirty feet from the end, a police car swung in front of me, blocking off the alley. A big man sat at the wheel, twisting his body to look at me. I was in full light, fully visible. I automatically felt guilty and afraid, and swiveled sideways to look down to the alley's other end, which was clear. I looked back at the man in the police car. He was motioning for me to approach him. I walked toward the car, telling myself that I had not done anything.

When I got closer, I saw that the man was Polar Bears, in uniform. He swung open the passenger door and circled a forefinger in the air, and I walked around the front of the car and got in beside him. "You've had brighter ideas," he said. "Suppose someone saw you? I'm trying to keep you from getting your head busted in."

"How did you know I was here?"

"Let's say it was a guess." He looked at me in a kindly, almost paternal fashion which was as genuine as a glass eye. "I got a call about an hour ago from a boy works at the filling station. Boy named Hank Speltz. He was a little upset. It seems when you brought in that VW, you gave him a phony name."

"How did he know it was phony?"

"Oh, Miles," Polar Bears sighed. He started up the car and rolled away from the curb. At the corner he swung into Main Street and we purred gently along past Zumgo's and the bars and the bakery and the Cream City brick façade of the Dairyland Laboratories. "You're a famous man, you know. You're like a movie star. You have to expect to be recognized." When we reached the courthouse and the city hall, he did not pull into the police parking lot as I had expected, but kept going on over the bridge. On that side of Arden, the shops drop away fast, after you pass the bowling alley and the restaurants and a few houses, and you are back in open corn country.

"I don't think it's a crime to have a car repaired under an assumed name," I said. "Where are we going, anyhow?"

"Just for a ride around the county, Miles. No, it's no crime, that's right. But since damn near everybody knows who you are, it's not very effective either. It just makes boys like Hank, who aren't too well supplied upstairs, sort of suspicious. And Miles, why in *hell* did you use that name?" On "hell" he banged one of his fists into the steering wheel. "Huh? Answer me that. Out of all the names you could have picked, why the devil did you pick Greening? That's what you don't want to remind people of, boy. I'm trying to keep all that in the background. We don't want that to come out."

"I think it came out the first second I showed up in Arden."

Polar Bears shook his head, disgusted. "Okay. Let's forget it. I told that Hank kid to forget about it. He's probably too young to know about it anyhow."

"So why are you upset?"

"Forget about my problems, Miles. Let's see if we can get any work done. You learn anything talking with Paul Kant?"

"He didn't do anything. He certainly didn't kill anybody. He's a sad frightened man. He isn't capable of anything like these killings. He's too scared to do anything but shop for his groceries."

"Is that what he told you?"

"He's too frightened even to bury his dog. I saw it just when I was leaving. He couldn't kill anybody."

Polar Bears tilted his hat back and hunched down further on the seat. He was too big to fit comfortably behind a steering wheel. By now we were well out in the country, and I could see the broad loops of the Blundell River between trees. "Is this where the fishermen found the body of the Olson girl?"

He tilted his head and looked at me. "No. That was a couple miles back. We passed the spot about five-six minutes ago."

"On purpose?"

"On purpose for what?"

I shrugged: we both knew.

"I think our friend Paul might not have told you all the truth," Polar Bears said. "If he was going out grocery shopping, wouldn't he manage to buy some dog-food?"

"What are you saying?"

"Did he offer you anything when you were visiting? Lunch? A sandwich? Coffee?"

"No. Why?" Then I saw why. "You mean he doesn't leave his house? You mean his dog starved to death?"

"Well, it might of starved, or somebody might of helped put it out of its misery. I don't know. But I do know Paul Kant hasn't been out of his house in about a week. Unless he sneaks out at night."

"What does he eat?"

"Damn little. I guess he must have some canned stuff in his kitchen. That's why you didn't get any lunch out of him. He's screwed down pretty tight."

"Well, how the hell can you—"

He held up one hand. "I can't make a man go out and buy groceries. And as long as he doesn't actually starve, it might be better this way. Keeps him away from trouble. You maybe saw one of our local vigilantes watching his house."

"Can't you chase them away?"

"Why should I? This way I know what the hotheads are doing. I think there are some things you ought to know about Paul, Miles. I doubt that he'd tell you everything himself."

"Everything he needed to."

Polar Bears swung the car into a crossroads and began to go back in the general direction of Arden. We had gone nearly as far as the little town of Blundell, and we had not seen another person yet. The police radio crackled, but Hovre ignored it. He drove still at the same unhurried pace, following the line of the river through the valleys. "I wonder about that. You see, Paul's had a few problems. Not the sort of thing a man is proud of. He's been in a little trouble. You know how he lived in that rundown old place with his mother for years—even dropped out of school to nurse her and work so he could pay her doctor bills. Well, when the old lady died, Paul hung around town for a little bit, sort of lost, I guess, but then he packed up and went to Minneapolis for a week. About a month later, he did the same thing. He sort of settled down into a pattern. The last time he went, I got a call from a police sergeant over there. It seems that they had Paul under arrest. It seems they'd even been looking for him." He glanced over at me, savoring the denouement. He couldn't keep from smiling. "Seems they had a character used to hang around Boy Scout meetings—in summer, you know, when they meet in school playgrounds. Never said anything, just watched through the fence. When some of the kids walked home, he'd sort of amble on behind 'em, not saying anything, just trolling after these kids. After a fair number of times, say half a dozen, one of the parents calls the police. And the guy ducks out of the way— police couldn't find him. Not then. Not until he tried something in a park with lots of mommies and kiddies and cops around. He damn near exposed himself. When they came up on him, it was old Paul, with his hand on his fly. He was their boy. He'd been going over to Minnesota to release his urges, you could say, and then coming back here until he had to do it again. He confessed, of course, but he hadn't actually done anything. But he was scared. He committed himself voluntarily to our state hospital and stayed put there seven months. Then he came back. He didn't have anywhere else to go. Now I suppose he forgot to tell you about that little episode in his life."

I just nodded. Eventually I thought of something to say. "I'll have to take your word that what you told me is correct." Hovre snorted with amusement. "But even so, what Paul did—what he *didn't* do, rather— is a million miles from rape. The same person wouldn't commit both kinds of crime. Not if I understand people at all."

"Maybe so. But nobody around Arden is going to rule it out, you understand? And there are things about these killings that people generally don't know. What we have here isn't a straightforward rapist. Even a rapist who kills. We got something a little fancier. We got a really sick man. Could be impotent. Could even be a woman. Or a man and a woman. I go for the single man idea, but the others are possible."

"What are you telling me?"

We were back on the fringes of Arden now, and Polar Bears was homing in toward the Nash as if he knew where it was.

"I got a theory about this boy of ours, Miles. I think he wants to come to me, he wants to talk about what he's been doing. He's got all that pressure, all that guilt building up inside of him. He's bursting a gut to tell me about it. Wouldn't you say?"

I didn't know, and told him so.

"Just consider it. Sick as he is, he's a mighty lonely man. He probably doesn't even enjoy what he's doing to these girls. But he knows he's going to do it again." Polar Bears looked at me; he was smiling and confidential and helpful. "There's a big head of steam in our boy. He's got to blow it off, but he knows it's wrong—sick. I'm the one he has to talk to, and he knows it. I wouldn't be surprised if he's someone I see now and then, someone who's around here and there, ready to share a few words. I might have seen him two or three times this week alone." He pulled up to a stopsign; across the road and down the block sat the Nash. I wouldn't have known how to find it. "Well, speaking of luck, Miles, isn't that Nash the loaner Hank gave you?"

"Yes. What are you going to do about the men who wrecked my car?"

"I'm looking into it, Miles. Looking into it." He rolled across the street and pulled up beside the old Nash.

"Are you going to explain what you said about the killer? About his not being a straightforward rapist?"

"Sure. Why don't you come over to my house for a bite to eat some night this week? I'll tell you all about it." He reached across me and opened the door. "My cooking won't kill you, I guess. I'll be in touch, Miles. Keep your eyes open. Remember, you can always call me."

His flat ingratiating voice stayed in my ears all the way home. It was almost hypnotic, like having your will taken from you. When I got out of the car at the farmhouse I was still hearing it, and I could not shake it even while I was pushing furniture around. I felt slightly engulfed by Polar Bears, and I knew the furniture would not come right, lock into the correct position, until I was free of him. I went upstairs and sat at my desk and looked into the two photographs. Eventually everything else went away, and I was left with Alison. Dimly, far away, the phone was ringing.

And the third time it happened like this:

A girl walked out of her home in the late afternoon and stood in the humid motionless air for a moment, wondering if it were not too hot to go bowling with her friends. Perspiration seemed to leap from her scalp. She remembered that she had left her sunglasses in her room, but she could not waste the energy to go back in and get them. She could feel her body sagging in the heat: and the pollen count was up nearly to 200. She would be sneezing by the time she got to the Bowl-A-Rama.

Maybe it would be better to simply stay in her bedroom and read. She was small for her age, and her pretty face had a piquant, passive cast which looked utterly at home in front of a book. She wanted to be a teacher, an English teacher. The girl looked back across the brown lawn to her house, and sunlight bounced off the plateglass window. There was not a shadow in sight. She sneezed. Her white blouse already adhered to her skin.

She turned away from the glare of the sun off the picture window and went toward town. She was following the direction she had seen Chief Hovre's car travel, two or three hours earlier. Girls in Arden did not like going anywhere alone since the death of Jenny Strand: friends waited at the bowling alley. But surely in the daytime one was safe. Galen Hovre, she thought, was not intelligent enough to catch the killer of Gwen Olson and Jenny Strand: unless the big man she had seen sitting beside the sheriff was the murderer.

She idled along looking at the ground, her thin arms swinging. She admitted to herself that she disliked bowling, and did it only because everyone else did.

She never saw what grabbed her——there was only

an awareness of a shape coming swiftly out of an alley, and then she was slammed against a wall and the fear was too bright in her mind for her to speak or cry out. The force with which she had been lifted and moved seemed scarcely human: what had touched her, what was bearing down on her, scarcely seemed the flesh of a fellow creature. Surrounding her was the pungent smell of earth, as if she were already in her grave.

Seven

My arms and legs could not move. Yet in another dimension, they were moving, not lying still on the floor of my workroom but taking me toward the woods. I witnessed both processes impartially, both the internal (walking into the woods) and the external (lying on the workroom floor), thinking that the only previous time such an experience had been given to me was when I had burst open the sea chest and looked at the photograph she had directed to be put on my desk. The air was sweet, perfumy, both in and out. The lights had all gone out and the fields were dark. At some point in the immeasurable, unreckonable amount of time since I had stood up to see why the mare was terrified, night had come. I was walking across the dark field toward the cottonwood trees; I parted thick weeds, I walked out onto a grassy root-hump and jumped easily across the creek. My body was light, a dream-body. There was no need to run. I could hear the telephone, owls, crickets. The night air was soft, so sweet it seemed liable to catch in the trees, like fog.

I passed easily beyond the next area of fields and entered the woods. Birches gleamed like girls. Who had turned the lights out? My right index finger registered the sensation of polished boards, but it was touching a ghostly maple. Leaving it behind, I walked on a mulch of leaves. The gradient began to change. A deer plunged deeper into the woods somewhere to my right, and I turned in that direction. Uphill. Through trees closer and closer, high life-breathing oaks with bark like rivers. I touched the flank of a dead maple, down across my path like the corpse of a soldier, and lifted myself with my arms so that I sat on it and then swung my legs over and let myself fall onto the springy floor again. My knees absorbed the shock. There was still the light problem, but I knew where I was going.

It was a clearing. A clearing perhaps sixteen feet across, ringed with giant oaks, the ashes of a fire at its center. She was there, waiting for me.

Magically, I knew how to get there: all I had to do was drift and I would be taken, my feet would guide me.

When the trees approached too near, I shoved them aside with my hand. Twigs caught in my jacket and hair, pulling at me as a thorny weed had captured my foot outside the Dream House. Leaves stirred in the thick perfumy air. Where my feet had been were sucking black holes. On the perpendicular sides of trees hung glistening mushrooms, white and red. I waded through ferns as high as my waist, holding my arms as if they cradled a rifle.

There was a darkening of the spirit. Going closer to where I had to go, I saw the edges of starlight on the bark-rills and began to be afraid. When I passed through a gap, it seemed to close behind me. The breathing life of the forest expressed an immensity of force. Even the air grew tight. I climbed over a lightning-blasted trunk. Living stuff coiled around my boots, golden roots proliferated over them. I stepped on a mushroom the size of a sheep's head and felt it become jelly beneath my weight.

The rough hand of a tree brushed my face. I felt my skin tear along my jaw, and crack like a porcelain cup. Branches closed over my head. The only light leading me was from leaves and ferns themselves, the light plants produce like oxygen. Another tree clicked into place behind me, blocking the way back. I went to my knees. By scraping along the soft damp forest floor, I got beneath the lowest branch of the sentinel tree. My fingers touched grass and stones; I pulled myself into the clearing.

When I stood, my shirt was green with moss. The bandage was gone from my left hand. I could feel snapped twigs and dried, crumbling leaves in my hair. I tried to brush them away, off, but my hands could not move, my arms could not lift.

The trees jostled and whispered behind me. The blackness was edged and pierced by a thousand sharp silvery lights on leaf-edge and the curve of tendrils. The clearing was a dark circle with a darker circle at its center. I could move, and went forward. I touched the ashes. They were warm. I smelled woodsmoke, and it was heavy and sweet. The dense forest behind and before me seemed to grow taut. I froze beside the warm ashes, bent forward over my knees and in total silence.

What will happen after she comes back? Rinn had asked me, and I felt a terror deeper than that of the first time in the woods. A high rustling whistling noise was coming toward me from where the leaf-light was strongest, a whispery sound of movement. My skin felt icy. The sound dragged toward me.

Then I saw her.

She was across the clearing, framed between two black birches. She was unchanged. If anything had touched my thin layer of cold skin, I would have cracked open, I would have shattered into a heap of white cold fragments. She began to move forward, her motion slow, unstoppable.

I called her name.

As she drew nearer the noise increased—that high whispery whistling scratched in my ears. Her mouth was open. I saw that her teeth were water-polished stones. Her face was an intricate pattern of leaves;

her hands were rilled wood, tipped with thorns. She was made of bark and leaves.

I threw my hands back and felt smooth wood. Air lay in my lungs like water. I realized I was screaming only when I heard it.

"His eyes are open," a voice said. I was looking at the open window above my desk, the curtains blowing and small papers lifting in the warm breeze. It was day. The air was its normal weight, unperfumed. "His eyes are wide open."

Another voice said, "Are you awake, Miles? Can you hear?"

I tried to speak, and a rush of sour fluid poured from my mouth.

The woman said, "He'll live. Thanks to you."

I sat up suddenly. I was in bed. It was still daytime. The telephone was ringing downstairs. "Don't worry about it," someone said. I turned to look; beside the door, her pale eyes reflectively on mine, the Tin Woodsman was closing a book. It was one I had given Zack. "That phone's been going all night and morning, I guess. It's Chief Hovre. He wants to talk to you about something. Was it an accident?" On the last sentence her tone changed, and her head tilted up. In her eyes I saw the fear of a complex betrayal.

"What happened?"

"You're lucky you weren't smoking. Pieces of you would probably be on top of Korte's barn by now."

"What happened?"

"Did you leave the gas on? On purpose?"

"What? What gas?"

"The gas in the kitchen, dummy. It was on most of the night. Mrs. Sunderson says you're alive because you're up here. I had to break a window in the kitchen."

"How was it turned on?"

"That's the big question, all right. Mrs. Sunderson says you were trying to kill yourself. She says she should have known."

I rubbed my face. It was unscratched. The bandage was still on my left hand. "Pilot light," I said.

"Blown out. Or gone out. Both of them. Boy. You should have smelled that kitchen. So *sweet*."

"I think I smelled it up here," I said. "I was sitting at my desk, and the next thing I knew I was lying on the floor. It was almost as though I left my body."

"Well, if you didn't do it, it must have happened by itself." She seemed relieved. "There's something wrong with this house. Just when you got home two nights ago, all the lights went on, all over the house."

"You saw that too?"

"Sure, I was in my bedroom. And last night, they all went off at once. My dad says the wiring never was any good in this old house."

"Aren't you supposed to be keeping away from me?"

"I said I'd leave as soon as you were all right. See, I was the one who found you. Old man Hovre phoned our house. He said you weren't answering your phone. He said he had important news for you. My dad was asleep, so I came over myself. It was all locked up, except for the porch. So I pushed up the window in the front bedroom downstairs, and that's when I smelled the gas. I went around to the kitchen and broke a window. To let air in. Then I held my breath and climbed in and ran into the living room and pushed up the window. A little later I came up here. You were on the floor in the other room. I pushed open the window in there too. I thought I was going to be sick."

"What time was this?"

"About six. This morning. Maybe earlier."

"You were still up at six o'clock?"

She tilted her head again. "I just got home. From a date. Anyhow, I just waited to see if you were alive, and then Mrs. Sunderson showed up. She went straight to the phone and called the police. She thought you did it on purpose. Tried to kill yourself. She'll be back tomorrow, she says. If you want her today, you're supposed to call her up. In the meantime, I told old man Hovre you'd call him when you felt better."

"Thanks," I said. "Thanks for saving my life, I guess I mean."

She shrugged, then smiled. "If anyone did, it was old man Hovre. He was the one who called me. And if I hadn't found you, Tuta Sunderson would have. Eventually. You weren't ready to die."

I raised my eyebrows.

"You were moving all over the place. And making noises. You knew who I was."

"What do you mean?"

"You were saying my name. At least that's what it sounded like."

"Do you really think I tried to kill myself?"

"No. I really don't." She sounded surprised. She stood up and tucked the book beneath her elbow. "I think you're too smart to do anything like that. Oh. I almost forgot. Zack says thanks for the books. He wants to see you again soon."

I nodded.

"Are you sure you're okay now?"

"I'm sure, Alison."

At the door she paused and turned toward me. She opened her mouth, closed it, and then decided to speak after all. "I'm really happy you're okay now."

The telephone began to trill again. "Don't worry about answering the phone," I said. "Sooner or later I'll get it. Polar Bears wants to invite me to dinner. And Alison—I'm very happy you were around."

"Wait until we're comfortable before you start asking the serious questions," said Galen Hovre two nights later, cracking ice cubes from a tray into a bowl. My intuition had been at least partially correct. I was seated in a large overstuffed chair in Polar Bears' living room, in that part of Arden where I had parked the Nash. Hovre's was a family house without a family. Newspapers several weeks old were piled on one of the chairs, and the red fabric of the couch had become greasy with age; the coffee table supported a rank of empty beer cans. Polar Bears' pistol hung in its holster from the wing of an old chair. The green carpet showed several darker patches where he had apparently made half-hearted stabs at washing out stains. On end tables on either side of the couch, two big lamps with stands shaped like wildfowl cast murky yellowish light. The walls were dark brown—Hovre's wife, whoever she had been, had fought for unconventionality. On them hung two pictures not, I was willing to bet, of her choosing: a framed photograph of Polar Bears in plaid shirt and fisherman's hat, holding up a string of trout, and a reproduction of Van Gogh's sunflowers. "I generally have a little drink after dinner. Do you want bourbon, bourbon or bourbon?"

"Fine," I said.

"Helps tamp down the grease," he said, though in fact he had surprised me by being an adequate cook. Pot roast, reasonably well made, may not be notably elegant, but it was not what I had expected from a two hundred and seventy-five pound man in a wrinkled police uniform. Burned venison steaks were more like it, I had thought: virile, but badly executed.

One reason for the invitation had been immediately clear: Polar Bears was a lonely man, and he kept up a tide of chatter all during the meal. Not a word about my supposed suicide attempt, nor about the girls' deaths—he had talked about fishing. Tackle and equipment, bait, sea-water vs. freshwater fishing, fishing then vs. fishing now, boats and "People on Lake Michigan claim those coho salmon taste pretty good, but give me a river trout any day," and " 'Course there's nothing like dry fly fishing for sport, but sometimes I like to take my old spinning rod and just sit by the shallows and wait for that wily old grandad down there." It was the talk of a man deprived by circumstances or profession of normal social conversation and who misses it badly, and I had chewed my way through several slices of juicy beef and a mound of vegetables in thick sauce while he let the tap flow and the pressure decrease.

I heard him tip a stack of plates into the sink and

run water over them; a moment later he came back into the living room carrying a bottle of Wild Turkey under his arm, a porcelain bowl of ice cubes in one hand, and two glasses in the other.

"Something just occurred to me," I said as he grunted, bending down over the table, and set down glasses, ice, and then the bottle with a deliberate thump.

"What's that?"

"That we're all men alone—single men. The four of us that used to know each other. Duane, Paul Kant, you and me. You were married once, weren't you?" The furnishings and the brown walls made it obvious, even the ducks mounting up one of the side walls; Polar Bears' house existed, it occurred to me, in symmetry with Paul's, except that Polar Bears' bore the traces of a younger woman's taste, a wife, not a mother.

"I was," he said, and poured bourbon over ice and leaned back on the couch and put his feet on the coffee table. "Like you. She ran off a long time ago. Left me with a kid. Our son."

"I didn't know you had a son, Polar Bears."

"Oh, yeah. Raised him myself. He lives here in Arden."

"How old is he?"

"Round about twenty. His mother left when he was just a little runt. She was no good. My boy never had much education, but he's smart and he works around town on a kind of handyman basis. Got his own place too. I'd like him to join the police, but he's got his own ideas. Good kid, though. He believes in the law, not like some of them now."

"Why didn't you or Duane remarry?" I helped myself to a good dose of bourbon.

"You could say I learned my lesson. Police work is hard on a wife. You never really stop working, if you see what I mean. And then, I never found another woman I could trust. As for good old Du-ane, I don't think he ever really did like women. He's got his girl to cook and keep house, and I reckon that's about all he wants."

I recognized that Polar Bears was making me feel very relaxed, giving me the spurious sense that this was nothing more than a casual evening between two old friends, and I looked at him from my chair. Light silvered the thick flesh on the top of his head. His eyes were half closed.

"I think you're right. I think he hates women. Maybe he's your killer."

Polar Bears gave a genuine laugh. "Ah, Miles, Miles. Well, he didn't always hate women. There was one that got to him, once upon a time."

"That Polish girl."

"Not quite. Why do you think his daughter's got that name of hers?"

I gaped at him, and found that his slitted eyes were watching me anything but sleepily.

"Truth," he said. "I think he even lost his cherry to that little Alison Greening. You weren't around every summer she was, you know. He was stuck on her, and I mean stuck. 'Course she mighta gone to bed with him, or done it standing up beside a haystack more likely, but she was too young for that to be public, and she treated him like shit most of the time anyhow. She just tore him up. I always thought that's why he went and engaged himself to that Polish girl."

The shock was still ringing in my chest. "You said he lost his virginity to Alison?"

"Yep. He told me himself."

"But she could have been no older than thirteen."

"That's right. He said she knew a lot more about it than he did."

I remembered the art teacher. "I don't believe it. He was lying. She used to laugh at him."

"That's true too. He was real burned up by the way she preferred you to him whenever you were around. Jealous. Crazy jealous." He bent forward over his belly and poured more bourbon into his glass, not bothering to add ice cubes. "So you can see why you shouldn't go tossing that name around. Du-ane might think you was deliberately rubbing salt in his wounds. Not to mention that you oughta think about protecting yourself. I hate to act like a spiritual adviser, Miles, but I think you might even try goin' to that church in the valley. People might let up on you if they see you acting more like them. Sit and absorb a little of Bertilsson's wisdom. Funny how all these Norskies took to that little Swedish rat. I can't see him for horse piss, but the farmers all love him. He gave me some story about your stealing out of Zumgo's. A book, he said."

"Ridiculous."

"So I told him. What's your side of this suicide business, anyhow, Miles? I don't suppose there's any truth in it."

"None. Either it was an accident, or someone was trying to kill me. Or warn me off." I was still mentally struggling to sit up.

"Warn you off what? You ain't *on* anything. I'm glad it didn't have anything to do with our talk yesterday."

"Polar Bears," I said, "did your father ever find out who called him, that night my cousin drowned?"

He shook his head, unhappy with me. "Get all that out of your head, Miles. Get it out of your system. We're talking about now, not twenty years ago."

"Well, did he?"

"Goddam it, Miles." He poured what was left of his drink down his throat and bent forward, grunting, to make another. "Didn't I tell you to leave that alone? No. He never did. That good enough for you? So you say this gas business was an accident. Right?"

I nodded, wondering what this conversation was really about. I had to talk to Duane.

"Well now, you see that's what I thought. I wish we could have kept Tuta Sunderson out of it, because she's bound to go around telling people what she thinks, and her version is a little hard on you. And right now, we've gotta take attention off of you. Aren't you gonna have any more of this good booze?"

My glass was empty.

"Come on. Keep me company. I gotta have a few drinks at night in order to get to sleep. If Lokken arrests you for drunken driving, I'll tear up your ticket." His big seamed face split into a smile.

I poured two inches into my glass and added a handful of ice cubes. The bourbon appeared to have as much effect on Polar Bears as Coca-Cola.

"You see," he said, "I'm tryin' my darnedest to keep you out of trouble. I like talking to you, Miles. We go back a long way. And I can't allow one of our good citizens of Arden to come in and sit here and see his police chief get sloshed, can I? We've got a good little understanding going. You forgive me for the Larabee business, and I'll listen to anything you have to tell me. I forgive you for boosting a book out of Zumgo's. You probably had a lot of things on your mind."

"Like getting anonymous blank letters."

"Like that. Uh huh. Real good. And like your wife dying. And right now, we got another problem here. One that means you gotta keep a low profile, old buddy."

"Another problem."

He sipped at his drink, and slid his eyes toward mine over the rim like a card player. "It's what I was tryin' to talk to you about two nights ago, old buddy. A new wrinkle. Are you startin' to shake, Miles? What for?"

"Just go on," I said. I felt as cold as in the old Updahl kitchen. "This is what you've been leading up to all night."

"That's not entirely fair, Miles. I'm just a cop trying to see all around a case. Trouble is, it keeps on growing."

"There's another one," I said. "Another girl."

"Maybe. Now you're mighty clever to get that out of me, because we're trying to keep it quiet for the time being. It isn't like the other ones. We don't have a body." He made a fist and coughed into it, stringing out the suspense. "We don't even know there *is* a body.

A girl named Candace Michalski, good looker, seventeen years old, just disappeared the other evening. Two-three hours after I dropped you off at the Nash a couple blocks from here. She told her parents she was going bowling down at the Bowl-A-Rama—we passed it going out of town, remember—and she never came back. Never even made it to the Bowl-A-Rama."

"Maybe she ran away." My hands were shaking, and I sat on them.

"Out of character. She was an honors student. Member of the Future Teachers of America. Had a scholarship to River Falls next year. That's part of the state university system now, you know. I took some extension courses in police science there some years back. A good girl, Miles, not the kind that lights out."

"It's funny," I said. "It's funny how the past keeps up with us. We were just talking about Alison Greening, who is still, ah . . . on my mind a lot, and you and Duane and I all knew her, and people are all remembering about her death—"

"You and Duane were a lot closer to her than I was." He laughed. "But you gotta take your mind off her, Miles."

My body gave a tremor. "And an Arden girl with a Polish name leaves town or disappears, like that girl of Duane's . . ."

"And you make a museum out of your grand-maw's house," he said almost brutally. "Yeah, but I don't exactly see where that gets us. Now here's my thinking. I talked to the Michalskis, who are all shook up, naturally, and upset, and I said that they should keep quiet. They won't tell anyone about Candy. They'll say she went visiting her aunt in Sparta—or anything like that. I want to keep the lid on it for as long as possible. Maybe the girl will write them a postcard from a nudist colony in California. Huh? Maybe we'll find her body. If she's dead, maybe we can smoke out her killer before anybody gets the chance to get all hysterical. I'd like a nice clean arrest, and I guess the killer would prefer that too. With the sane part of his mind, anyhow." He levered himself off the couch and put his hands in the small of his back and stretched. He looked like a tired old bear that had just missed a fish. "Why did you want to go and steal from Zumgo's, anyhow? That was shit-stupid. Anyone would think you were asking to be put away."

I shook my head. "Bertilsson is wrong. I didn't steal anything."

"I'll confess to you, I wish that boy would come up to me and say, I did it, now get it over with. He *wants* to. He *wants* me to get him. He'd love to be sitting right where you are, Miles. He's all screwed up inside. He's about ready to snap. He can't get me out of his mind. Maybe he killed that Michalski girl. Maybe he's got her hid away someplace. Maybe he doesn't know what to do now that he's got her. He's in a bad spot. I feel sorry for the bastard, Miles, honest I do. If we do get a suicide, I'll say, that was him. I missed him, dammit. But he missed me too. What time is it?"

I looked at my watch. Polar Bears moved over to his front window and stood leaning against the glass, looking out into night. "Two."

"I never get to sleep until four or five. I'm screwed up nearly as bad as him." The gunpowder odor seemed particularly strong, along with the smell of unwashed skin. I wondered if Polar Bears ever changed his uniform. "How's that project you mentioned? Comin' along okay?"

"Sure. I guess so."

"What is it, anyhow?"

"Historical research."

"Real good. I still need your help, though. I hope you'll stay with us until this is all cleared up."

He was watching my reflection in the window glass. I glanced at his revolver hanging in its holster from the side wing of a chair.

I said, "What did you mean the other day when you said something about the killer's not just being an ordinary rapist? That he might be impotent?"

"Well, you take rape, Miles," Polar Bears said,

moving heavily across the room to lean on the back
of the couch. "I can understand rape. It's always been
with us. I'll tell you what I couldn't say to a woman.
These cases didn't have anything to do with rape. These
things were done by somebody with a bad head problem. Rape isn't perverted, the way I look at it—it's
almost a normal thing. A girl gets a fellow all heated
up so he can't control himself, and then she hollers
rape. The way these girls dress is almost incitement to
rape. Hell, the way some girls *look* is an incitement to
rape. A fellow might misunderstand what some bottom-
swinging little critter is all about, what she wants. He
gets all steamed up and can't help himself. Fault?
Both parties! That's not exactly a popular point of
view these days, but it's sure enough the truth. I've
been a cop long enough to see a hundred cases of it.
Power, they say. Of course it's about power. All life
is about power. But these cases now weren't done by
any normal man. See Miles, these girls didn't have any
form of intercourse at all—the examiner at the state
hospital in Blundell, Dr. Hampton, didn't find any
traces of semen. They were violated by other means."

"Other means?" I asked, not really sure I wanted to
hear any more.

"A bottle. A Coke bottle. We found one smashed
up beside both Gwen Olson and Jenny Strand. On
Strand, something else was used too. A broomhandle,
something like that. We're still looking for it in the
field off 93. Then there was some knife work. And
they were both beaten up pretty badly before the real
fun started."

"Christ," I said.

"So it might even be a woman, but that's pretty far-
fetched. It's hard to see a woman being strong enough,
for one thing, and it doesn't really sound like a woman,
does it? Well." He smiled at me from his position
behind the couch, leaning forward on his arms. "Now
you know as much as we do."

"You don't really think Paul Kant did these things,
do you? That's impossible."

"What's impossible, Miles? Maybe I did it. Maybe you did, or Du-ane. Paul's all right as long as he stays inside and keeps out of trouble." He pushed himself off the couch and went into the kitchen. I heard an explosive bubbling sound and realized that he was gargling. When He came back into the living room his blue uniform shirt was unbuttoned, revealing a sleeveless undershirt straining over his immense belly. "You want some sleep, Miles. Take care you don't run off the road on your way home. It was a nice evening. We know each other better. Now scat."

Through the huge magnifying lenses, Tuta Sunderson's eyes looked like goggling fish. Sulky, she forced her hands into the pockets of her gray cardigan. For the three days following my late-night conversation with Polar Bears, she had sullenly arrived every morning, noisily tramped around the kitchen, wordlessly cooked my breakfast, and then busied herself cleaning the kitchen and the bathroom while I experimented with the placement of the furniture. The old bamboo and fabric couch went against the far wall, to the left of the small shelves. The glass-fronted case (I remembered it holding Bibles and novels by Lloyd C. Douglas) faced into the room from the short wall by the porch door; the only thing resembling an easy chair sat on the other side of that door; but the other chairs and small tables seemed too numerous, impossible to place—a spindly-legged table with a magazine rack? A cane-backed chair? I was not sure I could even remember them in the room, much less where they had been situated. Perhaps a half dozen other small articles of furniture presented the same problem. Tuta Sunderson could not help.

"It wasn't always the same way. There is no right way."

"Just think. Try to remember."

"I think that little table there went sort of alongside that couch." She was humoring me, half-reluctantly.

"Here?" I moved it under the shelves.

"No. Out more."

I pulled it forward.

"If I was Du-ane, I'd have your head examined. He spent pretty near his whole rebate on that nice furniture. When he told my boy about it, Red went down and got some real nice bargains for me, too."

"Duane can move this stuff back downstairs when I leave. That table doesn't look right."

"Looks good enough to me."

"Because you don't understand."

"I reckon there's lots I don't understand. You'll never get your writing done if you do this all day long."

"Why don't you change my sheets or something? If you can't help me, at least you could get out of my way."

Her face seemed to fill with water, like a sack.

"I reckon you left all your good manners in New York, Miles." With that, she visibly gave up on me for the moment, and turned toward the window. "How long before that little car of yours gonna be ready from the filling station?"

"I'll try them in a few days."

"Then will you be leaving the valley?" She cocked her head, watching something on the road.

"No. Polar Bears wants me to stay. He must be bored with his usual company."

"You and Galen pretty close?"

"We're like brothers."

"He never invited anyone to his house before. Galen keeps himself to himself. He's a smart man. Guess you had a ride in his police car. Folks in Arden told Red."

I moved a chair to a spot beside the oil heater, then moved it nearer the bedroom door. "You seem to have cars on the brain today."

"Maybe because I just saw someone stop and put something in your mailbox. Not the mailman. It was a different car. Why don't you go out there where it's warm and see what you got?"

"Now you tell me," I said, and went toward the

porch. I stepped outside into the sunlight. For the past two days, Tuta Sunderson had taken to wearing a sweater while she worked, in part to irritate me with the anomaly of a cardigan in hot summer weather, in part because the farmhouse was genuinely cold and damp: it was as if a breeze came slicing down from the woods to pitch camp in the house. Behind me I could hear her saying, just loudly enough for me to hear, "Some more of your fan mail."

Which, in the event, was what it turned out to be: fan mail. It was a single sheet of cheap lined paper torn from a school exercise book, and printed on it was BASTERD YOURE IN OUR SIGHTS. Yes, a familiar image from the movies; I could almost feel the cross-hairs centering on my chest. I looked down the road, saw the nothing I expected to see, and then leaned forward with my arms on the mailbox, making my breathing regular. Twice in the past two days I had received silent telephone calls, bringing me down from my new project to a noise of muffled breathing on which I could smell onions, cheese, beer. Tuta Sunderson said people all talk, and I could guess that there were rumors of the Polish girl's disappearance. Tuta's attitude itself, more abrasive since my "suicide attempt," showed that she had attended to these whispers: she had just thrown back to me my remark about Red's manners.

As I walked back toward the farmhouse I could see her mooning at me through the window. I slammed the porch door, and she scuttled over to the cupboards and pretended to dust the shelves.

"I don't suppose you recognized the car?"

Her flabby upper arms wobbled; her rump bobbed in sympathetic motion. "It wasn't from the valley. I know all the cars hereabouts." She peeked at me over her fat shoulder, dying to know what I had found in the mailbox.

"What color was it?"

"It was all dust. I couldn't see."

"You know, Mrs. Sunderson," I said, putting it very slowly so she would not miss a word, "if it was your

son or any of his friends that came in here that night
and turned on the gas, they were attempting murder.
The law takes a hard line on that sort of thing."

Furious, baffled, she turned around. "My boy's no
sneak!"

"Is that what you'd call it?"

She whirled around again and began to dust the
dishes so vigorously that they rattled. After a moment
she permitted herself to speak, though not to face me.
"People say something else happened. They say Galen
Hovre is going to get him soon. They say he sits down
there in his office knowing a lot more than he tells."
Then another wall-eyed peek at me. "And they say
Paul Kant is starving himself in his mother's house. So
if it happens again people will know he was inside and
didn't do it."

"What a field day they're having," I said. "What
fun they're all having. I envy them."

She shook her head maddeningly, and I would gladly
have gone on in that vein, but the telephone rang. She
glanced at it and then at me, telling me she would not
answer it.

I put the sheet of paper down on the table and picked
up the receiver. "Hello." Silence, breathing, the smells
of onions and beer. I do not know if these were truly
the odors of my caller, or if they were only those I
expected from someone who made anonymous telephone calls. Tuta Sunderson pounced on the sheet of
paper.

"You miserable boor," I said into the mouthpiece.
"You have pigshit where you should have an imagination."

My caller hung up; I laughed at that and at the expression on Tuta Sunderson's face. She put down the
misspelled note. She was shocked. I laughed again, tast-
ing something black and sour at the back of my throat.

When I heard the porch door slam I waited until I saw
her toiling up the road, the lumpy cardigan over one
arm and the handbag jigging on its strap. After a long

while she moved out of the frame of vision the window gave me, struggling in the sunlight like a white beetle. I put down my pencil and closed the journal. Standing on the cool porch, I looked up toward the woods—all was still, as if life stopped when the sun was so high. Sound told me that it did not: out of sight down the road, Duane's tractor put-putted from the far field, birds said things to one another. I went down the rutted drive, crossed the road, and jumped the ditch.

On the other side of the creek, I could hear crickets and grasshoppers, and small things whirring in the grass. I went up the bifurcated hill; crows took off from the alfalfa, screeching, their bodies like flak, like ashes in the air. Sweat dripped into my eyebrows, and I felt my shirt clammily adhering to my sides. I thumped down into the dip, and then began to rise again, walking toward the trees.

This was where she had twice led me. Birds twittered, darting through branches far above. Light came down in that streaming way it does only in forests and cathedrals. I watched a gray squirrel race out onto a slender branch, bend it under his weight, and then transfer to a lower, stouter branch like a man stepping out of an elevator. When the ground began to alter, so did the trees; I walked on spongy gray mulch between oaks and elms; I skirted pines and conifers and felt thin brown needles skid underfoot. As when I lay on the polished floor, I waded through high leafy beds of ferns. Berries crushed against my trousers. A lightning-blasted old ruin of an oak lay splintered and jagged in my path, and I jumped on top of it, feeling the softness of rotting wood. Filaments of green snagged and caught in the eyelets of my boots.

Going as I had gone in vision that night, I passed the thick unmoving trees until I saw where they seemed to gather like a crowd at an accident: I slid through a gap, and was in the clearing. The sunlight, after the filter of the network of the leaves, seemed violently yellow and intense, lionlike, full of inhuman energy. Tall grass tipped under its own weight. Insect noises hovered in vibrato over the clearing. A chirring unmoving noise.

At the center, in the charred place, the ashes showed a still red core, like the ashes in Rinn's old woodstove. It had Alison's warmth. Galen Hovre was wrong about Duane and my cousin. Or Duane, all those years ago, had lied.

Oddly, perhaps predictably, when I had dreamed about walking up into the woods the journey had a direct, palpable actuality, and when I actually went up there it felt like dreaming. I thought, almost fearing it, that I would sense some deeper closeness to Alison Greening if I approached the clearing where I had met her dreadful apparition in my vision; that space was hers, and I thought of it as the source of the chill which penetrated the old farmhouse. If there is another world, a world of Spirit, who is to say that its touch may not shake us to our boots, that its heat may not come to us as the cold of quarry water? But discounting that nightmare vision of Alison as a creature stitched together from leaves and bark, indirection brought me closer to her, evoked her more satisfactorily, than a crude search through the woods and clearing. I had begun a memoir, a task she had motivated (I could remember her telling me, one high summer day when we climbed the hill behind the valley and, carrying shovels, searched for Indian mounds, that she was going to be a painter, and I a writer), and it seemed to cement us even further, since—at the most obvious level—it meant that I thought about her even more than I might otherwise. She was the groundbass of what I wrote. It was as though I were reeling her in, sentence by sentence. And then, one morning after suffering through a breakfast presided over by a Tuta Sunderson who had accepted seven one-dollar bills from me and then wordlessly handed back two as if they represented an immoral suggestion, I had driven the Nash loaner over the Mississippi bridge on Highway 35—a wonderful American sight, those islands showing their wooded backs like green water buffaloes in the brown river—to Winona, Minnesota, looking for the records necessary to the Alison-environment. If I'd had to, I would have gone all the way to Minneapolis. Albums on the Pacific label from the 'fifties are rare items. An initial glance through the racks in a Winona record store unearthed none, but then I saw the sign saying Second Hand Department Downstairs, and went down to flip through, in a basement illuminated by a single bulb, crate after crate of albums with worn sleeves and crumbled spines. Surrounded by cast-off Perry Comos and Roy Acuffs and Roger Williamses, two records shone like gold, and I grunted with such loud approval that the owner appeared at the top of the stairs to ask if I were all right. One was an old Dave Brubeck record I remembered Alison telling me she had loved *(Jazz at Oberlin)* and the other—well, the other was a true find. It was the Gerry Mulligan quartet album on Pacific which Alison had urged me to buy, the one with a cover painting by Keith Finch. Finding that record was like finding a message from her scrawled on a page of my manuscript. It was the record, above all others, which evoked her, the one she had most cherished. The owner of the record store charged me five dollars for the two records, but I would have paid twenty times that. As much as my writing, they brought Alison nearer.

"What *is* that stuff you play all the time?" asked the Tin Woodsman. She was standing on the porch on Saturday night, peering in through the screen door. "Is that jazz?" I put my pencil into my manuscript and closed it. I was sitting on the old couch downstairs, and the kerosene lamps shed a muted orange glow which softened her features, blurred already by the mesh of the screen. She wore a denim shirt and trousers, and looked more feminine, in that soft light, than I had ever seen her. "Look," she said, "it's okay. I mean, Dad's in Arden for some kind of meeting. Red Sunderson called him just before dinner. All the men are talking about something. They'll probably be at it for hours. I heard you playing that record the other day. Is that the kind of music you like? Can I come in?"

She entered the room and sat facing me from a wooden rocker. On her bare feet were tan clogs. "What is it, anyhow?"

"Do you like it?" I really was curious.

She lifted her shoulders. "Doesn't it all sound sort of the same?"

"No."

"What's that instrument playing now?"

"A guitar."

"A guitar? That's a guitar? Come on. It's a . . . um, a whatsit. Some kind of horn. A sax. Right?"

"Yes. It's a baritone saxophone."

"So why did you say it was a guitar?" Then she smiled, seeing the joke.

I shrugged, smiling back.

"Shit, Miles, it's cold in here."

"That's because it's damp."

"Yeah? Hey Miles, did you steal out of Zumgo's? Pastor Bertilsson's telling everyone you did."

"Then I must have."

"I don't get it." She looked around the room, shaking her head, her jaws working on a piece of gum. "Hey, you know this room looks really neat this way. It's just like it used to be. When I was a little kid and Great-Gramma was still alive."

"I know."

"It's neat," she said, still examining the room. "Didn't there used to be more pictures? Like of you and Dad?" When I nodded, she asked, "So where are they?"

"I didn't need them."

The gum snapped. "Boy, Miles, I don't know about you. You're really superstrange. Sometimes you remind me of Zack, and sometimes you just talk crazy. How did you know where everything went in here?"

"I had to work at it."

"It's sort of like a museum, isn't it? I mean, I almost expect to see Great-Gramma!"

"She probably wouldn't like the music."

She giggled. "Hey, did you really steal from Zum-go's?"

"Does Zack steal?"

"Sure." She made her sea-water eyes very wide. "All the time. He says you have to liberate things. And he says if you can take things without being caught, then you have a right to them."

"Where does he steal from?"

"Places where he works. You know. Stuff from people's houses, if he's working for them. Stuff from the gas station, if he's working there. You mean, you're a college professor and all and you steal things?"

"If you say so."

"I can see why Zack likes you. That would really turn him on. Some big Establishment guy ripping off stores. He thinks he might be able to trust you."

"I really think you're too good for Zack," I said.

"You're wrong, Miles. You don't know Zack. You don't know what he's into." She leaned forward, putting each hand on the opposite shoulder. The gesture was surprisingly womanly.

"What's the meeting in Arden about? The one Red and your father went to."

"Who cares? Listen, Miles, are you going to church tomorrow?"

"Of course not. I have my reputation to think of."

"Then try not to get stinko again tonight, huh? We gotta plan. We're gonna take you somewhere."

Portion of Statement of Tuta Sunderson:

July 18

Well, what my boy thought was that there was some kind of coverup. That was the word he used to me, Galen Hovre, like it or not. Coverup. 'Course it wasn't, we know that now, but look at what we had then—nothing! After those two murders, there's poor Paul Kant holed up in his mother's house, there's Miles batching it in his grandmother's house and riding around in police cars and who knows what all, turning that house into something Duane didn't want it to be, and people just thought something had to be done. And we all thought you were hiding something from us. And you were!

Anyhow, one of Red's friends had the car idea, and Red told him, let's wait until we know for sure what's going on, and let's have a general meeting to talk about it. All the men. They'd get together, see? To sort of piece out the rumors.

So they met in the back of the Angler's. Red says they had thirty-forty men at the meeting. They all looked up to Red, on account of his finding Jenny Strand.

Now, who's heard what? says Red. Let's get it all out. Let's get it where we can see it and not just gossip about it. Now, a few of the men had heard that the police were sitting on something. Let me see. Did one of the deputies tell his girlfriend? Something like that. I'm not saying it was that, mind. So one of the men says, who knows about anybody hiding away—not acting normal and neighborly.

And someone says, Roman Michalski hasn't been to work this week.

Sick? they ask.

No, nobody heard of him being sick. He's just holed up. Him and his wife.

Now, if we're talking about people being holed up, I could have told them about Miles. You bet. He just set there after he got all the furniture just the way he wanted it, the way his Gramma had it. He was real white, sitting there in that damp old house, drinking himself to sleep every night, and playing those goofy records all day. He looked like he was in a trance or something all the time. A big man like that, and he looked like he'd jump out of his skin if you said boo. And his language! Oh, he knew he wasn't going to get away with anything.

*When I found out he'd had a girl in his bed I
told Red right away.*

*Anyhow, like you know, Monday night some of
the men paid a call on Roman Michalski.*

After showering on Sunday morning I went upstairs
and hugged my bathrobe about me while I examined
my clothes. Mrs. Sunderson had wordlessly washed my
muddy jeans and shirt and folded them on top of the
bureau. The jeans had a quarter-sized hole at one cuff;
looking at it awakened uneasy memories of my scramble
through the woods; I was grateful that I had gone back
to the clearing and found no more than a dying picnic
fire. I fingered the hole in the jeans then withdrew my
hand. I remembered a portion of Polar Bears' advice
to me, and wandered indecisively to the closet where
I'd put the one suit I had brought with me. It was
seven-thirty; I had just time enough to dress and make
the service. It had to be done correctly—I had to be
dressed correctly, I could display no nervousness, my
attitude must shout innocence. Just thinking about it
while looking at the suit in the closet made me nervous.
You're like Paul Kant if you don't go, stated a clear
voice in my mind.

I took the suit from the hanger and began to dress.
For a reason probably closely related to vanity, in
New York I had packed, along with clothing appropriate to the farm, my most expensive things—eighty-
dollar shoes, a lightweight pinstripe from Brooks, several of the custom-made shirts Joan, being nicely ironic,
had once had made for me for Christmas. I certainly
had not foreseen wearing them to Gethsemane Lutheran
church.

After I had knotted a thick, glossy tie and put on the
jacket I looked at myself in the bedroom mirror. I resembled a Wall Street lawyer far more than a failed
academic or murder suspect. I looked innocent, big
and bland and prosperous and washed in milk. A baby
for the work of the Lord, a man who would absent-
mindedly mutter a prayer while sinking a difficult putt.

On the way out of the house I slipped the copy of *She* into my jacket pocket: a sliver of Alison for company.

I pulled the Nash into the last space in the gravel parking lot before the church and got out into the hot sun and began to walk over the crunching white stones to the church steps. As they did every Sunday, the men were standing on the wide high steps and on the concrete walk, smoking. I could remember them standing there, smoking and talking, when I was a child; but those men had been the fathers and uncles of these, and they had dressed in sober, poorly cut suits of serge and gabardine. Like the previous generation, these men had the badges of their profession, the heavy hands with stiff enormous thumbs and the white foreheads above sunburnt faces, but Duane's was the only suit among them. The rest wore sport shirts and casual slacks. Walking toward them, I felt absurdly over-dressed and urban.

One of them noticed me, and his cigarette had frozen in mid-arc to his mouth. He muttered to the man beside him, and I could read the three syllables of Teagarden on his lips.

When I reached the concrete walk to the church steps, I here and there recognized a face, and greeted the first of these. "Good morning, Mr. Korte," I said to a squat bulldog-like man with a crewcut and heavy black glasses. Bud Korte owned a farm a mile or two down the valley from the Updahl land. He and my father had often gone fishing together.

"Miles," he said, and then his eyes shot wildly away toward the cigarette he was pinching between two fingers the size of small bananas. "Howdy." He was as embarrassed as a bishop just greeted familiarly by a hooker. "Heard you was back." The eyes shot away again, and landed with painful relief on Dave Eberud, another farmer I recognized, now looking in his horizontally-striped shirt and plaid trousers as if his mother had dressed him in too much haste. Eberud's snapping turtle face, twisted slightly in our direction, snapped forward. "Gotta have a word with Dave," said Bud Korte, and left me examining the shine on my shoes.

Duane, in his double-breasted suit, its jacket unbuttoned to reveal wide red braces, stood halfway up the church steps; his posture, one foot aggressively planted on a higher step, his shoulders brought forward, plainly said that he did not want to acknowledge me, but I moved toward him through men who drew together as I passed.

When I began to go up the steps I could hear his voice. ". . . the last auction. How can I wait it out? If beef goes down below twenty-seven a pound, I'm through. I can't raise all my own feed, even now with that new land, and that old M I got is fallin' apart." Looming heavily beside him was Red Sunderson, who stared at me, not even bothering to pretend to listen to Duane's complaints. In the sunlight, Sunderson looked younger and tougher than he had at night. His face was a flat angry plane of chipped angles.

He said, "We're mighty fancy today, Miles."

Duane irritably glanced at me, and then shifted his cocked leg. The sunburnt part of his face was unnaturally red. "I considered we might see you here sometime." But it's too late now, his tone said.

"I said, we're mighty fancy today."

"It's all I brought with me besides jeans," I said.

"Ma says you finished playing with that old furniture."

Duane made a disgusted, angry sound with his lips. Behind me, a man drew in a hissing breath like a secret laugh.

"What's an old M?" I asked.

Duane's face became a deeper shade of red. "A goddamned tractor. A god-damned tractor with a busted gearbox, if you wanta know. Since you're through wrecking my furniture, maybe you'd like to junk up my tractors too, huh?"

"Been in the woods lately, Teagarden?" asked Red Sunderson. "Been gettin' any up in the woods?"

"What's that about the woods?" asked my cousin.

Red was still staring at me from his flat chipped face incongruously mounted with his mother's blobby nose.

Some tribal signal was drawing the men at the bottom toward the steps; at first I thought they were coming for me, but when the first shouldered past without looking at me, I knew that the services were about to begin, and it was time to rejoin the women. Red turned away as if he could no longer bear to look at me, and I was left with red-faced furious Duane. I said, "I have to talk to you about something. About Alison Greening." "Hell," he uttered, and then, "Don't you sit with me, Miles," and stomped up the stairs with his friends.

I could hear them whispering as I followed them into the church. By either gossip or telepathy, they all knew who would be the last man to enter the building, and the women were all craning their necks to look at me. On several of their plain country faces, I caught expressions of horror. Duane went his shovel-handed way down to the right aisle. I went to the left, already sweating through the tailored shirt.

Halfway up toward the front I slid into a pew and sat down. I could feel their faces pointing at me, white and red, and tilted my head back and examined the familiar interior. White arched wooden ceiling, white chaste walls, four stained-glass windows on either side with Norwegian names at the bottoms: in memory of Gunnar and Joron Gunderson, in memory of Einar and Florence Weverstad, in memory of Emma Jahr. Up in Bertilsson's sanctuary behind the altar, a huge sentimental painting of Jesus anointing St. John. A white bird like one of the town hall pigeons hovered above the pale symmetrical face.

When Bertilsson popped like a figure on a German clock through his entrance at the front of the church, he unerringly looked at me first. The telepathy had reached him too. After that, much standing up and sitting down, much responsive reading, much singing. A wizened woman in a purple dress gave abrupt, unmusical accompaniment on a small organ. Bertilsson kept watching me with oily eyes: he seemed to brim with a generalized emotion. His ears were very red. The four or five other people in my pew had moved farther and farther away from me, taking advantage of all the standing and sitting to shift a few inches each time.

My shirt felt like paper about to shred; a fly buzzed angrily, obsessively, somewhere up near the ceiling; whenever I leaned back, I stuck to the wood of the pew. Above the blond wood of the pew before me protruded a boy's vacant face, regarding me with dull eyes and open mouth. A drop of saliva hung on the full part of his lower lip.

After "O God Our Help in Ages Past" Bertilsson motioned for us to sit, using the gesture with which an actor silences applause, and moved to the pulpit. Once there, he deliberately removed a handkerchief from his sleeve, dabbed his shiny forehead, and replaced it. More time-wasting while extracting his sheaf of notes from within his loose garments. All this time, he was looking directly at me.

"The text for the day," he said, his voice light and confidential, "is James II, verses one to five. 'My brethren, have not the faith of our Lord Jesus Christ, the Lord of glory, with respect to persons. For if there come into your assembly a man with a gold ring, in goodly apparel, and there come in also a poor man in vile raiment . . .' "

I tuned him out and let my head fall forward, wishing that I had not taken Polar Bears' advice. What good could come of this? Then I was needled by a sharp awareness that Polar Bears had told me something far more important—a fact that connected to another fact. It was like a thorn in my side, nagging at me. I tried to go over the conversations I'd had with Hovre, but Bertilsson's sermon kept breaking in.

He had managed to wrestle the Good Samaritan into James II, I noticed, quite a feat even for someone as glib as Bertilsson. It seems the Samaritan was not a superficial respector of persons. "But this works in reverse, my friends." I looked up at his odious, glistening moonface and silently groaned. He was still fixing

me with his eyes. "Yes, my friends, we must not con-
demn the Samaritan to seeing but one side of the coin."
I closed my eyes.

Bertilsson rolled on inexorably, and it was only his
pauses while he rummaged for the ripest vocabulary that
told me he was improvising. I looked up and saw him
folding his notes, unconsciously making them into neat
square packages with sharp edges. The boy before me
permitted his chin to drop even further.

Then I realized what Bertilsson was going to do,
and he did it while I witnessed the malice leaking
from the glistening eyes and the rolling voice. "Is not
there one among us in fine raiment, one who cannot
hide his anguish beneath fine clothing? Is not there one
among us needful of the Samaritan's touch? A man in
pain? Brethren, we have with us a man sorely troubled,
who imagines life not God's gift, as we know it to be.
A sparrow's life, a child's life, all are precious to Him.
I speak of a man whose whole soul is a cry of pain, a
cry to God for release. A sick man, my brethren, a
man sorely ill. My friends, a man in need of our Christian love . . ."

It was unbearable. The fly still angrily thrummed
against the ceiling, wanting out. I stood up, stepped
out of the pew, and turned my back on Bertilsson. I
could hear the glee in his voice, far below the message of love. I wanted to be up in the woods, holding
my hands above the warmth of an ember. A woman
began to chatter like a bird. I felt shock radiate between
the white walls. Bertilsson rolled on, calling for my
blood. I walked down the side aisle, going as quickly
as I could. At the front of the church I swung open the
big door and stepped outside. I could sense them all
twisting their necks, looking at me. A vision of fish.

Back across the gravel to the ugly little car, and
home in sweltering sunlight. I yanked off my jacket and
threw it into the back seat. I wanted to be naked, I
wanted to feel mulch and pine needles beneath the soles
of my feet. Halfway to the farmhouse on the valley
road, I began to shout.

Eight

As I went across the lawn toward the house I could hear the stereo going. Someone was playing the song "I'm Beginning to See the Light" on the Gerry Mulligan record. My anger at Bertilsson's inspiration left me all at once: I felt tired, hot, directionless. The smell of bacon cooking drifted toward me with the sound of Chet Baker's trumpet. I came up onto the screen porch and felt suddenly cooler.

Alison Updahl, chewing on something and dressed in her uniform, appeared in the doorway of the kitchen. Her T shirt was pale blue. "Where were you, Miles?" I just went past her. When I reached the old bamboo couch I collapsed into it, making its joints creak and sing. "Would you mind if I turned off the music? I don't think I can listen to it now."

"You don't mind my—" She pointed to the turntable and lifted her shoulders.

"Not enough to actually object," I said. I leaned over and lifted the tone arm with trembling fingers.

"Hey, you were in church," she said grinning a little. She had noticed my necktie and striped trousers. "I like you in those clothes. You look sort of classy and oldfashioned. But isn't it early for church to be out?"

"Yes."

"What did you go there for anyway? I don't think they want you there."

I nodded.

"They think you tried to kill yourself."

"That's not all they think."

"Don't let them bug you. You and old man Hovre are in real good, aren't you? Didn't he invite you to his house?"

The bush telegraph. "How do you know that? Did I tell you?"

"Everybody knows that, Miles." I sagged back into the couch. "Hey, it doesn't mean anything. Not really. They just talk." She was trying to lift my mood. "It doesn't mean anything."

"Okay," I said. "Thanks for the positive thinking. Did you come over just to play the records?"

"You were going to meet me, remember?" She pulled her shoulders back, smiling at me, and put her hands in the small of her back. If the clothing she wore had seams, they were straining. Her blood smell hovered between us, neither increasing nor decreasing. "Come on. We're going on an adventure. Zack wants to talk to you."

"Women would make great generals," I said and followed her back outside.

Minutes later I was driving past the church. The sound of singing carried all the way to the road. She looked at the cars in the parking spaces, stared at the church, and then turned to look at me with genuine astonishment. "You left early? You walked out?"

"What does it look like?"

"In front of everybody? Did they see?"

"Every single one of them." I loosened the knot of my tie.

She laughed out loud. "Miles, you're a real cowboy." Then she laughed some more. It was a pleasant, human sound.

"Your pastor seems to think I'm a sex murderer. He was shouting for the noose."

Her high approving good humor suddenly died. "Not

you not you," she said, almost crooning. She twisted her legs up beneath her. Then she was silent for a long time.

"Where are we going?"

"One of our places." Her voice was flat. "You shouldn't have gone. It just makes them think you're trying to trick them somehow."

It was better advice than Polar Bears', but it was too late. She let herself slump over so that her head rested on my shoulder.

I had undergone too many swift alterations and swings of feeling, and this gesture nearly made me weep. Her head stayed on my shoulder as we drove toward Arden through the rising, sun-browned hills. I was looking forward to seeing her march into Freebo's as though beneath her sandaled feet were not wooden boards but a red carpet. This time, I considered, we would both need the mysterious protection of "who Zack was" to get into Freebo's.

Yet it was not Freebo's to which she was taking me. A mile outside of Arden we approached a juncture I had not yet permitted myself to notice, and she straightened up and said "Slow down."

I glanced at her. Her head was turning, showing her blunt profile beneath the choppy blond fringe of hair. "Left here."

I slowed the Nash to a crawl. "Why here?"

"Because no one ever comes here. What's wrong with it?"

Everything was wrong with it. It was the worst place in the world.

"I'm not going up there," I said.

"Why? It's just the old Pohlson quarry. There's nothing wrong with it." She looked at me, her face concentrated. "Oh. I think I know why. Because it's where my aunt Alison died. The one I was named after."

I was sweating.

"Those are her pictures in your upstairs room, right? Do you think I look like her?"

"No," I breathed. "Not really."

"She was bad, wasn't she?" I could sense her heating up again, pumping out that odor. I stopped the car. Alison said, "She was like you. She was too freaky for the people around here."

"I suppose." My mind was working.

"You in a trance or something?" She biffed my shoulder. "Get out of it. Turn up. Turn up the path."

"I want to try something. An experiment." I told her what I wanted her to do.

"You promise you'll come up afterwards? You won't just drive away? It's not a trick?"

"I promise to come up afterward," I said. "I'll give you five minutes." I leaned across and opened her door. She crossed the deserted road and began to march stiffly up the track to the quarry.

For two or three minutes I waited in the heat of the car, looking unseeing down the highway. A wasp flew in, all business, and bumped his head against the windshield several times before losing his temper and zooming by accident out the window on the other side. A long way down the highway a broiler farm occupied the fields to the left, and specks of white which were chickens/ moved jerkily over the green in the sunlight. I looked up toward a flat blue sky. I heard nothing but the mindless twitter of a bird.

When I got out of the car and stood on the sticky tar of the highway I thought I could hear a faint voice calling; if it was a voice, it seemed indistinguishable from the landscape, coming from nowhere in particular; it could have been a breeze. I got back in the car and drove up the track to the quarry.

The day I had returned to the Updahl farm I had expected a surge of feeling, but experienced only flatness and disappointment; the act of stepping out into the terrific heat of the flat grassy area near the quarry hit me with an only half-anticipated force. I anchored myself in the present by placing the palm of my right hand on the baking metal of the top of the Nash. It all looked very much the same. The grass was browner, because of the summer's dry heat, and the outcroppings of speckled rock appeared more jagged and prominent. I saw the same flat gray space where the workmen's sheds had stood. The screen of bushes above the quarry itself had grown spindly, the small leaves like brush-strokes, dry and brown, papery. Drawn up nearer to them than my car was a dusty black van. I pulled my hand off the hot metal of the car and walked on the path through the bushes to the rocky steps down to the lip of the quarry.

They were both there. Alison sat with her feet in the water, looking up at me with expectant curiosity. Zack, a bisected white exclamation point in his black bathing suit, was grinning, snapping his fingers. "It's the man," he said. "It's my main man."

"Did you shout?"

Zack giggled. "Wowee." *Snap-snap* of his fingers.

"Did I shout? I screamed my head off!"

"How long?"

"A couple of minutes. Couldn't you hear?"

"I don't think so," I said. "You screamed as loud as you could?"

"I'm practically hoarse," she answered. "If I yelled any longer, I would have ripped something."

Zack bent his legs and sat down on the black pile of his clothing. "It's the truth, man. She really hollered. What's it about, anyhow? What's your stunt?"

"No stunt," I said. "Just finding out about an old lie."

"You're too hung up on the past, Miles." His grin grew more intense. "Jesus, man, look at those clothes. What kind of clothes are those for a swim?"

"I didn't know I was going swimming."

"What else do you do at a quarry?"

I sat down with my legs before me on the smooth hot lip of rock. I looked up at the bushes overhead. They would have been hidden up there, waiting to jump down. That was where they had been. I wanted to be anywhere but where I was. I could smell the water and it was Alison's smell.

"I haven't been here for twenty years," I said. "I don't know what you do here."

"It's a great place to groove on ideas," Zack said, stretched out whitely in the sun. His ribs showed under the skin like sticks and his arms and legs were skinny and covered with thin black hair. His body looked obscene, spidery. Beneath the black strip of bathing suit lay a prominent sexual bulge. "I thought it was time we saw each other again." He spoke like a general summoning his adjutant. "I had to thank you for the books."

"That's okay," I said. I removed my tie and dropped it and the jacket I had been carrying by my side. Then I pulled my shirt out of my trousers and unbuttoned it halfway down to let air enter.

"Miles went to church," Alison said from the quarry's edge. "Old Bertilsson preached about him again."

"*Hah hah hah!*" Zack exploded with laughter. "That old fart. He oughta be making shitty little doilies, hey? He's a feeb. I hate that sucker, man. So he thinks you're the Masked Marauder, huh?"

Alison asked, "Did you bring towels?"

"Hey? Sure I brought towels. Can't go swimming without towels. Brought three of them.' Zack rolled over on his belly and examined me. "Is that right? Am I right about him, my main man?"

"More or less." It was too hot for my heavy shoes, and I unlaced them and pulled them off.

The Woodsman said, 'Well, if you brought towels, I'm sure going to swim. My throat hurts from all that yelling.' She looked over her shoulder at Zack, who indulgently flipped his hand in a do-what-you-want gesture.

"I'm gonna go skinny," she said, and glanced at me. She still had not got over her desire to shock.

"You can't scare him, he's the Masked Marauder," said Zack.

She stood up, displeased, leaving dark high-arched footprints on the stone, and pulled the blue shirt over her head. Her breasts lolled large and pink against her chest. She pushed her jeans down unceremoniously, revealing all of her stocky well-shaped little body.

"If you're the Masked Marauder, haven't you been busy lately?" asked Zack.

I watched Alison go padding to the edge of the quarry and stand, judging the water for a moment. She wanted to get away from us.

"That's not actually funny," I said.

She raised her arms and then used her leg muscles to spring out into the water in a clean dive. When her head broke water, she began to breast-stroke across the quarry.

"Well, what about that guy, anyhow?"

"What guy?" For a moment my mind blurred and I thought he meant Alison Updahl.

"The killer." He was lying on his side, gleeful. He seemed to be supercharged with sly, flinty enthusiasm, as if secrets were bubbling inside him. His eyes, very large now, appeared to be chiefly pupil. "He kinda turns me on. He's done something else, you know, something most people don't know about yet."

"Oh?" If that were widely known, Polar Bears' strategy was a failure.

"Don't you see the beauty of that? Man, that D. H. Lawrence would have. The guy who wrote those books. I been reading those books. There's a lot in them."

"I don't think Lawrence ever sympathized with sex killers."

"Are you sure? Are you really sure? What if a killer was on the side of life? Hey? See, I looked at that *Women in Love* book—I didn't read all of it, I just read the parts you underlined. I wanted to get inside you, man."

"Oh, yes." It was an appalling notion.

"Doesn't he talk about beetles? That some people are beetles? Who should be killed? You gotta live according to your ideas, don't you? Take the idea of pain. Pain is a tool. Pain is a tool for release."

"Why don't you stop talking and come in and swim?"

Alison called from the center of the quarry. Sweat poured down my face.

Zack's intense black eyes focused unblinkingly on me. "Take your shirt off," he said.

"I guess I will," I said, and unbuttoned it the rest of the way and dropped it on top of my jacket.

"Don't you think the people who are just stupid beetles should be killed? That's why I dig this guy. He just goes out and does it."

We had left Lawrence a long way behind, but I wanted only to let him rant, so that he would be done earlier. "Has there been another one? Another murder?"

"I don't know, man, but answer me this. Why would he fuckin' stop?"

I nodded. Suddenly all I wanted was to be in the water, to feel the quarry's cold water about me again.

"Maybe my favorite part of the book was about blood-brotherhood," Zack said. "I dug that nude wrestling part between two men. You underlined almost all of that."

"I suppose I might have," I said, but he had switched gears again.

"He's free, you see, whoever this guy is, he's free as hell. Nobody's gonna stop him. He's thrown out all of the old shit holding him back. And if he thought anybody was gonna stand in his way, bang, he'd get rid of him."

This conversation was reminding me uneasily of my afternoon with Paul Kant; it was even worse. Where Paul Kant had been low-voiced and depressed, this skinny boy was simply shivering with conviction.

"Like Hitler did to Roehm. Roehm was in his way, and he just smashed him with his foot. The Night of the Long Knives. Bang. Another beetle dead. You see the beauty in that?"

"No," I said. "There isn't any." I had to get away from him, and when Alison shouted to us again, I said, "It's too hot for this. I think I'll swim a little."

"You gonna skinny-dip?" His mad eyes were taunting me.

"Why not?" I said, irritated, and shucked the rest of my clothing. Infuriatingly, Zack stood when I did, and slithered out of his skimpy black bathing suit. We dove into the water together. I felt more than saw the Woodsman watching us from the center of the pool.

The water hit me like an electric jolt. The memories of the last time I had been in the quarry hit me too, with an even greater force, and I could see her as I had seen her then, her hands and feet flashing. Then I recognized that I was seeing not *my* Alison, but my cousin's daughter, an altogether more adult female form. Underwater, I frog-kicked away, wanting to experience the rush of emotion away from the other two. It was like a clamp around my chest, and for a moment, fleeing the legs dangling in the water, I thought I would be killed by my own emotion. My heart fluttered, and I kicked away for another second and then surfaced, breathing noisily.

Zack's grinning face was four feet away, looking absurdly young beneath his streaming black hair. His eyes seemed to have no white at all. He said something inaudible, choked by his own pleasure.

Then he repeated it. "This is where it happened, isn't it, Miles?" He was exuding crazy glee.

"What?" I said, my stomach frozen.

"You and Alison's aunt. Hey?" His mouth was lifted in a loose insane smile.

I turned away and began to swim as strongly as I could toward the lip of the quarry. His voice was calling, but not to me.

Water was thrashing behind me. Now he was calling to me. "You don't talk, do you? You don't talk, do you?" His voice was loud and brutal.

Eight feet from safety I felt a hand catch my ankle. When I kicked out with my free leg, another hand grasped my calf, and then I was yanked backward and down. While two hands held my legs, other hands pushed my shoulders, and I felt a heavy body riding my back, beginning to squeeze my chest. The one on top leaned forward to wrap arms around my neck, and cushiony breasts pressed against me. I bucked underwater, but she clamped me with greater force, expelling the rest of the air from my lungs. Games, I thought, and breast-stroked, thinking that my breath would outlast hers. Zack still clung to my ankles. I kicked idly, resolved not to give them the satisfaction of a struggle. Then I realized that she was close enough to the surface to raise her head and breathe, and a spurt of fear made me fight.

I shook violently, but she forced me deeper into the tunnel of water. The hands on my legs let go, and I knew that Zack too was going up to breathe. My chest fought for air. In moments, Zack appeared before me under the water and raised his arms to my shoulders. I swung at him, but the blow was ridiculously slowed by the water. He dug his fingers into my shoulders and held me helpless, prone in the water. Astride me, the Woodsman squeezed and squeezed.

If I had been alone with the Woodsman, I could have thrown or pulled her off, but while Zack held me and pinned my arms, I could do nothing but struggle, making my air problem worse. As I grew weaker, Zack moved in nearer and put his hands on the small of my back, pulling me down even further. I realized with shock and horror that he was erect when a fleshy club bumped my hip.

In the next instant I breathed in a gulp of burning water, and I knew that they were going to kill me.

Then their hands and arms fell away, the weight of Alison rolled off my back, and I was helped to the surface.

I held to the rock edge of the quarry, coughing painfully. Water came up like vomit. Getting out of the quarry was impossible; I clung with my weak arms and my head lolled against my shoulder. After a moment I could lever myself up far enough so that my forearms were flat on the hot stone, and I bent my head to rest on them. Through half-opened eyes, not really recogniz-

ing what I saw, I noticed Zack sliding out of the water
and up onto rock as easily as an eel. Then he bent
down and braced himself to take the arm of the naked
girl. That bastard nearly killed me and it turned him
on, I thought, and an emotion half fear and half anger
gave me the energy to struggle up onto the edge of
stone. I lay in the sun, shivering, my skin burning where
it touched the hot smooth rock.

He sat down beside me. I saw only a spidery flank
with thin black hairs streaming across white skin. "Hey,
Miles. Hey, man. You okay?"

I rolled away, onto my back. The hot stone seared
me. I closed my eyes, still coughing. When I opened
my eyes, they were blocking the sun, standing above
me. They were black against the flat blue sky. Alison
knelt to cradle my head. "Let me alone," I said. I
wriggled away. "Did you plan that?"

"It was just fun, Miles," he said. "We were playing."

"Poor old Miles, he 'most drowned," crooned Alison,
and came toward me again and pushed herself against
me. I was engulfed in cool wet skin. Involuntarily, I
looked at Zack. "I'm sorry, man," he said, unselfcon-
sciously manipulating his testicles. I turned my eyes
away and found myself staring at Alison's soft heavy
breasts and firm belly. "Give me a towel," I ordered.
Zack stepped away toward the pile of clothing.

Alison brought her face closer to mine. "This is
where it happened, isn't it? You can tell Zack. You
could tell him anything. That's why he wanted to meet
you here. He heard about it at Freebo's. That's why
he knows you understand him. He wants you to be
brothers. Didn't you hear what he was saying before?"

I fought to stand up, and after a moment she released
me. Zack was coming toward me, a pink towel in one
hand. The other hand held an open switchblade. I
stepped backwards.

When Zack saw what must have been in my face,
he tossed me the towel and said, "Hey, man. I want
to help you take off the bandage. It's not doing you
any good any more."

After knotting the towel around my waist, I looked at my left hand. It was caught in a soggy limp mass of gauze, a webby useless thing already half off my palm. Zack took my hand in his and before I had time to push him away, neatly sliced the mess of gauze away from my palm. Then he ripped away the tape in one quick motion.

Above the base of my thumb was a reddish triangle of new skin, defined by a thin red line on all three sides. I gingerly touched the spot with incurling fingers. It was delicate, but it had healed. Zack threw the drowned package of tape and gauze up into the bushes. I looked at him and his eyes were crazy and gleeful. His face was very young, framed by long smooth Indian's hair.

"You're my best friend," he said. He held out his left palm, and the image of him as a thin dead-white Indian lurched into stronger focus in my mind. He stood there, skinny, his ribs thrusting beneath his skin, dripping, dangling, armored in loony radiance. His dog's eyes filled with shining light. "I'll prove it to you, Miles. We can be brothers." He raised the switchblade like a scalpel and deliberately sliced his left palm. Then he dropped the blade and continued to hold his palm out toward me, inviting me to press mine against it. Alison screamed when she looked up at the sound of the knife clattering and saw blood dripping onto the flat rock.

"Miles!" she screeched. "Go to the truck! Get the bandages! Go!"

Zack's face did not alter by a millimeter: he was still encased in the armor of crazy light. "You did it," I said, still grasping the dimensions of what I had seen. "It's you."

"Miles," Alison sobbed, "run, run, please run."

Zack stood shining at me with dog's eyes and loose smile. To escape the light of the smile I ran around him, around the Tin Woodsman who was rushing toward Zack, and sprinted in bare feet and flapping towel up to the black van.

When I yanked down on the handle of the rear doors

and pushed them open, something that had been wedged against one of them fell out into the dust. I looked down and saw a familiar shape just ceasing to roll. It was one of the old wide-hipped eight-ounce Coke bottles.

"What did you do that for?" she asked, still naked, the water dried by the sun from all but her darkened hair, as the paperback of *She* began to sink into the water of the quarry. I was conscious of Zack behind us, standing near his dropped knife on the hot stone, and I was aware of having too many reasons to be able to roll them up into a single answer. I was sending a chip of Alison into the place where she had died; I was furious with them both and with myself for not knowing how to reckon with what I suspected, the sight of the Coke bottle having brought back clearly what Polar Bears Hovre had told me; I was simply overcome with anger and disgust and throwing away something I valued was the simplest way to express that I had looked into the face of damnation. When I had crawled into the back of the van, I had seen, glittering amidst the rubble of spare parts, one of the thousand-faceted doorknobs I had removed from my desk.

"Get away from him," Zack said. "Ally, get your ass over here."

"Why?"

"Alison," I said softly, "Zack is in trouble. I think you should keep away from him."

"You don't understand him. Nobody does."

"Just take my advice," I said, "please," very aware in spite of everything of the Maillol-like body of the naked girl I was bending toward.

That night and the next I dreamed of being back in the drifting blue horror, suspended, dead, guilty beyond the possibility of help or forgiveness. It was the quarry, the deep pitiless water of the quarry, and it was where I had let her die, the greatest sin of my life, the one before which I had been most helpless, and the greatest crime I knew. The crime for which she could not forgive me. Even in sleep I believe I wept and ground my teeth. They had been up there, and I had not been able to send them away, those murderers of both her life and mine. It was a bottomless guilt. I would be freed of it only by her return. I had twice immersed myself in the cold water of the quarry, twice I had breathed it in, and both times I had emerged alive: that too was a crime, when she had not.

Sunday night I came miserably awake near two o'clock, smelled the air like a forest animal, and got downstairs in time to turn off the gas cocks on the stove. The recurrence seemed to prove that the cause was a simple mechanical failure, if one that could have had fatal results. What had awakened me, and therefore saved me, was the ringing of the telephone. I had once told Alison that if I got one of "those" calls at night, I would not answer it. But after twisting the handles on the stove and shoving open a window to admit the cool meadow air, I was in the perfect mood for handling Onion Breath. "Stinking skulking creeping weasel," I pronounced into the phone, "crawling cowardly weak crippled ugly snake." Incapable of syntax but with a good stock of adjectives, I went on until he (she) hung up. I could not then return to bed and that dominating nightmare. The kitchen was very cold; I waved newspapers to dispel the gas, and closed the window. After wrapping a blanket from the downstairs bedroom around my shoulders, I returned to the kitchen, lit a kerosene lamp and a cigarette, and combined some further elements of the Alison-environment, gin, vermouth, twist of lemon peel, ice. Her drink, with which I had been dosing myself nightly. Wrapped in the blanket, I sipped the martini and sat in one of the kitchen chairs near the telephone. I *wanted* another call.

Half an hour later, when the person might have judged me to have returned to sleep (I thought), the telephone rang again. I let it trill three, then four times, then twice more, hearing the noise of the bell spread through the cold farmhouse. Finally I raised my arm and detached the receiver and rose to speak into the horn. But instead of breathing I heard what I had heard once before, a whuffling, beating noise, inhuman, like wings thrashing in the air, and the receiver was as cold as the sweating glass of my martini and I was unable to utter a word, my tongue would not move. I dropped the icy receiver and wrapped the blanket tightly around myself and went upstairs to lie on the bed. The next night, as I have said, following the day which was the first turning point, I entered the same drifting guilt-ridden dream, but I had no anonymous calls, from either living or dead.

On the day—Monday—which marked my slide into knowledge and was the interregnum between these two awful nights, I came down from my work for lunch and asked a stony-faced Tuta Sunderson how to turn off the gas before it reached the stove. She became even more disapproving, and gruntingly bent over the range and pointed an obese finger down at the pipe descending from the wall. "It's on this pipe. What for?"

"So I can turn it off at night."

"Ain't fooling me," she muttered, or I thought she did, while she turned away to jam her hands into the pockets of her cardigan. More audibly, she said, "Made a big stir in church yesterday."

"I wasn't there to notice. I trust things went well without me." I bit into a hamburger and discovered that I had no appetite. My relationship with Tuta Sunderson had degenerated into a parody of my marriage.

"You afraid of what the pastor was saying?"

"As I recall he made a very sweet comment about my suit," I said.

As she began to lump herself toward the door, I said, "Wait. What do you know about a boy named Zack? He lives somewhere in Arden, I think. Tall and skinny, with an Elvis Presley hairdo. Alison's boyfriend. He calls her 'Ally.' "

"I don't know that boy. If you're going to waste good food, get out of the kitchen so I can do my work."

"Good God," I said, and left the table to stand on the porch. That cold breath of spirit which could only be felt on these twenty square yards was strongly present, and I knew with a certainty for once filled not with joy but resignation that Alison would appear on the date she had set twenty years before. Her release would be mine, I told myself. Only later did I recognize that when Tuta Sunderson said that she did not know that boy, she meant not that the boy was a stranger to her, but that she knew him well and detested him.

Yet if my release were to be total there were things I needed to know, and a series of bangs and clatters from the long aluminum rectangle of the pole barn suggested an opportunity for learning them. I left Tuta Sunderson's complaining voice behind me and stepped off the porch and began to walk through the sunshine toward the path.

The noises increased as I drew nearer, and eventually the sound of Duane grunting with effort joined them. I threaded through the litter of rusting parts and junked equipment at the pole barn's front end and walked onto the packed powdery brown dust which is the barn's only floor. Under the high tented metal roof, Duane was working in semi-dark, slamming a wrench on the base of a tractor's gearshift. His peaked cap had been thrown off earlier, and lay in the dust near his boots.

"Duane," I said.

He could not hear. The deafness may have been as much internal as caused by the terrific banging clatter he was making, for his face was set into that frustrated angry mask common to men who are singlemindedly, impatiently, making a botch of a job.

I said it again, and his head twisted toward me. As I stepped toward him, he turned his face away silently and went back to banging on the base of the gearshift.

"Duane, I have to talk with you."

"Get out of here. Just get the hell out." He still

would not look at me. The hammering with the wrench became more frenzied.

I continued to come toward him. His arm was a blur, and the noise echoed against the metal walls. "God damn," he breathed after I had taken a half-dozen steps, "I got the son of a bitch off."

"What's wrong?" I asked.

"The god-damned gearbox, if you really wanna know," he said, scowling at me. His tan shirt was stained irregularly with perspiration and a black smear of grease bisected his forehead at the white line where his cap stuck. "It's jammed in first, and on these old Ms you gotta go in from the top here and slide a couple of plates around to get the slots lined up, see, but what the hell am I talking about this with you for anyhow? You wouldn't know a gearbox if you saw it outside of Shakespeare."

"Probably not."

"Anyhow, on this one here, I have to take off the whole shift mechanism because everything's rusted shut, but in order to do that, you have to get the nuts off first, see?"

"I think so."

"And then I'll probably find out the battery's dead anyhow, and my jumper cables got burned to shit the last time I used them on the pickup and the plastic melted all over the terminals, so it probably won't work anyhow."

"But at least you got the nuts off."

"Yeah. So why don't you go break up some more furniture or something and leave me work?" He jumped up on the side of the tractor and began to twiddle the burring on the wrench down to the size of the nut.

"I have to talk with you about some things."

"We don't have anything to talk about. After that act of yours in church, nobody around here has anything to talk with you about." He glared down at me. "At least not for the present."

I stood and watched as he removed the troublesome nut, dropped it on a greasy sheet of newspaper by the tractor's rear wheels, and, grunting on the seat, lifted the shift levers and an attached plate up out of the body of the machine. Then he bent down and knelt before the seat. "Shit."

"What's wrong?"

"It's all grease in there, and I can't see the slots, that's what's wrong." His pudgy face revolved toward me again. "And after I fix this damn thing, the same thing will happen next week, and I'll have to do it all over again." He began to scrape oily sludge out with the point of a long screwdriver. "Shouldn't even be grease like that in here." He impatiently took a rag from the hip pocket of his coveralls and began to work it around in the hole he had opened up.

"I want to ask you about—" I was going to say, about Zack, but he interrupted me.

"Not what you said at the church. There's nothing to say about that."

"Alison Greening?"

His face hardened.

"You never slept with her, did you?" Looking at him kneeling like a squat filthy toad on the tractor, it seemed an impossibility. He began to scrub harder, his face frozen. "Did you?"

"Yeah. Okay." He plucked the rag out and threw it aside. "So what if I did? I didn't hurt anybody. Except myself, I guess. That little whore treated it like it was a new comic book or something. And she only did it once. Whenever I wanted to do it afterwards, she laughed at me." He looked at me, hard. "You were the golden boy, anyhow. What do you care? She made me feel like shit. She liked making me feel like shit."

"Then why did you name your daughter after her?"

He began to tug at something within the body of the tractor. He was trembling.

Of course. I had known it yesterday, when I had looked up at the dying bushes and seen a white shirt flitting in memory between them. "You followed us out to the quarry, didn't you? I know that that story about the driver hearing screams was a lie. I proved that you can't hear screams from up there down on the road."

His face, even the white parts, was turning red.

"So someone else was there, someone surprised us. It was you. Then you ran away and called the police when you knew she was dead."

"No. No." He slammed his fist into the tractor's seat, making a million small metal parts jangle. "Goddam you, you had to come back here, didn't you? You and your stories."

"Twenty years ago, somebody told a story all right. And has been telling it ever since."

"Wait." He glared at me, his face still massively red. "Who told you about me and Alison, anyhow?" I did not speak, and saw comprehension battle fury in his face.

"You know who told me. The only person you told. Polar Bears."

"What else did Hovre say?"

"That you hated her. But I knew that. I just didn't understand the reason."

Then he said too much. "Hovre talked about her?"

"Not really," I said. "He just let it slip that . . ." I looked at Duane's face, full of sly questions and frightened questions, and I understood. Understood at least part of it. I heard the cough from one side of the quarry's top, the whistle from the other.

"You try to go and prove anything," Duane said. "You can't prove a thing."

"Polar Bears was with you," I said, almost not believing it. "Both of you came to the quarry. And you both jumped us. You both wanted her. I can remember Polar Bears coming around day after day, staring at her . . ."

"I gotta fix my tractor. You get the hell out."

"And everybody up here thinks it was me. Even my wife thought it was me."

Duane stolidly replaced the gear levers and plate and started to tighten the nuts. He looked shaken, and he would not meet my eyes. "You better talk to Hovre," he said. "I ain't sayin' no more."

I felt, in the big dim dusty interior of the pole barn, as I had when the Woodsman and Zack had held me under water, and I made it to an oil drum before my legs gave out. Duane was not bright enough to be a good liar, and his stolid stupid refusal to talk was as good as a confession. "Jesus," I breathed, and heard my voice tremble.

Duane had opened up the engine of the tractor; his back was to me. His ears flamed. As in the Plainview diner, I could sense violence gathering between us. At the same time, I was aware of the force with which sensory impressions were packing into my mind, and I clung to them for sanity: the big dim space open at either end, the thick powder of brown dust on the floor, fluffy and grainy at once, the litter of machinery lying around, discs and harrows and things I could not identify, most of it in need of paint, with rusty edges; in a corner, the high tractor; a sparrow darting through as I sat on the oil drum; my throat constricted and my hands shaking and my chest inflamed; the searing metal walls and high empty space above us, as though for a jury of observers; the man in front of me, hitting something deep inside the smaller tractor he was bent before, sweat darkening his shirt, dirt and grease all over his coveralls and the smell of gunpowder overtaking all other odors. The knowledge that I was looking at Alison's murderer.

"It's crazy," I said. "I didn't even come here to talk to you about this. Not really."

He dropped the wrench and leaned forward on the tractor's engine block, supporting himself with his arms.

"And it doesn't matter any more," I said. "Soon it won't matter any more at all."

He would not move.

"God, this is strange," I said. "I really came here to talk to you about Zack. When you brought up the other thing I thought I'd ask you about what Polar

Bears said . . ." He pushed himself back from the tractor and for the space of a taut second I thought he
would come for me. But he went to the side of the barn
and returned with a hammer. And began to pound
savagely, as if he did not care what he was battering
or saw something besides the tractor beneath the hammer.

From down the path at my grandmother's house I
faintly heard a screen door slam. Tuta Sunderson was
going home.

Duane heard it too, and the sound seemed to release
him. "All right, you son of a bitch, ask me about Zack.
Hey? Ask me about him." He gave the tractor a
thwacking, ringing blow with the hammer.

He turned to face me at last, his feet stirring up dust
like smoke. His face was inflamed and explosive. "What
do you want to know about that no good bastard? He's
as crazy as you are."

I heard the calls and whistles of that terrible night,
saw the white shirt flitting behind the screen of bushes,
heard the coughing of a boy hidden behind those
bushes. As they watched with the hunger of twenty-
year-old manhood the naked girl flashing like a star in
the black water. The quick, quiet removal of clothes,
the leap upon her and the boy. Then knocking him out
before he even saw what had happened and hauling up
his body onto the rock shelf before turning to the girl.

"Do you want to know what's funny about people
like you, Miles?" Duane half-screamed. "You always
think that what you want to talk about is important.
You think that what you want to say is like some kind
of god-damned present—huh?—to people like me. You
think people like me are just goons, don't you, Miles?"
He spat thickly into the dust and gave the tractor another ringing blow. "I hate you god-damned professors,
Miles. You fucking writers. You people with your fifty-
cent words and your 'What I wanted to say was really
this, not this.'" He turned furiously away and reached
inside the tractor to draw out a clamped pipe. This he
rapped twice with the hammer, and I understood that

something had broken off inside the clamp. He stamped, puffing up dust, his frustration growing. "I have half a dozen punches around here, and do you think I can find one of them?" Duane stamped over to the darkest section of the barn and rooted in a pile of loose equipment. "So you want to know about Zack, hey? What do you want to know about him? About the time he barricaded himself in his house and they had to go·in with axes to get him out? That's when he was nine. About the time he beat up an old woman in Arden because she looked at him funny? That's when he was thirteen. About all the stealing he did, all along? Then there's the fires he used to go for, yeah, he went for 'em so much he sometimes didn't wait for other people to start 'em, and then there's——" He dipped forward suddenly, like a heron after a frog, and said, "God damn, I found one. Then there's Hitler, I thought we won that war and it was all over, but no, I guess if you're real smart, smarter than a dumb shitkicker like me anyhow, you know Hitler was the good guy and he really won because he provided this and that, I don't know. Understanding. Then there's the social worker he had once, said because he didn't have a mother he grew up mean as a snake——" Now he was approaching the tractor again, taking up the clamped pipe—

—coughing, up behind the bushes, impatiently unbuttoning the white shirt and unlacing his boots, hearing the signal of a whistle that now, in two minutes, five minutes, they would jump on the girl and stop her contempt in the simplest way they knew, hearing her voice saying *Do birds cough?*—

I heard him make a noise in his throat. The pounding stopped. The hammer thudded to the ground, the pipe sprang back. Duane hopped away from the tractor, gripping the wrist of his splayed left hand with his right, and moved with surprising speed past me and out into the sun. I went after him; his body seemed compressed, under a suddenly increased gravity. He was standing spread-legged beside the rusted hooks and curls of metal, examining his hand, turning it over. He had sliced the skin at the base of his thumb. "Not so bad," he said, and pressed the wound against his coveralls.

I did not know then why I chose that moment to say "Last night the gas went on again," but now I see that his accident reminded me of mine.

"Everything's fouled up in that house," he said, holding his hand tightly against the filthy coveralls. "I oughta tear it down."

"Someone told me it might be a warning."

He said, "You're liable to get all the warnings you can use," and stepped off toward his house, having given me another as useless as the rest.

I went back to my grandmother's house and called the Arden police station. What I wanted was not to accuse Polar Bears or to seek a futile revenge by cursing at him, but simply to hear his voice again, with what I now knew or thought I knew in my mind while I listened to it. I felt as bottomless as the quarry was said to be, as directionless as still water, and I do not believe that I felt any anger at all. I could remember Polar Bears striking his steering wheel, enraged, saying, "Don't you know better than to use that Greening name? That's what you don't want to remind people of, boy. I'm trying to keep all that in the background." That was Larabee at work, keeping things out of sight —he would say, using his Larabee-side as he had while defending it, for my own good. But Hovre was not in his office, and Dave Lokken greeted me with a cold reluctance which barely permitted him to say that he would tell the Chief that I had called.

Upstairs, my workroom looked very little as it had on the day I had set it up. The books once piled on the floor were either given away or stacked in a far corner to gather dust. The typewriter was in its case on the floor, and I had thrown away all the typist's paraphernalia. I was writing my memoir in pencil, being too clumsy a typist to be able to work at the speed required. All of the thick folders of notes and drafts, along with my laboriously compiled packs of file cards, I had burned a week and a half before. I read somewhere that birds shit before they fly, and I was engaged in a parallel process, stripping myself down for take-off, making myself lighter.

I often worked until I fell asleep at my desk. That was what I did Monday night, and I must have come awake about the time the men from Arden and the valley thrust their way into Roman Michalski's house and ruined Galen Hovre's plans by giving flesh to the rumors they had all heard. My eyes burned, and my stomach felt as though I had been swallowing cigars, a sensation precisely reproduced in my mouth. The room was icy, my fingers were cold and stiff. I stood up and turned to the window. I realized that Polar Bears had not called back. In half-light the mare tossed her head in the field. When I looked across the far fields I saw her again, standing in that vulpine way, not bothering with the shield of the trees, and staring directly at the house. I could not take my eyes from her, and stood in the blast of cold, feeling her energy come streaming toward me, and then I blinked and she was gone.

Nine

After the noise of Zack's receding motorcycle pulled me from the second night in a row of that dreadful dream, I lay in the gray light of early morning, experiencing what seemed an utter desolation. For the second time the thought of Alison Greening brought with it no current of joy and anticipation. The wrong things had happened; I was in the wrong room, the wrong place; I was the wrong man. It must be the way a young soldier feels when after he has enlisted out of a glorious mish-mash of ideals, adventurousness and boredom, he finds himself cold, hungry, shouted at and on the verge of battle. I simply could not think of what to do. I had been going to tell Polar Bears what I knew about Zack—but did I really know it? (Yes. I did. Anyway, I thought I did.) But my relation to Polar Bears had irrevocably changed. I could remember all too clearly his telling me that rape was normal. Had he been telling himself that for twenty years?

I saw that both Duane and Polar Bears must have hated my coming back to Arden. I was the last person they wanted to see again. Especially since I had begun speaking about Alison Greening almost from the moment I arrived in the valley.

And then I thought of the slight vulpine figure I had seen last night, leveling her face toward the farmhouse

like a loaded gun, and thought too of the vision I'd
had when the gas had almost killed me. And of the
lights in my grandmother's house flashing on, all at
once, making the place look like a boat floating out of
its harbor. I was unforgiven.

I wondered how well I knew—had known—my
cousin Alison. Again I saw that face of sewn leaves
coming toward me, and I hurriedly left the bed, threw
on my robe, and went downstairs.

I thought: now you are almost afraid of it.

And thought: no. You have always been afraid of it.
My bare feet were very cold.

When the telephone rang, I hesitated a moment
before lifting the receiver from its hook. Polar Bears,
up early from another sleepless night. *Do birds cough?*,
that ardent high electric voice in my ears. But I smelled
blubber, and knew that I did not yet have to solve the
problem of what to say to Galen Hovre. She said, "Mr.
Teagarden? Miles?"

"Present."

"I can't come to work today. I won't be there this
morning. I'm sick."

"Well," I began, and realized that she had already
hung up. Stupidly, I stared at the receiver, as if it
could explain Tuta Sunderson's behavior.

The explanation came about an hour later, after I had
dressed and was seated upstairs, trying to smother
thought by the familiar tactic of concentration on work.
I had succeeded in this often enough during my marriage. Intellectual labor is a common technique for
the avoidance of thinking. Yet I had more problems
fighting for mental space than Joan's infidelity with
various Dribbles had given me, and I had written less
than half a page of my record before I put my head
down on the desk, my face damp with sweat and the
desolation back in full strength. I groaned. The admission that I might—did—feel unease, disquiet, fear, all
of those, at the enactment of the vow between my
cousin and myself had opened up a vast psychic hole.

I remembered Rinn's harsh words—I felt as though I were thrust back into the world of the "blue horror" dream, as though mere wakefulness could not separate me from it. I was still a guilt expert; that was a vocation which outlasted the academic.

Alison Greening *was* my life; her death had thrown me forever out of significance, out of happiness; but suppose Rinn was right, and that significance and happiness had been flawed and illusory from the beginning. Suppose that by returning to the valley I had brought death with me? Or if not death, its taint? The terror I had felt in the woods flicked at me again, and I pushed myself away from the desk and left the study. All the way down the stairs I felt pursued by that slight figure, that atom of the woods.

Downstairs, I was jerked back into the present. I knew why Tuta Sunderson had refused to come to work. They were there, out on the road, waiting like vultures.

Because that is what they resembled, vultures, sitting in their cars just past the walnut trees. I could not see their faces. They had switched off their motors. I imagined them assembling at the prearranged time, each pulling up on the road before the house, coming from all over Arden, all up and down the valley. Somehow, they had heard about Candace Michalski's disappearance. My throat dried. From where I was standing at the kitchen window I could see perhaps twenty of them, each alone in his car, all men.

At first, like a child, I thought of calling Rinn—of invoking that safety.

I swallowed, and went into the living room and opened the door to the porch. Now I could see them all. Their cars filled the road. Some of them must have gone down to Duane's driveway to turn around, because they were bunched in a thick pack, all facing the same way, three abreast in places where I could see only the tops of the farthest cars glinting light. From them rose wavy lines of heat. Menace came from them like a physical force. I stepped backwards into the dark of the room, and saw them still, framed in the doorway. The men in the cars visible to me sat twisted sideways on their seats, looking toward the porch.

One more impatient than the rest honked his horn.

And then I knew they would not leave their cars, for no one answered the single horn blast with his own: they were just going to sit out there.

I walked out onto the porch where I would be visible. Another car honked, one of those nearest the house. It was a signal: *he's out:* and I could see some of the hunched figures in the cars swing their heads sideways to stare at me.

I went back into the kitchen and dialed Polar Bears' office. A voice I recognized as Lokken's answered me.

"Hell no, he ain't in here. All hell's broke loose since last night. He's out with two of the others, lookin' for that girl."

"The news got out."

"It was that damn Red Sunderson did it, he and a lot of the boys called on the family last night, and now they got all stirred up, runnin' around and demandin' things and holy man, we been workin'—hey, who is this, anyways?"

"Get in touch with him fast and tell him to call Miles Teagarden. I've got some trouble here." And I know who did it, I said silently. "And I might have some information for him."

"What kind of information would that be, Teagarden?" I had ceased to be Mr. Teagarden.

"Ask him if a doorknob could have been used on those two girls," I said, and heard my heart thudding.

"Why, you lose a doorknob, Teagarden?" came Lokken's insufferable yokel's voice. "Whyn't you call up your friend Larabee and ask him to find it for you? You outa your skull or something? The Chief ain't gonna do you no favors, Teagarden, don't you know that?"

"Just get him over here," I said.

Some of the men could see me telephoning, and I

held the receiver for a few moments after Lokken hung up and stood directly in front of the window with the black cone of plastic to my ear. Two of the cars in front of the column came to life, and drove off after their drivers had tapped their horns. Two others crept up to take their places. I juggled the hook and then dialed Rinn's number. I could see the man nearest to me watching my arm move. He too tapped his horn and drove off in the direction of the highway. The front end of a blue pickup appeared in his space. Rinn's telephone trilled and trilled. I didn't know what I expected from her anyway. I hung up.

I heard cars gunning their engines and tires crunching the road. My throat felt looser. I took a cigarette from the pack in my shirt pocket and lit it with a kitchen match. Cars were still moving off and turning around out on the road, and as I exhaled I saw the blue truck move past the frame of the window, then two cars at once, tan and dark blue, then a gray car with spectacular dents in its side. For two or three minutes I waited and smoked, hearing them wrangle their way out, backing up onto the lawn, noisily bouncing on the drive to the garage, turning around.

When I thought they were all gone I saw the nose of a dark Ford pull into the frame of the window and stop.

I went out onto the porch. Three of them had stayed behind. When I pushed open the screen door, not really knowing what I intended to do, two of them left their cars. The third, whose pickup was nearest the drive, backed his truck around the last of the walnut trees and came about five yards up the drive. When he hopped out of the cab I saw that it was Hank Speltz, the boy from the garage. In front of the house, the lawn had been ripped into muddy tracks.

"Go on up that way, Hank, and we'll jump the ditch," called one of the two men out on the road. The boy began coming warily up the drive, his hands spread.

One of the men jumped the ditch and began coming through the line of walnut trees, the second following a little behind. They looked like the men I had seen outside the Angler's Bar, the men who had stoned me—big middle-aged roughs, with bellies hanging over their belts and plaid and tan shirts open past their breastbones. A circle of red just below the neck, and then the dead white skin usually covered by undershirts.

"Hovre is coming here," I called. "You'd better get out with the others."

A man I did not recognize called back, "Hovre ain't gonna be here in time to stop us doin' what we're gonna do."

"Where you got the Michalski girl?" shouted the man hanging back.

"I don't have her anywhere." I began to sidle toward the garage and the path to Duane's house. Hank Speltz, his face hanging open-mouthed like a wrestler's, was coming up. I tossed the remaining two inches of cigarette onto the torn lawn, and went nearer the garage.

The man in the plaid shirt who had spoken first said, "Come at him slow," and Hank Speltz halved his pace, shuffling like a bear from side to side. "Get the hell on up here, Roy," he said. "Where you got her?"

"He's got her hid somewhere inside. I tol' you."

"I've never seen her." I kept moving to the side.

"He's going to that garage."

"Let him go. We'll get him there." He had a red hook-nosed face with deep lines, a bully's face—the face of the schoolyard terror who had never grown up. The two of them were coming at me slowly across the lawn. "Keep an eye on him in case he runs toward that Nash," shouted the man in the cap.

"Whose idea was this?" I called.

"Ours, smartass."

Then I was close enough to the garage and I hit the clip off the lock and opened the door. I looked at the curl of smoke coming from my cigarette and knew what I was going to try to do. "Go in there and we got you cornered," the leader crowed. Knowing that any sudden movement would make them rush me, I backed into the open garage and went into its gloom. The three ten-gallon gascans were where I remembered them from the day I had broken open the sea chest. I picked one of them up: full. With my back to them, I bent down and screwed off the cap. When I emerged carrying the heavy can, one of them guffawed. "Gonna put gas in your car, Teagarden?"

Only the man in the plaid shirt saw what I was going to do. *"Shit,"* he yelled, and began to run at me.

With as much force as I had, I threw the gascan toward the curl of smoke. I supposed that the odds were no worse than they were if I'd bet on a horse. Fluid began to spray out in wheels and loops.

For a moment we were all standing still, watching the gasoline come spraying out of the sailing can, but when the *crump* of the explosion came I was already running up the path toward Duane's house. I heard them shouting behind me. A bit of flying metal whizzed past my head. One of them was screaming.

I had just about time enough to get to the near side of Duane's house; when I glanced over my shoulder, I saw them coming through the fire, two of them. The man in the cap was rolling on the ground. Pieces of scattered fire dotted the lawn all the way to the row of walnut trees. Now they were stopping to kneel by the man in the cap.

If I had been right that Duane's basement was originally a root cellar like my grandparents', I would be able to get into it from the outside.

"Duane ain't gonna help you, you son of a bitch!" came a distorted, yelling voice.

I came running past the dogwood and sweetpea and onto Duane's lawn.

"Cuz he's gone!"

I don't know what I was picturing: hiding down there, finding a burrow, defending it with an ax. As I raced across the short lawn I saw that I had been right. The white-painted boards of the entrance cover—the old access to the cellar—extended from the base of the house, just visible around the corner on the side facing the road. I came skidding around the corner and the door I yanked on swung easily upwards.

I fell down the earthen steps and rolled beneath the hanging axes. Then I remembered. The far wall, where my desk had been, in cases like mummies. I scrambled up from my knees and ran, crouching, over to the shotguns.

I took one up case and all and dipped my hand into the box of shells and ran back to the earthen steps. Like moving up from water into light, going back toward the slanting rectangle of blue air and sunlight.

I had the twelve-gauge out of the case as the men and Hank Speltz came running around the corner of dogwood and sweetpea. I broke the gun and slotted two shells into the barrels. "Stop right there," I said, and raised the gun and pointed it at the chest of the man in the plaid shirt. Then I rose up from my belly on the earthen steps and came out of the cellar. My breathing was so harsh that I could scarcely form words. They dropped their arms and stood momentarily still, shock and anger in their faces.

"Now get the hell out of here," I said.

They were beginning to circle. They were as wary as beasts.

"I've never seen that girl," I said. "I've never seen any of them. I only knew about the Michalski girl because Polar Bears told me she was missing." Put the gun against my shoulder, pointed it at the opening in the plaid shirt. Expected the recoil. "Get together and stay together. Stop moving around like that."

They obeyed. I could see the man in the cap limping up behind them, his hands in the air. His tan workshirt was flecked with black, blood leaking through some of the holes. His hands were blackened too. He stood by the dogwood with his hands up. "Walk backwards," I said. "All the way to your cars."

Hank Speltz took a step backwards into the dogwood, looked around wildly, and then began to edge around to the path. The others moved with him, following me with their eyes.

"If you're so innocent, how come you stuck around up here?" asked the man in the plaid shirt.

I gestured with the shotgun.

"Screwing that old crazywoman up in the woods," said Hank Speltz. "That's how come. And what about Gwen Olson and Jenny Strand?"

"You're asking the wrong man," I said. "Now I want you to start moving backwards toward the cars."

When they did not move I shifted the barrels to the right, flicked the safety, and pulled one of the triggers. The recoil nearly jerked the shotgun from my hands. The sound was louder than the explosion of the gascan. All of them moved smartly away from the dogwood. I saw that I had shredded the leaves and ruined the blossoms, leaving broken twigs and the smell of powder hanging. "You damn near killed Roy back there," said the one in the plaid shirt.

"What was he going to do to me? Move." I raised the barrels, and they began to step backwards down the path.

Over their shoulders I could see the mess of the long front lawn. A ragged, irregular black circle ten yards from the drive showed where the ten-gallon can had exploded. Smaller burned patches, a greasy yellow in color, were dotted all over the lawn, churned and rutted by their tires. A large hole had been blown in the mesh of the porch screen. The animals had disappeared down into the far end of the side field.

"We ain't through yet," said the man whose name I did not know.

"Hank, get in your pickup and drive out," I said. "I'll be coming in to pick up my car soon, and I don't expect any trouble."

"No," he said, and sprinted toward the truck in the driveway.

All three of us watched him roar away scattering dirt as he turned onto the valley road.

"Now you, Roy." The man in the cap looked at me glumly, lowered his hands, and walked heavily over the lawn to pass between the walnut trees. He stopped to

stamp out the small flames licking up at the base of one
of the trees.

"Now it's your turn," I said to the remaining man.

"Whyn't you just kill us?" he asked belligerently.
"You like killin'. We all know about you. You got
sumpun wrong in your head."

I said, "If you don't get out of here right now, you
won't believe what's happening to you. You'll probably
live for a minute or two, but you'll be glad to die when
they're over." I cradled the gun in my arms and leveled
it at his belt. And then I did an astounding thing—a
thing that astounded me. I laughed. Self-disgust hit me
with such force that I feared for a moment that I would
vomit.

Portion of Statement by Hank Speltz:

July 15

*I was standin' there watchin' Miles and I says to
myself, boy, if you ever get outa this I promise I'll
go to church every Sunday, I'll pray every night,
I'll never say another dirty word, I'll be good forever, because you never seen anything like the way
that Miles looked, crazy enough to chew glass,
eat gunpowder, that's how he looked. His eyes
they was just slits. His hair was flyin' all directions. When he let go with one of those barrels,
I thought, uh oh, the next one's for me. Because
he knew me from the filling station. I didn't even
wanna be there in the first place, I just went because Red Sunderson said, he said we'll all park
in front of his place and scare hell out of old
Miles. And we'll break him down for sure. He's
got that girl put away somewhere. So I said, count
me in. Then when the other ones all pulled out,
I saw Roy and Don were stayin', so I thought I'd
stick around for the fun.*

*He was a trapped rat. Like something mean
backed up into a corner. Man. He blew shit out*

*of everything with that gascan—he didn't care
what happened. He coulda killed himself too!*

*So when he let me go I just took off, yessir,
right off, and I figured, let someone else find that
girl. But I did a little something extra to that beat-
to-shit VW of his after I got to town. I fixed it
real good. I fixed it so's he couldn't go but thirty-
forty miles an hour, and wouldn't run very long
at any one time too. One thing I am's a good
mechanic.*

*But I knew that crazy sonofabitch done it. And
if you ask me, he was askin' to get caught. Else
why would he put that name Greening on the
repair slip? Answer me that.*

A screaming voice: "Miles, you bastard! You bastard!": Duane.

"Calm down." Another voice, deeper, lower.

"Get the shit out here! Now!"

"Just simmer down, Duane. He'll come."

"Goddam you! Goddam you! You crazy?"

I cautiously open the door and see that Duane in
fury appears to be reduced in size, a small square jigging knot of red-faced anger. "I told you, goddamit! I
said, stay the hell away from my girl! And second, what
the hell is all this? He whirls around, his rage giving
him agility, and the gesture of his arms encompasses,
as well as the greasy yellowish and black burns on the
ripped lawn and the marks of the explosion—the gaping hole in the screen, twisted pieces of the gascan—
the figure of Polar Bears in uniform behind him, and
Alison Updahl hurrying up the path toward her home.
She glances over her shoulder, nearly there already,
sending me a look, half fear, half warning.

"Just sitting in their cars, goddam it—just sitting
out there—no goddam trouble—and what the hell did
you do? Make a goddam bomb? Look at my lawn!"
He stomps heavily, too furious to speak any longer.

"I tried to call you," I say to Polar Bears.

"You're lucky I don't kill you now!" Duane screams.

"I'm lucky they didn't kill me then."

Polar Bears firmly positions one hand on Duane's shoulder. "Hold your horses," he says. "Dave Lokken told me you called up. I didn't expect there'd be any trouble, Miles. I figured you could take a bunch of our country boys starin' at you from the road."

"Sittin' there—just sittin' there," Duane says, quietly now that Polar Bears is gripping his shoulder.

"I didn't think you'd declare war on 'em."

"I didn't think you'd go crawlin' around after my girl either," Duane hisses, and I see Polar Bears' fingers tighten. "I warned you. I told you, stay off. You're gonna get it—for sure."

"They didn't just sit there. Most of them left when they saw me dialing the telephone, but three of them decided to come for me."

"See who they were this time, Miles?"

"That boy from the garage, Hank Speltz, a man named Roy, and one I didn't know. One of those who threw stones at me in Arden."

"*Stones . . . stones*," hisses Duane, his contempt so great that it is almost despair.

"How d'ya manage all this?" He lifts his chin toward the lawn where tire tracks and brown muddy ruts loop crazily.

"They did most of it themselves. They drove all over it. I guess they were in a hurry to get out before you showed up. The rest I did. I flipped an open gascan from the garage on top of a burning cigarette. I didn't even think it would work. You knew they were going to be here, didn't you?"

"You got me again. Sure I knew. I figured they'd just help keep you—"

"Out of trouble. Like Paul Kant."

"Yeah." His smile almost expresses pride in me.

"You and Duane were together? With Alison?"

"Keep her name out of your mouth, damn you," Duane says.

"Just having a beer in the Bowl-A-Rama."

"Just having a beer. Not working on your story."

"Even a cop doesn't work all the time, Miles," he says, and I think: no. You do work all the time, and that's why you are dangerous. He takes his paw off Duane's arm and shrugs his shoulders. "I wanted to explain to Du-ane here that you and me are sort of helpin' each other out on these killings. That's a big plus for you, Miles. You shouldn't want to take that plus away from yourself. Now I hear you been talking to Du-ane about some crazy idea you got. You been talking about just the exact thing I told you not to talk about, Miles. Now that kinda makes me question your judgment. I just wanta be sure you've seen the error in your thinking. Old Duane here didn't tell you you was right, did he? When you hit him with this crazy idea?" He looks at me, his face open and companionable. "Did you, Duane?"

"I said he should talk to you."

"Well, you see, you got him all suspicious and worked up."

"I knew it out at the quarry, really. I had the girl shout. You couldn't hear her on the road."

Duane stamps in a furious muttering half-circle. "Undressed. You were undressed."

"Hold on, Duane, you'll make it worse. Old Miles will just go on drawing the wrong conclusions if you get sidetracked. Now, Miles, Duane says he never said you was right in your ideas. Now let's ask him. Were you out there that night?"

Duane shakes his head, looking angrily at the ground.

"Of course you weren't. It's all in the records my father made. You went out on 93 and turned the other way, toward Liberty. Right?"

Duane nods.

"You were mad at that little Greening girl, and you just wanted to get the hell away from her. Right? Sure," as Duane nods again. "See, Miles, if you just tell a girl to yell without her knowing anything about why, she's not liable to really give her best, like a girl would if she's bein' attacked. You see the error there? Now,

I don't want you to go on talking about this, because you'll just dig yourself into a deep hole, Miles."

There is no point in prolonging this charade. "That little Greening girl," the figure of lean intensity I have seen leveling her muzzle toward the house? That little Greening girl, the fire in the woods and the blast of freezing wind? I can smell cold water about me.

I think that which I do not wish to think; and remember Rinn's words. My guilt drowns me.

Duane, for different reasons, also does not wish to continue. "To hell with this," he says. Then he straightens up and his pudgy red-and-white face flames at me. "But I warned you about seeing my daughter again."

"She asked me to come with her."

"Did she? Did she? That's what you say. I suppose you say you didn't take off your clothes in front of her."

"It was just for swimming. She took hers off first. The boy undressed too."

In front of Duane, I cannot tell Polar Bears my fears about Zack. I have already said too much, for Duane looks ready to flail out again.

I am trembling. I feel cold wind.

"Yeah, okay," Duane says. "Sure. Whatever you say." He turns his upper body toward me. "If you fool around with her, Miles, I won't wait for anyone else to get you. I'll get you myself." Yet there is no real conviction in this threat, he does not care enough; treachery is what he expects from women.

Polar Bears and I watch him tramping up the path. Then he turns to me. "Say, you look kind of peaked, Miles. Must be all that skinny-dipping you do."

"Which one of you raped her?"

"Hold on."

"Or did you take turns?"

"I'm beginning to question your judgment again, Miles."

"I'm beginning to question everything."

"You heard me mention that hole you could be digging for yourself?" Polar Bears steps toward me, big

and solid and full of serious concern, and I see dark
blue blotches of perspiration on his uniform shirt, dark
blue smudges beneath his eyes. "Jesus, boy, you gotta
be crazy, throwing bombs at the citizens here, gettin'
yourself in trouble . . ." He is moving with a cautious,
wary slowness and I think *this is it: he's going to break,
he's going to fight me.* But he stops and rubs a hand
over his face. "Pretty soon this is all gonna be over,
Miles. Pretty soon." He steps back, and the sour com-
bination of sweat and gunpowder engulfing me like
smoke recedes with him. "Miles. Jesus Christ. What
was that you were telling Dave Lokken about something like a doorknob?"

I cannot answer.

That night and every night afterward I turned off the
gas where Tuta Sunderson had shown me. In the mornings, when she heaved herself into the kitchen and began to cough and stamp her feet and shuffle around
and clear her throat and produce the entire array of
noises expressive of sullen discontent with which I had
become familiar, among them was always the sharp
grunt of suspicious disapproval—and contempt?—that
accompanied her discovery that I had done so. I would
have fired her but for my certainty that, like Bartleby,
she would have come anyhow. The day after the visitation by Hank Speltz and the others, I heard the coughing, feet-stamping, etc., and went downstairs to ask
her if she had known what was going to happen.
Foolish me. "Did I know what? What was going to
happen? So what happened?" She had made no comment on the condition of the lawn or the hole in the
porch screen. I told her that I imagined her son had
been involved. "Red? Red doesn't get messed up in
anything. Now how many eggs do you want to throw
away today?"

For days I did nothing but work; and I worked undisturbed, for it seemed that no one would talk to me.
Apart from her morning demonstrations of how much
noise she could produce, Tuta Sunderson was silent;

Duane kept away, even turning his head so he would not have to look at me on the infrequent times he passed the old farmhouse. His daughter, presumably beaten or warned off in a less physical manner, also avoided me. Sometimes, from my bedroom window I could see her criss-crossing the path to go to the equipment barn or the granary, her body looking rushed and inexpressive, but she never appeared downstairs in the kitchen or on the porch, chewing something from my larder. At night, I was often awakened from dozing at my desk, the martini glass beside me and the pencil still in my hand, by the sound of Zack's motorcycle cutting off when it came parallel to me. I wrote. I dozed. I drank. I accumulated guilt. I hoped that soon the Michalskis would get a postcard from their vanished daughter. I hoped that Polar Bears was right, and that it would soon be over. I often wanted to leave.

At night, I experienced fear.

Rinn had given up answering her telephone, and I kept telling myself that I would visit her tomorrow. But that too I feared. The anonymous calls ceased, both from Onion Breath and from the—whatever the other thing was. Perhaps there was a fault in the old telephone.

I received no more blank letters, and only one more bit of fan mail. It was printed on lined paper with torn perforations along one side, and it read W E ' L L G E T Y O U K I L L E R. I put it in an envelope and mailed it with a note to Polar Bears.

It seemed to me that I had died.

Many times, I thought: you were wrong, back at the quarry. That he had Coke bottles in his truck is no proof; the doorknob taken from wherever I had put it is no proof. And then I thought of him slicing open his hand.

I said: it is not your problem. And then thought of his dedicating a record "to the lost ones."

And thought of Alison Greening coming toward me, a creature of sewn leaves and bark. But the thoughts which followed this could not be true.

It was impossible to talk with Polar Bears. He did not respond to my note or to the printed threat.

When the telephone finally rang on a Monday afternoon, I thought it would be Hovre, but when I was greeted by another voice pronouncing my name, I thought of a bent hungry man with tight curling black hair and aging face. "Miles," he said. "You told me to call you if I ever wanted help." His voice was dry and papery.

"Yes."

"I have to get out of here. I'm out of food. I lied to you that day—I said I went out, but I hadn't in a long time."

"I know."

"Who told you?" Fear made his voice trill.

"It doesn't matter."

"No. No, it probably doesn't. But I can't stay in town any more. I think they're going to do something. Now even more of them are watching my house, and sometimes I see them talking, planning. I think they're planning to break in. I'm afraid they'll kill me. And I haven't had anything to eat for two days. If—if I can get away can I come there?"

"Of course. You can stay here. I can get a gun."

"They all have guns, guns are no use . . . I just have to get away from them." During the pauses I could hear him gasping.

"Your car doesn't work. How can you get here?"

"I'll walk. I'll hide in the ditches or the fields if I see anyone. Tonight."

"It's ten miles!"

"It's the only way I can do it." Then, with that ghastly wanness, that dead humor in his voice, "I don't think anyone will give me a ride."

About nine-thirty, when the light began to fail, I started to expect him, though I knew that he could not possibly arrive for many hours. I walked around the old house, peering from the upstairs windows for the sight of him working his way across the fields. At ten, when it was fully dark, I turned on only one light—in my study—so that he would not be seen crossing the lawn. Then I sat on the porch swing and waited.

It took him four hours. At two o'clock I heard something rustle in the ditch behind the walnut trees, and my head jerked up and I saw him moving across the ripped lawn. "I'm on the porch," I whispered, and opened the door for him.

Even in the darkness, I could see that he was exhausted. "Stay away from the windows," I said, and led him into the kitchen. I turned on the light. He was slumped at the table, panting, his clothing covered with smears of dirt and bits of adhering straw. "Did anyone see you?" He shook his head. "Let me get you some food." "Please," he whispered.

While I fried bacon and eggs, he stayed in that beaten position, his eyes fluttering, his back bent and his knees splayed out. I gave him a glass of water. "My feet hurt so much," he said. "And my side. I fell into a rock."

"Did anyone see you leave?"

"I wouldn't be here if they did."

I let him recover while the eggs fried.

"Do you have any cigarettes? I ran out six days ago."

I tossed him my pack. "Jesus, Miles . . ." he said, and could go no further. "Jesus . . ."

"Save it," I said. "Your food's about ready. Eat some bread in the meantime." He had been too tired to notice the loaf set squarely in the middle of the table. "Jesus . . ." he repeated, and began to tear at the loaf. When I put the food down before him, he ate greedily, silently, like an escaped convict.

When he had finished I turned off the light and we went into the living room and felt our way to chairs. I could see the tip of his cigarette burning in the dark room, tilting back and forth as he moved in the rocker. "Do you have anything to drink? Excuse me, Miles. You're saving my life." I think he began to cry, and I was glad the lights were off. I went back to the kitchen and returned with a bottle and two glasses.

"That's good," he said when he had taken his.
"What is it?"

"Gin."

"I never had it before. My mother wouldn't let alcohol in the house, and I never wanted to go to the bars. We never had anything stronger than beer. And that was only once or twice. She died of lung cancer. She was a chainsmoker. Like me."

"I'm sorry."

"It was a long time ago."

"What are you going to do now, Paul?"

"I don't know. Go somewhere. Hide. Try to get to a city somewhere. Come back when it's over." Cigarette glowing with his inhalations, dipping forward and back as he rocked. "There was another one, another girl. She disappeared."

"I know."

"That's why they were going to come for me. She's been missing more than a week. I heard about it on the radio."

"Michael Moose."

"That's it." He gave a crackly humorless laugh. "You probably don't know Michael Moose. He's about three hundred and fifty pounds and he chews peppermints. He's grotesque. He's got flat slicked-down hair and pig's eyes and a little moustache like Oliver Hardy's. He's right out of *Babbitt*. He imitates Walter Cronkite's voice, and he'd never get a job anywhere but Arden, and kids laugh at him on the street, but he's better than I am. To Arden. They think he's funny-looking, and they make jokes about him, but they respect him too. Maybe that's too strong. What it is, they take him as one of them. And do you know why that is?"

"Why?"

His voice was flat and bitter. "Because when he was growing up they knew he went out on dates, they know the girls, and because he got married. Because they know, or say, that he's got a woman over in Blundell who's a telephone operator. Red hair." The cigarette waved in the air, and I could dimly see Paul Kant raising the glass of gin to his lips. "That's it. He's one of them. You know what my crime is?" I held my breath. "I never had a date. I never had a girl. I never told a dirty joke. I never even had a dead girl, like you, Miles. So they thought I was—what they thought. Different. Not like them. Like something bad they knew about."

We sat there in silence for a long time, each of us only a vague form to the other. "It didn't start that way, you know. It didn't matter that I was less, shall we say robust, when we were all little kids. In grade school. Grade school was paradise—when I think about it, it was paradise. It got bad only in high school. I wasn't *cute*. I wasn't like Polar Bears. No athlete. I didn't chase the girls. So they started to talk about me. I noticed that people didn't want me around their kids about the time I had to leave school." He bent, and felt for something on the floor. "Would you mind if I had another drink?"

"It's right on the floor beside your chair."

"So now when this admirable character goes around ripping up little girls, they assume it's me. Oh yes, Paul Kant. He's never been quite right, has he? A momma's boy. Not quite normal, in a society that makes being normal the most virtuous quality of them all. And then there was another thing—some trouble I had. Stupid scum. They put me in a police station. They hit me. For doing nothing. Did they tell you about that?"

"No," I lied. "Not a word."

"I had to go to a hospital. Seven months. Little pills every day. For doing nothing. Stares when I got out. Only job I could get at Zumgo's. With those leering women. Jesus. Do you know how I got here tonight? Had to sneak out of my own house. Wind through the streets like a dog. Know about my dog, Miles? They killed him. One of them. He came up at night and strangled my dog. I could hear him crying. The dog." I could imagine the little monkey face contorting. The smell of gin and cigarettes drifted through the dark room. "Jesus." I thought he might have been crying again.

Then: "So what do you say, Miles Teagarden? Or do you just sit and listen? What do you say?"

I said, "I don't know."

"You were rich. You could come here in the summers and then go back to one of your private schools and then go to some expensive university and smoke pipes and join a fraternity and get married and get a Ph.D. and live in apartments in New York and go to Europe and wreck cars and buy Brooks Brothers suits and, I don't know, do whatever you do. Teach English in a college. I'm going to have some more of your gin." He bent, and I heard the bottle clinking against the glass. "Oh. I spilled some."

"It doesn't matter," I said.

"It wouldn't to you, would it? I'm getting drunk. Is it you, Miles? Is it you? Come on."

"Is what me?" But I knew.

"Are you the admirable character? Did you take time off from your *Atlantic Monthly* life to come out here and rip up a few little girls?"

"No."

"Well, it's not me either. So who is it?"

I looked down at the floor. Before I had decided to tell him about Zack, he was speaking again.

"No, it's not me."

"I know that," I said. "I think—"

"It's not me, no way is it me. They just want it to be me. Or you. But I don't know about you. Still, you're being nice to me, aren't you, Miles? Being so nice. Probably never had someone strangle your dog. Or do people like you have dogs? Borzois, wolfhounds. Or a cute little cheetah on a leash."

"Paul, I'm trying to help you." I said. "You have a ludicrous misconception of my life."

"Oops, sorry, oops, mustn't be offensive. Just a poor country boy, I know. Poor dumb pitiable country schmuck. I'll tell you why no way it's me. This is it,

boy. I'd never go after a girl. That's why. You hear
what I'm saying?"

I did, and hoped he would not torture himself by
going further.

"You heard that?"

"I heard."

"You understand?"

"Yes."

"Yes. Because I'd do it to boys, not girls. Isn't that
funny? That's why it isn't me. That's what I've always
wanted, but I never did that either. Never even touched
one. I wouldn't hurt any of them, though. Never hurt
them."

He sat there, slumped in the rocking chair, the cigarette glowing in his mouth. "Miles?"

"Yes."

"Leave me alone."

"Is it important to you to be alone now?"

"Get the hell out of here, Miles." He was crying
again.

Instead of leaving the room, I got up and walked past
his chair and looked through the window facing the
porch and the road. I could see nothing but the darker
square mass of my own face reflected in the glass and
the torn meshes of the screen beyond it. Beyond that,
everything was black. His mouth made noises on his
glass. "Okay," I said, "I'll leave you alone, Paul. I'll
be back though."

I went upstairs in the dark and sat at my desk. It
was three-fifteen. There was the morning to worry
about. If the men from Arden broke into Paul's house
and found that he had gone, the news, I was certain,
would reach Polar Bears almost immediately. And if
they were going to break into his house, it could only
mean that they had been persuaded somehow that he
and not I was responsible for the girls' deaths. But
then they might think of looking for Paul at my house
—and I could see nothing but disaster for both of us
if a gang of Arden hooligans stormed into the house
and found the two of us. A shotgun from Duane's base-

ment would not rescue me again. I heard the sound of a car starting up outside, and I jumped. It faded.

Fifteen minutes passed. Time enough, I thought, for Paul to have recovered. I stood up, and recognized how weary I was.

I came down the stairs into the dark room. I saw the tip of a cigarette glowing at the edge of the ashtray. The odors of gin and smoke seemed very thick in the air of the cold small room. "Paul?" I said, going toward the rocking chair. "Paul, let me get you a blanket. I have a plan for tomorrow."

And then I stopped. I could see the top of the rocker against the window, and it was unbroken by the silhouette of his head. The rocker was empty. He was no longer in the room.

Immediately I knew what had happened, but I switched on one of the lights anyway, and confirmed it. The glass and three-fourths empty bottle sat on the floor beside his chair, the cigarette had burned nearly to the rim of the ashtray. I went into the kitchen, and then opened the door to the bathroom. He had left the house shortly after I had gone upstairs. I swore out loud, half in anger at myself for leaving him, half in despair.

I went through the porch and out onto the lawn. He could not have gone far. And I remembered the sound of the car that I thought I'd heard upstairs, and began to run across the lawn.

When I got to the road, I turned right by reflex and pounded down toward the Sunderson farm, in the direction of Arden, for perhaps forty seconds. But he could have gone the other way, deeper into the valley —I didn't even know what lay in that direction; and I recognized that he could also have gone into the fields, as he had done on the way from Arden earlier that night. I thought of him hiding behind a building or crouching in a field, riven by fear and self-loathing, and told myself that he had nowhere, really nowhere to go. He would come back before daylight.

I turned around on the dark road and began to

trudge home. When I reached the drive to my grandmother's house I hesitated, and then walked a bit
further up the road in that direction. It was hopeless. I
could see nothing. I could find him only if he allowed
me to. I turned back and went up the drive and sat on
the porch swing to wait. An hour, I told myself; it
won't be as much as an hour. I would sit and wait.
As tired as I was, it was unthinkable that I could fall
asleep.

But an hour later I was jerked awake by a sound I
could not at first identify. A high agitated wailing, the
sound of mechanical fury, mechanical panic, it came
from somewhere off to my right, but was loud and
near enough to distort my sense of place: for a moment I thought I was in New York, awake before dawn
in New York. It was a New York sound, and as I
gradually located my surroundings I located the sound
too. It was the siren of a fire engine.

I found that I was standing up on the porch in the
gray light of very early dawn, listening to a fire engine.
Fog lay across the fields, and carpeted the valley road.
As I listened, trying to position the sound of the fire
bell, it abruptly cut off. I wheeled around and banged
open the door to the living room. Bottle and glass on
the floor, dead cigarette on the rim of the ashtray. Paul
Kant was still gone.

Numbly, knowing that I had to hurry, I stepped
down the porch's single step. Fog lay in the ruts on
the lawn and concealed its burned patches. I went
stumbling toward the drive, completely forgetting the
car I must have walked right past, and went out onto
the road. Then I began to run. Just visible down the
road, in the direction of the highway, red suffused the
dark gray air.

By the time I reached the Sunderson house I had
to stop running, and I walked as quickly as I could
without increasing the pain in my chest until I reached
the shell of the schoolhouse; then I jogged as far as
the church. The red sandstone bluff hid the redness of

the sky. *Andy's,* I thought, and forced myself to run
again. I heard men moving, machinery working. When
I came around the sharp corner of the bluff I began
to run harder. The fire engine was drawn up into the
parking lot beside Andy's and a police car had pulled
in slightly ahead of it, to the side of the gaspumps. I
heard fire, that terrible raging noise of devouring. But
it was not Andy's that was burning. I could see the
flames jumping behind the high white front of the general store.

I thought, remembering: it might have been a motorcycle I heard, not a car. I had been too groggy to tell
the difference.

I rushed past the front of Andy's and around the
side.

At first I saw only the blazing façade of the Dream
House, rushing into extinction as Duane must so often
have wished it to do. It looked transparent, skeletal.
The frames of the doors and windows hung darkly, like
bones suspended in the red-orange flames. Three fire-
men in rubber boots and iron hats played a useless hose
on the blaze. Steam rose with the smoke. Then I saw
Polar Bears calmly watching me from beside the fire-
truck; he was out of uniform, dressed in a shapeless
sports jacket and brown trousers, and I could tell by
looking at him that he had not been to bed. His in-
somnia had kept him up, working at his bottle of Wild
Turkey until the call from the fire department had
come. It was still dark enough for the flames to redden
the ground and the sky and the back of Andy's store,
and as I walked nearer, I felt the heat. Dave Lokken,
in uniform, stood talking to Andy and his wife, both
wearing bathrobes and shocked unmoving faces, directly at the back of the store. The fire stained their
faces peach. All three noticed me at the same time
and stared at me as if I were a ghoul.

Polar Bears motioned me to him. I kept watching the
fire; the first boards collapsed inward, sending up a
huge shower of sparks.

"Fire bells wake you up?" he asked.

I nodded.

"You got here in a hell of a hurry. Sleeping in your clothes?"

"I wasn't in bed."

"Me neither," he said, and gave me one of his sad paternal smiles. "Care to hear the story? I'll have to tell you anyhow. You'll be interested."

I was looking dumbly at a mess of gray army blankets thrown in a heap halfway between the burning Dream House and the back of Andy's, and I nodded.

"Of course these boys aren't really going to do anything with that hose," he said, "but they might keep the flames from jumping to Andy Kastad's store. That'll be the best they could do. The call came too late for them to save that little abortion of Du-ane's, but I reckon nobody'll be too sorry to see that go, least of all Du-ane. It should of been pulled down long before this. What happened was, Andy and his wife woke up in time to save themselves—claim they heard a noise and *then* they heard the fire. Both jumped out of bed. They look through the window. Get the scare of their lives."

I glanced back at Andy and his wife, and thought it was probably true.

"So old Margaret calls the volunteers while Andy runs out the back to do something—he doesn't know what. Piss on it, maybe. And he sees something. Can you guess what?"

"No." Polar Bears was using his favorite trick of building up suspense.

"No. No indeed. Say, by the way, Miles, I don't suppose you happened to see your friend Paul Kant tonight?" His head was cocked, his eyebrows raised, his manner entirely unembarrassed by the digression. Another favorite trick.

"No."

"Uh huh. Real good. Anyhow, like I was saying, Andy comes boiling out of his back door, all set to pour beer or something all over the fire, and he sees this object in the doorway of the house. Now he's like you. He can't guess what it is either. But he thinks he'd better have a closer look. So he runs up, takes a grab and pulls it away. Half of it's on fire. And when he sees it good and plain, he runs back inside and calls me up too, only Dave and I are already rarin' out here."

"What's the point of all this folksy crap, Polar Bears?" The heat of the fire seemed to be intensifying, grilling the side of my face.

"I thought you mighta guessed." He put a big hand on my bicep and began to lead me toward the store. "The point is that you got nothing more to worry about, Miles. Everything's over. I picked the wrong horse, but you're out in the free and clear as of this moment. It's like I told you. I missed him, but he missed me too."

I stopped and looked up into his massive face and saw, operating far beneath the confidential tone and manner, bafflement and anger. He jerked me forward, commanding me to join his charade. I stumbled, and he gripped my arm more tightly. "We're at the sixteenth of July, old buddy, so if you got nothing holding you here after the twenty-first, I guess you'll be leaving us. That's less than a week. Long enough to keep your mouth shut, I guess."

"Polar Bears," I said, "I don't know what you're talking about, but I think I know who you're looking for."

"Who I was looking for," he said.

We were nearly at the heap of blankets, and I was aware of Lokken shooing Andy and Margaret Kastad away. They bustled off somewhere behind me, seemingly glad to leave.

"That was a man he found in there," Polar Bears said, and bent over like a man about to pick a coin off the sidewalk.

"A man?"

Wordlessly Polar Bears folded back the edge of the blanket.

I was looking at his face. Part of his hair was burned away and his cheek was bloody. His eyes were still open. I felt my knees try to vanish, and I remained standing up only by great effort. Polar Bears touched me across the line of my shoulder blades and I again felt his suppressed anger. It came out of him like the touch of a branding iron. I heard him say, "That's your ticket out of here, Miles," and glanced at his fire-reddened features and then back at Paul's body.

"What's that on the side of his head?" I asked, and heard my voice tremble. "It looks like he was clubbed."

"Falling board."

"They didn't start to fall until I got here."

"Then he fell down."

I turned away.

"One more thing, Miles," said Polar Bears beside me. He bent over again, flipped back the edge of blanket, straightened up, and used his foot to kick over another section of gray wool. "Look. Something else Andy pulled out." He took my arm and revolved me like a toy. It took me a moment to recognize what lay exposed beside the kicked-back gray blanket, because the metal had been blackened by the fire. It was the second ten-gallon gascan from the garage beside the farmhouse.

"How he started the fire," said Polar Bears. "Plain as day."

"What is? That gascan's from my home."

"Sure it is. He snuck out, stole that can of gas, came back here, spilled it around and set it alight. He might as well have confessed. He couldn't take it any more."

"No, no, no," I said, "Polar Bears, he *was* at my place earlier. He was trying to escape before that gang of thugs beat him up or killed him. He wasn't guilty, he didn't have anything to confess."

"Give it up, Miles," Hovre said. "You already told me you hadn't seen him. It's too late to lie about it."

"I'm not lying now."

"You were before, but you're not now." His voice was toneless and disbelieving.

"He left my house a little after three. Somebody must have been following him all the time. Somebody killed him. That's what he was afraid of. That's why he ran. I even heard the car." My voice was rising.

Polar Bears scuffled a few paces away. I saw that he was struggling to keep himself under control. "Now, Miles," he said, turning around to face me again, "it seems to me, just to get back to reality here, that the coroner might go one of two ways on this one. You listening? He might judge this as suicide or accidental death in the commission of a crime, depending on how much he wanted to protect the reputation of Paul Kant. Either way he's got to weigh in the evidence of that gascan."

"Those are the only two verdicts you think he might consider?"

"Yep."

"Not if I can help it."

"You won't be able to do anything here, Miles. You better finish off that research of yours and get out."

"Who's the coroner here?"

Polar Bears gave me a flat angry triumphant glare. "I am."

I could only stare at him.

"In a county of this size, it didn't make much sense to have two men both drawing public salaries."

I turned wordlessly to look at the fire. It was much lower now and the doorframe and all of the roof had collapsed into the roaring heart of the building. My skin felt half-roasted, face and hands. My trousers were hot where they brushed my legs. I sensed the Kastads shying away from both me and the fire.

"He was at my house," I said. I could not bear it any longer. I started to walk towards him. "He was at my house, and you raped my cousin. You and Duane. You killed her. Probably accidentally. But this makes two deaths you want to shovel dirt over. This time it won't happen."

His fury was more frightening than Duane's because it was quieter. "Dave," he said, looking over my shoulder.

"You can't pin it all on an innocent man because he's conveniently dead," I said. "I know who it is."

"Dave." Lokken came up behind me. I could hear him walking over the gravel.

"It's that boy Zack," I said. "There's one other possibility, but it's too crazy . . . so it has to be Zack." I heard Lokken whisper something in surprise behind me. "He had those Coke bottles in his truck, and a doorknob . . ."

"Do you know who Zachary is, Miles?" interrupted Polar Bears, his voice flat as a tombstone.

"He likes fires too, doesn't he?" I said. "Duane said he liked them so much sometimes he didn't wait for someone else to start them."

Dave Lokken grabbed my arms. "Hold him, Dave," said Polar Bears. "Hold him good." He came up close to me, and Lokken pinned my arms back, holding me so tightly I could not move. "You know who Zachary is?"

"Now I do," I tried to say.

"He's my boy," said Polar Bears. "My son. Now I'm going to teach you when to shut up."

In the second before he hit me I saw his face irradiated with rage and I had time to wonder if Duane would have told me the final detail if he had not cut his hand. Then I couldn't think about anything but the pain. Afterwards he told Lokken to let me fall, and I toppled over onto the gravel. I could not breathe. I heard him say, "Lokken, get your fat ass out of here fast," and I opened my eyes and saw his shoes. One of his toecaps lifted and came down on my face. I could hear Lokken running off. Polar Bears' odor poured over me. The foot lifted from my face. His voice came straight into my ear. "You would have been a lot better off if you hadn't never come here, Miles. And I think you better act like you know it." I could hear him breathing hard. Wild Turkey mingled with the smell of gunpowder. "Miles, god-damn you, if you say one more word about those god-damned *Coke* bottles or god-damned *doorknobs* I'll break you in half." His breathing became ragged and harsh, and his belly strained out against his belt with the force of it. "And your cousin died twenty years ago, Miles. You say one more word about her and you're through. Now remember this and remember it good. Whoever it was that was there when your cousin died saved your life by dragging you up onto the shelf. Maybe they wouldn't repeat the favor. Maybe they'd just drop you back in the water." Then he grunted, standing up, and was gone. I closed my eyes. I could hear tires spraying gravel.

When I opened my eyes again I touched my face. I felt slick blood. Then I sat up. I was alone. Duane's Dream House was only a burning jumble of boards emitting a plume of dark smoke. Paul's body was gone, and so was the heap of blankets. I was absolutely alone, lying on the white gravel beside a dying fire.

Ten

The final stage began.

When I reached home, I washed the blood from my face and went upstairs to bed and stayed there thirty-six hours. I was without friends—Paul was dead, Duane hated me, and Polar Bears had revealed himself as an enemy too complex to see clearly. I felt his touch burning me like a branding iron, and that touch was worse than his blows. My only protection was Rinn, a woman more than ninety years old. Yet if Polar Bears and Arden in general had absolved me of suspicion, why did I need protection? From Zack? I had done my worst there. I rolled under the damp sheets, groaning. I felt great dread.

I know that I waited, hearing nothing but the sound of my own voice saying to Polar Bears over the body of Paul Kant that there was another possibility, but it was too crazy, and knowing that it was there that my real dread originated . . . and lay rigid with tension. But nothing happened. There is no other possibility, I told myself. Gradually I calmed, eventually I went back to sleep.

I woke, aware of the smell of cold water inundating the room. "Alison," I said.

A hand touched my shoulder. This happened. I rolled over and reached out and touched—I touched the body of a girl. A slight cold body, much colder than my hands. I was in that condition of only partial wakefulness when reality is at its most tenuous. I was conscious only of having been forgiven, and of her presence. My hands went, on their own impulse, to her face and felt what I could not see, the taut cheekbones bracketing that wild contradictory magical face, then her smooth hair. I felt her smile loosing itself under my palm, and there was no doubt that it was the smile of Alison Greening. A great general feeling of blessedness suffused my entire body. I touched her slim legs, embraced her lithe waist, cradled my head in the dip of flesh at the base of her neck. I have never felt such joy.

Actually, I have felt precisely that joy, and for the same reason: during the years of our marriage, I would at times come groggily half-awake and brush against Joan and think *Alison,* and embrace her, feeling in her longer taller body as we made love the lineaments of the dead girl I needed. At such moments, I experienced the same numb ecstasy, the same blessing; but on this night, the sensations were even more particularized, and as I embraced her shoulders and entered her, the small hands on my back and the slender body beneath mine were undoubtedly Alison's. Everything else vanished, all the wretchedness of the past week. If we had been on a battlefield I would not have noticed the gunfire and exploding shells.

As her body warmed, the strangeness began. It was not that her body changed—it was not as crude as that—but that it seemed at times during the night double-exposed, shifting imperceptibly in shape so that in one half of a second it was that body I had seen flashing in the water and in the other half it was fuller, so that a leg drawn up against my flank seemed to increase in weight, to press with greater urgency. The breasts against my chest were small, then heavy, then small; the waist, slim, then sturdy; but it is more accurate to say that both were present at once and when

I was aware of this double-exposure I dully imagined it as a flickering between the two halves of a second.

Once, for only a moment that was submerged deep into an onrushing succession of longer moments—a moment like the smaller fraction concealed within a fraction—my hands seemed to touch something besides flesh.

Hours later I opened my eyes and saw young skin beneath me, a curve of flesh which resolved itself into a shoulder. Hands were kneading my back, a round knee lifted between my legs. The bed was a bath of odors. Sexual perfume, that raw, pungent odor, talcum powder, young skin, newly-washed hair. And the smell of blood. I jerked my head up and saw that the girl beneath me, even now sliding her hand to excite me once again, was Alison Updahl.

I scrambled off. "You."

"Mnnn." She crept forward into me. Her eyes were flat and pale as ever, but her face was soft.

"How long have you been here?"

She laughed. "I wanted to surprise you. But last night you didn't even act surprised. Just starved. You really make a girl feel welcome."

"How long have you been here?"

"Since about one last night. Your face is all cut up where Mr. Hovre hit you. You know that dumb deputy he has, Dave Lokken? He's been telling everybody. About two days ago. About how Mr. Hovre hit you. How it was Paul Kant all along. So I thought I'd help you celebrate. Even though you tried to make him think it was Zack. But that was just stupid."

"I want you to leave."

"Oh, it's okay. I mean, he won't know anything about it. It's Thursday morning, and on Thursday mornings he always goes over to the Co-op. He doesn't even know I'm out of the house."

I looked at her carefully. She seemed to be entirely comfortable, unaware of any oddity.

"You were here all night?"

"Huh? Sure I was."

"You didn't feel anything strange?"

"Only you." She giggled, and put an arm around my neck. "You're pretty strange. You shouldn't have said that about Zack to Mr. Hovre. Zack really likes you. He even read some of those books you gave him, like he told you. He usually only reads books about crime, you know, murder and stuff. Did you say it because of out at the quarry? What we did? We were just fooling around. You were cute then. Even after, when you were mad, you were looking at me—you know. 'Course I didn't have any clothes on. Like now."

She grimaced, apparently having scratched herself on something in the bed, and brushed off her hip with her hand; the gesture uncovered all of her compact upper body, and I felt an involuntary flame of sexual interest—the Woodsman was right. I had been starved. I still felt as though I had not made love in months. I reached over and cupped one of her breasts. The smell of blood began to pour outward again. My only excuse is that we were in bed together, and that she was being deliberately seductive. It was an experience entirely different from that of the night before. Her body was altogether foreign to me, our rhythms did not match, and I kept being thrown out of stride by sudden charges and spasms from her. Eventually I rolled over and let her direct things, as she evidently wished to do. It was an awkward performance, I suppose unhelped by my doubts about my own sanity. I had been so certain that my partner had been my cousin; when I tried to recall the "double exposure" sensation, it seemed very vague. But one thing was certain—Alison Updahl was a sexual stranger to me, less melodic with her body.

When it was over, she sat up in the bed. "Well. Your heart wasn't in that one."

"Alison," I said, having to ask it, "did Zack do those things—the killings? Because Paul Kant didn't, in spite of what Polar Bears thinks."

Her tenderness had vanished before I had finished

speaking. She swiveled her legs over the side of the bed, making it impossible for me to see her face. I thought that her shoulders were trembling. "Zack only talks about stuff, he never does it." She lifted her head. "Hey, what do you have in this bed anyhow, I was scratching myself on it all morning." She stood up, turned to face me, and threw back the sheet. On the bottom sheet lay a scattering of thin brown twigs—about enough to cover the palm of a hand. "Time you changed your sheets," she said, in control of herself again. "They're starting to sprout."

I looked with a dry throat at the small things beside me on the rumpled sheet. She turned away.

"Alison," I said, "answer something for me."

"I don't want to talk about those things."

"No. Listen. Did you and Zack request a song on the radio about two weeks ago? From A and Z, for all the lost ones?"

"Yes. But I said I can't talk about that—please, Miles."

Of course Alison had no notion of what those finger-like twigs meant to me, and when I got hurriedly out of bed she at first ignored me as she dressed. "Not exactly chatty, are you? Except for stupid questions," she said, yanking a T shirt over her head. "Not exactly big on smalltalk, hey Miles?" She squirmed into her jeans. "You just like to ruin things. Well, you don't have to worry. I won't invade your privacy any more." Then, when I did not protest, she looked at me more closely. "Hey Miles, what is going on? You looked just as spooked as you did that first day you came back."

"I'm not surprised," I said. "I have the same reason. For your own good, you'd better leave."

"For my own good? Jesus, are you ever a case."

"No doubt," I said, and she stamped her feet into clogs and clattered down the stairs without saying goodbye.

Other explanations—there had to be other explanations. I had picked up the twigs on my clothing as I had walked into the woods, or simply while walking around the farm. Or they had adhered to my clothing when Polar Bears had permitted Dave Lokken to let me fall. I stood up and brushed them from the sheets. Eventually I straightened the bed, dressed, went into my office and took a pencil and some sheets of paper downstairs to try to work at the kitchen table. Tuta Sunderson showed up not long after, and I asked her to change the sheets.

"Heard you was over at Andy's the other morning," she announced, hands on hips. "Lot went on there, I guess."

"Um," I said.

"You'll be grateful for some of it, I guess."

"Nothing like a good beating."

"Red says that Paul Kant should have been run off a long time ago."

"That sounds like good old Red."

"I think he killed himself. That boy Paul was always a weak one."

"Yes, that's one of your favorite theories, isn't it?"

Portion of Statement by Tuta Sunderson:

July 18

The way I saw it, I wasn't going to rush into thinking something just because everyone else did. There wasn't any proof, was there? I think Paul Kant just snapped—he was too weak to take the pressure, and he broke. He never even confessed, did he? No. And you still hadn't found that other girl yet. I keep an open mind.

Anyhow, I was goin' to keep on watching Miles. In case he decided to run or something. So I went over on Wednesday morning just like always, and I'll tell you what I was thinking about—that torn-up picture of Duane's girl I found. That just sat in my mind, bothering me. I mean, what goes through a man's mind when he tears up a picture of a girl? You think about that.

So, like I said, I saw the girl leave his house that morning just when I was walking up the road. I says to myself, you've been where you shouldn't be, little girl, and I stayed out there on the road a little bit so he wouldn't know I saw, and when he sent me up to change his sheets I knew just what they'd been up to. You can lie all you want to, and some do, but you can't fool the person who washes your sheets.

I made up my mind I'd talk to Red. I knew sure as shooting that he'd get real mad, but I wanted him to decide if we should tell Duane. He's the man now.

Half a dozen times that day I nearly left, got into the car and took off for someplace—it did not matter where. But I still did not have my car and I still thought there might be other explanations than the one which had leaked into my consciousness on the night when I had looked through the window of my room and seen that slight figure blasting cold jealous energy at me from the edge of the woods. That was when the conscious fear had started.

And it remained, refusing to be salved by theories. It followed me downstairs and upstairs, it was with me while I bolted my food, and when I sat and wrote, it stood behind me, sending its chill straight through my clothing.

She is your snare, Aunt Rinn had said. All of my life had demonstrated the truth of that statement.

Which put me where I had started, with the overwhelming memory of the terror I had felt, that night in the woods. I tried to reconstruct those moments. Later, I had explained it to myself as a fantasy cooked up out of literature, but *at the time*—that was important, at the time I had sensed nothing literary but instead the pure and overwhelmingly terror of evil. Evil is what we call the force we can discover when we send our minds as far as they can go: when the mind crumbles before something bigger, harder than itself, unknowable and hostile. Had I not courted that evil, by willing my cousin back into life? She did not promise comfort, I knew, thinking again of the figure at the edge of the fields; she did not promise anything I could comprehend.

I still could not admit to myself what I had begun to imagine. That night, the night which changed everything, began calmly enough, in the manner of most of my evenings. I had half-heartedly munched an assortment of things in the kitchen—nuts, a couple of limp carrots, some cheese—and then wandered outside onto the lawn. The night was warm and full of the scents of hay and mown grass, and I could hear crickets chirruping and invisible birds lifting off the walnut trees. I rubbed my face and went down to the road. I could not see the woods, but I knew they were there. From the center of the warm night, an icicle of cold reached out to touch my face. Now that the inhabitants of Arden and the valley had decided that I was innocent of the girls' deaths, I felt more watched, more under observation, than ever before.

I thought of the twigs in my bed, and went back up the drive.

I pulled my chair up to the desk. Mechanically, I began to resume writing. After some minutes I became aware of an intensification of the atmosphere: the air in the room seemed charged, crowded with unseen activity. The overhead light appeared to waver, darkening my shadow on the page before me. I blinked and sat up straight. I could smell cold water all about me.

A palm of cold wind struck the pencil from my hand, an elbow of wind cut into my body.

The light darkened as my shadow had, and I was immediately aware of Alison's presence fighting to enter me. My face and hands were icy. I tipped backwards in my chair, windmilling my arms. She was coming in through nose and eyes and mouth; I screamed with terror. A stack of paper shot up into the air and fragmented. I felt my mind become elastic, skidding, stretching out of my control. She was within my mind, within my body: beneath my animal terror, I felt her hatred and jealousy. My feet kicked out at the desk, and the door racketed away from the trestles. The typewriter thudded to the ground. My head struck the wooden floor. When my right arm found a stack of books, they geysered up into the air. I felt her hatred on all my senses: the darkness, the burning cold of my mouth and fingertips, the flooding smell of water, a rushing noise, the taste of fire in my mouth. It was punishment for the last sad copulation, that spiritless animal joining. She was boiling within me, and my arms thrashed and my back arched and slammed against the wood. I sent papers flying toward the window, toward the lightbulb. My body was sent rolling across the floor. Saliva, mucus, tears slid across my face. For an instant I was above my body, seeing it thrashing and writhing across the littered floor, watching my slimed face contort and my arms hurling books and papers, and then I was back in the boiling, thrashing mess, suffering like an animal in a fit. Her fingers seemed slipped into mine, her light, violent bones overlay mine.

My ears were pressed forward, fluid filled my nose, my chest burst.

When my eyes opened it was over. I heard myself panting, not screaming. I had not sensed her leaving, but she had left. I was looking at a quiet edge of the moon through the window above the toppled desk.

Then my stomach violently unlocked itself, and I barely made it downstairs in time. A bitter brown colloidal juice shot upwards into my mouth. At that moment I was seated on the toilet, feeling watery liquid expel itself from the other end of my body with an equal force, and I turned my head toward the sink, my eyes closed and a sickly perspiration blossoming on my face.

When I came limply out of the bathroom into the kitchen I had to support myself by leaning against the sink as I drank glass after glass of cold water. Cold water. The smell pervaded the house.

She wanted me dead. She wanted me with her. On that night which seemed a century ago, Rinn had warned me. *She means death.*

And the other things—the girls' deaths? I looked that dread in the face, fully, for the first time. I sat in the room I had labored to prepare for her and numbly tried to accept what I had refused to think about before: the other possibility I had mentioned to Polar Bears. I had awakened Alison's spirit, that terrible force I had felt in the woods, and I knew now that spirit was rancid with jealousy of life. On the twenty-first she would appear—and would have anyhow, I now saw, even if I had not worked at reconstructing the old interior of the farmhouse—but as the date drew nearer, she was growing in strength. She could take life. That, she had been able to do from the day I had begun to draw near the valley.

I sat in the cold room, paralyzed straight down to the core. Alison. I thought: the twenty-first begins at midnight on the twentieth. One day away from the day just beginning to appear in stripes of dark purple over the woods blackening the hills.

As the morning drew closer I moved out onto the porch. The bands of purple increased in width; the wide fields, striped yellow and green, grew in visibility and detail. Fog lay upon them in trails of misty gray, wisps of cotton snagged in the corn.

Footsteps awoke me. My hands and feet were cold. The sky had become a flat uniform pale blue, and the mist was gone from everywhere but the very edges of the woods. It was going to be one of those days when the moon is visible all morning, hanging in blue sky like a white dead stone. Tuta Sunderson was coming heavily up the drive, trudging as though her shoes were encased in concrete. Her bag jigged at her side. When she saw me, her mouth clapped shut and her face hardened. I waited for her to open the screen door and come onto the porch.

"You don't have to come here any more," I said. "The job is over."

"What do you mean?" I could see suspicion darken her goggling eyes.

"Your employment is terminated. I don't need you any more. The job is *finis. Kaput.* Ended. Over. Finished. Done."

"You been sitting here all night?" She crossed her arms over her chest, an operation requiring an impressive amount of effort. "Drinking gin?"

"Please go home, Mrs. Sunderson."

"You afraid of my seeing something? Well, I've already seen it."

"You haven't seen anything."

"You look kinda sick. What did you do, swallow a bottle of aspirin or something?"

"I don't know how suicide ever got along without you."

"By rights I should get the whole week's wages."

"Indeed you should. In fact you should get two weeks' wages. Forgive me. Please take fourteen dollars." I reached in my pocket, drew out bills, counted out two fives and four ones and handed them to her.

"One week's, I told you. That's five dollars. You're paying for today, Friday and Saturday besides the three days I worked." She took one of the fives and dropped the rest of the money beside me on the porch swing.

"Splendid. Please go and leave me alone. I realize that I've been awful to you. I couldn't help it. I'm sorry."

"I know what you're doing," she said. "You're as filthy as any beast of the field."

"That was eloquent." I closed my eyes. After a while the noise of her breathing changed, and I could hear her turning around. I was getting better. Now I could smell anger. Thank you, Alison. The screen door banged shut, I kept my eyes closed as I heard her walking down the drive.

Who slept together?

One crushed an anthill.

One broke a chair.

One was afraid.

One swam in blood.

One had cold hands.

One had the last word.

When I opened my eyes she was gone. A dusty brown Ford, the mailman's car, came up the road and passed the impaled metal receptacle without braking. No more fan mail, no more letters from my cousin. Yes. It made sense. Her body—her skeleton, after twenty years—was in a graveyard in Los Angeles, beneath a headstone I had never seen. So she had to put herself together out of the available materials. Or be just a wind, the cold breath of spirit. Leaves, gravel, thorns. Thorns for tearing.

I stood up and went down from the porch. I said in my mind: thorns for tearing. I felt as though I were walking in my sleep. The door on the driver's side of the Nash had slipped out of alignment, and it dipped when I opened it, creaking loudly in a voice like rust.

For a moment I could not remember where I was going, and simply put-putted up the road, going slowly and serenely as Duane on the big tractor. Then I remembered. The last, the only help. I depressed the accelerator, made the car rattle, picked up speed as I went past the Sunderson house. Mrs. Sunderson was at one of the windows, watching me go by. Then the shell of the school, the church, the tight curve at the sandstone bluff. I passed Andy's, and saw him pumping gas. His face was like clotted milk. Behind him was a large black area of dead land. His clotted-milk face swung around, tracking me as I passed.

When I came to the narrow path going up between the fields to the trees I swung hard on the wheel again and began to bounce along, going in the direction of the sun. A few ears of corn in the row nearest the

road had been struck down, broken off at the stalk, and
they lay flattened and sprawling at the field's edge.
Here and there, whole rows had been trampled down;
stick-leg cornstalks tilted crazily. Soon I reached the
first of the trees, and then the fields vanished behind
me and I was threading between big oaks. The narrow
early sunlight filtered by the boughs and leaves came
down in ribbons. I parked on the slope beside the tall
red henhouse. When I got out of the car I could hear
the gabbling of the birds. A few terrified hens ran away
into the woods, lurching from side to side.

I looked in the henhouse first. I pulled open the
doors and stepped inside, hit once again by the stench.
It seemed even stronger than on the day when I had
clumsily helped her cull the eggs. Two or three birds
flapped their wings, high up on their nests. Beaked
heads swiveled, button eyes stared fixedly. Slowly, I
backed out, the fixed eyes glaring at me from the sides
of their old men's heads. I closed the door as gently
as she had taught me.

Two chickens were roosting on the hood of the Nash.
I went up the path toward her house. Here the sunlight
was blocked from entering directly, and there was only
a golden hovering rustle overhead, where the leaves
formed another sky. The little house seemed dark
and empty.

One had cold hands.

One had the last word.

On a counter in the kitchen stood a plate stacked
with something wrapped in a red and white gingham
cloth. I touched the cloth. It was dry. I folded it back,
and saw mould sprinkled green on the surface of the
top piece of lefsa.

She was in the bedroom, lying in the middle of the
double bed. A yellowed sheet, a patchwork quilt, covered her. My nostrils caught an odor like a deep bass
chord. I knew she was dead before I touched her and
felt the stiffness of her fingers. The white hair was
spread thickly on the embroidered pillow case. Two,
three days dead, I thought. She might have died while

Paul Kant's body was being dragged from the flames of the Dream House, or while I was fitting my body within a ghost's. I put down her stiff hand and went back into the dark kitchen to telephone the Arden police.

"Uh, goddam," said Dave Lokken after I had spoken two sentences of explanation. "You're there now? With her?"

"Yes."

"You say you found her?"

"Yes."

"Any, uh, marks on her? Any signs of, uh, assault? Any indication of cause of death?"

"She was about ninety-four years old," I said. "I suppose that'll do for cause of death."

"Well goddam. Goddam. You say you just found her now? What the hell were you doing up there anyways?"

For the last protection. "She was my grandmother's sister," I said.

"Uh, family reasons," he said, and I knew he was writing it down. "So you're up there in those woods now? That's where her farm is, right?"

"That's where I am."

"Well, goddam." I couldn't figure out why he was so agitated by my information. "Look. Teagarden, you don't budge. Just stay there until I can get out there with an ambulance. Don't touch anything."

"I want to talk to Polar Bears," I said.

"Well, you can't. You get that? The Chief ain't here now. But don't worry, Teagarden, you'll be talkin' to the Chief soon enough." He hung up without saying goodby.

Lokken had been like a being from another, more furious world, and I went back into Rinn's bedroom and sat beside her on the bed. I realized that I was still moving with the numbness which had settled on me during my almost sleepless night in the living room I had prepared for Alison Greening, and I nearly stretched out on the bed beside Rinn's body. Her face seemed smoother in death, less Chinese and wrinkled. I was conscious of the bones pushing through the skin of her face. I touched her cheek and then tried to pull the sheet and quilt up over her head. They were pinned beneath her arms; and I remembered Lokken's telling me not to touch anything.

It was over an hour before I heard vehicles coming up the drive from the valley road, and went onto her porch to see a police car drawing up alongside the Nash, followed by an ambulance.

Chubby Dave Lokken bounced out of the police car and waved angrily at the two men in the ambulance. They got out and crossed their arms and leaned against the side of the ambulance. One of them was smoking, and the leafage of smoke from his cigarette wound up to the dense covering of trees. "You, Teagarden," Lokken shouted, and I turned my head to look at him. For the first time I saw the rumpled-looking man wearing a suit who stood beside the deputy. He had a Marine crewcut and wore thick glasses. "Teagarden, get the hell out here!" Lokken shouted. The man beside him sighed and rubbed his face, and I saw the black bag in his hands.

I came down from the porch. Lokken was nearly hopping with rage and impatience. I could see his breasts bulging in his uniform shirt. "All right. What's your story, Teagarden?"

"What I told you."

"Is she in the house?" asked the doctor. He looked very tired, and as though Dave Lokken had begun to wear on him.

I nodded, and the doctor began to move up the path.

"Hold on. I got a few questions first. You say you found her. Is that right?"

"That's what I said and that's right."

"You got a witness?"

One of the ambulance men snickered, and Lokken's face began to flush. "Well?"

"No. No witnesses."

"You say you just came here this morning?"

I nodded.

"What time?"

"Just before I called you."

"I suppose she was dead when you got here?"

"Yes."

"Where were you coming from?" He put great weight on the question.

"The Updahl farm."

"Anybody see you there? Wait up, doc. I wanta finish here before we go in. Well?"

"Tuta Sunderson saw me. I fired her this morning."

Lokken seemed puzzled and angered by this detail, but he decided to ignore it. "You touch the old woman in any way?"

I nodded. The doctor looked at me for the first time.

"You did, huh? You touched her? How?"

"I held her hand."

His color darkened, and the ambulance man snickered again.

"What made you decide to come up here this morning anyhow?"

"I wanted to see her."

"Just wanted to see her." His flabby incompetent face shouted that he would love to swing at me.

"I've had a rough morning," said the doctor. "Dave, let's get this over with so I can get back and write my reports."

"Uh huh," said Lokken, violently nodding his head. "Teagarden, this here honeymoon of yours might come to a sudden end."

The doctor looked at me with an almost professional curiosity, and then he and Lokken went marching up to the house.

I watched them go, and then looked at the ambulance men. They were both concentrating on the ground. One glanced at me and then snatched his cigarette from his mouth and scowled at it as if he were thinking of changing brands. After a moment I went back inside the house.

"Natural causes," the doctor was saying. "Looks like no problems with this one. She just ran out of life."

Lokken nodded, writing on a pad, and then looked up and noticed me. "Hey! Get out of here, Teagarden. You ain't even supposed to be in here!"

I went out onto the porch. A minute later, Lokken bustled past me to wave in the ambulance men, who disappeared behind for a second and then reappeared carrying a stretcher. I followed them into the house, but did not go as far as the bedroom. They needed no more than seconds to place Rinn on the stretcher. The sheets and quilt had been replaced by a white blanket, pulled up over her face.

As we stood watching them carrying her down to the ambulance, Lokken was a symphony of small movements: he tapped a foot, buffed a shoe on his trouser leg, patted his fat thigh with his fingertips, adjusted his holster. I understood that all this expressed his reluctance to stand so near me. When the doctor came out saying, "Let's shake it, I got four hours' work on the other one," Lokken turned to me and said, "Okay, Teagarden. But we got people who will say they saw you going up into those woods. Don't you go anywhere but back home. Got me? Hey, Professor? You got me?"

All of which was explained by a visit I received later that day. I had been picking up the papers in my office, just gathering them up by the armful and dropping them into bushel baskets. The typewriter was useless now; the carriage had been bent so that the roller would not advance, and I threw the machine into the root cellar.

When I heard a car driving up toward the house I looked out the window: the car had already drawn up too close to the house to be visible. I waited for a knock but none came. I went downstairs and saw a police car drawn right up before the porch. Polar Bears was sitting on the near front fender, wiping his forehead with a big speckled handkerchief.

He saw me come out onto the porch, put his hand down, and shifted his body slightly so that he was facing me. "Step outside, Miles," he said.

I stood right in front of the screen door with my hands in my pockets.

"Sorry about old Rinn," he said. "I suppose I should apologize about Dave Lokken, too. Dr. Hampton, the county M.E., says my deputy was a little rough with you."

"Not by your standards. He was just stupid and pompous."

"Well, he's no mental giant," Polar Bears said. There was a quiet watchful quality—a restraint—to his manner which I had not seen before. We stayed where we were and regarded each other for a bit before he spoke again. I didn't give a damn for him or anything he said. "Thought you'd like to know. The M.E. says she died forty-eight, maybe sixty hours ago. The way he puts it together, she probably knew it was happening and just got into bed and died. Heart attack. Nice and simple."

"Does Duane know?"

"Yep. He got her transferred to the funeral parlor this afternoon. She'll be buried day after tomorrow." His big head was tilting, looking at me with squinting eyes. Beside him, his hat pointed toward me so that I could see light reflected from the star-shield pinned to the crown.

"Well, thanks," I said, and moved to go back inside.

"One more thing."

I stopped. "Yes?"

"I oughta explain to you why Dave Lokken was acting sorta extra uptight."

"I'm not interested," I said.

"Oh, you're interested, Miles. See, we found that Michalski girl this morning." He sent me one of his low heavy smiles. "Funny sort of coincidence there. She was dead, naturally. But I don't expect that's a surprise."

"No. Nor to you." I felt the dread again, and leaned against the screen door.

"Nope. I expected it. The thing is, Miles, she was right up there in those woods—not three hundred yards from Rinn's little cabin. We started workin' our way in from 93—" pointing with one arm—"and we just *pored* through them woods, see, lookin' at every little twig, and this morning we found her buried under loose dirt in a sort of clearing up there."

I swallowed.

"You know that clearing, Miles?"

"I might."

"Uh huh. Real good. That's why old Dave was sorta salty with you—you were up there with one body, and we found another one so close you could spit that far. It's just a little natural clearing, got some campfire remains in the middle of it. Been used pretty regular, by the look of it."

I nodded. I kept my hands in my pockets.

"Could be you used to go up there. Now that don't make any difference but for one fact. Oh, and Miles, she was worse than the other two. Her feet were burned. Come to think of it, her hair was burned too. And, let me see. Oh yeah. She was sorta kept there. This friend of ours, he tied her to a tree or something and—I'm only guessing—went up at night to work on her. For more than a week."

I thought of the slight figure drawing me up toward the clearing, and of how I had taken the warm ashes as a sign of her healing presence.

"You wouldn't happen to have any idea about who'd do a thing like that, would you?"

I was going to say *yes,* but instead said, "You think it was Paul Kant?"

Polar Bears nodded like a proud schoolmaster. "Real good. Real good. See, that brings up the little fact I mentioned before. What do we need to know?"

"How long she's been dead."

"Miles, you shoulda been a cop. See, we don't think she died of—our friend's little experiments. She was strangled. Big fucking bruises on her throat. Now our friend Dr. Hampton isn't sure yet when that might have happened. But suppose it happened after Paul Kant killed himself?"

I said, "It's not me, Polar Bears."

He just sat there blinking, feigning polite attention. When I said no more, he folded his hands into his lap. "Now, we both know who it isn't, don't we, Miles? I had a talk with your prime suspect yesterday. He told me that those Coke bottles came from Du-ane's cellar, where you could get at 'em pretty easy, and he says you threw out that doorknob yourself. They were Du-ane's. Says he doesn't know how they got in his truck. And I know he hasn't been up in the woods at night, because he confessed to me what he's been doing with his nights." He smiled again. "He and Du-ane's girl used to go down to that shack behind Andy's. Do pokey-pokey all night. Paul Kant sort of ruined their fun."

"Nobody living is the one you want," I said.

He squinted up his entire face, then let out a dis-gusted grunt and put his hat back on his head. "Miles, if you go crazy on me you're gonna ruin all the fun." On went his sunglasses. He pushed himself off the fender. He looked like something you'd run from on a dark night. "Why don't you take a little trip with me?"

"A trip?"

"A little jaunt. I want to show you something. Get into my car."

I just looked at him, trying to figure it out.

"Get your ass in the car, Miles."

I did as I was told.

He spun the squadcar out onto the highway without speaking to me, his face a tight mask of distaste. All of those unhappy odors began to build up. We went toward Arden at a good twenty miles over the speed limit.

"You're taking me to her parents," I said.

He did not reply.

"You finally decided to arrest me."

"Shut up," he said.

But we did not stop at the police station. Polar Bears zoomed straight through Arden, and we picked up more speed as we left town. Restaurants, the bowling alley, fields. The farms and the corn took over again. Now we were in the same country he had driven me through before, the afternoon I had talked to Paul Kant: wide fields green and yellow, and the Blundell River shining through a screen of trees. Eventually Polar Bears took off his hat and sailed it onto the back seat. He ran a palm over his forehead. "Too damn hot," he said.

"I still don't get it. If you were going to work me over you could have done it miles back."

"I don't want to hear your voice," he said. Then he glanced over at me. "Do you know what's in Blundell?"

I shook my head.

"Well, you're gonna find out."

Exhausted-looking cows swung their heads to watch us pass.

"The state hospital?"

"Yeah, that's there." He would say no more.

Hovre hit the accelerator even harder, and we sped past the sign at the Blundell town limits. It was a town much like Arden, one main street lined with stores, wooden houses with porches on a small grid of streets. Lightbulbs on a string and a row of banners hung before a used-car lot, the banners too limp to flap. A few men in straw hats and working clothes squatted on the curb.

Polar Bears took the first road out of town, and then guided the patrol car into what looked like a park. The road turned narrow. It was edged with a long green lawn. "State hospital grounds," he said noncommittally. "But you and me ain't going there."

I could see the big gray buildings of the hospital complex appearing through the trees to my left. They had a Martian remoteness. Sun umbrellas dotted the lawn, but no one sat beneath them.

"I'm gonna do you a real favor," he said. "Most tourists never get to see this feature of our county."

The road divided, and Polar Bears turned into the left fork, which soon ended in a gray parking lot before a low gray building like an ice cube. Shrubs around the sides of the cube struggled in the hard clay. I realized where I was a half second before I saw the metal plate staked into the ground in the midst of the shrubs.

"Welcome to the Furniveau County Morgue," Polar Bears said, and got out of the car. He went across the tacky asphalt of the lot without looking back at me.

I reached the door just as it closed behind him. I pushed it open and stepped into a cold white interior. Machinery hummed behind the walls.

"This here's my assistant," Polar Bears was saying. I realized after a moment that he meant me. He had his sunglasses off, and he rested his hands on his hips. In the antiseptic cold interior of the morgue, he smelled like a buffalo. A short dark-complected man in a spotted white coat sat at a battered desk in an alcove and incuriously looked at him. The desk was bare except for a portable radio and an ashtray. "I want him to have a look at the new one."

The man glanced at me. It didn't make any difference to him. Nothing made any difference to him.

"Which new one?"

"Michalski."

"Uh huh. She's back from the autopsy. Didn't know you had any new deputies."

"He's a volunteer," said Polar Bears.

"Well, what the hell," the man said, and pushed himself away from the desk. He went through green metal doors at the end of the hall. "After you," said Polar Bears, waving me through.

It was useless to protest. I followed the attendant down a cold row of metal lockers. Hovre followed, so close that he nearly walked on my heels.

"You braced for this?" he asked me.

"I don't see the point," I said.

"You pretty soon will."

The dark-complected man stopped before one of the lockers, took a ring of keys from his pocket, and unlocked the door.

"Belly up," said Polar Bears.

The little man pulled the long tray out of the locker. A dead naked girl was lying on the slab. I had thought they covered them with sheets. "God," I said, seeing her wounds and the scars from the autopsy.

Polar Bears was waiting, very still. I looked at the girl's face. Then I began to perspire in the icy room.

Polar Bears' voice came: "She remind you of anybody?"

I tried to swallow. It was more than enough proof, if I needed any more proof. "Did the first two look more or less the same?"

"Pretty close," said Polar Bears. "That Strand girl was as close as a sister might be."

I remembered the violence of the hatred I had felt when she had seemed to storm inside me. She had come back all right, and she had killed three girls who had an accidental resemblance to her. I would be next.

"Interesting, isn't it?" said Hovre. "Close 'er up, Archy."

The dark little man, who had been standing with his arms braced against the front of the locker as if asleep on his feet, pushed the tray back into the locker.

"Now let's go back to the car," said Polar Bears.

I followed him out into the blast of heat and sunlight. He drove me back to the Updahl farm without saying a word.

After he turned up the drive he cut the patrol car onto the lawn before the porch and got out as I did. He came toward me, a big intimidating physical presence. "Suppose we just agree to stay put until I get the final word from the M.E."

"Why don't you put me in jail?"

"Why, Miles, you're my assistant on this case," he said, and got back into his car. "In the meantime, get some sleep. You look like hell." As he twirled the car into the drive, I saw the grim, entirely satisfied smile on his lips.

I woke up late in the night. Alison Greening was seated on the chair at the foot of the bed. I could just distinguish her face and the shape of her body in the moonlight. I feared—I do not know what I feared, but I feared for my life. She did nothing. I sat up in the bed: I felt terribly naked and unprotected. She seemed utterly normal; she looked like an ordinary young woman. She was looking straight at me, her expression placid and unemotional, abstracted. For a moment I thought that she looked too ordinary to have caused all the upheavals in me and in Arden. Her face was waxen. Then my fear came booming back into me, and I opened my mouth to say something. Before I could form words, she was gone.

I got out of bed, touched the chair, and went across the top of the house to my office. Papers still lay on the floor, papers spilled out of bushel baskets. She was not there.

In the morning I gulped down a half-pint of milk, thought with distaste of food, and knew that I had to get away. Rinn had been right, all that time ago. I had to leave the valley. The sight of her calmly, emotionlessly sitting on the chair at the foot of the bed, her blank face washed in moonlight, was more frightening than the frantic assault on my room. I could see that face, drained by the pale light, and it held no feeling I recognized; the complications of emotion had been erased. There was no more life in it than there was in a mask. I set down the bottle, checked my pockets for money and keys, and went outside into the sunlight. Dew lay shining on the grass.

Highway 93 to Liberty, I thought, then down to where I could pick up the freeway to La Crosse, and then I'd cross the river and head for a small town where I would leave the Nash and telegraph the New York Chemical for money and buy a second-hand car and go to Colorado or Wyoming, where I knew nobody. I backed out into the valley road and picked up speed, heading for the highway.

When I checked the rear-view mirror as I passed the church, I saw another car keeping pace with me.

I accelerated, and it kept the distance between us
steady. It was like the prelude to that awful night when
I had lost her, the night when we had made the vow.
As the other car picked up speed and came closer, I
saw black and white and knew that it was a police
car. If it's Polar Bears, I thought, I'll attack him with
my bare hands. I pushed the accelerator to the floor,
and yanked at the wheel as I went around the curve
by the sandstone bluff. The Nash began to vibrate.
The patrol car pulled up easily and began to nose in
before me, forcing me to the side of the road. I spun
into Andy's and went around the gaspumps. The patrol
car anticipated me and moved ahead to block my exit.
I looked around, considering backing up and swinging
around into the side parking lot, but his car would
have caught the old Nash in thirty seconds. I turned off
the ignition.

I got out of the car and stood up. The man behind
the wheel of the patrol car opened his door and rose
up into the sunshine. It was Dave Lokken. Walking
toward me, he kept his right hand on his holster.

"Nice little race." He was imitating Polar Bears, even
in his slow walk. "Where do you think you were going?"

I slumped against the hot metal of the Nash. "Shopping."

"You wasn't thinking about leaving, I hope. Because
that's why I been sittin' out near your place for two
days, to make sure you don't even think about it."

"You were watching me?"

"For your own good," he said, grinning. "The Chief
says you need a lot of help. I'm gonna help you stick
around where we can keep an eye on you. The medical
examiner is supposed to call the Chief real soon now."

"I'm not the one you're looking for," I said. "I'm
telling you the truth."

"I guess you're gonna tell me it was Chief Hovre's
boy Zack. I heard you say that a couple of nights back.
You might just as well of put a gun to your head. His

boy is all the family the Chief's got. Now get back and get home."

I remembered the pale mask looking at me from the foot of the bed; and then I looked up toward the windows of Andy's store. Andy and his wife were standing up there looking down at us, one face showing horror, the other contempt.

"Come on and help me get my car back," I said and turned my back on him.

After a couple of steps I stopped walking. "What would you say if I told you your Chief raped and killed a girl?" I asked. "Twenty years ago."

"I'd say you was lookin' to get your head blown off. Just like you been doin' since you got here."

"What would you say if I told you that the girl he raped—" I turned back around, looked at his angry yokel's face and gave up. He smelled like burning rubber. "I'm going into Arden," I said. "Tag along."

I saw him driving along behind me all the way to Arden, at times speaking into his radio microphone, and when I haggled with the boy Hank Speltz, he stayed in the car and parked across the street from the garage. The boy at first told me that the "repairs" to the VW would cost me five hundred dollars, and I refused to pay it. He shoved his hands into the pockets of his coveralls and looked at me with sullen hatred. I asked him what he had done. "Had to rebuild most of the motor. Patch what I couldn't rebuild. Lots of stuff. New belts."

"I imagine you're being funny," I said. "I don't think you could rebuild a cigarette."

"Pay up or no car. You want me to get the police?"

"I'll give you fifty dollars and that's it. You haven't even shown me a worksheet."

"Five hundred. We don't use worksheets. People around here trust us."

It was my day for being reckless. I went across the street and opened Lokken's door and made him follow

me back to the garage. Hank Speltz looked as though
he regretted his remark about getting the police.

"Well," Speltz said after I had forced Lokken to
listen to an account of our interchange, "I was chargin'
you in advance for the body work."

Lokken looked at him disgustedly.

"I'll give you thirty bucks," I said.

Speltz howled, "You said fifty!"

"I changed my mind."

"Make out a bill for thirty," said Lokken. The boy
went inside to the garage's office.

"It's funny," I told Lokken, "you can't do any wrong
in this country if you've got a cop beside you."

Lokken waddled away without replying, and Speltz
reappeared, grumbling that the new windows had cost
more than thirty dollars.

"Now fill it up," I said. "It's on my credit card."

"We don't take out-of-state credit cards."

"Deputy!" I yelled, and Lokken glowered at us from
behind the wheel of his car.

"Shee-ut," the boy said. When I pulled the battered
car up to the pumps, he filled the tank and returned
with the credit card apparatus.

Out on the street, Lokken pulled his car up beside
mine and leaned toward me. "I had some news on my
radio a while back. I probably won't be watching you
any more." Then he reversed, turned around, and sped
away down Main Street, going in the direction of the
police headquarters.

I discovered what Hank Speltz had meant about re-
building the engine when I pressed the accelerator going up the hill past the R-D-N motel. The car died, and
I had to coast over to the curb and wait several minutes before it would start again. This was repeated
when I went up the hill toward the Community Chest
thermometer and the Italian distance, and again when
I was coming down the last hill toward the highway.
It cut out a fourth time when I pulled into the drive,
and I let the car coast to a stop on the lawn.

Another police car was drawn up in my usual place

before the garage. I saw the Chief's star on the door.

I began to walk toward the figure sitting on the porch swing. "Everything work out okay at the filling station?" asked Polar Bears.

"What are you doing here?"

"Good question. Suppose you come inside and talk about it." Part of the façade had been put aside: his voice was level and weary.

When I came up inside the porch I saw that Polar Bears was sitting beside a pile of my clothing. "That's a brilliant idea," I said. "Take away a man's clothes and he can't go anywhere. The riverbank school of detection."

"I'll get to the clothes in a minute. Sit down." It was an order. I went to a chair at the end of the porch and sat facing him.

"The medical examiner phoned in his report a couple hours ago. He thinks the Michalski girl died on Thursday. Might have been as long as twenty-four hours after Paul Kant meatballed himself."

"A day before you found her."

"That's right." Now he was having difficulty concealing his anger. "We were a day late. We might not have found her at all if someone hadn't decided to tel us that you liked to go up into those woods. Maybe Paul Kant would still be alive too if we'd been there earlier."

"You mean maybe one of your vigilantes wouldn't have killed him."

"Okay." He stood up and walked toward me, his feet making the boards squeak. "Okay, Miles. You've been having lots of fun. You've been making a lot of wild accusations. But the fun's almost over. Why don't you wrap it all up and give me a confession?" He smiled. "It's my job, Miles. I'm being real nice and careful with you. I don't want any sharp Jew lawyer from New York coming out here and saying I walked all over your rights."

"I want you to put me in jail," I said.

"I know you do. I told you that a long time ago.

There's only one little thing you gotta do before your conscience gets a nice rest."

"I think——" I said, and my throat went as tight as Galen Hovre's face. "I know it sounds crazy, but I think Alison Greening killed those girls."

His neck was swelling. "She wrote, I mean she sent, those blank letters. The one I showed you and the other one. I've seen her, Polar Bears. She's back. The night she died we made a vow that we'd meet in 1975, and I came back here because of that, and . . . and she's here. I've seen her. She wants to take me with her. She hates life. Rinn knew. She'd . . ."

I realized with shock that Polar Bears was enraged. In the next second, he moved with more rapidity than I would have thought possible in a man of his size, and kicked the chair out from under me. I went over sideways and rolled into the screen. He kicked out, and his shoe connected with my hip.

"You god-damned idiot," he said. The smell of gunpowder poured over me. He kicked me in the pit of the stomach, and I jackknifed over. Splinters from the boards dug into my cheek. As on the night of Paul's death, Polar Bears bent over me. "You think you're gonna get out of this by playing crazy? I'll tell you about your tramp cousin, Miles. Sure I was there, that night. We were both there. Duane and me. But Duane didn't rape her. I did. Du-ane was too busy knockin' you out." I was struggling to breathe. "I hit her on the head just after Duane clubbed you with a rock. Then I had her. It was just what she wanted—she was only fighting because you were there." He picked up my head by my hair and slammed it down onto the boards. "I didn't even know she was out until it was all over. That little bitch was teasing me all summer, the little cunt. Maybe I even meant to kill her. I don't even know any more. But I know that every time you said that little bitch's name I could have killed you, Miles. You shouldn't have gone messing around with what's past, Miles." He banged my head on the boards once again. "Shouldn't have gone messing." He took his hand off my head and inhaled noisily. "It's no good your tryin' to tell this to anybody, because nobody'll believe you. You know that, don't you?" I could hear his breathing. "Don't you?" His hand came back and slammed my head down again. Then he said, "We're moving inside. I don't want anybody to see this." He picked me up and dragged me inside and dropped me onto the floor. I felt a sharp, bursting pain in my nose and ears. I was still having trouble breathing.

"Arrest me," I said, and heard my voice bubble. "She'll kill me." The weave of a hooked rug cushioned my cheek.

"You want things too easy, Miles." I heard his feet moving on the floor, and tensed for another kick. Then I heard him going into the kitchen. Water splashed. I opened my eyes. He came back drinking from a glass of water.

He sat on the old couch. "I want to know something. How did it feel when you saw Paul Kant on the night he died? How did it feel, looking at that miserable little queer and knowing he was in hell because of what you did?"

"I didn't do it," I said. My voice was still bubbling.

Hovre emitted an enormous sigh. "You're making me do all this the hard way. What about the blood on your clothes?"

"What blood?" I found that I could lever myself up to a sitting position.

"The blood on your clothes. I went through your closet. You got some pants with blood on 'em, a pair of shoes with what could be bloodstains on the uppers." He put the glass down on the floor. "Now I gotta take those to the lab over in Blundell and see if they come out the blood type of any of the girls. Candace Michalski and Gwen Olson were AB, Jenny Strand was type O."

"Blood on my clothes? Oh. Yes. It happened when I cut my hand. The first day I came here. It dripped onto my shoes when I was driving here. Probably on my trousers too."

Hovre shook his head.

"And I'm AB," I said.

"How would you happen to know that, Miles?"

"My wife was a do-gooder. Every year we gave a pint each to the blood center in Long Island City."

"Long Island City." He shook his head again. "And you're AB?" He pushed himself up from the couch, walked past me to get to the porch.

"'Miles," he called to me, "if you're so simon-pure innocent, why are you in such a hurry to be put in jail?"

"I already told you that," I said.

"Kee-rist." He returned holding my clothes and shoes. I felt the pain in my head jump in anticipation as he came toward me. "Now I'm gonna tell you the facts of life," he said. "Word is gonna get around. I'm not going to do anything to stop it. I'm not even going to have Dave Lokken sitting on his fat ass down the road. If anyone comes out here to find you, that's all right with me. A little jungle justice wouldn't bother me a bit. I'd almost rather have you dead than in jail, old pal. And I don't think you're stupid enough to think you can get away from me. Are you? You couldn't get far in that beat-up car anyhow. Hey?" His foot came toward me, and stopped an inch short of my ribs. "Hey?"

I nodded.

"I'll be hearing from you, Miles. I'll be hearing from you. We're both gonna get what we want."

After I soaked for an hour in a hot bath, letting the pain seep away into the steam, I sat upstairs and wrote for several hours—until I saw that it had begun to get dark. I heard Duane shouting at his daughter. His voice rose and fell, monotonously, angrily, insisting on some inaudible point. Both Duane's voice and the on-coming of dark made it impossible to work any longer. To spend another night in the farmhouse was almost impossible: I could still see her, sitting in the chair at the foot of my bed, looking blankly, even dully, at me, as if what I were seeing were only a waxen model of her face and body, a shell a millimeter thick behind which lay spinning stars and gases. I put down the pencil, grabbed a jacket from my plundered closet and went downstairs and outside.

The night was beginning. The dark shapes of clouds drifted beneath an immense sky. Above them hung a moon nearly washed of color. A single arrow of cool breeze seemed to come straight toward the house from high in the black woods. I shuddered, and climbed into the battered Volkswagen.

At first I thought of simply driving around the county roads until I was too tired to go further and then sleep the rest of the night in the car; then I thought I might go to Freebo's and speed oblivion by purchasing it. Oblivion could scarcely cost more than ten dollars, and it was the best buy in Arden. I rattled onto 93, and turned the car toward town. But what sort of reception could I expect in Freebo's? By this time, everybody would know about the medical examiner's report. I would be a ghastly pariah. Or an inhuman thing to be hunted down. At that point the car went dead. I cursed Hank Speltz. I did not even begin to have the mechanical competence to fix whatever the boy had done. I pictured driving back to New York at a steady rate of thirty-five miles an hour. I'd need another mechanic, which meant that I would have to commit most of the money remaining in my account. Then I thought of the waxen face concealing stars and gases, and knew that I would be lucky ever to get back to New York.

That night I made an appeal to compassion, a second appeal to violence.

Finally I got the car started again.

As I sped down one of the Arden back streets I saw a familiar shape passing a lighted picture window, and I cut over to the curb and jumped out of the car before the motor was dead. I ran on the black asphalt in the middle of the road and crossed his lawn. I pressed Bertilsson's bell.

When he opened his door I saw surprise alter his features. His face was as much a mask as hers. He ignored his wife's calls of "Who is it? Who is it?" behind him.

"Well," he said, grinning at me. "Come for my blessing? Or did you have something to confess?"

"I want you to take me in. I want you to protect me."

His wife's face appeared over his shoulder, at some hidden opening in their house, a corner or a door. She began to march forward.

"We've heard the distressing details of the Michalski girl's death," he said. "You have a nice sense of humor, Miles, coming here."

I said, "Please take me in. I need your help."

"I rather think my help is reserved for those who know how to use it."

"I'm in danger. In danger of my life."

His wife's face glared at me now from over his shoulder. "What does he want? Tell him to go away."

"I rather think he's going to ask to be put up for the night."

"Don't you have a duty?" I asked.

"I have a duty to all Christians," he said. "You are not a Christian. You are an abomination."

"Tell him to go away."

"I'm begging you."

Mrs. Bertilsson's head jerked upward, her face cold and hard. "You were too sick to take our advice when we saw you in town, and we're under no obligation to help you now. Are you asking us to let you stay here?"

"Just for a night."

"Do you think I could sleep with you in my house? Close the door, Elmer."

"Wait—"

"An abomination." He slammed the door. A second later I saw the drapes meeting in the middle of the window.

Helpless. Helpless to help, helpless to be helped. This is the story of a man who couldn't get arrested.

I drove to Main and stopped the car in the middle of the empty street. I honked the horn once, then twice. For a moment I rested my forehead on the rim of the steering wheel. Then I opened the door. I could hear the buzz of a neon sign, the momentary beating of wings far overhead. I stood beside the car. Nothing around me moved, nothing demonstrated life. All of the shops were dark; on either side of the street, cars pointed their noses at the curb like sleeping cattle. I shouted. Not even an echo answered. Even the two bars seemed deserted, although illuminated beer signs sparkled in their windows. I walked down the middle of the street toward Freebo's. I felt drifting blue gather around me.

A stone the size of a potato was caught in the grid of a drain by the curbside. It might have been one they had thrown at me. I tugged it out and hefted it in my hand. Then I hurled it at Freebo's long rectangular window. I remembered throwing glasses at the wall of my apartment, back in the passionate days of my marriage. There was an appalling noise, and glass shivered down onto the sidewalk.

And then everything was as it had been. I was still on the empty street; the shops were still light; no one was shouting, no one was running toward me. The only noise was the buzzing of the sign. I owed Freebo about fifty dollars, but I would never be able to pay him. I could smell dust and grass, the odors blown in on the wind from the fields. I imagined men inside the bar, backed away from the windows, holding their breath until I left. Inside with the scarred tables and the jukebox and the flashing beer signs, all waiting for me to leave. The last of the last chances.

On the morning of the twenty-first I woke up in the back seat of the car. I had been permitted to survive the night. Shouts, angry yells from Duane's house up the path. His problems with his daughter seemed terrifically remote, someone's else's problem in someone else's world. I leaned over the carseat and pulled the

door release, pushed the seat forward, and got out. My
back ached; I had a sharp, persistent pain behind my
eyes. When I looked at my watch I saw that it was
thirteen hours to dark: I would not run from it. I
could not. The day, my last, was hot and cloudless.
Sixty feet away, the chestnut mare leaned its head
over the fence of the side field and regarded me with
silky eyes. The air was very still. A big horsefly, greenly
iridescent, began to bustle across the top of the car,
concentrating on the bird droppings. Everything about
me seemed a part of Alison's coming, clues, sections
of a puzzle which would lock into place before midnight.

I thought: if I get back into this car and try to drive
off, she will stop me. Leaves and branches would block
the windshield, vines would trap the accelerator. My
visual sense of this was too powerful—for an instant
I saw the homely interior of the VW choked with a
struggling profusion of foliage, and I gagged on the
spermy odor of sap—and I snatched my hand away
from the top of the car.

I did not see how I could endure the tension of the
intervening hours. Where would I be when she came?

With the desperate foolhardiness of a soldier who
knows that the battle will come whether or not he is
prepared for it, I decided what I would do at nightfall.
Really, there was only one place for me to be when it
happened. I had waited twenty years for it, and I knew
where I would go to await the final moment, where
I had to go, had to be when the noise of rushing wind
came and the woods opened to release her for my own
violent release. There were no more last chances.

Time passed. I moved dazedly around the house, at
times wondering vaguely why Tuta Sunderson had not
appeared, and then remembering that I had fired her.
I sat on the old furniture, and fell bodily into the past.
My grandmother slid a pan into the oven, Oral Roberts declaimed from the radio, Duane slapped his
hands together from a chair in a dark corner. He was

twenty, and his hair swept upward from his forehead
in a pompadour. Alison Greening, fourteen years old,
magically vibrant, appeared in the doorway (man's
button-down shirt, fawn trousers, sexual promise making the air snap about her), and glided through on
sneakered feet. My mother, hers, talked on the porch.
Their voices were bored and peaceful. I saw Duane
look at my cousin with a look of hatred.

Then I found myself in the bedroom with no memory
of having climbed the stairs. I was staring at the bed.
I remembered the feeling of breasts against my chest,
first small, then cushiony, how I had fit myself into a
ghost's body. She was still moving downstairs; I heard
her light footsteps crossing the living room, heard her
slam the porch door.

You got into trouble again last year. My face had
blazed. *Summer's lease is fading, dear one.* I went
across into my office and saw papers spilling out of
bushel baskets. *Do birds cough?* I saw only one con-
clusion. I was in check. Still, in memory, she glided
downstairs. I felt as though absorbent cotton encased
me, as though I were moving through treacle, thick
dust . . .

I went back to the bedroom and sat in the chair
which faced the bed. I had lost everything. My face
felt mask-like, as if I could peel it off like Rinn's balm.
Even as I began to weep, I recognized that my features
had become as blank and empty as her own, the night
I had seen her gazing carelessly at me from this chair.
She has entered me again, she is downstairs drinking
Kool-Aid in the bubble of time that is 1955, she is
waiting.

Some hours later, I am sitting at my desk and looking
out the window when I hear Alison Updahl scream.
A moment later, my senses awakening from their fog,
I see her tearing down the path to the barn. In the back
her shirt is ripped, as though someone had tried to
swing her around by it, and it flaps as she pelts away.
When she reaches the barn she does not stop, but races

around the side and goes over a barbed wire fence to get into the back field and run in its declivities and grassy rises up toward the blanketing of woods on that side of the valley. These are the woods where Alison Greening and I, each carrying a shovel, had climbed to look for Indian mounds. When the Woodsman reaches a little rise and begins to run down into a hollow packed with massed yellow blossoms, she tears off the flapping T shirt and throws it behind her. I know at that second that she is crying.

Then a secondary, nearer motion: I see Duane, dressed in his working clothes, coming indecisively down the path. He carries a shotgun under one arm, but he seems in an uneasy relationship to it. He marches forward ten feet, the shotgun pointing the way, and then he pauses, looks at it, and turns his back on me. A few paces up the path, then another turn and the resumption of the march in my direction. Then he looks at the shotgun again. He takes another three steps forward. Then he sighs—I see his shoulders lift and depress—and tosses the gun into the weeds by the garage. I see his mouth form the word *bitch*. He glances at the old farmhouse for a moment as if he is wishing that he might see it too in flames. Then he looks up at the window and sees me. I immediately smell gunpowder and burning flesh. He says something, jerking his body, but the words do not carry through the glass, and I thrust open the window.

"Get out here," he says. "God damn you, get out here."

I go downstairs and out onto the porch. He is pacing over the ruin of the front lawn, his hands deep in the coverall pockets, his head bent. When he sees me, he gives a powerful sideways kick to a ridge of dirt left by a skidding tire. He glares at me, then bends his head again, and swivels his foot in the ridge of dirt. "I knew it," he says. His voice is hoarse and choking. "Damn women. Damn you."

His face seems to be flying apart. His condition is unlike the fury I had seen earlier, and more like the suppressed dull rage I had witnessed in the equipment barn, when he flailed the tractor with a hammer. "You're filth. Filth. You made her filthy. You and Zack."

I come out of the porch into waning sunlight. Duane seems nearly to be steaming. To touch him would be to burn your hands. Even in my foggy state, concentrated on what will happen four or five hours later, I am impressed by the high charge of Duane's emotional confusion. His hatred is nearly visible, but as if suffocated, like a fire under a blanket.

"I saw you drop the gun," I say.

"You saw me drop the gun," he mimics. "You saw me drop the gun. Big fucking deal. You think I couldn't kill you with my bare hands?" With ten per cent more pressure behind it, his face would explode and go sailing away in a hundred pieces. "Hey? You think you're gonna get away that easy?"

Get away with what, I could ask, but I am riveted by his despair.

"Well, you ain't," he says. He cannot control his voice, and it spirals up into falsetto. "I know what happens to you sex creeps in jail. They'll make hash out of you down there. You'll wish you were dead. Or maybe you'll be in a nut house. Huh? Either way, you're gonna rot. *Rot.* Every day you'll be a little sorrier you're still alive. And that's good. Because you don't deserve to die."

The quantity of his hatred awes me.

"Oh, it's gonna happen, Miles. It's gonna *happen.* You had to come back here, didn't you? Wave your god-damned face, your god-damned education, in front of me? You bastard. I had to beat it out of her, but she told me. She admitted it." Duane brings himself forward toward me, and I see the colors alternating on his face. "Guys like you think you can get away with anything, don't you? You think the girls will never talk about it."

"There was no 'it,'" I say, finally understanding.

"Tuta saw her. Tuta saw her come out. She told

Red, and my friend Red told me. So I know, Miles, I know. You made her filthy. I can't even stand to look at you."

"I didn't rape your daughter, Duane," I say, scarcely believing that this scene is happening.

"You say. So tell me what happened, shithead. You're good with words, you gotta command of the language, tell me what happened."

"She came to me. I didn't ask her to. I didn't even want her to. She climbed into my bed. She was used by someone else."

Of course Duane misunderstands me. "Someone else—"

"She was used by Alison Greening."

"Goddam, goddam, goddam," and he jerks his hands out of his pockets and strikes himself on either side of his head. "When they got you locked up to rot, I'm gonna burn this place to the ground, I'm gonna bull-doze it over, all you city people can go to hell, I'm—" He is calmer. He takes his fists from his temples, and his eyes blaze at me. They are, I notice for the first time, the same color as his daughter's, but as filled with abstract light as Zack's.

"Why did you decide not to shoot me?"

"Because that's too easy on you. You didn't come back here, stir it all up, just to get shot. The worst things in the world are gonna happen to you." His eyes blaze again. "You don't have to think I don't know about that little fucker Zack. I know about how she sneaks out. You don't know anything I don't, even if you buy 'em drinks and that. I got ears. I hear her crawling back into her room in the mornings—she's just dirt, like all the others. Starting with the one I named her after. They're all dirt. Animals. A dozen of 'em wouldn't make one good man. I don't know why I ever got married. After that Polish bitch I knew all about women. *Dirty,* like you. I knew I couldn't keep her and you apart. Women are all the same. But you're going to pay."

"Do you hate me so much because of Alison Greening?" I ask. "Pay for what?"

"For being you." He says this flatly, as if it is self-explanatory. "It's all over for you, Miles. Hovre is gonna put you away. I just talked to him. Twenty-four hours at the most. If you try to run, they'll get you."

"You talked to Hovre? He's going to arrest me?" I feel the beginnings of relief.

"You bet your ass."

"Good," I say, startling Duane. "That's what I want."

"Jesus man," Duane utters softly.

"Alison Greening is coming back tonight. She's not what she used to be—she's something horrible. Rinn tried to warn me." I look into Duane's incredulous face. "And she's the one who has been killing those girls. I thought it was Zack, but now I know it was Alison Greening."

"Stop-saying-that-name," Duane says.

I turn around and begin to sprint toward the house. Duane shouts behind me, and I yell back to him, "I'm going inside to call Hovre."

He follows me inside and glares at me suspiciously as I dial the number of the police station. "Ain't gonna do you no good," he mutters, stumping around the kitchen. "Only thing you can do now is wait for it. Or get in that heap of yours and try to run. According to Hank you can't do more than forty in her, though. You wouldn't get to Blundell before Hovre caught you." He is talking as much to himself as to me; his bowed back faces me.

I am listening to the ringing of the telephone, expecting Dave Lokken to answer; but Polar Bears' voice comes to me instead. "Chief Hovre."

"This is Miles."

Duane: "Who you talkin' to? Is that Hovre?"

"This is Miles, Polar Bears. Why aren't you on your way out here?"

There is a baffling pause. Then he says: "Why, Miles.

I just been hearing about you. Seems you couldn't stop. I reckon your cousin Du-ane is there with you."

"Yes. He is."

"Fuckin'-A I am," says Duane.

"Good. Say, we got results on that blood. It's AB, all right. It'll take another day to break it down further to see if it's male or female, the lab boys say."

"I don't have another day."

"Miles old friend, I'd be surprised if you had another five minutes. Isn't Duane carrying a twelve-gauge? I told him to bring one when he went down to see you. The law can overlook some things a man might do, if he's been pushed too far."

"I'm asking you to save my life, Polar Bears."

"Some might say that you'd be a whole lot safer dead, Miles."

"Does Lokken know what you're doing?"

I hear the wheeze of his coughing. "Dave had to go all the way to the other end of the county today. Funny thing."

"Tell him to get out here now," Duane says. "I can't stand having you in the house any more."

"Duane says you should come now."

"Why don't you and Duane keep up your conversation? Sounds real fruitful to me." He hung up.

I turn around, still holding the receiver, and see Duane looking at me with dull eyes in a flushed face. "He's not coming, Duane. He thinks you're going to shoot me. He wants you to do it. He sent Lokken off on a wild goose chase so nobody will know how he arranged things."

"You're talking guff."

"Did he tell you to bring a shotgun?"

"Sure. He thinks you killed those girls."

"He's more devious than that. He told me about Alison Greening. He told me what happened. He'd rather have me dead than in jail. If I'm dead, I'm still guilty of the killings, but I can't talk to anybody."

"You shut *up* about that," he says, his arms swinging at his sides. "Don't say one word about that."

"Because you hate thinking about it. You couldn't do it. You couldn't rape her."

"Huh," Duane snorts, his face red and strained. "I didn't come here to talk about this. I just wanted to hear you admit you put the dirtiest part of yourself into my girl. Do you think I liked beating it out of her?"

"Yes."

"What?"

"Yes. I think you did enjoy it."

Duane whirls and presses the palms of his hands against a kitchen cupboard, supporting his weight on his arms, as I had seen him do against the engine block of a tractor. When he turns around again he is doing his best to smile. "Now I know you're crazy. Boy, that just says it all. Maybe I oughta kill you, like you say Hovre wants."

"Maybe you should." I am transfixed by his ghastly attempt at relaxation. His face is colorless now; it looks as though you could pluck gobbets off it, like clay. His personality, which I had thought as stolid and bull-like as his body, appears to be breaking up, shaking apart into its facets.

"Why did you let me come here at all?" I ask. "Why didn't you write back to say that someone else was staying in the house? And why did you pretend to be friendly when I first came?"

He says nothing; he simply looks at me, dull and sullen anger expressed by every inch and angle of his body.

"I'm as innocent of the deaths of those girls as I was of the death of Alison Greening," I say to him.

"Maybe that was the first warning you had," Duane says. "I'm gonna be listening for the sound of that junker of yours, so you'd best sit tight until Hovre comes to get you." Then a smile which appears almost genuine. "I'm gonna enjoy that." His gray face breaks, alters, as a perception hits him. "By God, if I'd of had my shotgun here, I would have cut you in two."

"Then Alison Greening would come for you tonight."

"It don't make any difference how crazy you pretend to be," Duane says. "Not now it don't."

"No. Not now."

When Duane left the farmhouse he said, "You know, my wife was as dumb as the others. That cow actually wanted it. She couldn't even pretend she was better than that. She used to yammer about how dirty I got out in the fields, and I used to say the dirt on me is nothing compared to what's in your mind. I just hoped she would give me a son."

When dusk began to devour the landscape, I knew that I had approximately three hours to get where I had to go. I would have to walk. Duane would hear the car, and telephone Hovre. They did not belong where I was going. The alternative was to wait in the farmhouse and take every creak of the boards for the sign of her coming. No. If she were going to appear and spring the trap of our old vow, the Pohlson quarry, where it started, would be where it would end. I had to go back, alone, to where it had begun, to see it as it was on that night, without the Woodsman and Zack, to stand in darkness on those flat slabs of stone and breathe that air. I felt almost that if I stood on that spot again, I might go back to the beginning and reverse things: might find an echo of the living girl, and reclaim myself and her in that salvation. Duane and his furious repressions, Polar Bears and his schemes, were tiny in the light of this immense possibility. I forgot them both five minutes after Duane left the farmhouse. Starving Paul Kant had worked through the fields; so would I.

It took me a little more than a quarter of the time it had Paul. I simply walked along the soft verge of the highway, going in dying light where I had to go; once a rattling slat-sided truck passed me, and I veered off into a cornfield until its red taillights disappeared around a bend. I had a pervasive sense of invisibility.

No clumsy hothead in a truck could stop me; no more than I could stop my cousin from asserting her claim. Fear sparkled beneath my skin; I walked quickly, scarcely aware of the gravel over which I moved; at the top of the long winding hill I touched the wood of the Community Chest sign and felt the dampness of woodrot. Lights burned in a farmhouse just visible in a black valley. For a second I had the sensation that I was about to leap from the hill's sheer side and fly—a dream of the inhuman, a dream of escape. Cold hands brushed my sides and urged me forward.

At the base of the drive leading up the smaller hill to the quarry I paused for breath. It was just past nine o'clock. In the darkening sky hung the white lifeless stone of the moon. I took a step up the drive: I was a magnet's negative pole, the lunar pole. My feet throbbed in their city shoes. A random branch of an oak stood out with supernatural, almost vocal clarity; a huge muscle rolled beneath its crust of bark. I sat on the edge of a pebbly granite shelf and slid off my shoes. Then I dropped them beside the rock and, finding what I had to find to move, moved. The air breathed me.

On tiptoe, with wincing feet, I went up the drive. Gravel gave way to dry grass. At the top of the drive I eased down onto my heels. The flat brown area was before me, the line of dying bushes at the far end. The sky was darkening fast. I realized that I was carrying my jacket in one hand, and I pulled it up over my shoulders. Air caught in my throat. Alison Greening seemed profoundly *in* the landscape, a part of all of it. She was printed deeply into every scrabble of rock, every tick of leaf. I went forward, the bravest act of my life, and felt invisibility stir about me.

By the time I reached the other side of the flat brown space, it had become dark. The translation from dusk to night was instantaneous, a subdivision of a second. My stockinged feet found a smooth rock slab. A blister burned at my heel. Its redness mounted up my leg, I could see that color rising and staining me, and I

went forward again over brown grass to the line of
bushes. My mind fluttered, and I snapped my head to
the right, and saw a pair of finches shooting off into
the bowl of the sky. Moonlight touched them for an
instant, then lay upon and silvered the threads and
bones of the sparse bushes. I took another step, and
was on the first rock, looking down at the cup of
black water which was the quarry. It was the center
of an intense, packed silence.

And of a great brightness. The moon, as medallion-
like as Alison's face, shimmered and glowed from the
water's center. My leg was shaking. My mind was no
more than a flat plate of images. It would have taken
me a minute to remember my name, that leap from
slippery *Miles* to froggy *Teagarden*. The stone beneath
me ground at my feet; I went down onto the next step,
and felt myself pulled toward the brightness. That flat
pane of water with its glowing center drew me on,
brought me down toward it. Another step. The entire
silent pool edged with smooth rock was as if humming—no, was humming, wedged in the divide between
the bottomless dark of the water and the flat shining
head of the moon. The world tipped to slide me down,
and I tipped with it.

Then I was there, on the bottom of the bottom of
the world. Cool rock pushed upward on the soles of
my feet. Heat burned at my temples and crisped small
hairs in my nose. Water slid across my wrists. My
fingers touched my sleeves, and they were dry. At the
bottom of the bottom of the world, my face turned to
the moon's cold effigy, I sat in a hard unreal brightness.

When my body began to tremble I planted my hands
on the shelf of cool rock and closed my eyes. The signs
of her coming were unimaginable: it seemed to me that
she might step out from the center of that gleaming
disc on the water. Rock flowed under my hands; with
my eyes clamped shut I was moving, part of a moving
element, the rock which fitted itself beneath my hands
and body like a negative, mirrored image. This sensation was very strong. My fingerprints folded into minute

grooves in the stone, hand-shapes met my hands, and when I snapped open my eyes again I thought I would see before them a sheer rise of rock.

I centered myself in my body, centered my body on the slab of rock. I felt the rock lift with my breathing, the veins in my hands connect to veins in the stone, and I ceased to move. I thought: I am a human mind in a human body. I saw white unreal brightness on my knees and my stockinged feet. High walls circled me, the water lay still, the only thing in the world beneath me. I knew that I had very little time left. The jacket lay across my shoulder like leaves. I had all the rest of my life to think; to wait.

But waiting itself is thinking, anticipation is an idea in the body, and for a long time even my pulse was charged with the energy of my waiting. I thought of hurtling through time; I was no longer trembling. My fingers slid into grooves in the stone. In the bowl of the quarry, the night was terrifically still. Once I opened my eyes and looked at my watch where dots by the numerals and slivers along the hands glowed green: it was ten forty-five.

I tried to remember when we had started to swim. It had to be sometime between eleven and twelve. Alison had probably died near to midnight. I looked up at the stars and then back down at the water where the moon floated. I could remember every word spoken on that night, every gesture. They had been crowded into my mind for the past twenty years. Twice, while lecturing to my sophomores, I had spun backwards to those busy minutes and seen them all again while my disembodied voice droned on, being witty at the expense of literature. It was true to say that I had been trapped here, in that section of time, ever since, and that what had frightened me in my classroom was no more than an image of my life.

It was all still happening, in a space behind my eyes that belonged to it, and I could look inward to see it and us. The way she looked, grinning at me as cool air settled on my shoulders. *Do you want to do what we do in California?* Her hands on her hips. I could see my own hands working at my buttons, my legs, the legs of a thirteen-year-old boy, hanging pale and slim to the rock slab. I looked up and she was a white arc just entering the water, a vision of a leaping fish.

That would be printed on two other minds as well as mine. They had seen us: our bodies cutting the water, our arms white, her hair a sleek mass against my face. From their angle we would be pale faces beneath water-darkened hair, two faces so close as to be flowing together.

I shook all over. I raised my arm and looked at my wrist: eleven o'clock. A patch of skin on the back of my neck began to jump.

I closed my eyes again and the energy of the stone again rushed up to meet my hands, heels, outstretched legs. My breathing seemed overloud, amplified by the complicated passages within my body. The whole area of the quarry was breathing with me, taking in and releasing air. I counted to one hundred, making each inhalation and exhalation last eight beats.

Very soon.

I saw myself as I had been a month earlier, when I had only half dared to admit that I had returned to the farm to keep an appointment with a ghost. And brought a string of deaths dragging like a tail behind me. Despite the pretense of the boxes of books and notes, I had not done even three good days' work on my dissertation: I had given it up on the feeblest of pretexts, that Zack's foolish ideas were too much like Lawrence's. Instead I had almost willfully turned the valley against me. And I *saw* myself: a large man with thinning hair, a man whose face immediately expresses whatever emotion has hold of him, a man rampaging through a small town. I had insulted more people in four weeks than I had in the past four years. I witnessed all of this as from the outside, saw myself bursting into stores and giving crazy messages from barstools, miming shoplifting, my face registering disgust.

Even Duane had done a better job of disguising his feelings. From the morning of my arrival, I had felt Alison Greening's approach, and that fact—the vision of her hovering at the edge of the fields—had sent me sliding as irrationally as a pinball.

I said her name, and a leaf rustled. The moonlight made my body look two-dimensional, a figure from a cartoon.

It had to be nearly the time. Eleven-thirty. Pressure suddenly happened in my bladder; I felt my face grow hot. I crossed my legs and waited for the pressure to ebb. I began to rock forward on my stiff arms. Nerves in the stone responded to my movement, and echoed it so that at first the stone rocked with me, and then took all the motion and rocked me itself. The need to urinate built into an ache. I was rocked more intensely, and it vanished. I lay back and let the stone fit a hollow for my skull. My hands, stretched by my sides, found their true places.

Very soon.

A cloud covered half the stars and slowly scudded past the dead circle of the moon. My body seemed already to have given up its life, and the stone to have taken it into itself. The cold quarry water was breathing through me, using me as its bellows; I thought I heard her walking toward me, but a breeze skimmed past, and still the complications of life, the complications of feeling streamed from my body into everything around. I thought: it cannot last, it is too much, death is necessary, necessary. Suddenly it seemed to me, at the bottom of my fear like a flash of gold, that I had returned to the valley knowing that I would die there.

I heard music and knew it came from the electric point of contact between my head and the rock above the water. Soon, soon, soon. My death came speeding toward me, and I felt my body lighten. The tremendous forces about me seemed to lift me an inch or two above the rock, the music sounded in my head, I felt my soul contract into a humming capsule just below my breastbone. So I remained for a long time, gathered to split apart at her touch.

I witnessed my heavy profane sarcastic deathbound naive person hurtling through Arden, hiding within the body of my grandmother's house, quailing on the floor of a forest, half-raping a coiling girl; I gasped because the sensation of levitating, all my cells linked by moonlight in a contract to ignore gravity, had endured so long.

All my being told me when midnight approached. I could not a second time will away the quick pain in my bladder, a leaf rattled in a twist of wind, and warm fluid rushed over my legs in a delicious letting go. I reached out for her, every second of her time ticked along my body. I caught only bright empty air.

And fell back to earth and unliving stone. In that giant embarrassment, the music ceased and I was conscious of my lungs pulling in air, the rock inert beneath me, the water black and cold, and I pushed myself backwards to rest my back against the wall of the quarry. The wet legs of my trousers hung on my legs. I'd had the time wrong. It must have happened later; but I caught the edge of desperation in the thought, and I leaned back and looked through the bleach of moonlight to the greatest loss in my life.

It was two minutes past twelve. She had not come. The twenty-first of July had slipped into the past and she was not coming. She would never come. She was dead. I was stranded alone in only the human world. My guilt, moving under some impetus of its own, shifted hugely within me and came to a new relationship with my body.

I could not move. I had invented it all. I had seen nothing at the edge of the fields—nothing but my hysteria. I pulled the jacket tightly around me, obeying a reflex left over from childhood.

The shock endured for hours. By the time my trousers had begun to dry, I realized that my legs and feet had gone to sleep, and I leaned forward and bent my knees with my hands. Intense pain arrowed out from my knees. I was grateful enough for it to try to stand. For a time I drowned my awareness in pain, moving awkwardly on someone else's legs. Then I sat on one of the stone steps and looked again into loss. I could not cry: too much of the loss was of myself. Whatever I was going to be, whenever I could think about becoming something I could call myself, I was going to be different. I had made up a self which relied on the possibility of Alison Greening for its shadings, and now I felt like a Siamese twin whose other half had been surgically severed, cast away. The guilt which I had carried for twenty years had drastically altered its dimensions, but I could not tell if it had grown larger or smaller.

I was going to have to live.

I spend the entire night by the quarry's side, though I knew from the moment I had seemed to fall back to earth—even before I had looked at my watch—that Alison Greening was gone from my life for eternity.

During the last hour I spent mourning Alison's second and final departure from my life, I was able to think about Arden and what had been happening there. Duane, Polar Bears, Paul Kant, myself. How after twenty years we had come together again in a tragic landscape. How we had all been marked by women. I saw the patterns tying us together, like Zack's "lines of force."

And I saw something else.

At last I understood that the murderer of the girls had been my cousin Duane. Who hated women more than any other man I had ever met, who had probably planned the murders of the girls who resembled Alison Greening from the day I had written him that I was coming to Arden. Duane's were the old Coke bottles, the axes, the doorknobs: Zack must have stolen the one I had seen from wherever Duane had hidden them.

Sitting by the quarry's side, still numb with the shock of loss, I saw it with a brisk, heartless clarity.

Alison gone, it could only be Duane. And his daughter had feared this, I saw—she had run from any discussion of the girls' deaths. What I had taken for a desire to appear more callous (therefore, she imagined, more adult) than she was made even more sense, given the fear that her father was a killer. She had really rebuffed any conversation about the dead girls.

I stood up: I could walk. A kind of strength blessed me. An entire era of my life, like a geologic period, was coming to an end—it would end with what I was going to have to do. I did not have the whisper of an idea of what I would do after that.

I walked down the side of the hill and found my shoes. In one night they had gone dead and curling, and when I forced my feet into them, the inner soles felt like the hides of dead lizards. They seemed not to fit, to have been shaped by another man.

When I stepped onto the highway I saw a high rattling truck coming toward me from the direction of Arden. It was a blood relative of the truck from which I had fled the previous night; I stuck out my hand, thumb up, and the man beside the wheel pulled up beside me. From the truck floated the earthy smell of pigs.

"Mister?" said the old man behind the wheel.

"My car broke down," I said. "I wonder if you're going anywhere near Norway Valley?"

"Hop yourself right in, young feller," he said, and leaned across to open the door for me.

I climbed in beside him. He was a wiry man in his mid-seventies, with white hair that stuck up like a scrubbing brush. On the steering wheel his hands were the size of steaks. "Up early," he said, not quite making it a question.

"I've been traveling a long time."

He started the truck rolling again, and its whole rear section began jouncing and squeaking.

"Are you actually going into the valley?"

- "Sure," he said. "I just been taking a load of porkers into town, and now I'm going home. My boy and me farm a piece of land about eight-ten miles down the valley. You ever been that way?"

"No," I said.

"It's nice. It's real nice down there. Don't know what a healthy young feller like you is doing bumming around the country when you could settle down on the best farmland in the whole state. Man wasn't born to live in cities, way I see it."

I nodded. His words unlocked in me the knowledge that I was not going to return to New York.

"I reckon you're a salesman," he said.

"Right now I'm between jobs," I said, and earned a bright look of curiosity.

"Shame. But you vote Democrat, we'll get this country back on its feet and young men like you will have jobs again." He squinted into the road and the rising sun, and the bouncing truck sent wave after wave of pig over us. "You remember that, now."

When he turned the truck into the valley road, he asked just where I wanted to go, exactly. "You might think about coming all the way with me, and we could set you up with a good cup of coffee. What say?"

"Thanks, but no. I'd like you to drop me off at Andy/s."

"You're the boss," he said, perfectly equable.

Then we were slowing down before Andy's gas-pumps. The seven o'clock sunlight fell on the dust and gravel. As I pulled down the door handle, he turned his brush-topped head slyly toward me and said, "I know you were fibbing me, young man."

I just looked at him in surprise, wondering what he could have read in my face.

"About your auto. You don't have any auto, do you? You've been thumbing your way right along."

I met his smile. "Thanks for the ride," I said, and stepped down from the cab and the thick odor of pigs into warm light. He rattled away, going deeper into the valley, and I turned to walk across the gravel and climb the steps.

The door was locked. I peered in through the glass and saw no lights. Andy had no CLOSED sign on the door, but I looked at the bottom panel of glass behind the screen and saw a dusty card which said Mon–Fri 7:30–6:30, Sat 7:30–9:00. I pounded on the screen door, rattling it. After forty seconds of steady pounding, I saw Andy waddling toward me through the crowded tables, peering at me to figure out who I was.

When he got close enough to identify me, he stopped. "We're closed." I motioned him forward. He shook his head. "Please," I shouted. "I just want to use your phone."

He hesitated, and then came slowly up toward the door. He looked worried and confused. "You got a phone down at Duane's place," he said, his voice muffled by the glass.

"I have to make a call before I get there," I pleaded.

"Who you going to call, Miles?"

"The police. Polar Bears Hovre."

"What're you gonna say to the Chief?"

"Listen in and you'll know."

He came the necessary two steps and put his hand on the lock. His face jerked, and then he slid the bolt and opened the door. "Screen door's still locked, Miles. I suppose if you're gonna call the police it's okay . . . but how do I know that's what you're gonna do?"

"You can stand right behind me. You can dial it for me."

He revolved the pinwheel catch. "Quiet. Margaret's back in the kitchen. She won't like this." I followed him inside. He turned his face toward me; he looked worried. He was used to making the wrong decisions. "Phone's on the counter," he whispered.

As he went toward it his wife called from the back of the store. "Who was it?"

"Drummer," Andy called back.

"For goodness' sake, send him off. It's too early."

"Just a minute." He pointed to the telephone; then whispered, "No. I'll dial it."

When he had the number he gave me the receiver and crossed his arms over his chest.

The telephone rang twice, and then I heard Lokken's voice. "Police?"

I asked to speak to Polar Bears. *If you want your killer,* I was going to say, *just do what I tell you. He'll be on his farm, driving his tractor or banging on some machinery.*

"Teagarden?" came the deputy's high-pitched astonished whine. "Is that you? Where the hell did you get yourself to anyways? You're supposed to be here, this morning. What the hell?"

"What do you mean, I'm supposed to be there?"

"Well, see—the Chief sent me out on this damnfool errand yesterday afternoon. I didn't get what I was supposed to get because it wasn't there in the first place, it never even *was* there, he just wanted me outa the way I guess. Anyhow by the time I got back it was near to midnight and he was hoppin' mad. Duane called him up and said you run off somewheres. So the Chief says, hold your horses, I'll know where he is. I think he went and got Du-ane to help him bring you in. So where are you now? And where's the Chief?"

"I'm at Andy's store," I said. I glanced over at him. His worried face was turned toward the rear of the shop; he was afraid his wife would appear and find me. "Lokken, listen to me. I know who should be arrested, and I think I know where the Chief would have gone. Pick me up at Andy's."

"You bet your ass I'm pickin' you up," said Lokken.

"You'll get your killer," I said, and handed the receiver back to Andy.

"Should I hang it up?" he asked, perplexed.

"Hang it up."

He clicked it down and then stared at me, becoming more conscious every moment of my beard-stubble and wrinkled clothes. "Thanks," I said, and turned away and threaded past the tables and went out, leaving him with his hand on the telephone. I went down the steps and out into the early light to wait for Lokken.

In eight minutes, which must have been a record, the deputy's squadcar came speeding down the valley road. I waved, and Lokken braked to a halt, raising a great white plume of dust. He jumped out of the car as I walked across the road toward him. "All right, what is this?" he demanded. "This just plain don't make sense. Where's Chief Hovre?"

"I think he imagined that I'd go back up to that clearing where you found the Michalski girl. Maybe Duane went with him."

"Maybe he did, maybe he didn't," said Lokken. His hand was on the butt of his gun. "Maybe we'll go there, maybe we won't. Why in hell did you call the station?"

"I told you." His hand curled around the gunbutt. "I know who killed those girls. Let's get in the car and talk about it on the way."

Very suspiciously, he stepped away from the side of the car and permitted me to walk around its nose. We got in at the same time. I leaned back against the hot plastic of the seat. "All right," Lokken said. "You better start talking. If it's real good I might listen."

"Duane Updahl did it," I said. His hand, holding the ignition key, froze on the way to the slot and he swiveled his head to gape at me.

"I wasn't even in town when Gwen Olson died," I said.

"That's why I'm listening to you," said Lokken. I returned his glance. "We just heard this morning from the Ohio state police. The Chief had them checking into your story about staying in a motel ever since you told him about it. They finally found a guy named Rolfshus says he recognized your picture. He runs a little place off the freeway. Well, this here Rolfshus says you might be someone checked in there that night."

"You mean Polar Bears was looking for that motel since the night I told him about it?"

"He's tooken statements too," said Lokken. "Lots of folks up here don't like you." He started the car. "I don't know what the Chief would say, but it sure as hell looks to me like you're okay on that Olson killing. So why the hell do you say it's Duane?"

I gave him my reasons as we spun down the road. His hatred of women, his hatred of me. The physical evidence. "I think he set up the whole thing to get me a life sentence in the booby hatch," I said. "And Polar Bears was hoping he'd shoot me, so that I couldn't say anything about how Alison Greening really died. He sent you off so you'd be far away when it happened."

"Christ, I don't know," said Lokken. "It's crazy. What's this about Alison Greening?"

So I told him that too. "And I think Duane has been half-crazy ever since," I ended. "When I wrote him that I was coming back, I think he just snapped."

"Holy man."

"I sort of snapped too. Otherwise I think I would have seen it earlier. I had a crazy theory, but last night it turned out to be wrong."

"Everything about this is crazy," Lokken said in despair. He pulled the car up on the shoulder of the road beside the rows of corn. Polar Bears' car sat, facing the way we had come, on the other side of the road. "Looks like you were right about the Chief, anyhow. You think they're both up there?"

"I think Duane would go with Polar Bears," I said. "It'd be too risky for him not to."

"Let's have a look. Hell, let's have a look." We got out of the car and jumped the ditch.

He said nothing, the run up toward the woods took much of his breath, but after we had forded the creek Lokken spoke again. "If what you say is right, Duane might of tried something on the Chief."

"I don't think he would," I said.

"Yeah, but he might of," he said, and drew his gun. "I don't exactly remember where the damn clearing was."

I said, "Follow me," and began to work up over the rise and toward the beginning of the woods. Lokken crashed along behind me.

When I reached the first of the trees I began to trot uphill, going in the direction of Rinn's old cabin. I had no idea of how the scene would be played. For once, I was grateful for Lokken's presence. It did not make sense that Polar Bears would have spent the entire night in the clearing. Gradually the big gnarled trees drew closer. I slowed to a walk. In places I had to part branches and tall weeds with my hands.

"Do you notice anything funny?" I said after a time.

"Huh?" Lokken's voice came from a good distance behind me.

"There isn't any noise. No birds, no squirrels. No animal noises."

"Huh," said Lokken.

It was true. Other times when I had come up into the woods, I had been aware of a constant natural chatter about me. Now it was as though all the birds and animals had died. In that dark place, surrounded by the looming trees, the silence was decidedly spooky.

"Gunshot scares 'em off," Lokken said. "Maybe there was some trouble." He sounded as apprehensive as I felt, and I knew that he still had the gun in his hand.

"We're pretty close to the clearing now," I said. "We'll know soon."

A few minutes later I saw the ring of trees around the clearing. "Right through there," I said, and looked around at Lokken. His face was red with effort.

"Yeah. I remember now." He cupped his hands around his mouth. "Chief? You there?" He got not even an echo; he shouted again. "Chief! Chief Hovre!" He looked at me hard, angry and frustrated, sweat running down his face. "Dammit, Teagarden, shake your butt."

Though I felt cold, I too had begun to sweat. I could not tell Lokken that I was afraid to go into the clearing. Just then the woods seemed very potent.

"Come on, we saw the car, we know he's here," said Lokken.

"Something's funny," I said. I almost thought I could smell cold water. But that was not possible.

"Come on. Let's go. Move it." I heard the revolver click against a tree as he shook it at me.

I went toward the circle of trees; light hovered in the clearing beyond them.

Then I went through the sentinel trees and stepped into the clearing. The sudden dazzle of light at first made it difficult to see. Smoke came from the banked fire at the clearing's center. I took another step toward it. I wiped my eyes. There was no humming, vibrant noise of insects.

Then I saw them. I stopped walking. I could not speak.

Lokken noisily broke into the clearing behind me. "Hey, what's goin' on? Hey, Teagarden, they in here? You—" His voice ended as if chopped off with an ax.

I knew why Lokken had vomited when he had seen the body of Jenny Strand.

Polar Bears was in front, Duane behind him fixed to a shorter tree. They were pinned to their trees, both naked, their bodies blackened and hanging like crushed fruit.

Lokken came up beside me, making a noise in his throat. I could not take my eyes from them. It was the most savage thing I had ever seen. I heard the handgun thump onto the earth. "What the—" Lokken began. "What—"

"I was wrong," I whispered. "Jesus Christ, I was wrong. She's back after all."

"What—" Lokken's face had turned a glistening, cloudy white.

"It wasn't Duane after all," I said. "It was Alison Greening. They came up here last night and she killed them."

"Jesus, look at their skin," moaned Lokken.

"She was saving me. She knew she could get me any time."

"Their *skin* . . ."

"She punished them for raping and killing her," I said. "Oh my God."

Lokken half-sat, half-fell into the tall grass.

"Now she'll be after Duane's daughter," I said, suddenly realizing that another life was probably lost. "We have to get down to the farm right now." Lokken was retching into the grass.

"How could someone—someone lift them two like that—"

"My crazy theory was right," I said to him. "We have to get to the farm right now. Can you run?'

"Run?"

"Then follow me as soon as you can. Go down and drive your car to Duane's place."

". . . place," he said. Then his eyes cleared a little, and he picked up the gun and waved it at me. "You wait. You don't go anywhere, hear?"

I bent over and pushed the gun aside. "I brought you here, remember? And do you think I'm strong enough to lift those two and pin them to trees like that? Now hurry up and get straight. If it isn't too late, we have to keep this from happening again."

"How—"

"I don't know," I said, and turned away from him, and turned again with an idea. "Give me your keys. You can hotwire Polar Bears' car."

When I got back down to the road I hastily got into the squadcar and twisted Lokken's key in the ignition. The motor started at once. I rolled away from Polar Bears' car and stepped the accelerator all the way down to the floor.

A tractor chugged down the road before Bertilsson's church; it straddled two lanes. I blew the horn, and the straw-hatted overweight man on the tractor's seat wagged his hand without looking back. I looked for the siren button and found it. The farmer jerked around on

the seat, saw the car, and steered the tractor to the side
of the road. I blasted the horn and zipped by.

When I drove up to the old farmhouse I could see
nothing unusual—the mare grazed among the cows, the
lawn lay ripped and burned, Alison was not in sight.
I swallowed, turning into the drive, afraid that I would
find her as I had found her father and Polar Bears. I
braked as I cut the car onto the lawn, and jumped out
before it had stopped rolling.

I could smell her—I could smell cold water, as if
rain had just ceased to fall. My legs nearly refused to
move, and in my stomach lay an iciness that fear had
deposited there.

I began to jog up the path to Duane's house. A door
slammed. I realized that Alison Updahl had seen the
squadcar pull into the drive. She came running around
the side of her house. When she saw me instead of
Polar Bears or Dave Lokken, she stopped running and
stood hesitantly on the path, looking worried, pleased
and confused all at once. The air seemed to tighten,
as it had on my first night in the woods: it seemed to
grow thick and tight with malevolence. "Run!" I
shouted to the girl. I waved my arms, semaphoring.
"Get going!" The smell of the quarry washed over us,
and this time she too caught it, for she half-turned and
lifted her head.

"Danger!" I yelled, and began to sprint toward her.
Wind knocked me down as casually as a breeze
flips a playing card.

"Miles?" she said. "My father didn't—"
Before she could say *come home,* I saw another
woman, a smaller woman, appear momentarily on the
path behind her. My heart froze. The shadowy second girl stood with her hands on her hips, looking at
both of us. She vanished in the next instant. Alison
Updahl must have felt some particle of the other's
force, and she twisted her upper body to look behind
her. I saw the terror begin in her—it was as though
life and will had suddenly drained from her. She had
seen something, but I did not know what. I got up

from the dust and stones of the path. "Take off," I shouted to her.

But it was too late. She was too terrified by whatever it was she had seen, and she could not move. "Alison!" I shouted, and it was not the living girl I addressed. "Leave her alone!"

There was a whirring, typhoon-like noise of rushing, rattling wind. I turned in its direction, and was aware of Alison Updahl, stunned like a bird before a snake, turning slowly too. In the long grass before the road, wind was making a pattern: carving circles in flattened grass. Leaves and twigs began to fly together. Out on the road, stones and chunks of tarry asphalt lifted and flew toward the circling pattern.

I called to Alison Updahl, "Come toward me." She jerked herself forward, stumbled. The air was filled with small flying bits of wood, with tumbling leaves.

Through the leafstorm I ran toward her. She had fallen on the path, and a shower of small branches and stones came cascading down upon her. I grasped her hand and pulled her upright.

"I saw something," she muttered.

"I saw it too. We have to run."

The whirling pattern exploded. Most of the twigs and leaves filling the air were blasted soundlessly away, and spun lifelessly down to earth all over the area between the two houses. Only a tall skeletal superstructure, a vague outline of brown and green, remained towering; then it too blew away. A few stones rattled around us. The noise of screeching air, as if we were in a hurricane, stayed with us. Again the grass was printing itself into wide circles.

Her mouth opened, but she could not speak.

I took her hand more firmly and started to run. As we came hurrying down the path. Dave Lokken pulled into the drive in Polar Bears' car. He still looked like a man climbing out of a three-day drunk. He looked at the girl and me, running as hard as we could in his direction. "Hey," he said. "We gotta get those bodies . . ."

The circling pattern on the grass moved in his direction. Then I saw the figure of the girl, still shadowy, that I had seen on the path appear beside his car. Immediately, both windshields shattered. Lokken screamed and covered his face with his arms. A force I could not imagine pulled him from the carseat and through the open window at his side. He rolled across the gravel of the drive. His nose was pouring blood.

I tried to take Alison Updahl toward the side field, seeing that it was useless to try to hide in the house. We had gone three paces, me tugging, she stumbling, when our hands were torn apart and a wind that stank of the grave and rotting meat buffeted me aside and knocked me against the tree where my grandfather used to hang his scythe. Something started to move across the grass toward Alison Updahl.

It was as though the rind of the world had broken away, just sheared away, houses, trees, dogs, people, jobs, sunlight, all of it, and only the most primitive and the darkest life was left, what remains when everything comprehensible and usual, the rind, has peeled off and what emerges is like what you see when you flip over a long flat rock in the woods. Lokken, lying down in thick vines behind me, his nose still gouting blood, saw what I saw and screamed a second time. I knew that he was covering his eyes.

Alison got to the porch and rushed inside. Whatever it was that followed her vanished like a smudge on a pane of glass.

A spout of material—grass, leaves, pebbles—lifted from the lawn and shattered against the side of the house.

There was one gascan left in the garage. I saw it in my mind and felt the way the grip would fit my hand, and without knowing what I would do with it or how it would help, I made myself run into the garage and lift it. It was full, as I knew it would be. By itself, the weight of the heavy liquid seemed to draw me outside again, as if it were pulling me down a slope.

I went toward the house. You have already done

this once, I told myself, you did it last night: but I knew that beside the quarry I had been ready to die and now I was not. I glanced back at Lokken; he was half crouching in the weeds into which she had rolled him, making noises in his throat. Blood covered his uniform shirt. No sound came from the house. I had a sudden mental vision of poor Duane, poor Polar Bears, pinned like fruit to the trees, their skin black and white, and obligation to the past—a feeling like love—moved me forward.

The smell was like water from graves, and it blanketed the porch. The gascan weighed heavily in my hand. I went through into the living room. Everything looked different. It was all there, nothing had been moved, but the room I had prepared for Alison Greening was now darker, meaner, shabbier; water stains blotted the walls. The smell was thicker inside than on the porch. Alison Updahl was cowering on a chair, her legs drawn up before her chest as if she would kick anything that came too close. I do not think that she saw me. Her face was a tight white shield. What she had seen when she had twisted around on the path was what Lokken and I had witnessed moving toward the house. "I'm not going to let her get you," I said. "I'm going to get you out." It was just noise.

I heard the windows breaking all over the house. The girl before me twitched: her eyes were all whites. "Stand up," I said. She put down her legs and tried to lever herself out of the chair. I turned away, satisfied that she could move and began to splash gasoline around the room. *If we have to go this way,* I thought, *it will be better than*—I saw the bodies pinned to the trees. I doused the furniture and splashed the gasoline on the back wall.

She was there, I knew; I could sense her in the house. It was that awareness of a hostile force I had had on the first night in the woods. Alison Updahl was up on her feet, her arms out in front of her like a blind woman's. The floor of the room was filmed with dirt;

I saw a triangle of moss sprouting in a corner of the ceiling.

Then I saw a shadow against the gasoline-spattered wall. Small, formless, but essentially manlike. I dropped the empty gascan and it rang on the floor. Outside, a branch thwacked against the white boards. "Miles," Alison Updahl said very softly.

"I'm here." Useless words of comfort.

Leaves pushed against the broken kitchen window and forced it in. I heard them boiling in the corrupt air.

The shadow against the wall grew darker. I caught the girl's outstretched arm and pulled her toward me. Her eyes were fluttering, but I could see their pupils. "That smell . . ." She was on the edge of hysteria, I could hear it slice in her voice. She moved her head and saw the darkening shadow on the wall. The earth on the floor was stirring, moving in dervish circles.

"I'm going to light a match," I said. "When I do, I want you to run out on the porch and jump through the screen. It's full of holes, it's weak. Then just keep running."

In horror she was watching the shadow darken. Her mouth opened. "I dug up a cowdog once . . . after I buried it . . ."

The shadow was three-dimensional, standing out from the wall like a relief. The rotten air filled with the rustling of leaves. With part of my mind I thought that the room looked like it had been pulled up out of a flooding river. I tightened my arm around Alison Updahl's shoulder. She seemed scarcely to be breathing. "Now get out," I said. "Fast." I pushed her toward the porch. The air hissed. The matches were in my hand. My fingers shook. I twisted five or six matches out of the book and managed to scratch them in a general way against the lighting surface. They went up into flame, and I tossed them toward the back of the room.

Heat and light exploded there. Beneath the whooshing sound of the gas igniting I heard the porch screen letting go as Alison tumbled through it.

Standing across the room from me was no shadow, no circling pattern on the grass, no tall outline of sticks, no dark thing from beneath the world's rind, but a living person. Maybe if I were closer to her I could have seen the seams and imperfections, the rough vein of a leaf or the discoloration in the white of an eye, but from where I stood she looked as she had in 1955, a perfect girl of bone and skin and blood. Even then, she stopped my breath, with the fire beating in on us, beating in. It was that face composed of a thousand magical complications. Not a man in fifty could have looked at it without aching—for the pain it would know, for the pain it would cause.

She was not smiling, but it was as if she were. Her gravity encompassed and suggested all feeling. Only gravity, the grave composure of such a face, can do this. Behind her figure small and slim the fire beat upwards on the wall. My skin baked in the heat.

With moveless fascination I saw that the tips of the fingers on one of her hands had caught fire. Without passion, with a clear quiet gravity which promised more than I could know or understand, she held me with her eyes and face.

Upstairs the house let go with a noise like a sigh. Fire sucked in a flaming orange stream up the narrow staircase. I stepped backwards, away from the flames. My eyebrows were crisping; I knew that my face was burned as if by the sun.

I understood, being looked at by her or what looked like her, that a contract was being made. I understood that she would rather have me dead, but that Duane's daughter, her namesake, was the reason I would live. Now her entire hand was blazing, lost at the center of a glowing circle of light. Yes, there was a contract: I did not wholly comprehend it, I never wholly would, but I was bound to it.

She let me back away as far as the door. The expression on the face so much like her face had not

altered by as much as a millimeter. The heat was unbearable, killing; I turned and ran, as much from the
sense of bondage as from the fire.

Like Duane's Dream House, the old farmhouse was
igniting behind me, and when I turned around on the
lawn to watch it go up, I saw that it too was a dream
house. I felt as though part of me was still inside it.
I was bound to it, bound for life, as I had been for
twenty years. Seven hours earlier I had thought I had
come to a new accommodation, and I now saw—still
only half-comprehendingly—that all accommodations
are the same accommodation. I felt simultaneously
heavier and lighter, with my face burned and my life
returned to me freighted with the responsibilities I had
always had because I had taken them, because I was
simply the person who had them. My cousin's daughter
was standing before the walnut trees, watching me with
disbelief. When I noticed the expression in her eyes,
I began to shake more noticeably. I turned away from
her regard and watched the house. Dave Lokken lay
whimpering behind us.

I thought of her in there, sealing me to my bargain.
The whole upper and rear portions of the house were
distorted by flame. I had laughed at Duane without
recognizing that I too owned a dream house; and he
had paid for my illusions, on the night when they were
strongest in me.

"There was a—a person in there," breathed Alison
Updahl. "I thought you were going to die."

"And I thought you were," I said. "I didn't know
I could really do anything to stop it."

"But you could."

"I was here. That was enough."

The house was roaring now, making a vast devouring sound. She moved right up next to me. "I saw
something horrible," she said. "Miles—"

"We saw it too," I told her, cutting off her gasp as
she remembered. "That's why he's like that." We both
glanced at Lokken, who was kneeling now and looking

at the house with red stunned-looking eyes. Blood and vomit covered his shirt.

"If you hadn't come just then . . ."

"You would have been killed. And so would I. That's what it was about."

"But now that—person—won't come back."

"I don't know," I said. "I don't think so. She'll never come back like that, anyhow."

The whole house was in the last stage before collapse, and I could feel the heat beating against my face. I had to immerse myself in cold water. Blisters were forming on the palms of my hands. Behind the flames the old building was so skeletal that it looked as though it could float.

"When I dug up our cowdog it smelled like that," Alison said. "Like inside."

Boards and rafters began to tumble inward. The entire porch leaned against the wall of flames, sighed like a tired child, and soundlessly sank down into flatness.

"If she doesn't come back like that, how will she come back?"

"As us," I said.

"Your father and I loved her," I said. "I suppose he hated her too, but he named you after her because he loved her first, before he hated her."

"And he killed her, didn't he?" she asked. "And blamed it on you."

"He was just there. It was really Zack's father. He was the one."

"I knew it wasn't you. I wanted you to tell me, out at the quarry. I thought it was my dad." I could see her throat fluttering, jumping like a frog's. "I'm glad it wasn't."

"Yes."

"I feel . . . numb. I can't feel anything yet."

"Yes."

"I feel like I could talk a lot or not say anything at all."

"I know," I said.

The sides of the house were still upright, bracketing two open rooms of surging and twisting fire. At the center of a strand of flame stood an immovable shadow, a brief column of dark. Dave Lokken staggered to his feet.

"Is my father . . . ?" She took one of my hands, and her touch was cool.

"We weren't in time," I said. "Lokken and I found your father and Polar Bears. Up in the woods. I wish we could have done something. Lokken will bring them down."

The shadow I was watching as she clung to me darkened in the midst of the fire. Her tears flamed in the damaged skin at the base of my neck.

I led her to my car. I could not stand there any more. His eyes stupid with shock, Lokken watched us getting into the VW. We too were in shock, I knew. My hands and face hurt, but I still could not feel the pain, it was only an abstraction of pain. I backed out into the drive and stopped to look at the house for the last time. Goodby, grandmother, goodby, dream house, goodby dreams, goodby Alison. Hello. Goodby. Goodby, Alison. Who would be back—as a gesture seen on a crowded street, or as a snatch of music heard from an open window, as the curve of a neck and the pressure of a pair of hands, or as a child. Who would always be with us, now. Neighbors were coming slowly up the road, some of them walking, holding dishtowels and tools in their hands, some of them getting out of their pickups with taut, worried faces. Red and Tuta Sunderson were moving slowly across the lawn, going toward Dave Lokken. The old farmhouse was nearly gone and the flames were low. I backed the car through the people and swung it out on the road so that it was facing deeper into the valley.

"Where are we going?" asked Alison.

"I don't know."

"My father is really dead?" She put a knuckle in her mouth, knowing the answer.

"Yes. So is Polar Bears."

"I thought he was the one—the one who killed those girls."

"I thought so too, for a little while," I said. "I'm sorry. Polar Bears thought so too for a little while. He was the one that finally put the idea in my head."

"I can't go back, Miles," she said,

"Fine."

"Will I have to go back?"

"You can think about it," I said.

I was just steering, just driving a car. For a while her crying was a wet noise beside me. The road seemed to wind generally westward. I saw only farms and a winding road ahead of me. After this valley there would be another, and then another after that. Here the trees grew more thickly, coming right down to the buildings.

She straightened her back on the seat beside me. There were no more crying noises. "Let's just drive," she said. "I don't want to see Zack. I can't see him. We can write back from wherever we get to."

"Fine," I said.

"Let's go someplace like Wyoming or Colorado."

"Whatever you want," I said. "We'll do whatever you want." The curve of a neck, the pressure of a pair of hands, the familiar gesture of an arm. The blisters on my hands began truly to hurt; the nerves in my face began to transmit the pain of being burnt; I was beginning to feel better.

At the next curve of the valley the car trembled and the motor died. I heard myself begin to laugh.